The Broken Halo

By FLORENCE L. BARCLAY

The Rosary
The Mistress of Shenstone
The Following of the Star
Through the Postern Gate
The Upas Tree
The Broken Halo

The Breaking of the Halo

Drawn by F. H. Townsend

Broken Halo

By

Florence L. Barclay

Author of "The Rosary," etc.

G. P. Putnam's Sons
New York and London
The Knickerbocker Press
1913

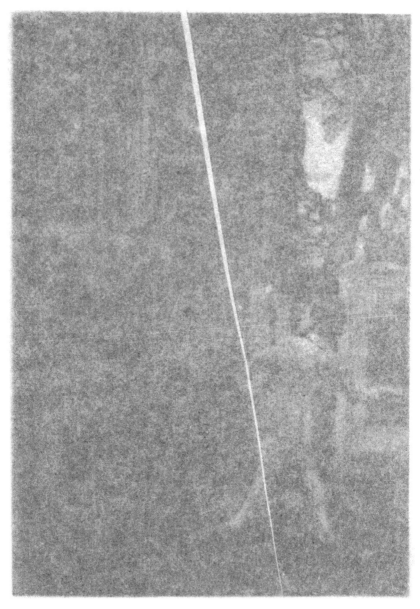

The Breaking of the Halo

Drawn by F. H. Townsend

The Broken Halo

By

Florence L. Barclay

Author of " The Rosary," etc.

✿

G. P. Putnam's Sons
New York and London
The Knickerbocker Press
1913

The Knickerbocker Press, New York

To

ONE WHO IS ABSENT,

YET EVER NEAR,

M. A. B.

CONTENTS

Contents

The Broken Halo

The Broken Halo

CHAPTER I

THE BELLS OF DINGLEVALE

A SUNDAY morning in Surrey—loveliest of English counties; a sunny, breezy day, early in June.

All nature browsed in peaceful Sabbath stillness.

The old shepherd, in clean smock-frock, whose only time-piece was in the sky, and who considered the sun to have been placed there for that object, shading his eyes and looking upward, would have judged the day to be within thirty minutes of noon. Also, a good half hour ago, the bells of Dinglevale had ceased pealing.

Very characteristic were the bells of Dinglevale, and inclined to be denominational in tone. The full peal of eight, in the belfry of the old church tower, was not, as a rule, rung before service. But, during ten minutes, the three lowest bells in the octave would declaim, with solemn persistence: "Come—to—church! Come—to—church!

Come—to—church!" After which the theme would change suddenly, five bells bursting out, in eager insistence: "Don't—go—to—chap—el! *Don't*—go—to—chap—el!" varied by an occasional return to: "Come—to—church!   Come—to—church! Come—to—church!"

Meanwhile the solitary bell of the chapel, beneath its little hen-coop, on the roof of that humble building, was doing its best, with the only tang it possessed, to say with unquenchable zeal, and persistent reiteration: "Come! Come! Come! Come!"

All the swinging and swaying, all the commotion and vibration; all the booming ecclesiastical reverberation, going on in the old church tower, failed to silence or to drown the brave little "tang, tang, tang," from beneath the hen-coop; the anxious "Come! Come! Come!" of the chapel bell.

But when the hour struck, all other sounds fell silent; and as the eleven strokes tolled slowly, belated worshippers hurried up the churchyard path to the porch, and disappeared through the red baize-covered swing doors, from out of which, as they pushed them open, came the mellow tones of the organ, in the opening voluntary.

In the chapel, the harmonium, assisted thereto by Miss Emily Dink, the chemist's pretty daughter —whose engagement to the minister was now looked upon as almost a certainty—had performed its introductory wheeze, and was conscientiously bleating through the tune of the opening hymn.

The "new minister"—so called, not because he was particularly new, but to distinguish him from the "old minister" some time deceased—was Irish. He had organised a sacred concert in the chapel during the first winter of his ministry; and, in explaining beforehand, to performers from a distance, the programme and attendant circumstances, he had remarked: "And I regret to say, the only piano we possess, is a harmonium."

None of these inner sounds, however, reached the hilltops; nor did they penetrate to the ears of the old shepherd, whose one concession to the Sabbath was a clean smock-frock, and who leaned over a gate, twirling a straw between his toothless gums; enjoying the present; ruminating in the past; wholly oblivious of the future.

Neither were they heard by a cyclist, who appeared on the horizon exactly thirty minutes after the bells ceased ringing, and rode so swiftly that, from being a mere speck on the sky line of that wide Surrey common, in less than no time he was skimming down the broad white ribbon of road, between the golden gorse, and heading straight for the long hill which drops you gently into Dinglevale.

He was a powerfully built youth, who rode with head erect, his right hand on the handlebar, his left plunged into the pocket of an old blue flannel coat, bearing on its breast the arms of some club or college. His white flannels, turned well up over old tennis shoes, had by no means the immaculate

Sabbath appearance of the shepherd's smock-frock. A blue flannel cap, also bearing a shield with arms embroidered, was stuck jauntily on the back of his head. His sunburnt face, brown and clean-shaven, his broad low brow, from which the dark hair rose thick and close-cropped, carried a look of indomitable vigour—masterful, virile, self-assured.

He treadled from the ankles, with that swift easy movement which sends the wheels flying round, without any apparent effort on the part of the rider.

His brown eyes, bright and keen of glance, took in the whole landscape as he rode, and the gay *joie-de-vivre* on his boyish face was so infectious, that jaded passers-by who saw it, smiled unconsciously, and went on their way realising that, after all, this really is a beautiful world.

As, immovable on the freewheel, he flashed past you down the hill, with the skimming motion of a bird on the wing, you would most probably have taken him for a crack tennis player, on his way to prove that he could hold the championship against all comers; or for the captain of a county cricket team, ready to justify his reputation as a demon bowler, or to carry out his bat for top score—not flushed with natural pride and elation, but as a quiet matter of course; a mere doing that which he had made up his mind to do.

You would have been correct in placing him as "captain," anyway; his foremost rule of life being: "I am the master of my fate; I am the captain of my soul!" He intended to succeed in everything he undertook. His clear eyes were always lifted fearlessly to the Top of the Tree. He was not there yet; in fact he was quite at the bottom. But he meant to get there.

But you would have been wrong—hopelessly wrong—in imagining that, on this particular Sunday morning, he was intent on sport.

As a matter of fact he was a hard-worked doctor, riding back to an unfinished breakfast, and to a cup of coffee, long grown cold.

He had lately taken a brilliant degree, with honours, but he had neither the money nor the influence required for the immediate acquisition of a practice of his own. He was, just now, acting *locum* for a country practitioner suffering from nervous breakdown, which had necessitated a long and complete holiday.

The practice was a large one, the experience varied and useful; so Richard Cameron, M.B., found there ample scope for his energy, and for the development of his up-to-date theories and ideas.

Moreover Dinglevale had been the home of his childhood, and he was spoken of with affection, by friends of by-gone years, as "Master Dick," which gradually became "Dr. Dick," as they learned to know him in this new capacity.

Thus he was trusted by the inhabitants of the whole neighbourhood, with a more complete and whole-hearted confidence than they would have bestowed upon an unknown *locum tenens* of so youthful and unprofessional an appearance, who might have ventured to their bedsides, in the place of their own staid and elderly medical adviser.

On this particular Sunday morning, Dr. Dick had planned to take a holiday. He was well ahead with his work. No one of his patients was likely to require him before the afternoon.

He came down to breakfast arrayed in old flannels, intending to mow and roll his landlady's lawn; then to lie on his back in the sun, and ruminate on things in general, and on his own brilliant future in particular.

He was halfway through his first cup of coffee when a note was brought in marked "urgent." It had been scrawled in hot haste, by a neighbouring doctor, suddenly incapacitated owing to an accident. It was a call to ride five miles, to a distant Rectory.

He reached the request to hasten to the Rectory, at the bottom of the first page.

"They may jolly well whistle!" said Dr. Dick. "Sanctimonious old Sabbath-breakers!"

Then he turned the page.

"*Double pneumonia and heart-failure. Practically no hope.*"

"No hope!" shouted Dr. Dick. "What's the fool talkin' about?"

He dropped the note on to his eggs and bacon, and dashed into the little den which—in view of tree-top eventualities—he already called his "consulting-room."

He had all the callous selfishness of youth, but life-saving was a passion.

He stuffed the very newest pattern of stethoscope into the breast-pocket of his blue flannel coat; various important remedies into his other pockets, and was carrying his bicycle bodily down the little garden path and out at the gate, when Miss Prettyman—who had meanwhile picked the note out of the dish, and dried it on the blotting paper—ran after him, imploring him to come back and finish his nice breakfast first.

Dr. Dick, as he rode away, consigned his breakfast to a place where it would at least have been kept warm; and Miss Prettyman went sadly in, to survey the half-finished condition of things, then considered herself fully justified in reading the note, seeing that she found herself with it, so to say, open in her hand.

By dint of hard riding, Dr. Dick turned in at the Rectory gate, half an hour sooner than the anxious watchers had dared to expect him.

His old tennis shoes made no sound as he walked into the room where the Rector's young wife lay fighting with death; and his strong brown hands were so gentle as he moved aside the lace of her nightdress, and knelt to listen to the fluttering heart, that she thought the touch was her mother's, and, not feeling equal to the huge effort of opening her eyes, failed to realise at first how powerful an ally had come to aid her in the desperate fight

—an ally who was to turn the almost certainty of defeat, into ultimate victory.

But the church bells had ceased ringing before Dr. Dick rode back to his unfinished breakfast; and the old shepherd had pronounced it half-past eleven, by his own particular time-piece, as the bicycle sped past him at the top of the hill.

The young doctor's observant eye took in every detail of the landscape, as he rode, and his active mind passed rapid comment thereupon.

"Now why on earth does this panorama of hill and vale proclaim so plainly that to-day is what my Grandaunt Louisa used to call 'the blessed Sabbath morn'? Look at those silly old cows! There they lie, chewing the cud in their best Sunday morning manner. Those sheep on the hill side, browse in sanctimonious solemnity; and as they move, with dainty pious tread, from tuft to tuft, their very bells seem to tinkle the Old Hundredth.

"And there stands the old church tower, lowering its ivy brows at an ungodly chap who dares to bicycle during service hours; smugly conscious that the deafening row it made just now has induced scores of poor mortals to pass in beneath it, and spend two hours of this glorious sunshine, cooped up between four walls, listening to a lot of rigmarole they don't attempt to understand.

"Yet the old church tower never looks smug, except on Sunday; the woods, hills, and meadows never hold their breath and remain so ghastly

still, except—oh, shade of my Grandaunt Louisa—
on the blessed Sabbath morn! It is all very well
for us chaps who preach the Gospel of Reason, to
avoid church, and play golf on Sundays, but so
long as cows cultivate a Sunday manner, sheep
tinkle psalm tunes, and the English landscape
keeps Sabbath, we shall be mere blots on the
scene, mere discords in the prevailing harmony.
Hullo! What's up?"

He was passing the churchyard, and his quick
eye had caught sight of a silent, but agitated,
little group in the church porch.

He dismounted, leaned his bicycle against the
fence, and strode quickly up the path.

CHAPTER II

THE LITTLE WHITE LADY

WHEN Dick Cameron reached the church porch, he found half a dozen people forming a useless crowd around a little white lady with drawn face, whose eyes were fixed in helpless agony. The old verger, in rusty black cassock, held a glass of water; a stout churchwarden blocked the doorway, keeping out most of the fresh air.

The Little White Lady sat huddled on the wooden seat, supported by an elderly female in black, who fanned her with a prayer-book, ejaculating "Gawd help us!" at intervals.

Dr. Dick shot a long blue arm between the rusty cassock and the churchwarden's black coat, and laid his fingers lightly on the pulse of the frailest, most ethereal little hand he had ever seen. Then he shoved them off to right and left, and, bending over the Little White Lady, rapidly unfastened the cameo brooch at her neck. Instantly a black cotton glove pushed him indignantly away, and he found himself confronted by the gaunt female in merino.

"My name, young man," she said, "is Ellen

Ransom; and I 'll have you to understand, that you don't lay hands on my poor lady!"

"Your name, young woman," said Dr. Dick, "doesn't interest me at all. It might be Maher-shalal-hash-baz, for aught I care, except that it would take a plaguy long time to call you, if one was in a hurry. But I'll have you to understand that your lady is now in my hands, and you are under my orders. So hurry up and get this lacy arrangement unfastened in ten seconds, or I shall get out a penknife."

The elderly maid gave him a look of fury, but something in the clear brown eyes which met hers, and in the forceful decision of the broad-shouldered youth, quenched her anger, and compelled her to obedience. She bent over her mistress and busied herself with the many fastenings, at neck and bosom, of the dainty gown.

As Dr. Dick stood back a moment, his shoulder pushed the baize doors partly open, and a whiff reached him, indicative of the closeness of the atmosphere within.

"Bah!" he said. "You could bail it out with a ladle! No wonder it has done for her. One might put up with their frowzy theology, if they didn't air it in such a poisonous atmosphere!"

He pulled the door to; but the next moment it opened softly and the schoolmaster came out, with uplifted finger, closing the door behind him.

"Dr. Dick," he said, in tones of dismay, "your remark was audible throughout the entire church!"

"Best text they've heard for a long time," said Dick, rapidly putting together his stethoscope. "Now, Jerry, if you can manage to run in that cassock, scurry along and fetch a pillow from somewhere—anywhere; the fat red velvet cushion in the pulpit will do, if no other is handy. Everybody else clear out, please, excepting Mrs. Hashbaz. The two things we now require are privacy and fresh air. Stop that organ, somebody! I can't hear myself speak. What? Hymn before the sermon? Rubbish! They can't have a hymn until my patient is better. Now, Mr. Churchwarden, you go in and say so, or I must. You will probably put it more tactfully and officially. Ah, Jerry! Good man! The very thing! Place it in that corner; then wait out of sight, until I call. Now, madam"—his voice and manner changed completely, as he bent over the Little White Lady—"we will soon give you relief."

The grey eyes looked up into his, with an expression of terrified anguish; the breathless lips seemed to implore not to be moved.

"Don't be frightened," he said, gently. "Leave her to me, Mrs. Maher-shalal."

Then he put his strong young arms around the Little White Lady.

It did not take Dick Cameron's quick ear long to find out all there was to know about the worn-out heart which feebly struggled to keep life in the frail body of the Little White Lady. He realised, in a very few moments, that he had rarely been more closely confronted with Death, than in that church porch, on this sunny summer morning.

His manner became very gentle, and his voice very low, but his movements were quick; there was no time to lose.

Taking a piece of lint from his pocket, he broke a tiny sealed vial, letting the contents soak into the lint. Then he held it, so that the Little White Lady gradually inhaled it.

Almost at once she began to breathe more easily; a faint colour came into her cheeks, and tinted her white lips. The grey eyes, losing the look of terror, closed for a moment, as she gave a soft sigh of relief. But soon they opened again, and looked up into the brown eyes bent so keenly on her face.

Then the Little White Lady smiled up at Dr. Dick.

"Wonderful," she whispered. "Wonderful!"

He signed to the maid to pass him the glass of water, produced out of another pocket a bottle containing a bright red liquid; poured away most of the water, adding to the remainder a carefully measured dose of the powerful heart stimulant. Slipping his hands behind the pillow, he lifted the Little White Lady's head and made her drink the dose. Then he laid his fingers gently on her pulse.

This time it was Dick who smiled down at the Little White Lady.

She opened her lips to speak, but he shook his head.

"No talking yet," he said.   Then turned to the maid.   "Where do you live?"

"Park Lane, sir," said Ellen Ransom, laconic, but respectful.   This astonishing young man, who had called her heathen names without the slightest provocation, who was dressed like a cricket match, and had no "by your leaves" for anybody, had certainly worked a miracle of healing on her dear lady.   Her honesty compelled her to admit it.   The "sir" in her reply, was the reluctant tribute of her honesty.

"Park Lane won't help us to-day, Mrs. Hash-baz.   You hardly came from there this morning."

"No heathen names, if you please, sir.   My name is Ellen Ransom.   And we came from the Manor House, sir, which we have took for six weeks."

"From the Manor?" said Dr. Dick.   "Ah, I heard it was let.   You arrived the day before yesterday, I believe.   And how did you get here, from the Manor?"

"Walked, sir.   My lady does not hold with having her carriage out on Sundays."

"Walked!"   Dr. Dick began a long drawn-out whistle, but checked it just in time.   "I see. I suppose it was a longer walk than your lady had lately undertaken? "

"It was, sir; but we rested often, on the way."

"I see. And then, overtaxed already, your lady came—from out the fresh air and sunshine—into an absolutely ill-ventilated place, in which all the oxygen was used up centuries ago! No wonder she—er—felt faint. When will these parsons learn that it is criminal not to have fresh air in their churches? The 'odour of sanctity,' as cultivated by them, is responsible for much suffering and disease. However, it now remains for us to get my patient safely away, before this whole congregation comes trooping out."

He stepped outside the porch and beckoned the verger, who was remaining discreetly out of sight.

"Jeremiah," he said, "go to Captain Desart, as fast as you can. Tell him I want his motor—the large Napier, closed—at the church gate, as rapidly as possible. If the Captain is out, find the chauffeur, and give him the order from me. Tell him not to wait to change into livery. Nothing matters, excepting that he must be here within a quarter of an hour. Run, Jerry, run!"

As it happened, Jeremiah chanced to meet the car at the lodge gates, just turning in. Hailing it, he delivered Dr. Dick's peremptory message, which was immediately obeyed. Captain Desart alighted and told his man to drive at once to the church. He, himself, could very well walk up the avenue.

Thus the car glided swiftly and silently up to the gate, within ten minutes of the despatch of Jerry; yet not a moment too soon. The doctor, listening anxiously, had heard the peroration of the sermon, followed by the rising of the congregation at the ascription.

He bent over the Little White Lady.

"Now, look here," he said, "I am going to carry you. No, it is no good protesting! I know you feel all right again, but I am not going to let you walk one step. Only—don't hold your breath when I lift you, or make all your muscles rigid, as if *you* were carrying *me!* Just let yourself go—quite limp and easy, and, remember, it is no more effort to me to carry you, than it would be to you to carry a kitten; perhaps not so much. Now then—don't be frightened."

Then the Little White Lady felt Dr. Dick's strong young arms beneath her, and experienced what it was to be lifted by one who knew, scientifically, exactly the right way to do it.

It seemed to her that she was wafted to the motor with an ease which savoured of magic; and though getting her safely into the car was more complicated, it was accomplished, with no conscious effort on her part. She lay back comfortably—Ellen Ransom seated beside her. Dr. Dick, jumping up outside, gave the word to start, and off they glided, just as the red doors opened wide, and the congregation streamed out, to lively strains of organ music

"By Jove, that was a near thing!" laughed Dr. Dick. "Drive slowly, Chambers! A sudden swerve, or a jolt, might mean death to the little old lady inside.　Now, I wonder," mused Dr. Dick to himself, "whether she knows how near she has been this morning to what Aunt Louisa used to describe, with gusto, as 'an Eternity of Sabbaths in the world to come'?　Well, anyway, let 's hope they 'll be better ventilated than are the Sabbaths here below."

CHAPTER III

WHEN Dr. Dick had carried the Little White Lady up the wide oak staircase of the Manor House and deposited her safely upon her bed, he left her to Ellen Ransom.

"I shall wait in the house an hour," he announced from the doorway. "I want to be quite satisfied as to how matters are going, after the heart has had time to rest, and to quiet down a bit. If you want any help, I shall be within call."

He closed the door, softly; then walked slowly along the wide passage, looking at the old pictures in heavy gold frames, mostly portraits of ancestors of the owner of the Manor House.

"Ugly old brutes!" thought Dr. Dick. "It would be uphill work mastering life and winning one's way in the world, if one had to walk about in lace frills, sporting such noses as these!"

At the top of the staircase, also in a gold frame, hung a full-length pier-glass. Dr. Dick grinned at his own handsome reflection.

"Well, I *am* grubby!" he said. "And I don't think anything of less professional aspect ever

18

forked out a stethoscope! No wonder the old dragon, Maher-shalal-hash-baz shrieked 'Hands off, young man!' and clawed me, with her black cotton glove. I wish I had time to go home and change, before my patient sees me again; but I can't safely be out of call, just yet. I may as well have a wash, though, if I can find a place."

In the hall, he met an elderly butler, grave and respectful, who glanced at his dusty flannels, then immediately looked away.

"Can I have a wash and brush up?" inquired Dr. Dick, serenely. "I was on my way home from a long bicycle ride, when your mistress unexpectedly needed me."

The butler led the way upstairs to a perfectly appointed bath-room, made sure that there were brushes, and all he could require, to his hand; then left him in possession.

"Was ever a fellow so tempted!" thought Dr. Dick, ruefully, as he took off his coat. "Imagine the joys of a tub—the absolute luxury of a glorious full-length up-to-your-neck bath, after Miss Prettyman's tin pannikins! Yet it would be a most foolhardy tempting of fate—and the Fates are being fairly propitious to-day. No sooner was I well in, and all over soap, than the door of that bedroom would fly open, and old Hash-baz would be shrieking for me to come at once. Tableau! A doctor in an old flannel blazer was bad enough; but a medical man in a bath towel! Even the mild grey eye of the Little White Lady would note so great a laxity as that, in the matter of pro-fessional attire. It could never be lived down. Dicky, my boy, you daren't risk it ! Your longing for a tub just now is beyond all earthly words to describe; but you could not love you tub so much, loved you not duty more!" "Isn't that a text? " inquired Dick, of his wet and glow-ing reflection, as he lifted his face from the basin, and scrubbed it vigorously with a rough towel. "It sounds uncommonly like what Aunt Louisa used to call 'a quotation from Holy Writ.' I suppose 'writ' was elegant slang for 'writing.' 'It is writ.' Yet she used to reprove *me* for saying 'bus' for 'omnibus.' Inconsistent old person ! . . . No, Richard Cameron, M.B.—now of Wood-bine Villa, Dinglevale, but eventually of Harley Street, W., you certainly could not risk appearing arrayed in a bath towel, at the bedside of a patient, who resides, when at home, in Park Lane ! But when you are established in a big town-house, where patients wait in crowds for the summons to your consulting-room—*then*, you can have a bath-room fitted up precisely on these lines; and every time you use it, you can say: 'I have arrived at this, because, in days gone by, I missed no chances, and I took no risks. Present success is the reward of a lofty sense of duty, which nobly disregarded mere creature comforts!"

His merry eyes laughed back from the mirror, as he vigorously brushed his damp hair, rejoicing in his improved appearance.

"Now, if I can steal a pin—'it is a sin, to steal a pin'—find the garden, and a Rayon d'Or rose, I ought to make a quite excellent impression on the Little White Lady, who will so far have recovered from her attack, as to have 'a heart at leisure from itself, to soothe and sympathise'—I should say 'admire.' . . . Oh, my forsaken—coffee and bacon! I hope they will realise that it is time for luncheon, and that a busy doctor occasionally has to forego breakfast."

In the hall, the butler waited.

"Your luncheon is served, sir, in the dining-room," and Dick turned joyfully to the room in which, through an open door, he could see the glint of glass and silver, and the sheen of snowy damask.

CHAPTER IV

THE BREAKING OF THE HALO

D R. DICK partook of that luncheon with a frankness of enjoyment, which was essentially youthful. But there was a more subtle element mingling with the natural zest of a large and healthy appetite. This luncheon, in the Manor House dining-room, paid off an old score of twenty years' standing.

"I'm even with that old woman, at last!" laughed Dr. Dick. "Here I sit, at her table, master of the situation! I hope this fine old silver belongs to her, and not to the Little White Lady. I only wish the old beast were here, to see me walking round, helping myself. '*What* a greedy little boy!' And I'm miles greedier now, than I was then!"

More than twenty years before, the lonely little bright-eyed boy, living with his granduncle and aunt at the Rectory, had been invited to a children's party, by the Lady of the Manor. She was one of those people whose kindnesses always take the form of insufferable patronage. She was condescendingly agreeable to small children who

22

quailed before her; but conceived an instant dislike to dark eyes which were lifted fearlessly to hers; to a young mind which calmly and obviously took her measure.

The sturdy, seven-year-old boy had arrived in high spirits, bent upon enjoying his unusual outing, to the full.

From the very outset, his pleasure had seemed to meet with continual and unaccountable checks. When he won a race, beating a boy older and bigger than himself, and came up glowing with the certainty of assured victory, he found himself disqualified for no apparent reason, the prize being given to the other boy.

When he joined with whole-hearted energy in a game, he was taken forcibly on one side, and requested not to be rough.

When he described, with shining eyes, to a little circle of admiring contemporaries, an exciting adventure he had had that morning, alone in a tradesman's cart with a runaway pony, the cold voice of his hostess from somewhere behind him and far above his head, remarked that little boys should not exaggerate.

But the climax had been reached at tea. His little soul was crushed, his self-esteem sorely wounded, his spirit goaded by a sense of injustice, by the failure to win the approbation, the admiration, the popularity and success which, even then, seemed to him essential. The Fates, in the person of his large and cold-voiced hostess, had been against him, eyeing him, at his best and brightest, with stony disapproval. But he meant to make up for all this at tea. He intended to have a large and complete tea, and to enjoy it to the full. He could rely upon his appetite. In its way, its proportions resembled those of the Lady of the Manor, and it never failed him. So, when the bell rang, and the children, leaving the joys of the old garden, all trooped into the dining-room, he was the first to dash in through the French window; and, as he climbed into his chair, and saw the ample supply of good things upon the table, all disappointments and mortifications were forgotten. Anyway, he was going to make a success of tea! His brown eyes shone. His busy little tongue was silent. He was making a record in the race through the prescribed routine of bread-and-butter, and bread-and-jam, to the much desired goal of the cakes.

In the middle of tea, the curate arrived, and was told off by the Lady of the Manor, who herself presided at the urn, to walk round the table, handing the good things to the children.

Now this curate chanced to be little Dick's especial friend and hero. He rode a bicycle, and could do so—when Dick was sole spectator—with one leg thrown gracefully over the handlebar. He possessed a deep bass voice, and sang warlike songs at the village concerts. When the curate mounted the platform to sing "The Lads in Red," little Dick, seated just beneath him in the centre of the foremost row, used to curl his toes firmly round the front bar of his chair, and hold on to the sides with both hands.   Each time the curate reached the refrain, "Here they come! Fife and drum!" Dick's throat would contract, and hot tears smart under his eyelids.   He could not have explained the sensation, but when the curate sang, in his most pounding voice, "Here they come! Fife and drum!" it gave him the same feeling as when he suddenly saw a crimson and gold sunset, or heard a brass band in the distance, coming nearer.

The curate made much of his rector's little grandnephew.   It was agreeable to be the object of adoring admiration, even though the admiration was only that of a small boy of seven.

But, at the Manor House, he took no notice of Dick; though the brown eyes had sparkled at his entrance.   His whole attention was given to the Large Lady of the Manor.   He watched her, much as Rough, the Rectory terrier, watched the cook when he expected scraps, or hoped for a bone.   Dick wondered at this.   He also wondered why the curate's hair was so carefully parted in the middle, and why he was wearing the beautiful silk waistcoat which, as a rule, he only wore on grand occasions in the evening; and why he laughed, loud and long, at things which were not funny; and why he fetched and carried, in a sort of anxious hurry, much as Betsy the scullery-maid did, when Aunt Louisa happened to be in the kitchen.

Dick did not understand that when a Lady of the Manor has the living in her gift, her stalest joke is fresh and funny, and her least command is law.

When the cake stage, reached at last, was well under weigh, the curate took a rest, and was graciously allowed a cup of tea. He stood to drink it, behind the children, at the side of the table, exactly opposite to Dick.

Then occurred poor little Dick's fiasco.

The richest and plummiest of the plum-cakes had been cut up and handed round. The dish had then been placed upon the table, well within Dick's reach. Two pieces only were left, one much larger than the other. Dick had had his eye on these for some time, anxiously weighing the question as to which was *the cake*, and which was *a slice*. The smaller piece stood up on the dish; the larger piece was lying down. Dick knew, in his secret heart, that the large piece was the cake; but he silenced that instinctive knowledge, and proceeded to reason that the cake itself would most certainly stand up in the dish, whereas a slice would undoubtedly lie down. This method of reasoning against instinctive certainties has brought about man's downfall from the first. It brought about Dick's. He reached out an eager little hand and took—the cake!

The small slice, left alone, looked very small. The large piece, on his little plate, looked larger than it had looked on the dish.

Then a cold, clear voice, from behind the urn,

said slowly: "*What* a greedy little boy!   He has helped himself to the cake!"

There was an awful silence.   It seemed as long as a sermon, or a nightmare.   Would nobody speak, or help, or say that the cake had been lying down and therefore might reasonably have been mistaken for a slice?

He lifted imploring eyes to his friend and hero, the curate.   "Here they come!   Fife and drum!" Oh stalwart comrade, come to the rescue of this little lad whose cheeks are red—flying the signals of childhood's horrified shame!

Then the curate laughed—a low, sneering snigger.

"A little pig, I call him!" he said.   "He should be made to stand and eat it in the corner."

Then all the injustice, the mortification, the failures, of the afternoon, rolled back in overwhelming waves upon the swelling heart of little Dick.   A fury of indignation arose within him, submerging all shyness and all shame.   His idol had fallen, his friend had failed him; and his hostess, who had asked him to tea, had called him greedy because he enjoyed her cake!   Oh, wicked world, governed by unjust grown-up people !   His hero had collapsed—flat as a punctured tyre; and he—Dick Cameron—who had often, himself, strutted as a hero before all these staring boys and girls, had been publicly shamed in their presence.

He seized the piece of cake and flung it at the curate.

It caught his cup, straight on the brim, working

threefold disaster; for, first the cup shot backward, emptying its contents over the curate's silk waistcoat; then it ricochetted off to the right, and broke into many pieces on the parquet floor; while the saucer flew out of his hand, and was reduced to atoms on the left.

Meanwhile Dick leapt from his chair, rushed to the door, wrenched it open and turned in the doorway, a little figure of blazing indignation.

"You've been beastly to me the whole afternoon!" he shouted at the Large Lady of the Manor, who had risen from behind the urn, and was gazing at him in blank astonishment.

The curate, paralysed into inaction, was feebly mopping his steaming waistcoat.

The frightened children sat round the table, wide-eyed and open-mouthed. One tiny girl, an especial little playmate of Dick's, gave a delighted laugh of enjoyment and irrepressible glee; then caught her breath, half frightened at her own amusement, wholly terrified for him.

The angry little figure in the doorway paused for breath; and for inspiration.

Then a favourite text of his Grandaunt Louisa's came into his mind. He hurled it at the Lady of the Manor, with all the force of absolute conviction and amazing inaccuracy.

"I shake off my shoes," cried the furious little voice, "from off my feet; and I hope you'll go to Sodom and Gomorrah!"

Then, as the curate made a dash for him, he

darted across the hall and out at the front door, scudded hatless across the park, like a frightened rabbit, dashed up the village street, not daring to look behind or pause for breath, and ran straight into Grandaunt Louisa, cutting roses in the garden.

For once the sight of Aunt Louisa was welcome. She was stern, but she was just; and so overwhelming a catastrophe had happened to him, that he longed to make a clean breast of it, and to tell her the whole thing, right from the beginning. It would be such a huge relief, and surely it would be possible to make Aunt Louisa understand.

But she took him by the hand, and led him into the house. She said she knew he had been naughty and had behaved badly at the party; that was a foregone conclusion. She would sift the matter presently. Meanwhile, he must go to his room and learn again the hymn he had repeated so inaccurately on Sunday. . . "Yes, 'We are but little children weak.' . . No, not a word!" She did not want any excuses.

The fact was, Aunt Louisa happened just then to be very much interested in her roses, and she could not see to trim them after sunset. A troublesome little boy could be talked to equally well in the twilight; rather better, perhaps, as he chanced to have such very bright brown eyes. So she found the hymnbook, put a marker in at the hymn he was to learn, and returned to her roses. She felt she had been calmly judicious.

Little Dick, thrown back upon himself, went slowly upstairs with the hymnbook.

He had to go slowly, because he put the hymnbook on each stair and stepped upon it. This took some time, but he always did it, when Aunt Louisa told him to take a hymnbook upstairs. He found that to have boldly trodden upon it on every step, helped him not to tear the hymnbook when he found himself alone with it in his own room. He used to pretend that he was St. George, and the hymnbook was the dragon—a very mild, dog-eared kind of dragon!

This method of taking a hymnbook upstairs, being a somewhat lengthy proceeding, little Dick had only just reached the verse about "our swelling hearts"—a verse he particularly disliked— when the curate came striding up the drive. He carried Dick's straw hat—the one with the blue ribbon, with H. M. S. DAUNTLESS stamped on it in gold. The elastic twisted round the curate's finger as he walked, making him even more angry than he already was. He did not know that you should never carry a straw hat by its elastic; especially if you are hurrying along, in an indignant flurry. The curate's coat-tails flew behind him, as he came up the drive.

Little Dick saw that the curate's coat-tails flew behind him, because he was looking out of the window. He had pitched the dragon up to the top of the wardrobe at "When deep within our swelling hearts"; then, counsels of prudence prevailing, had climbed on to the high window-sill to locate it—with a view to its ultimate rescue with a broom handle—just as the curate pranced in at the gate.

The curate was shown straight into Granduncle Andrew's study. Little Dick knew this, because, by then, he was peeping through the banisters.

After a very short time—about twenty heart-thumps—the study door opened and Uncle Andrew came out, calling: "Lou-wheeze-ah!" in his horriblest voice. Aunt Louisa hurried in, dropping her scissors and her garden gloves on the way.

Then the study door was shut again.

Little Dick flew back to his room, knelt down beside his bed, and began to pray in a great hurry.

"O God, please let the Judgment-day happen, before the study door opens again! . . . O God, please let the heavens and the earth pass away, before they come up to look for me!"

He held his breath to listen.

Yes! The study door had opened. Aunt Louisa was coming up the stairs. He could hear her chains tinkling and the rustle she always made, except when she walked about in her dressing-gown.

He prayed one last frantic prayer.

"O God, let the Twinkling-of-an-eye happen, before Aunt Louisa gets to here! I won't mind being left behind alone, so long as Aunt Louisa and Uncle Andrew's caught away. O God——"

But the "Twinkling-of-an-eye" did not happen. Aunt Louisa rustled in.

She found little Dick kneeling beside his bed, his curly head buried in the counterpane, his small, brown fingers nervously pulling at the little white balls.

Without a word, she took him by the hand and led him down the stairs. Grandaunt Louisa had a firm belief in the effectiveness of preserving a majestic silence—when she was not quite sure what to say.

She led little Dick into the study, where Uncle Andrew and the Fallen Idol waited.

Here, in Dick's presence, the curate gave, with zealous gusto, a recital of the happenings of that afternoon. And very bad it sounded; yet it was all true. Not a thing could Dick deny; whereas his own version of the story—all he had borne and endured—was too intangible, too difficult of expression, ever to explain to Uncle Andrew and Aunt Louisa. If he could have climbed upon his mother's lap, felt her soft arms around him, and her cheek upon his hair, he could have told her everything. But the nearest approach to his mother's lap for him, now, was when he ran away sometimes in the twilight, and climbed up on to her grave; and you can't tell things to a grave.

So when Granduncle Andrew, in his awfullest voice, called him "sir," and asked what he had to say for himself, he held up his head and made his case worse by saying, with absolute clearness and finality: "They were perfectly beastly, and I hate them."

Whereupon, at a sign from Uncle Andrew, Aunt Louisa rustled from the room, still maintaining the effective silence, and went back to her roses. She hurried a little, after picking up her gloves and scissors, and began at the rose-tree furthest from the study windows.

Then Uncle Andrew proceeded to give Dick the most severe caning he had as yet experienced in the whole seven years of his chequered little life; while the curate looked on with a righteous sense of satisfaction; afterwards returning to report to the Lady of the Manor that he had personally supervised the meting out of condign punishment.

When they had finished with him, Dick escaped by the back-door, crept through the dark wood where the nut trees grew, and where you had to push aside the boughs to find the path; slipped through the gap in the hedge, into the quiet churchyard, and stumbling along among the mounds, came at last to the white marble of his mother's tomb, where it stood in solitude, opposite the great chancel window.

Here he flung himself down, slipped his arms around the base of the cross and clung to the cold marble, sobbing, in the desperate helplessness of childhood's grief.

It was the more terrible when it came at last, this complete breakdown, because it had been held in check so long.

3

He had felt like it, ever since the Large Lady decided, in her cold voice, that he had not started fairly, and gave the popgun to Bobbie Desart. True, Bob had whispered to him, at the first opportunity: "She's a cheat, and I'll lend it to you!" but that didn't alter the fact that he had won it, and ought to have been in a position to lend it to Bobbie, who was two years older.

He had felt still more like it, when Aunt Louisa had sent him upstairs to learn a hymn, when he wanted to tell her the whole story of what had happened. It was because the dog-eared dragon was so dreadfully near the truth when it mentioned "tears of passion in our eyes," that he threw it on to the top of the wardrobe.

But later, when Aunt Louisa rustled away, leaving him to his fate, it was quite easy to be brave, because he hated Granduncle Andrew, and despised the curate, who had called him a pig, to please the Large Lady of the Manor. Hatred and scorn are wonderful helps to bravery, enabling you to be H. M. S. DAUNTLESS, even when Uncle Andrew gets out the cuttingest of all his canes.

So, though the Rector of Dinglevale drew blood from the motherless little boy left in his charge, he did not draw a sob or a cry for mercy; and, being a weak and an angry man himself, he tried to thrash the courage out of the seven-year-old boy, with treble the blows he would have inflicted if each blow had produced a shriek.

Yet now the breakdown came, it was the more overwhelming.

At first he clung to the marble, and sobbed convulsively.

Then he flung his sore little body down upon the turf, and lay with his face buried in the cool moss.

At last he ceased sobbing and began to talk to the dead mother, lying below.

"D'you know, Mummie," he said, in a broken little voice, yet which hardened as he talked: "I'm never going to pray again, in all my whole life, 'cept 'Jesus tender shepherd' that *you* taught me. An' that mus' do for night and morning, 'cause I can't say: 'Take me by the hand and lead me.' I'm sorry, Mummie dear, but it makes me think of Aunt Louisa's jammed old hand takin' hold of mine. 'Jammed' is what Cook calls things when she thinks they're cool and takes hold of them, and they're not. They're hot! It's very amusin' to be in the kitchen, then."

The tear-stained little face, pressed against the moss, broke into a watery smile. Then the helpful vision of Cook—taking hold of a thing she supposed to be cool, and finding it hot—faded; and the little face hardened again. He went on talking, but to himself alone; no longer to his mother.

"I'm never going to pray again," said the small boy of seven; "but *I'll* make Judgment-days happen, when I'm big; and, if I choose, *I'll* make heaven and earth pass away! And

I'll make Twinklings-of-an-eye happen, just whenever I want 'em to. And I won't get left behind, unless I choose. I'll come out on top of everything and everybody—always. And I'll do it without Aunt Louisa, and without Uncle Andrew, and without God. And I'll love nobody—ever; because nobody loves me. . . . And now I'm going to get up; and I'm never going to cry again in my whole life. But because I've *had* to cry this time, I'm now going to do the wickedest thing that can be done, in this world."

He got up promptly; climbed on to his mother's grave, and sat there. It hurt him to sit on the hard stone, so he took off his little jacket, rolled it up and made a cushion.

Then he sat for a long time, ruminating in the gathering twilight—a silent huddled little figure in a flannel shirt.

Suddenly his face brightened. He had lifted his eyes to the East window, and—he had thought of the wickedest thing that could be done in this world!

"I shall go to hell, for sure, if I do it," he whispered; "but that won't matter. Uncle Andrew and Aunt Louisa won't be there. And Mummie will come and pay me happy little visits. And there'll be no texts or hymnbooks, but I should think there'll be all the nice *wrong* things that Aunt Louisa won't allow, and specially doing of 'em on Sundays."

He smiled, and pushed back his tumbled curls.

Then he looked up again at the fine old stained-glass window. The central figure was that of Saint Peter, patron saint of the church, holding tightly to his keys.

Now little Dick, ever since he could remember, had particularly disliked this great tall figure of
· Saint Peter. He disliked it for three reasons.

First and foremost, he hated people who carried keys about. They had always either locked you in, or locked you out. If it was sunshine and hay-making, or other boys going to play cricket, they had locked you in. If it was jam or sweets or plums, they had locked you out.

Secondly, Saint Peter wore neither trousers nor knickerbockers, nor even flannel shirts. He wore a long blue dressing-gown, exceedingly like Aunt Louisa's, and he held it up in front with the keys, just as Aunt Louisa held hers up with a candle-stick. This, in a man, was a bit of odious affecta-tion, particularly in church. (Dick did not say "odious affectation," but he thought the childish equivalent.)

Thirdly, and most important, Saint Peter was bald. Dick could not abide bald people. Uncle Andrew was bald. But Uncle Andrew was bald in an open way. He did not attempt to disguise the fact. He even drew attention to it, by rubbing his baldness, round and round and round, with the palm of his hand. This made a hissing sound, like a small steam-engine, in an otherwise silent room. Uncle Andrew always did it, on those rare occasions when Aunt Louisa tried to argue. A person could not go on arguing for long, when Uncle Andrew started rubbing his bald head. He also did it when other people came to preach, if he did not like their sermons. Dick used to hear it happening, far away up in the chancel. Then Aunt Louisa used to say afterwards: "What did you disapprove in the sermon, dear?" If Uncle Andrew was feeling pleasant, he would tell her, and it was generally the only thing Dick had thought interesting. But if Uncle Andrew was *not* feeling pleasant, he only stared at Aunt Louisa, and said: "What should lead you to suppose I disapproved, Louisah?" Whereupon Aunt Louisa would look frightened and say: "Oh—I don't know, dear!" Dick felt this was not truthful of Aunt Louisa, because he knew, quite well, why Aunt Louisa knew; and he knew Aunt Louisa quite well knew why she knew! But grown-up people are like that. It is just the very people who talk to you most solemnly about what a wicked little boy you are, because you said you wiped your feet on the mat when you didn't, who say they really don't know, when they *do!*

Well, anyway, Uncle Andrew was openly and loudly bald. Aunt Louisa also had some baldness. Little Dick had discovered that, when he slept in her room at the seaside, where she took him after he had had measles. But Aunt Louisa pinned on a bunch of curls to hide her baldness. Saint Peter did not pin on curls, but he wore a plate—a large round yellow plate—at the back of his head, all tilted up. This shining plate had always been a cause of secret annoyance to little Dick. It did not hide the baldness, therefore it was ineffective. It was fastened by no visible means, so it always worried you, when you should have been attending to other things, by making you wonder how it stayed there. It was not a hat, because it was not *on*. It was just a gold tin plate, balanced at the back of the apostle's bald head.

Now, the sudden inspiration which had come to little Dick on this sad evening, when the traditions of his small life went to pieces, was that the wickedest thing in the whole world to do, but also a thing fraught with keen satisfaction, would be to put a stone clean through Saint Peter's gold tin plate.

He considered it for a long time, seated upon his little coat, on the marble coping of his mother's grave.

Twilight fell. The golden and red of the sun-light faded from behind the dark boughs of the Scotch firs. He could only just see the outline of the Apostle's massive figure. No light shone through from the church. But, clearer than the rest, showed the round plate. Even from behind you could not see any indication as to how it was fastened on.

Suddenly, with a movement of decision, little Dick stood up; and, as he stood up, he said,

"Oou!" and nearly sat down again. Uncle
Andrew had very effectively seen to that.

Stiff with pain, he carefully rubbed himself up
and down, with both little brown hands. Then
slipped on his coat, and went to find a stone.

"I am like David," he said, as he searched,
"and old Peter is Goliath; but I shall not choose
five smooth stones out of a brook, because there
is no brook, and I intend to do it with *one*."

His active little mind ran rapidly along the lines
of the Old Testament story. He almost felt himself an Israelitish hero, as he took up his position
well in front of the gigantic figure, looming large
on the dark window.

"Comest thou to me with a plate?" challenged
the clear treble of his fearless little voice.

Then, bending back his arm, he took careful aim;
his hand shot out from the shoulder; the stone
flew from it, crashed clean through the halo above
Saint Peter's head, and went rattling down on to
the tessellated pavement of the chancel.

Then little Dick ran home, crept in by the back
way, and put himself supperless to bed.

When Aunt Louisa at last went to look for him,
she found him fast asleep, one arm flung over his
curly head. His flushed little face wore a look of
triumphant peace. He had gone to bed in his
flannel shirt.

Aunt Louisa bent over him and smoothed his
tumbled curls. She had had no children of her
own.

Dick stirred restlessly, and half opened his eyes.

"Comest thou to me with a plate?" he said; then slept again.

"Poor little boy," murmured Aunt Louisa. "He is still thinking of the tea-party."

Then she found his little nightshirt, and tried to slip it on, without waking him. But she soon discovered why Dick had gone to bed in his day-shirt. It had stuck to him, in dark red lines.

Aunt Louisa shivered, as she drew the bed-clothes over him again.

"Andrew is a hard man," she thought, in the secret of her own sad heart. But what she *said*, was: "Poor little boy! I hope he has learnt his lesson."

Had little Dick been awake, he might have remarked: "Grown-up people don't often say what they *really* think!"

CHAPTER V

"I AM THE MASTER OF MY FATE"

NOW, strangely enough, the demolition of Saint Peter's halo was not discovered until three whole days had gone by.

At that time the little church of Dinglevale was used on Sundays only, which possibly accounted for the fact that the people of Dinglevale were inclined also to relegate their religion to the one day of the week.

When, on Saturday morning, the old woman who cleaned the church, unlocked it and went in, she sensed an airiness, which was not there as a rule; she saw a shaft of unadulterated sunlight, streaming down the chancel, and, drawing nearer, perceived a large hole immediately over the bald head of the Apostle, while, lying on the chancel floor, were the fragments of the shattered halo, and a large, smooth stone.

She ran and found her husband, the clerk, pouring out to him an incoherent story. He, being a man who refused on principle to believe anything he had not himself seen, who also invariably formed his own opinions and contradicted those of others, curtly requested her—in three words—to hold that portion of her face which must be allowed free play if conversation is to be possible, put on his coat, and marched over to the church.

There he took stock of the disaster, brought to bear upon it his faculty for deductive reasoning, on which he specially prided himself, then expressed his opinion: firstly, that the window had been broken; secondly, that it had been broken by a stone—otherwise why should a stone be lying there? Thirdly, that the stone, being *inside*, had most probably been thrown through the window from the *outside*. All this he stated in a belligerent manner to his silent wife, as if daring her to contradict him. He then asked her to tell him why she supposed eyes were ever given at all, to people who appeared to be unable to use them? But this was one of those statements which are merely couched in the form of a query, in order the more effectively to humiliate the person concerned; for when, after the momentary pause required to accentuate her stupidity and his acumen, she opened her mouth to reply, he again requested her to hold her jaw. Then he and she hurried to the Rectory.

Uncle Andrew came out of his study, calling loudly for Aunt Louisa to accompany him to the church.

The Rector perforce drew the same conclusions as the clerk, Aunt Louisa silently agreeing.

The news spread like wildfire. By the afternoon, many people remembered having seen a disreputable looking tramp hanging about the churchyard the day before. By evening, several people had noticed a stone in his hand, and, by Sunday morning, a quite reliable witness had heard him threaten to "do" for somebody—or something.

Meanwhile Aunt Louisa identified him as a man who had begged at the back door, and to whom she had sternly refused money; but, as he had said—probably untruly—that he and his wife and little child were starving, and had tramped since early dawn without food of any kind, Aunt Louisa —though fully alive to the reprehensible behaviour of the man in having a hungry wife and child, and to the iniquity of tramping from one place to another, instead of living in a comfortable home —had been moved to pity, and had presented him with a cold suet dumpling.

This last piece of evidence convinced the whole parish that the unknown tramp had, without question, broken the church window. A few recipients of Aunt Louisa's charities, even dared to whisper that he had probably done so, *with* the dumpling.

The tramp was the culprit; and he, and his hungry family, had tramped away beyond reach of punishment. Nothing remained to be done, save to open a fund for repairing the halo.

Nobody thought of Master Dick.

And as little Dick, during the long morning ser-

vice, lifted his eyes to the beautiful hole above the
bald head of Saint Peter, where the hated plate
had been, he felt, alas, no prickings of conscience,
and no remorse; but a secret sense of power.

He had done this entirely himself. It had happened in the "Twinkling-of-an-eye." It was the
first of the "Judgments" which he would bring
about, unaided, if he chose. And, meanwhile, he
no longer feared Grandaunt Louisa, or the unknown terrors with which she had heretofore
made his spirit quail. After this—he looked up
at the hole, through which the golden sunlight
streamed, making of the sacred dust a glorious
shining shaft of dancing motes—after this, the
very worst must eventually happen to him. And
there is a calm of mind which comes with certainty; even when that certainty is—the very
worst.

Looking down at the little face beside her,
Aunt Louisa was struck by its quiet happiness.
She felt that her many lessons were at last bear-
ing fruit in this wayward little heart.

The first of the morning Psalms was being
recited. It happened to be the 139th. The Fallen
Idol was declaiming loudly: "Try me, O God, and
seek the ground of my heart; prove me, and
examine my thoughts."

Little Dick, intent on the hole in the window,
had forgotten his Prayer-book; but Aunt Louisa's
admonitory forefinger, in Sabbath garb of sombre kid, descended thereupon, with heavy and

suggestive point, just in time to ensure the uplifting of his clear little voice in the final response:
"Look well if there be any way of wickedness in
me; and lead me in the way everlasting."

During the Gloria which followed, Dick lifted
his brown eyes once more to the broken halo of
Saint Peter, and a wistful smile illumined his
features.

Aunt Louisa would usually have felt it her duty
sternly to check smiling in church, but something
in the quality of that smile arrested her. It was
so very seraphic, so peculiarly radiant, so completely assured. It was the smile of a heart which
had nothing to fear, and therefore nothing to hide.

Then the flute-like treble of Dick's voice at her
elbow reached her.

"As it was in the beginning, is now, and ever
shall be, world without end. Amen!" sang little
Dick, with head erect, and shoulders squared.

Unwonted tears welled up in Grandaunt Louisa's
pale eyes. "Out of the mouth of babes and suck-
lings," she thought, "Thou hast perfected praise."

But, as a matter of fact, to that alarming "Look
well," little Dick's dauntless soul had added,
fearlessly: "Let 'em! I'm not afraid!" And, in
that moment, every shred of belief in Grandaunt
Louisa's carefully inculcated gospel of terror, fell
from him forever—"world without end. Amen."

And that day had proved the turning point in
the boy's young life. For some mysterious reason
—possibly because he no longer feared them—

misunderstandings, petty tyrannies, burdensome
oppressions, no longer assailed him. Each day
seemed crowned by small successes, and, as truly
says that tritest of all sayings: "Nothing succeeds
like success." So, though the halo of belief in love,
and truth, and goodness, was irrevocably gone
from it, Dick's boyhood was a gay and a happy
one. His father's return with his regiment, from
India, removed him from Dinglevale and from the
guardianship of his granduncle and aunt. His
onward progress from preparatory to public school,
and from public school to university, was a fine
crescendo of triumph. He decided to enter the
medical profession, at an age when most boys are
reading books of adventure, and eager to go to sea.

"There is nothing in the world so interesting as
people," remarked Dick, at the age of twelve. "I
like to know all about 'em, outside and in."

There was very little he did not know, of what
science could teach, when he had taken his degree
with brilliant honours and served his apprentice-
ship, under several big men, in surgical and clinical
work. But the moment had arrived when the next
step toward that consulting-room in Harley Street,
and the eventual top of the tree, was to obtain a
practice, or a share in a practice, in town.

Soon after he had secured a much-needed holiday and relaxation in the light work of this Dinglevale *locum tenency*, he heard of an opening in
Kensington which seemed to be, in every respect,
precisely what he wanted. The practice was an

excellent one; the neighbourhood highly desirable; the senior partner a man he knew well, able but lethargic, inclined to gravitate at 4 p.m. toward houses in which he knew the tea to be good, and a certainty; the armchairs, comfortable; the patients charming; the cases not complicated; there remaining until too late for a further round of visits. Dr. Dick, who had long ago gauged his man, knew it would require but very little manœuvring to have all the important cases in his own hands. A little tact, a few casual suggestions, instant deference should the senior partner's self-esteem take fright, a little flattery, if necessary, combined with a modest undervaluing of his own work—and the thing would be done. His superabundant energy would pander to the other man's lethargy, and, before he realised what was happening the junior partner would be at the top; and a step down or back was a move unknown to Dr. Dick.

An apparently insuperable obstacle in the way of this excellent plan lay in the fact that this partnership in the Kensington practice could only be obtained for a sum far beyond Dick's means, beyond anything which he had any prospect of being able to afford.

This seemed to him, however, a mere detail. He had made up his mind to have that practice, and when he made up his mind to have a thing, he usually had it, well within the appointed time.

Ever since the day of the smashed halo, that evening when the small boy made up his mind that

"Judgment-days"—yes, and even the "Twink-lings-of-an-eye"—should happen at his behest, unaided by Divine interposition, or any known exterior forces, few things had been able to with-stand Dick's imperious will.

"Twinklings-of-an-eye" undoubtedly took place, when occasion demanded. As, for instance, when walking unannounced into the private laboratory of a fellow-student, he found a small and helpless dog, who had strayed away from the care of a devoted little mistress, suffering untold and illegal agonies at the hands of this Scientific Investigator. A little child, her arms clasped around an empty dog-basket, had cried herself to sleep that evening, fearing lest Fido, who always slept so happily near her own little white bed, after sharing her supper, should on this night have no comfy bed, and be obliged to go to sleep hungry—little dreaming that poor wandering Fido was at that moment suffering torments compared with which a death from starvation would have been merciful indeed.

Dick took in the situation at a glance. Then the "Twinkling-of-an-eye" happened. The Scientific Investigator was not "caught up," but he was very promptly knocked down. Dick's fist shot out, and caught him full between the eyes. Then with a swift merciful stroke, he brought relief to the tortured body and release to the agonized spirit of little Fido.

The Scientific Investigator had no redress. He knew his methods were illegal. He knew every

4

honest man in his profession would approve Dick Cameron, and execrate himself. Raw steak and curses were his only solace for the plum on his forehead and his two black eyes; a sullen determination to double-lock the door next time, his only consolation. Thus Dick made enemies and friends, in his onward march; and went ahead gaily, caring nothing at all for either.

And "Judgment-days" happened also.

When Granduncle Andrew, after a truly impressive funeral, joined Grandaunt Louisa in the quiet vault in which, during five years, she had rested undisturbed, the Lady of the Manor presented the living of Dinglevale to the curate, long her pet and protégé. So the Fallen Idol now reigned at the Rectory and ruled in the parish.

But when Dick Cameron arrived as medical *locum tenens*, and the present Rector of Dinglevale, calling upon his "young friend of former years," unfortunately found him at home—why, then the Judgment-day happened for the Fallen Idol. He came face to face with the exact meaning of the passage upon which he happened to have preached on the previous Sunday: "Every idle word that men shall speak they shall give account thereof in the day of judgment."

Dr. Dick, in the undesired rôle of "young friend of former years," had various forcible home truths to tell the Fallen Idol. It is quite impossible to record the conversation, because Dick's share of it would require so much bowdlerizing, that very

little would remain to print; and the Rector, after
a first amazed protest, became inarticulate, being
engrossed in a hasty search for his soft clerical
wide-awake, which he had confidingly deposited
upon the writing-table, and which Dick had
dexterously flicked into a dark and dusty corner,
behind Miss Prettyman's tortuous red velvet sofa.
Was it not the Fallen Idol who had once come
striding up the Rectory drive, twisting around an
angry finger the elastic of a little hat, bearing the
brave device: "H.M.S. DAUNTLESS"?

Ah, me! Some men's sins go before to judgment; and some men's follow after.

The Rector hastened from Woodbine Villa,
strode down the garden path, and out at the little
gate, even more rapidly than he had hurried from
the Manor to the Rectory in the wake of his
"young friend of former years," a cruel Nemesis
of unjust retribution to the child who had trusted
him as hero and comrade. He then proceeded to
warn his parishioners against calling in, should
illness occur, the impious young man who pro-
fessed to have undertaken good Dr. Thompson's
work. Whereupon—on the same principle as the
unfailing advertisement of the ban or the Censor
—half-a-dozen people promptly fell ill and sent
for Dr. Dick, who was kept quite busy diagnos-
ing parochial curiosity, and prescribing for honest
annoyance at clerical interference.

This return to Dinglevale had awakened vivid
memories of those first seven years of childhood—

happy memories, most of them. Every tree and every furze bush seemed a friend. The well-remembered ha'penny buns, brown, shiny, and full of currants, still sat in tempting rows in Mrs. Berry's window. The first time Dr. Dick walked down the village street, he went in and bought a dozen, for the sake of the small boy who once, when his only halfpenny was spent and gone, had sworn so to do, some day; sworn it solemnly, his nose flattened against that identical window-pane.

"Greedy little beast!" said Dr. Dick crossly, as he prescribed for himself that evening. "But we have to see that he keeps his word; each oath of long ago fulfilled to the letter, cost what it may."

And now, sitting in the dining-room at the Manor House, he felt he was indeed paying off an old score. Not once had he been in that room since he had stood in the doorway, flinging defiance at the hostess who had invited and then shamed him.

No wonder the whole scene came back so vividly.

He walked round the table, cut himself a slice of cake, and returned to his seat, laughing.

" '*What* a greedy little boy!' " he said. "I can hear her now! Jove! how I hated that woman!"

He felt grateful toward the Little White Lady upstairs—so small, so frail, her hold on life so uncertain and precarious; yet it was she who had enabled him to pay off old scores upon two of the actors in that bygone tragedy; for it was the ponderous droning of the Fallen Idol which had been interrupted by his remarks and prohibitions from the porch, and it was in the domain of the Large Lady of the Manor that now, as sole doctor in charge, he was entitled to give peremptory orders.

As he pinned a golden rose into his old flannel coat, he began to think of the Little White Lady as a sort of mascot. Was this chance meeting with her going to affect in some unexpected way, his whole career? Park Lane! A good address!

He drew an easy chair near to the table, within reach of the fruit and decanters, lay back in its comfortable depths, and took out his cigarette-case, but returned it unopened to his pocket. He would have enjoyed smoking in the Large Lady's beautiful dining-room, beneath the frowns of her pretentious ancestors; but he had to listen to that fluttering heart again, and he shrewdly suspected that the Little White Lady would prefer that he should not smell of tobacco, however fragrant.

At that moment, the door opened and Mrs. Maher-shalal-hash-baz appeared, more forbidding than ever in demeanour, but almost deferential in manner. She closed the door and advanced into the room.

"My lady is pleased to wish to see you again, sir," she began; then paused, as if she had something further to say.

Dr. Dick turned toward her, all attention.

"Certainly. I will come up at once. But you wish to say something more, Mrs. Ransom? Don't hesitate. You and I must work together, you know. You can speak to me quite freely."

He looked into the grim face, and smiled. Dr. Dick had a very winning manner when he pleased.

The grim face relaxed.

"What ever did you give 'er?" she inquired, in an impressive, confidential whisper. "To think of the long hours of agony she suffers in them attacks, and there she was in two minutes a-looking up, and smiling! It passes me. And to think I tried to stop you, never knowing you was a doctor!"

"My good woman," said Dr. Dick, regarding her with interested appreciation, "how could you possibly guess that anything out of a frock-coat was a doctor? You were perfectly right in hesitating to permit interference on the part of a passing bicyclist in old cricket flannels. I commend your vigilance."

Mrs. Maher-shalal-hash-baz expanded still further.

"And you ridin' for pleasure, with all them things in your pockets! And many's the time old Dr. Baines 'as arrived, in tall hat and black coat, and 'There, Mrs. Ransom!' says he, 'if I aint bin an' forgotten m' telescope!' Just when her poor heart was at its worst!"

Dick's face was grave to portentousness.

"That was almost criminal carelessness in Dr. Baines," he said. "No wonder it made you anxious. Everything required for your lady should be at hand, the very moment it is needed; especially a telescope."

"Which brings me," said Ellen Ransom, "to what I have come to say."

This was precisely the point to which Dr. Dick desired to bring her. But Ellen Ransom was a person who must not be hurried.

"You look tired," said Dr. Dick, drawing out a chair from the table with his foot. "You have been standing for hours. Sit down."

"Not on mahogany, thank you, sir. I know m' place. And begging your pardon, I am never tired except in m' own room, or in the presence of m' inferiors."

She drew her angular form up to its full height, suffusing a look of proud vigour into her worn old face.

Dr. Dick, reclining in his armchair, looked up at her with undisguised admiration.

"You are a Spartan, Mrs. Ransom," he said; "but I should take it as a great compliment, if you would allow yourself to be tired when with me. However we are keeping your lady waiting. What do you wish to ask me?"

Ellen Ransom looked steadily over his head, and considered. She appeared to be consulting the Lady of the Manor's pretentious ancestors.

At length she spoke, more slowly than ever.

"When an attack is over, sir," she said, "my poor lady lives in terror of another, especially at nights, till time goes by, and she kind of forgets how bad it was. Could you be so good as to leave us a dose or two of that stuff, to have handy in case of need? Just the feel of it there, would help her."

"No," said Dr. Dick, "I couldn't do that. What I used was a very powerful heart stimulant, and only a doctor could judge whether the condition of the moment called for it. A lot of harm is done by putting these emergency remedies into the hands of people who cannot possibly know how or when to use them. I might as well leave you a lancet or a—a telescope."

Mrs. Ransom consulted the portraits on the opposite wall. Then she said: "In that case, sir, if I may make so bold as to ask, would you be willing—so as to be handy in case of need—to sleep in the house here for a few nights, until my lady gets back her nerve? Not that we should expect to have to disturb you, but just to feel that you and the remedy was handy."

Now it must have been the innate boyishness in Dr. Dick, which caused his mind to jump at once to the thought of the jolly big bath upstairs, the abundance of hot and cold water taps, the luxurious appliances he had so reluctantly eschewed, lest they should stand in the way of his professional duties. Oh, well-deserved reward of devotion to duty! Farewell to the limitations of Miss Prettyman's tin pannikin! Abundance should be his, night and morning.

These gay trivialities shouted riotously in his inner man. Outwardly he grew more decorously professional than ever.

"That might be possible, Mrs. Ransom," he said, "if your lady particularly desires it. I am not expecting any night-calls just now; and to-morrow Dr. Thompson returns, which sets me free at once, if I wish it; though, as a matter of fact, I am staying on for a bit, while he gets back into harness. Also there is one special case I want to see through. In fact," he glanced at the clock, "I am due, four miles from here, at half-past three."

Ellen Ransom stood her ground, ignoring the clock.

"Then you won't be leaving this village yet awhile, sir?"

Dick Cameron considered. "I need not go back to town for three or four weeks, if I am wanted here," he said, quietly.

Ellen Ransom started.

"Town?" she said. "Town! What town?"

"My good woman," laughed Dr. Dick, "there is but one 'town' in this little island! London, of course."

"Are you a London doctor, sir?"

"Why, certainly I am a London doctor, Mrs. Ransom. I am down here on a holiday."

"Now the Lord be praised!" exclaimed Ellen Ransom devoutly. "My poor lady said, 'Now if only that young man was a London doctor, Ellen, just when we are losing Dr. Baines'—not that we think Dr. Baines no loss—'I don't know *what* I would not give,' said my poor lady, 'to have that young man within call of Park Lane.'

And to think—Well, there! As I say: the Lord
be praised!"

"The Lord has nothing to do with it, my friend,"
smiled Dr. Dick. "I am going to buy a most
excellent practice in Kensington, and, as I shall
probably find it necessary to keep an electric
landaulette, we may consider that I shall be
within easy call of Park Lane."

He lay back, his hands behind his head, looking
up at the gaunt elderly woman, infinite amusement
in his bright brown eyes. He wondered whether
she took the electric landaulette, seriously;
whether she really thought that young doctors,
who earned their bread and butter by taking
village *locum tenencies*, could buy West End
practices in this airy fashion.

Yes—she appeared to have swallowed it! His
eyes sparkled with amusement.

Suddenly their expression changed and hardened; the fun died out. He looked fixedly before
him, as if struck by an arresting thought.

Then a dull red crept slowly up beneath his tan.

Why had he called the Little White Lady his
mascot?

Why had he been returning from a heart case,
with his pockets crammed full of remedies just
when she was collapsing in the church porch?

Why did they keep their tiresome churches so
stuffy?

He rose suddenly to his feet, squaring his
shoulders, with a characteristic gesture, and

plunging both hands into the pockets of his old flannel blazer.

"Come on, Mrs. Ransom," he said, boyishly. "We mustn't stay gossipping here. Don't tell that little lady of yours how long we talked. Doctors and nurses—capable nurses, you know—must be free to have a private consultation sometimes. And, look here! You needn't say that you suggested that I should sleep here to-night. It will please her better if I propose it myself, as a really needful precaution. By the way, what is your lady's name? . . . 'Erriot'? How do you spell it? . . . Oh, I see. 'Herriot.' Well, now take me up to Mrs. Herriot, and we shall soon know how matters are going."

"Queer old fish!" thought Dr. Dick, as he followed the gaunt figure upstairs. "Walks like a grenadier, and looks like a jailor. One almost expects a bunch of keys hanging at her girdle. How in the name of all that's French and fashionable, came the Little White Lady by such a maid?"

At the door of her mistress's bedroom, Ellen Ransom turned and confronted him. The process of mounting the stairs seemed to have wound her up, once more, to grimness. She was stiff and forbidding, as she paused, her hand upon the door handle.

"You will please to remember, sir," she said, threatening, yet respectful, "that my lady is *not* deaf, and particularly dislikes being talked to as if she were. It *is* possible to have white hair and yet keep your hearing—a thing Dr. Baines never *could* remember!" This in a confidential aside, almost startling in its suddenness.

Dr. Dick, his brown eyes on a level with her green ones, smiled at her, friendly and unafraid.

"Hadn't he white hair, himself?" he suggested.

"Neither black, white, nor grey," whispered Ellen Ransom. "He was as bald as my thumb."

Then, opening the door of her mistress's bed-room, she announced: "The Doctor, ma'am," and, standing aside, gravely signed to Dr. Dick to enter.

CHAPTER VI

"GOLDEN ROSES"

A LARGE, low room; the sort of bedroom one expects in an old Manor House. A bow-window overlooking the garden and shady lawn; a high, plain window facing the park and drive.

The windows were mostly open, green venetian blinds down, on the sunny side. The hum of bees stole in, from the large magnolia blossoms outside the bow.

The room was darkened, yet full of sunbeams; quiet, yet filled with sounds of summer; cool, yet suggesting the June day without.

An ineffable sense of peace prevailed; an atmosphere created, not by surroundings, but by one mind.

Dr. Dick stepped quietly across the old-fashioned Brussels carpet, with its chess-board pattern of faded green; a medallion, a streamer of ribbon, and wreath of pink roses, in each square.

The large four-poster, its canopy almost touching the ceiling, its curtains of much-calendered, early-Victorian chintz, was exactly the kind of bed in which you would have expected to find the

Large Lady of the Manor—had you been under the alarming necessity of having to seek for her in bed at all. She would fairly well have filled it.

But the Little White Lady seemed lost, on the vast expanse of billowy pillow, the ocean of spotless counterpane. She looked like an exquisite Watteau, over-margined and over-framed.

The frail whiteness of her cheek was tinted a bright pink, by a flush of nervous anxiety. Ellen had been gone so long, and it was such a very unusual experience to be expecting a visit in her bedroom from a big sunburnt youth in cricketing flannels, with close-cropped hair and handsome eyes, who called her maid by a long, almost unknown, Scriptural name, used unrepeatable language to church officials, and looked as completely unlike a medical man, as anything she had ever seen.

On the other hand, never had firm fingers, falling on her wrist, brought her such an instant sense of hope and confidence, never had her anguish and its cause, been so immediately comprehended and located, without the asking of a single question; and never—oh, never!—had blessed relief been brought so speedily, as by the remedy he had administered.

Therefore, much as she shrank from the idea of this great boy tramping into her bedroom in his flannels, she dared not let his skill pass from her, while there remained a possibility of the recurrence of her hour of need.

Nevertheless, the faint tint in her cheeks brightened, and her heart fluttered like a frightened bird, snared by a schoolboy, as Ellen Ransom announced in her most lugubrious voice: "The Doctor, ma'am"; then retired, closing the door behind her, leaving her mistress confronted at last by the perplexing problem as to which of the many nervous sentences she had prepared, would really be the most suitable with which to open the conversation with her new medical man.

Dr. Dick soon settled that question. As he walked across the room, in his noiseless tennis shoes, he saw the anxious flush on the face of the Little White Lady.

"Now, don't speak," he said, almost before he reached the side of the great four-poster. "I can't allow a word until your heart is quieter; and not then, unless there is something you particularly want to say."

This was a great relief. Mrs. Herriot had always found it difficult to talk to boys. She did not understand slang, and it unnerved and alarmed her.

The blue flannel coat, now at her bedside, with College arms embroidered on the left breast-pocket, reminded her of how she once attended a public school cricket match. Her carriage was drawn up in the shade, beneath the great trees at the side of the beautiful playing field, and she watched the game in comfort. Being a particular friend of the Head Master, and one of the most important personages present, quite a number of people were brought up to her carriage to be introduced, among them, during the interval, the Captain of the School Eleven.

Mrs. Herriot, in a moment of enthusiasm, had asked to shake hands with the hero of the day. But when the tall boy stood before her, looking so much larger and—and hotter than out in the field; when everybody awaited, in interested silence, her congratulatory remarks—speech failed the Little White Lady.

Then, in an anxious endeavour to say the right thing, to show an intelligent yet maternal interest in the game, she leaned forward and asked with gentle solicitude: "Does the ball hurt you when it hits you?"

The hero grinned, looking uneasily to right and left.

"Pensware," he said.

Now the Little White Lady, daintily seated beneath her parasol, had not the faintest idea what "Pensware" could mean. It was explained to her afterwards, that the younger generation do not believe in using sentences of more than two syllables, and that "Pensware" was merely a contraction of "It depends where," i.e., where the ball happens to strike. Not knowing this, she concluded "Pensware" to be a strong and unknown schoolboy phrase, implying that the hurt was excessive. So, leaning still further forward, she remarked sympathetically: "I am very sorry to hear that."

This closed the conversation abruptly. The hero fled to his fellows. Just at the end of the second innings, when he felt confident of carrying out his bat for a hundred, he was out "leg before" for 99!

That ball hurt. He made a stronger remark about it than "Pensware!"

This scene flashed through Mrs. Herriot's mind as she looked up into Dick's brown eyes, and was peremptorily told not to talk.

Dick moved a chair to the side of the bed, took her right hand gently in his, and laid the fingers of his left upon her wrist.

Mrs. Herriot closed her eyes, and lay quite still upon the pillows. The young man's touch was very firm and reassuring. When she could not see the sunburnt boyish face and handsome eyes, her confidence in him, as an undoubtedly clever medical man, returned.

Dr. Dick studied closely the frail face upon the pillows. Its delicate loveliness touched and surprised him. In the church porch she had looked like a faded and crumpled lily. Now she was like a lily, revived by shade and water; frail, yet fair and fragrant. In the church porch, he had thought her quite old—seventy, or thereabouts. In bed, she looked far younger. At first sight he would have said hardly more than fifty. As a matter of fact, her real age was midway between his two guesses.

The shell-like complexion, the perfectly formed

s

features, the delicately chiselled outline of profile, gave the effect of a lovely cameo. The silvery hair, soft and abundant, was smoothed demurely out of its natural waves, and dressed with old-fashioned simplicity, close to the small, graceful head. The face was scarcely lined at all, the Little White Lady's wrinkles being mostly crinkles of fun, when her soft grey eyes danced with amusement, and her whole face broke into a smile.

Yet, in repose, as Dr. Dick now studied it, it told a tale of suffering. The upright line of pain between the eyebrows, revealed to the practised eye, weary heart-trouble of long standing; while the droop of the sweet lips told of a life of sadness, probably borne in uncomplaining silence. Yet it was not a face which sorrow had hardened. Disappointment had left no trace of querulous bitterness. Its pre-eminent characteristic was peace.

Dr. Dick took his fingers from her wrist, released her hand from his, leaned back in his chair, and waited.

The Little White Lady, opening her eyes, looked full into the watching eyes of the young doctor.

Then they smiled, a slow, silent, comprehending smile, which increased in understanding humour, as the moments passed, and drew them infinitely nearer than hours of conversation could have done.

At length Dr. Dick said: "I think I may let you talk now, Mrs. Herriot, if you have anything really important to say."

And the Little White Lady said: "What a perfectly lovely golden rose!"

"Isn't it?" laughed Dr. Dick, glancing complacently at his buttonhole. "I hoped you would notice it. I prigged it from the tree outside the dining-room window, as an apologetic palliative to my ancient flannels."

"Why do you wear ancient flannels on Sunday?"

"Because my Grandaunt Louisa, of blessed memory, dinned it into me when I was a small boy, that Sunday was a 'day of rest,' and there is nothing in the world so restful as wearing your very oldest clothes, and taking the most violent exercise you know. So, as I had had a busy week, I planned for once to mind my Aunt Louisa, and to keep the Sabbath. To that end, I started the day in flannels, meaning to spend the morning mowing my landlady's lawn."

"Instead of which——?" queried Mrs. Herriot.

"Instead of which," continued Dr. Dick, promptly, "I went for a glorious bicycle ride across the common, where the gorse is golden and where the larks shoot up from every tuft and go carolling into the sky. And I said strong things to a flock of sheep on a slope of the down, because, being Sunday, they tinkled the Old Hundredth on their sheep-bells, which seemed so unnecessary, out in the radiant liberty of air and sunshine. I timed my return so as to skim down the hill when all the good folk were safe in the Second Lesson;

but as I passed the church porch I saw—well, that I was wanted."

The Little White Lady considered this.

Then: "Oh, I thank God you passed!" she said. "But it seems to me so wonderful that, even on a holiday ride, expecting no medical work, you yet had with you all that was necessary. It gives one such an extraordinary sense of confidence in you; such a feeling that, in any emergency, you would be there with everything required to meet it."

"There is nothing wonderful in that," said Dick. "A doctor must always be prepared for emergencies. As my Grandaunt Louisa used to say when her pastry turned out heavy: 'It is an uncertain world!' Bar pastry, there is nothing so uncertain as how people's bodies are going to behave. A doctor can never say, either by day or by night, that he is expecting no medical work."

"Ah, but I assure you," insisted Mrs. Herriot, "they do not always come prepared, even to important cases. My own medical man, now about to retire——"

But Dick held up his hand. "I know, ma'am," he said, in excellent imitation of Ellen Ransom, "*I* know! Dr. Baines has, on occasion, even arrived without his telescope! Next time *I* call," said Dr. Dick, "I shall come armed with binoculars."

Mrs. Herriot laughed, in much amusement. "Poor Ellen! She is a faithful soul, but peculiar. May I ask why you called her 'Maher-shalal-hash-baz'? "

"Because," said Dr. Dick, "she 'rushed upon the prey'; I being the prey. She clutched at me with the sort of glove which it always sets my teeth on edge even to think about. She called me 'young man,' and told me her own name in a voice of fury."

"My dear 'young man,'" said Mrs. Herriot, "what a remarkable knowledge of Scripture you must have! Not one Bible student in fifty would have ever heard of Maher-shalal-hash-baz; not one in a hundred would know the meaning of the name."

"My Bible knowledge," replied Dr. Dick, "depended entirely upon my youthful capacity for wrong-doing, and upon my excellent aunt's idea, at the moment, as to which portion of the Bible could provide the most suitable punishment for each particular offence. If I used a naughty word, I had to learn all the Bible names beginning with the same letter as my word, and their meaning. They often sounded worse than the original offence. For calling my Sunday School teacher a mummy, I had to learn all the M's and thus became acquainted with Maher-shalal-hash-baz."

"Why did you call your Sunday School teacher a mummy?"

"Because she *was* one," replied Dr. Dick. "In fact, the Egyptian dynasties weren't in it! She was absolutely antediluvian! Had I then had the superior knowledge I now possess, I should probably have called her a Dinotherium, and learnt all the D's!"

The Little White Lady's eyes were sad, yet tender.

"Poor little lad!" she said. "Was that your introduction to the Bible? What a desecration of the Book which is above every book! How was a little child under such conditions, to grow up loving God's Holy Word?"

Dick, remaining discreetly silent, offered no opinion upon that knotty point.

Presently Mrs. Herriot returned to the subject of the happenings of the morning.

"And it seemed so wonderful," she said, "to see all those appliances and remedies being produced from the pockets of that dear, blue coat! It was really a case of 'Can there any good thing come out of Nazareth?' "

Dr. Dick threw back his head and laughed. "Why should my innocent old flannel blazer be likened to that wicked city?" he asked.

"Ah, but it was *not* a wicked city!" exclaimed Mrs. Herriot eagerly. "There you have one of the most mistaken and libellous misreadings of a New Testament passage. Nazareth was a beautiful village in Galilee, sacred to us as having been the home of the Virgin Mary, the scene of the Annunciation, the abode of our blessed Lord Himself, during the years of His childhood and early manhood. There is no reason whatever to suppose that it had an evil reputation. But

Nathanael was an earnest student of prophecy. He knew that the Messiah was to be born at Bethlehem. His question might be paraphrased: 'Can the *genuine* thing—the Messiah we are expecting—come out of Nazareth?' Whatever may be the exact meaning of *agathon*, the entire sense of the passage proves that the question bore no relation whatever to the character of the village. It was simply a matter of geographical agreement with prophecy."

"I see," said Dr. Dick. His eye was on the leaping pulse in the transparent wrist upon the coverlet. No need to finger it, in order to count its beats. Evidently the question as to the correct readings of Bible passages was one upon which the Little White Lady felt strongly.

"I see," said Dr. Dick. "I am glad you have given me this explanation of the statement. Hitherto I have accepted the conventional belief that Nazareth was known to be a wicked little place, and that Nathanael—in common with many good people of the present day—concluded, therefore, with a thoroughness of sweeping condemnation, that no possibilities of good could, under any circumstances, be found in it. Good heavens!" said Dr. Dick, with a sudden flash of indignation, "how like many so-called Christians, who, if once they have discovered—or imagine themselves to have discovered—wrong, never again expect any good whatever from that quarter!" Then, seeing the pain and distress on the gentle face of the

Little White Lady, he laughed lightly and added:

"Yes, I am glad you have told me; because the only ideas I had on the passage came from a sermon I heard my Uncle Andrew preach in Dinglevale church, when I was a small boy. He took as his text: 'Can there any good thing come out of Nazareth?' And Nazareth stood, I remember, for all the places of which Uncle Andrew disapproved—various strongholds of iniquity abroad, and, coming nearer home, pubs., and the dissenting chapel."

"Oh, shame!" cried Mrs. Herriot, sharply. "Never tell that story again ! I cannot bear it. I am a staunch Churchwoman myself, but never would I say one word to undervalue the good work of others, who are equally honest in their beliefs and in their endeavours, although their beliefs may not, at all points, coincide with my own, and their endeavours may not be carried out along lines which appeal to me personally. Nothing fills me with greater indignation, than religious intolerance."

"Then there is no subject we must more carefully avoid just now," said Dr. Dick, catching a waving hand in his, as a boy catches a white butterfly, and laying it gently back upon the bed. "Let us return to the original matter under discussion. This new and charitable rendering of the passage, lifts all possible suggestion of ill-repute from my ancient but hitherto respectable coat, stamping it merely as a coat, from which you would not have expected genuine medical appli-

ances to issue. However, so long as they were
genuine, and proved to be what was needed, it
matters very little where they came from, or how
they chanced to be there. The important point
is: that they must be within reach, in case you
should want them again. Which brings me—as
Mrs. Ransom would remark—to what I have
come to say! You have satisfactorily recovered
so far, Mrs. Herriot, from this morning's attack,
but I should feel uneasy, were I beyond call during
the night, in case of the return of any of those
trying symptoms. Will you think it presumption
on my part if I suggest sleeping in the house
to-night, in order that you may know that your
maid could call me instantly, should need arise?"

The Little White Lady's eyes filled and over-
flowed with tears of relief.

"My dear young doctor," she said, "far from
thinking so kind a suggestion presumptuous on
your part, it is the very thing I have been trying
to tell myself I must not venture to ask of you.
The relief to me would be beyond all words.
But is it not expecting too much—with the entire
medical work of this village——"

"Not a bit," said Dr. Dick. "Old Thompson
returns to-morrow; after which I merely stay on
to oblige, and to see through a few special cases,
about which I am extra keen. I do not anticipate
any night calls, and can easily leave word where I
may be found, in case of unexpected emergency.
Now I must be off to Hazelmoor, and then to

a few old chronics, in order to impress upon them that they are not likely to die to-night. But I will be back in time to have a look at you the last thing, unless sleep comes to you very early. Should that happen, you must not be disturbed. I shall have a word with your maid, now, and give her a few instructions."

He rose and replaced the chair, then stood beside the bed, looking down upon the Little White Lady.

She put her hand into his.

"You are very good to me, my young doctor," she said, "very good. And I do not even know your name."

"Richard Cameron," he answered; "but most of the good folk around here call me 'Dr. Dick.' I lived amongst them as a small boy, and Surrey people are very faithful to old friends. My Grand-uncle Andrew was about the crustiest thing going in the way of parsons, but to hear the old villagers talk, you would think he had been a saint of the first water; while my Aunt Louisa, who never gave even gruel without the strictest inquiries, com-bined with a reproving aspect which implied that it was criminal improvidence to be either sick or hungry, is remembered as a gracious lady, who moved about the parish with her lap full of loaves and roses, like Saint What's-her-name?"

"Perhaps," said the Little White Lady, gently, "there was more saintliness in both, than their little nephew ever saw."

"Perhaps there was," agreed Dr. Dick. "Their little nephew started life as a halo-smasher! But I am letting you talk too long. I must be off. Lie very still during the rest of the day, Mrs. Herriot. Listen to the birds and bees, watch the sunshine and the shadows, and the tree-tops waving. But make no exertion, either mental or physical. Good-bye."

. . . .

Mrs. Herriot was lying very still, her eyes on the tree-tops, when Ellen Ransom walked in, carrying a silver vase, filled with golden roses.

She drew forward a small table, placed the vase upon it, and was about to leave the room in silence, when Mrs. Herriot spoke.

"Who sent me these lovely roses, Ellen?"

"The Doctor, ma'am," replied Ellen, with the ready energy of one released, by a question, from an irksome promise of silence. "Went through the dining-room window, while giving instructions —me follerin'. Outs with a big clasp-knife and begins slashin' at the rose tree, talkin' all the time. In through the window again—me after 'im. Pours water and a pinch of salt into this silver vase, in spite of me remarking 'twas for ornament, not use. Plumps in the whole bunch of roses, and with a touch here and a touch there, makes 'em into a bookay. Then says he: 'Carry these up to your mistress, Mrs. Ransom; fit emblem of her own golden heart—only you needn't say I said so.

Put them on that little table which stands between the window and the bed; and never again let me see *her* in a room with not a flower in it!' 'Beggin' your pardon, sir,' says I, 'but you're the first doctor I've come acrost who prescribed flowers.' 'I prescribe anything I choose, Mrs. Ransom,' says he. 'I prescribe trained nurses, if I think necessary, as you'll find out quick enough, if you don't carry out my orders without discussing them!' But he said it with a twinkle which pretty well showed he was pleased. An' he'll be back to-night and as many more nights as we like; which I must say, ma'am, lifts a load off me."

"Ellen," inquired Mrs. Herriot, her eyes on the golden roses, "did you tell Dr. Cameron, before he came upstairs, that we were hoping he would be able to sleep in the house to-night?"

"Well, ma'am," replied Ellen Ransom, in her slow, deliberate voice, "I did not say *you* had said so, but I made so bold as to suggest it on m' own, and he took to the idea at once and said, Why, yes, of course he would, and with pleasure. There 's nothing that young man wouldn't do, ma'am, to get a person well. He's worth a baker's dozen of Dr. Baines!"

Receiving no reply to this assertion, Ellen went to the door, paused on the threshold, as if arrested by a sudden thought, hesitated a moment, then said, hurriedly: "If it is not troubling you, ma'am, what is a 'Spartan'?"

"A Spartan, Ellen," replied the gentle voice

from the bed, "is a very brave and heroic person, who can bear or suffer anything in the cause of duty."

Ellen Ransom, more erect than ever, marched proudly from the room.

Left alone, Mrs. Herriot lay very still, her eyes on the golden roses in the massive silver vase.

At last she turned her head on the pillows, folded her hands, and gently closed her eyes. A sad smile played around the soft line of her lips.

"Poor little 'halo-smasher'!" she murmured. "Where was his mother all the time, I wonder? He must have needed all the tenderness the most tender mother could give."

Then the sunny room grew very still; and presently the Little White Lady fell asleep, before reaching the conclusion of her first prayer for Dr. Dick.

CHAPTER VII

DICK AIRS HIS OPINIONS

"THE saddest part of it all, to me," said Mrs. Herriot, "is that I fear the halo stands for an outward and visible sign——"

"Of an inward and spiritual grace?" questioned Dick, laughing.

"Of an inward and spiritual *loss*," amended Mrs. Herriot, gravely. "Think of all you lost, on that one day, poor little boy! Belief in the kindness, justice, and hospitality of your hostess; faith in the loyalty and honour of your friend and hero; trust in the love and tenderness of your guardians and relations. But worst of all—oh, worst of all!—child though you were, loss of faith in the love of God, in Divine interposition, and in the efficacy of prayer."

They were having tea in the garden—the Little White Lady and Dr. Dick. She reclined on a wicker couch, well propped with gay cushions. On a low rustic table at her left, stood a tea tray, placed so that she could reach the teapot with ease.

To the right of the couch, Dr. Dick was reclining, at full length upon the soft velvet of the turf, raised on one elbow, his cup and plate beside him. He had been round to cut himself a large piece of cake, remarking as he did so, in a shocked falsetto: "*What* a greedy little boy!" Then, as a concession to Mrs. Herriot's look of astonishment, had told her the whole story.

In the course thereof, the Little White Lady laughed till she wept, then wept without laughter; and, at the crashing of the stone through the halo of Saint Peter, a settled sadness fell upon her quiet face.

Nearly a month had passed since she was taken in charge in the church porch by her young doctor. Under his careful treatment she now felt better than she had done for years. Long since, he had stopped all drugs, insisting only on two things as of paramount importance: fresh air, the first; complete rest, the second. The charming old garden and the perfect summer weather, favoured the first. The second was rendered possible by the fact that as soon as she was dressed in the morning, had rested during a few minutes on the sofa in the bow-window, and was beginning to long to be in the garden, beneath the shade of the gently moving trees, a gay knock would resound upon the door, and Dr. Dick would walk in.

"Ready for the *h*elevator, ma'am?" he would say, quoting a remark which had amused them of Ellen Ransom's, who sighed after modern conveniences, unknown to the old Manor House. Then he would pick her up in his strong arms, and

carry her downstairs, and out through the French
window to the couch beneath the beech tree, where
Ellen was placing the cushions, having already put
her knitting and the book she was reading on the
rustic table, side by side with the silver vase,
filled with freshly gathered roses.

Here Mrs. Herriot lunched, and took tea; though
latterly she had had leave to walk quietly over the
smooth level turf if she wished the position of her
couch changed; or to pass slowly within doors, if
she preferred the restfulness of the cool drawing-
room, with windows open and blinds down.

But when evening came, the same strong arms
lifted her gaily, carrying her upstairs and deposit-
ing her on the couch, beside which he would linger
a few moments to make sure she was comfortable,
and likely to have a good night.

It sometimes seemed to Mrs. Herriot strange
how dependent she had become upon him—this
young doctor of whom, after all, she knew practically nothing. From the first there had been very
little of the professional aspect about their inter-
course, which had become almost at once, an intimate friendship—careful, attentive, deferential, on
his part; grateful, affectionate, dependent, on hers.

He felt for her what he had perhaps never felt, in
the same degree, for any one else on earth—a
sincere admiration for the qualities of her mind and
soul, which caused him, unconsciously, to rate
them as of higher value than the frail body which
contained them.

She felt for him all the grateful admiration which a chronic sufferer feels for the man who has understood her case, with a quickness of comprehension and an ability to relieve, such as she had never before experienced; coupled with an amused enjoyment of his vivid, vigorous nature, and an almost wistful tenderness over the fact that the infant son, lost to her at birth, many years before, might now have been surrounding her, in her loneliness, with just this gay strength of splendid manhood. The mother-love in Mrs. Herriot was beginning to awaken and to outpour its pent-up fragrance over Dr. Dick.

He was as unconscious of its essential nature as he was of the botanical classification of the roses, lilies, and sweet-scented pines, which made the summer air of the old Manor garden fragrant and life-giving. His eye rested on a clump of lilies-of-the-valley growing in the shade, each arched stem of pearly bells half hidden by its overshadowing leaf of tender green; he saw them, without realising how far-reaching was their sweet, mysterious fragrance, or that he himself was breathing it in as a part of the delight of this summer sunset breeze. In like manner he saw the delicate white face and the silvery hair, beneath soft lace; he felt the helpful atmosphere of sympathy and understanding gently surrounding him as he talked with the Little White Lady. He expanded to the influence without definitely analysing its source

6

"And how came it," inquired Mrs. Herriot presently, "that, so soon after the happenings of that eventful day, you left Dinglevale and did not return during all the intervening years ?"

"In the late autumn of that year," replied Dick, "my father's regiment returned from India. He had been so broken by my mother's unexpected death that he had not felt able to come home on leave; and even then he could not bring himself to come down to Dinglevale. I believe, at dead of night, he paid one moonlight visit to her grave. But he would never see Uncle Andrew or Aunt Louisa. He could not forgive them for having failed to let him know how quickly she was fading. You see, it had been the difficult question so often entailed by foreign service: should she go with her husband, or stay with her little child? Her own frail health gave the casting vote in favour of the latter course. She bade him farewell, and remained with me. Her own parents were not living, so her uncle and aunt gave her a home at Dinglevale Rectory.

"But she pined for the strength and tenderness which had been daily, hourly life to her. My father was a very vivid, vital person. She faded silently, without complaint. Aunt Louisa dosed her with homœopathy—not pillules, even, but tiny globules ! She kept them in a row of little bottles in a black leather case. You had to put out your tongue, and Aunt Louisa laid one, or two, or—in extreme cases—three globules upon it, with an exceedingly small metal spoon, taken from a little home of its own in the lid of the case. When Aunt Louisa laboriously scooped up the globules out of the bottle, counted them, and laid them on your tongue, you felt solemnly certain that it would probably be fatal to take four, if Aunt Louisa's ancient little sage-green book had said three. Yet, once, when left alone in her room with a longing for sweeties upon me, I emptied the entire contents of most of her little bottles down my infant throat, and felt none the worse for the achievement, until Granduncle Andrew had dealt with me on the matter, in his study, three or four days later; the smug little empty bottles having meanly told their tale.

"Well, as I say, Aunt Louisa dosed a breaking heart with homœopathy—and in more ways than one; for her tenderness and sympathy were also homœopathic in quantity.

"Uncle Andrew, on the other hand, dosed it with stern theology, his treatment being allopathic, and partaking of the nature of salts and senna—not to say brimstone !

"Her little boy gave her all the love he knew; but he was a mere infant, and his tiny arms, however loving, could not replace those big strong arms so far away.

"So she failed and faded, and finally fell asleep, never to wake again. And when I broke away from a strict imprisonment of three or four days in the nursery, made my way to her room, and shouting: 'Mummie! Mummie!' climbed on to the bed, I found it empty.

"Then my nurse, who had followed to recapture me, told me that it was no use looking there any more, as my mamma was now asleep under the grass in the churchyard; adding, in an audible aside to the housemaid: 'And a deal better off there, poor thing, than a-fretting of her heart out, above ground.'

"Later on, Aunt Louisa told me that my mother had gone to heaven to dwell with God, and that if I became a very good little boy, obedient in all things to herself, and attended carefully to what Uncle Andrew said when he preached on Sundays, I might also, some day, go to heaven and dwell with God.

"This seemed to me an alarming and altogether undesirable eventuality. Moreover, I believed nurse, and completely disbelieved Aunt Louisa. Nurse's story seemed so far more natural and likely. My Mummie had always loved lying on the grass, among the buttercups and daisies, and would lie there for hours while I played around her, and stuck dandelions in her soft brown hair; until Aunt Louisa would arrive upon the scene, exclaiming: 'My dear Eleanor, get up immediately! This long grass is probably damp, and that child is crumpling your gown and reducing your hair to a sad state of disorder.' It did not seem surprising, under these circumstances, that my patient, tired, little Mummie should prefer lying *under* the grass, where Aunt Louisa could not insist upon her getting up, to lying *on* it; even though, in her more secluded resting-place, her little boy could no longer stick dandelions in her hair. Besides, I several times overheard Uncle Andrew and Aunt Louisa discussing the details of 'poor Eleanor's resting-place,' and of how they intended to mark the spot where she lay, by erecting a massive marble cross. I therefore believed Nurse; and —I believe her still."

Dick stopped abruptly, and threw a large crumb at a thrush, which had been gradually hopping nearer and nearer, watching him with bright black eyes and head on one side.

The thrush seized the crumb, and hopped rapidly off towards the shrubbery. In his place advanced a veritable phalanx of sparrows, chirping, twittering, fluttering, squabbling, and all the while hopping fearlessly nearer and nearer to the couch beneath the tree—to the blue serge sleeve on the grass beside it, to the brown hand which held the bread-and-butter.

Dick laughed, broke the bread-and-butter into small pieces and pelted them with it.

"Cheeky little beggars!" he said. "I declare that one caught a piece, as a dog might catch a biscuit! They'll sit up on their tails and beg, next! And it isn't only sparrows. Here come a pair of bullfinches, two wagtails—jolly little black and white beggars, all the time on the wag— a robin, a pair of chaffinches, and a blue-tit.

How on earth do you make all the birds so tame?"

The Little White Lady wiped away her tears, and steadied her quiet voice.

"By keeping absolutely still at first; never making a sudden movement when they begin to come near. By never failing or disappointing their eager little expectations. If they found seed in a certain place yesterday, they may be sure of it in the same place to-day. If a bath of refreshing water is on the lawn to-day, it will be pure and bright and freshly filled to-morrow."

Mrs. Herriot paused, looking down wistfully upon the broad shoulders and dark head on the lawn beside her couch. Then she added, slowly: "Also, I think, continually, thoughts of love and sympathy and tenderness toward them. I try to understand their point of view—even a sparrow has a point of view! I try to make them feel that they need not be afraid of me, because I love them and want them. That, because not one of them is forgotten before God, therefore—little chirping eager sparrows though they are—not one of them can be forgotten by me. They more than repay my love and care, when, having learned to believe in it, they come to me with trust and with confidence."

"Lucky little beggars!" said Dr. Dick, and threw a piece of cake so straight and true, that he momentarily knocked over a bold cock sparrow.

"What happened after your father's return?" presently inquired Mrs. Herriot.

"He sent for me. He was quartered in Edinburgh. In that romantic and beautiful city, we spent jolly years together, and I went to school. Nothing could have been a greater contrast to Dinglevale Rectory than garrison life in Edinburgh. My father and I hit it off together, from the first. We were great chums. I believe I was ridiculously like him. The mess used to call me 'Chip.'"

"Why 'Chip'?"

"'A chip of the old block,' you know. He was not much over thirty when he came home. He had married very young. As I grew older, he seemed to grow younger. We were much of an age, when I went to the University to study for my degree; and he with his regiment to South Africa. His grave is in the Transvaal. He was leading one of the splendid blunders right at the beginning, and they got him clean through the heart. It was exactly as he would have liked it best, seeing it had to be. He was charging, yards ahead of his men. The bullet went clean through my mother's miniature, which he always wore under his tunic. It came back to me with a black hole right through the soft lace at her breast; her smiling young face above it, quite unconcerned. It would make a prettier story if the miniature had stopped the bullet. But it didn't, you see; and I lost my best chum."

"Surely," suggested the Little White Lady, gently, "the affection between you and your father gave you back your belief in human love and tenderness?"

Dr. Dick considered this.

"It was not exactly affection," he said, at last. "We understood each other perfectly, we amused each other, we were immensely proud of each other. We would have fought one another's battles against all the world—yet I cannot remember one moment of what you would call tenderness. I suppose all his capacity for that sort of thing slept under the grass at Dinglevale. I have seen him wince and turn away if he came unexpectedly on any billing and cooing, or even at sight of a woman fondling a little child. I suppose there are blows which turn all that part of a man's nature permanently to stone."

"It is a great loss to live a loveless life," remarked Mrs. Herriot.

"I don't agree with that," said Dr. Dick.

Then he laid down the law, with the cocksureness of youth and inexperience.

"All love is selfish," said Dr. Dick.

Mrs. Herriot pondered this trenchant remark in silence, drawing toward her the bouquet of golden roses, placed always at her elbow by the forethought of the young man who did not believe either in love or in unselfishness.

For a moment she buried her face in their fragrance; then, lifting her head, smiled indulgently at the well-knit figure lying prone upon the grass, yet kept the smile out of her voice as she remarked: "A startling statement, my dear young doctor. Can you substantiate it?"

"Certainly," replied Dr. Dick. "Let us begin with lovers. I maintain that lovers are selfish, not only toward all the world, but toward each other. In fact, the large majority of lovers, especially the women, are not in love with each other at all. They are merely in love with being loved. This fact explains most cases of jilting. A man comes along who can make love in a more delightful way — who has made a fine art of it; and the girl who is in love with being loved, leaves No. 1, and takes up with No. 2. Take away love from a pair of lovers, and what is left?"

The Little White Lady's eyes danced amid crinkles of fun; but she kept the laughter out of her voice.

"It sounds like the dear, delightful Red Queen's subtraction, in *Through the Looking Glass*," she said, "but I suppose a man and a woman are left; and, if no love remains between them, they had better part and go different ways without delay."

"Ah, ha!" cried Dr. Dick. "Now we arrive at the great marriage problem. There, incompatibility of temperament comes in. I suppose you favour easy divorce."

Mrs. Herriot flushed. "No," she said. "There

the Divine comes in. 'Those whom God hath
joined together, let no man put asunder.' "

"Which applies, undoubtedly, to marriages
made in heaven," retorted Dr. Dick. "But how
about those whom passion, or mammon, match-
making relations, or force of circumstances, have
joined together?"

"We cannot set aside a perfect law, because of
the many hopeless travesties of its high conditions," she answered. "No two people should
enter into the sacred bonds of matrimony, unless
that which is holy and Divine forms their primary
connecting link. Unless God Himself, and the
Love which is of God, joins them together, let
them not venture to embark upon so perilous
a voyage, lest they make shipwreck."

Dick picked a daisy, and threw it at a sparrow.

"Oh, well," he said, "I am not in a position to
argue the point, because I don't believe in the
two main factors in your case. Let's return to
my first contention: 'All love is selfish.' You
told me to prove it. Well, as I say, lovers are
selfish. Girls are mostly in love with being loved,
or—to put it more kindly, and at the same time
include an even larger number—in love with love.
Men are in love with conquest. When they have
obtained complete mastery, they tire of their
victory and turn to conquests new. And—even
when love outlasts the first year of marriage, it
is a selfish thing. Have you ever known a husband
who was not selfish?'"

Mrs. Herriot considered this in silence. Then, honestly: "No," she said, "the husbands I have known have all been selfish."

"There!" cried Dick, triumphant, reaching for a fir cone. The sparrow appeared to have swallowed the daisy, and liked it. "And then look at parents and their children. I go into heaps of interiors, as they say in France. No, I am not alluding to operations, but to the family circle, the intimate hearth and home of which England makes a speciality. And I maintain that the love of parents for their children is mostly an awfully selfish thing. So long as the sons and daughters—young or full-grown—please them in all things, cross them in nothing, assert no individuality, make no independent plans; obey without question, agree without comment, submit without demur—all is well. 'Ephraim is a pleasant child.'

"But let them cross the imperious parental will, ever so little, and at once 'the iniquity of Ephraim is discovered;' 'Ephraim is a cake not turned!' 'O Ephraim, what shall I do unto thee? I will set a rider upon Ephraim!'" Dr. Dick paused for want of breath.

"Did you call your Sunday School teacher a naughty name beginning with 'E'?" suggested the Little White Lady, sweetly.

Dick's eyes twinkled.

"No," he said. "But I put all the earwigs I could find into Aunt Louisa's large work-basket

—the very full one—and I had to learn by heart every mention of Ephraim in Hosea. It took days. But please don't change the subject. We may dismiss parental love as selfish. Now we come to friends. Do not most friends love one another merely for the pleasure, advancement, or help they can get out of each other?"

"Well," mused Mrs. Herriot, "until a moment ago I was under the impression that I enjoyed a very delightful friendship with my young doctor. But I suppose, if I am cornered, I must admit that I undoubtedly value his clever understanding and treatment of my case, though my belief in him—or is it my own vanity?—makes me loth to agree that his only interest in the matter, concerns the fee I am to have the pleasure of paying him."

Dr. Dick sat up promptly, scattering the birds, right and left, into the bushes.

"Oh, I say, Mrs. Herriot! That's too bad! One of the first rules in an abstract argument is never to reduce it to a specified case. And to come down to personalities, is worse still. 'Present company excepted' is always understood, without being expressed, when sweeping generalities are being made. And you must admit— you *must*—that you know perfectly well that *we* are the bright and shining exception to this general rule."

He knelt on one knee, searching her face with his keen brown eyes.

"You didn't mean it?" he said.

He laid his hand over her fluttering white fingers.

"You didn't mean it, Mrs. Herriot?"

He bent over her, insisting. "Say you were chaffing, or I shall take the next train back to town. There is nothing in the whole world I value so much as your friendship."

Then they both saw the French window of the drawing-room slowly open, and the Fallen Idol, making his ponderous way across the lawn, in their direction.

"Jupiter!" exclaimed Dr. Dick, and dropped like a stone. "I shall lie low! Don't give me away. The couch hides me completely; and he had not already seen me. He is exceedingly near-sighted. He only sees a yard or so beyond his own nose. He won't come round this side. All the chairs are on the other. Now, what the dickens brings him here? Just say you were only chaffing, before he arrives."

An insisting hand came up from below, and was laid upon the lace of her sleeve. The Little White Lady dislodged it with a playful pat; then, turning upon her couch, viewed with some apprehension and no little surprise, the unheralded approach of the Rector of the parish.

CHAPTER VIII

THE FALLEN IDOL DISCOURSES

THE Fallen Idol walked gingerly over the smooth lawn, as if picking his way among hot ploughshares. He seemed to be feeling his feet rather large. His ingratiating smile came on before. So did his sonorous voice, as soon as he was within speaking distance.

"I fear finding my way to you thus, unannounced, is a somewhat unwarrantable intrusion, Mrs. Herriot."

The Little White Lady's expressive silence, gave consent. She waved him to a wicker chair at a little distance from her couch.

The Fallen Idol drew it nearer and sat down, his toes turned inwards and his knees well together; laid his soft hat upon them, and his black gloves upon his hat. Then he smiled, in benign nervousness at Mrs. Herriot.

"The fact is, dear Mrs. Herriot," he said, "I have, as you may or may not be aware, called many times. But your butler, or, at all events, a very respectable elderly man whom I concluded was your butler, has invariably informed me that

you were 'not at home.' To-day, in answer to my
ring, the door was opened by a young woman."

The Fallen Idol paused, impressively.

Mrs. Herriot's couch seemed to vibrate with
the upheaval of silent laughter, so near it on the
grass, on the further side from the wicker chair.

"Jarvis was out," she remarked, in a voice
which trembled.

"Ah, is that so? Well, Jarvis being out, the
door was opened to me by a young woman,
who chanced to be one of my own parishioners;
in fact, one whom I recently prepared for con-
firmation."

"That was Mary, my temporary housemaid."

"That was, as you say, Mary; and Mary very
properly requested me to enter, and to await in
the drawing-room a person whom she called Mrs.
Ransom, and whom she proposed to fetch."

Mrs. Herriot hurriedly drew the silver vase
towards her, and buried her face among the roses.
Dr. Dick had so recently and so inimitably imper-
sonated the Fallen Idol, for her benefit, that the
conversation of the original proved almost too
much for her.

"Left in the drawing-room by Mary," continued
her visitor, "I looked from the window, and
fancied I espied you beneath the trees. I ventured, therefore, I hope not too boldly, to make
my way out; thus securing the pleasure at last,
dear Mrs. Herriot, of finding you at home."

The Rector lifted his gloves and arranged them

in a fresh position upon the crown of his soft felt hat, while awaiting a response from Mrs. Herriot.

"I am very sorry," she said, with gentle courtesy, "that you should have made so many fruitless attempts to see me. Jarvis should have told you, at once, that I am not allowed visitors."

"Something of the kind was mentioned," replied the Rector. "But a pastoral visit partakes of a different nature, and cannot be considered an ordinary call."

"I see," said Mrs. Herriot.

"My object in approaching you, dear lady," continued the Fallen Idol, "is two-fold. First, I desire to express my sincere regret that you should have been taken so seriously unwell during your first attendance at my church; secondly, I hope to interest you in the workings of the parish of which you are a temporary, but much valued, parishioner."

This was in the Fallen Idol's best "Therefore, my brethren" manner.

A melodramatic sigh came wafting up from beside the couch, and reached the ear of the Little White Lady. She glanced apprehensively at the Rector, then let her right hand drop in gentle admonition, but withdrew it when ready fingers were promptly laid, in mock anxiety upon her pulse.

"Let me then say, first of all," continued the Rector, "how deeply we regretted your serious indisposition, more especially as it occurred during the absence of our excellent Dr. Thompson, leaving you, I fear, in the hands of his not very desirable *locum tenens.*"

Mrs. Herriot bridled, instantly. Her very lace suddenly became starched.

"I found his *locum tenens* exceedingly efficient and attentive," she said. "In fact he understood my case with an accuracy, and relieved my sufferings with a rapidity, such as I had never before known during my long and varied experience of medical men."

The Fallen Idol folded his hands upon the soft crown of his hat, and smiled benignly.

"Ah, is that so?" he said. "I am glad indeed to hear that you detected no lack of skill on the part of my young friend of former years. Unfortunately his personal character is very far from being such as we, who have known him from boyhood, could desire. And, in a doctor, personal character is everything—everything. But we will let that pass," continued the Fallen Idol, with a gentle wave of the hand. "I should regret to be under the necessity of enlightening you further on the point. I gather that the young man in question has now returned to town."

Mrs. Herriot's complete silence, and the keenly indignant light in her eyes, rendered it evident even to the obtuse perceptions of the Fallen Idol, that he had made a serious mistake. He shifted uneasily beneath that keen gaze, lifted his hat and crossed his knees.

7

Then the eyes softened suddenly; a little smile, hovered about the firm lips. ·

Unconsciously she had let her right hand fall again. Dr. Dick had at once taken it firmly in his, drawn it down, and very gently kissed it.

This little intimate touch of sympathy and mutual understanding, rekindled Mrs. Herriot's almost extinguished sense of humour, arming her with a fresh stock of patience.

The Rector saw the kindly gleam in her eyes, the sudden softening of her whole face, and, unconscious of any presence other than his own, naturally took this change of demeanour as a gratifying tribute to himself. Uncrossing his knees, he leaned forward, with an ingratiating smile, and proceeded to develop his second point.

Mrs. Herriot listened to the long dissertation on the workings of Dinglevale parish, with a tender, humorous smile upon her lips, a delicate pink tint in either cheek, betokening pleasure, mingled with a touch of excitement. As a matter of fact she heard very little of the Rector's monotonous monologue.

This kissing of her hand by the young man who lay at full length on the grass behind her, was to her a little touch of spontaneous affection, as sweet as it was unexpected. Had he presumed to do such a thing during one of the hours of their ordinary intercourse, she would probably have resented it as an unwarrantable liberty on the part of her young doctor. But in this mutual adventure, the farcical situation brought about by the intrusion upon their privacy of the Fallen Idol, it partook of the spirit of Fun just then dancing around them—even as the sunbeams flickered through the gently moving leaves of the old beech tree. Yet it also expressed his confidence in her trust in him, notwithstanding the aspersions just cast upon his character, and his tender and reverential regard for herself, despite the crude cynicism of the views he had so recently expressed.

To the Little White Lady's sensitive instincts, this slight incident seemed to promise well for the gentle hold she was endeavouring to obtain over this self-reliant, frankly agnostic nature, now brought into such close contact with the earnest faith, and belief in eternal truths, which were hers.

So she passed one frail hand over the back of the other, with gentle touch, smoothed the lace at her wrist, and looked with loving, unseeing gaze at the black, unattractive figure of the Rector of Dinglevale.

"Therefore, my dear lady," he concluded, "I venture to enlist your kind sympathy, in the hope that you may feel inclined to help forward my work in this parish, by means of a much-needed subscription. You are probably not aware that I entered upon this task under circumstances of peculiar—yes, I may say *peculiar*—difficulty. My predecessor had been many years in possession of the living. He was a man who took little or no interest in the place or people."

Mrs. Herriot started, recalled her wandering attention, and concentrated her mind upon her visitor.

A sense of intent listening was in the air behind her.

But the Fallen Idol, completely unconscious of any atmospheric disturbance, droned on complacently.

"I found all parish matters greatly neglected, no funds in hand for present needs, but a considerable debt, caused by past unnecessary and unwise expenditure. There is, unfortunately, among many of my cloth, so complete a lack of business habits, so great a laxity in the matter of rendering account of the money which passes through their hands, that it almost amounts to——"

With an imperative gesture, Mrs. Herriot raised her hand, compelling her visitor to silence.

"Pray leave this topic," she said. "I have no wish to hear these accusations against your predecessor. They cannot in any way concern me."

But the Fallen Idol smiled, blandly.

" 'Accusations' is a strong word, dear Mrs. Herriot. I am merely explaining to you, in absolute confidence, the reason of my sad lack of funds, in a living which you may possibly have supposed to be well endowed. It is charitable to hope no actual dishonesty was intended, but——"

Then Dick sat up, with startling suddenness.

"Now it is my turn," he said, "to have a share in this highly interesting conversation, and I am

going to ask you a riddle. 'When is a parson *not*
a parson?' The answer rhymes with 'Choir.'"

He leapt to his feet and strode round the
couch.

"Do you give it up? Why, when he is a
Liar! You can spell it 'lyre,' if you like, and con-
nect it with psalmody. But I spell it l-i-a-r, and
walk it off the premises! Come, sir. My patient
has had as long and as edifying a pastoral visit as I
can allow. I must ask you to accompany me to the
nearest spot from which you can leave these
grounds and return to the sanctuary of your late
Rector's study. As we go, you will oblige me
with full details concerning my uncle's debts and
defalcations. Uncle Andrew was a hard man, as I
have reason to know; but this is the first imputa-
tion I have ever heard, made against his honesty
or his honour. . . . No! Mrs. Herriot will excuse
any formal leave-taking. Be good enough to
come this way."

The Little White Lady, with fluttering heart
and a sharp stab at her breast, watched them
walk across the lawn; Dick, tall and erect, indignant fury in every line, yet keeping himself well
under control, his hands thrust deep into the
pockets of his blue serge coat; beside him the
shamed black figure, with shambling gait, and
hurried, deprecatory gesture.

Breathless, Mrs. Herriot saw them go; trembling
for that which might happen when they had
turned the corner.

But in less than five minutes, Dick came back alone, whistling gaily, his hands still in his pockets.

"So sorry," he said. "I hope it hasn't upset you. The sanctimonious old humbug knew as well as I do, that Uncle Andrew spent more on this parish than he ever received from it. He grumbled at Aunt Louisa's housekeeping bills, and grudged me the price of a peg-top, but he was generous to a degree where the needs of the church and people were concerned. He had a considerable private income of his own, out of which for years, he paid a generous stipend to his curate. Toad! If he really believes in a place of departed spirits, surely his conscience will play Witch of Endor for him to-night, as he sits in the old study armchair, and will call up Uncle Andrew to stand before him in a harp and a crown, or whatever they wear down there, with a cash-box in one hand and his account-book in the other."

Dick flung himself into the vacated wicker-chair, threw back his head and laughed; but there was more of anger than of mirth in his laughter. Also he failed to mark the faint grey shadow, creeping over the face of the Little White Lady.

"So much for friendship!" pursued Dick. "So much for loyalty! So much for honesty toward the Dead! What a fine commentary on our previous conversation."

"Hush," she whispered, "hush, dear boy! You have had it all your own way hitherto. Now let *me* speak. Dismiss from your mind the unworthy person who interrupted us, and let me answer your arraignment of all human love. I admit that often, earthly love falters and fails. Unaided human nature is, at best, but a poor frail thing. Self is hydra-headed. We deem it slain, and lo, it raises yet another head, with poison in its fangs! But there *are* devoted mothers, there *are* unselfish wives; ay, and there are noble Christ-like men, in whom the self-love is overcome by the Divine. I believe in that which has been beautifully called, 'the expulsive power of a new affection.' Nothing can drive the self out of us, save the inflow of the Christ Life, the very nature of Him of Whom His bitterest enemies said, as He hung dying: 'He saved others; Himself He cannot save.' It was said as a taunt and a jeer, flung at the dying Christ; yet it defined the very mainspring of His great Atonement, the deepest secret of our redemption —a Love which, forgetful of self, regardless of suffering, stoops to utter depths of self-abnegation, for the salvation of others. When we rise to a love which can do that, we approximate, at last, to the Divine. . . . Now take me indoors, my dear young doctor. I fear you and your Fallen Idol have tired me out."

.   .   .   .

That night, for the first time, Ellen Ransom had to call Dr. Dick.

It was a stern fight, involving much agony for the patient, and desperate moments of anxiety for the two who watched and helped.

At dawn she fell asleep, her hand in Dr. Dick's; Ellen Ransom standing, a grim sentinel, at the foot of the bed.

As he bent over her, to make sure the breathing was easy and regular, there flashed into Dick's mind her last words under the beech tree that afternoon: "He saved others; Himself He cannot save." What connection had those words with the sufferings of the Little White Lady? None—so far as Dr. Dick could see.

He did not realise then, how much that frail heart was ready and willing to bear, if, at any cost to herself, one soul could be brought from the darkness of doubt and unbelief, out into the clear shining of her own perfect faith.

But she slept at last, and he left her to Ellen Ransom.

CHAPTER IX

THE LADY OF THE MANOR LUNCHES

THE Large Lady of the Manor sat at luncheon in her own dining-room, there entertained by an exceedingly good-looking young man, who had introduced himself merely as the bearer of Mrs. Herriot's apologies for being unable to appear, and who acted temporary host to the Lady of the Manor, in her own house, with charming ease and cordiality.

Urgent need had arisen for papers of importance put away in the safe at the Manor. A letter, therefore, arrived for Mrs. Herriot, asking whether the owner of the place might be permitted to call, between trains, and have access to her safe. The trains mentioned would bring her to the Manor at one o'clock, taking her away again at two-thirty. Mrs. Herriot had, therefore, no option in the matter. She was obliged to request the Lady of the Manor to give her the pleasure of her company at luncheon. The Large Lady was a person who firmly gave no option where her meals were concerned. She wrote back thanking Mrs. Herriot for her kind thought, and expressing pleasure at having this opportunity of making her acquaintance.

But the day fixed—being that which followed the pastoral visit of the Fallen Idol—found Mrs. Herriot absolutely unable for any effort, other than being gently lifted to her couch near the window, by Dr. Dick. Arrived there, the waving tree-tops were almost more than she could bear. She turned toward the quiet room, closing her eyes.

Dr. Dick stood watching her; then leaned over and carefully lowered the venetian blind, opening the laths to let in the breeze, and the golden shafts of sunlight.

She looked up, smiling her thanks.

"Restless things, trees," he said. "Must keep at it all the time, if the least breath of wind gives them an excuse. And you feel to-day as if their energy is a drain on your vitality. Fidgety people are always like that. They tire out the calm souls whose strength is to sit still, while they themselves seem inexhaustible. Well, the breeze and the sunshine are good for you, and the trees can be shut out. How about our friend the thrush? Shall I go and tell him to stop whistling? I once stayed at a water-cure in Leipzig, where we all lived by laws and regulations. Cards of rules, printed in German and English, hung in the bath-rooms. Foremost among these was: 'You may not sing or *pipe* in your bath.' And they call themselves a musical nation! I always whistle in my bath. So I broke that rule every day. But I think I shall go and tell the thrush he may not 'pipe' in his bush this morning."

She smiled again and closed her eyes. Then opened them quickly, with a sudden look of apprehension and dismay.

"Oh, I had forgotten—so trying—luncheon to-day. Mrs.—you know—Mrs.——"

"Yes, I know. Don't bother to remember her name. A particular old friend of mine! Don't give her another thought. I will make your apologies, explain the case, and entertain her at luncheon."

But the anxiety by no means left the weary eyes of the Little White Lady. They searched his face. She was too weak to make an effort to array her thought in tactful and disguising language. It spoke itself in words which revealed it exactly as it lay in her mind.

"Will you—promise—to behave—properly?"

Dr. Dick grinned, in huge delight. It was just what Aunt Louisa might have said, twenty years before, had he been going to lunch with the Large Lady of the Manor.

"Yes, I will behave perfectly," he said. "I won't be greedy, and I won't throw cake about; and I will ask no awkward riddles. The Large Lady will not remember me. For aught she will know, our acquaintance will be virgin soil. I shall lay myself out to make an excellent impression. I shall win the warm regard of the Large Lady of the Manor. Don't you worry. Lie here and rest, and don't give her another thought. By tea-time we shall be able to give the thrush leave to pipe again."

Thus it came to pass that the Lady of the Manor had scarcely been long enough in her own drawing-room to make sure that the parquet was not scratched, and that there were no spots of ink on the writing-table or little corners torn off the blotting-paper in her silver-mounted blotter, when the door opened to admit—not the little old lady with whom she was expecting a dull, though it was to be hoped ample, tête-à-tête luncheon—but an exceedingly well set-up, good-looking young man, into whose bright brown eyes, as he proceeded to explain the situation, and make Mrs. Herriot's excuses, leapt a look of admiration by no means lost upon the Large Lady. The manner she had assumed in expectation of the entrance of Mrs. Herriot, fell as a cloak from off her portly person. A luncheon with young *Mr.* Herriot, would be infinitely more entertaining. All smiles and affability, she extended a friendly hand.

"I am grieved to hear of your mother's indisposition," she said. "She must certainly make no effort on my account. And I am charmed to make your acquaintance, Mr. Herriot. I had not heard of you before, or realised when your mother took the house that you were to be here with her, or the billiard-room should certainly have been left open. I hope you find the place in every way to your liking?"

Dick assured her that he did, and that billiards were by no means essential to his happiness. Also that his presence at the Manor was really owing to the precarious condition of Mrs. Herriot's health. But he let "your mother" pass, uncorrected. The Large Lady's mistake exactly suited his plans.

While he explained and assured, his eyes dwelt upon her with that look of undisguised, almost involuntary, admiration, which is balm to the possessor of expensive and time-involving charms.

"Young Mr. Herriot" was undoubtedly behaving nicely, and our friend Dick was not at that moment altogether a humbug; for, indeed, he marvelled in his heart at the rejuvenation which the passing of twenty years had wrought in the appearance of his hostess of the Manor.

In the long ago days her hair had been grey, her figure portly, and she had had what little Dick described as "a wobbly tooth." Now her hair was of golden hue, her figure, large still, but knit together in that hardness of outline only to be found where Art has a daily, hourly conflict with Nature; while, within the gates of her wide and constant smile, a solid row of uncompromising teeth stood sentinel.

As Dick surveyed this new and revised edition of the Large Lady of the Manor, he found himself contrasting her elderly youthfulness with the young old age of the Little White Lady upstairs, the recollection of whose delicate charm brought a look into his brown eyes which completed the subjugation of the Large Lady of the Manor.

Young Mr. Herriot was delightful! How strange that none of Mrs. Herriot's friends should have mentioned him. Possibly he lived abroad—foreign diplomatic service, very likely—and had been summoned home on account of his mother's serious illness. However that might be, he was an exceedingly charming young man—and the Lady of the Manor, having accomplished her visit to the safe, passed into the dining-room, fully expecting to enjoy herself at luncheon.

This expectation was not disappointed. Young Mr. Herriot's conversation proved both vivacious and amusing. Taking his cue from the Large Lady's deportment and demeanour, he treated her, not with the deference which age demands from youth, but as a contemporary; and so innocently, and as a complete matter of course, did he do this, that the Lady of the Manor congratulated herself, more than once, upon having left the Oxford Street person and gone to that clever creature in Bond Street, whose methods were more thorough, yet far more certain to escape detection.

The gay luncheon was almost over. The Large Lady was peeling a peach, and had just called young Mr. Herriot "a foolish boy," with a glance which took the sting from the adjective and invited a repetition of the folly, when, drawing the cake toward him, he cut himself a big piece, remarking as he landed it safely on his plate: "This reminds me of something which happened in this very room, more than twenty years ago. It must have been long before your time. Such a funny story. I heard it from young Dick Cameron, who studied medicine with me at Aberdeen. His granduncle was rector here, in those days, and Dicky, as a very small boy, lived at the Rectory, and a precious dull time he appears to have had of it, poor little chap! An invitation to a party must have been a momentous event, which no doubt partly accounts for his vivid remembrance of the utter fiasco, at the close of the day to which he had so eagerly looked forward. He and lots of his little boy and girl friends had been asked to games in the garden and tea at the Manor House. It must have been before your time, for, if I remember rightly, he described his hostess as an old thing of fifty or more. He used to call her 'The Large Lady of the Manor.'" Young Mr. Herriot paused, turning his attention to an energetic attack upon the cake.

His visitor murmured something about her mother-in-law.

"Ah, no doubt. Well, I hope you were not deeply attached to your mother-in-law. Because, if you were, I must not tell the story, which would be a pity, as it is really worth hearing, and it would be amusing to tell it in the very room in which it all happened."

No, the present Lady of the Manor had never known much of her mother-in-law, and would love to hear the story. But her hand shook, as she peeled the peach, which slipped from beneath her fruit-knife, and almost shot on to the floor.

"Well, then, I hope you won't mind the rather uncomplimentary names Dick Cameron called her; in fact, I think when you have heard the story you will agree that she fully deserved them." With which preface, young Mr. Herriot launched forth into a vigorous description of the children's party given in that beautiful garden so long ago; the unjust decisions, the keen mortification of the eager little boy; the scene at the tea-table; the final fiasco; the cruel punishment. The Lady of the Manor aged beneath his watchful eye.

"She *was* an old tartar, wasn't she?"

The Lady of the Manor agreed that she was. She seemed to be having some difficulty in finishing her peach. Young Mr. Herriot progressed gaily with his cake.

"And though it seems a trivial, childish incident, it cost that little chap his faith in all things. He hated that old woman; he lost his friend and hero, the curate; his little prayers weren't answered; all things seemed against him. He finished up the day, sobbing on his mother's grave. He is now an avowed agnostic, and I believe he dates his first loss of faith to that experience. Don't you think it is a pity your mother-in-law gave a children's party?"

The Large Lady, consulting her watch, thought it was.

"Is she still living? . . . No? Do tell me where she is buried. . . . In Ireland? Oh, I am sorry! I should like to have visited her grave, and laid a ha'penny bun upon it, for my friend Dicky's sake!"

The Lady of the Manor said he was "naughty," but her sprightliness had gone from her. Then she expressed anxiety about her train. She felt sure the fly must be at the door. Would Mr. Herriot kindly ring and inquire?

Mr. Herriot rang, but under protest.

"Must you catch that particular train? I was hoping for a jolly afternoon together, under the trees." His brown eyes pleaded. But the Lady of the Manor was pale and obdurate.

The fly had arrived. A few minutes later he put her into it. He pressed her hand at parting.

"You are sure you are not vexed with me for having told you that story about your mother-in-law?"

His handsome head and broad shoulders were thrust in at the still open door.

The Large Lady smiled a crooked smile.

Not at all. She had been amused—that is to say, of course it was sad—very sad.

"How kind you are," said young Mr. Herriot. "I shall tell Dick Cameron that I told you, and that you sympathised. Good-bye. You can't possibly know how much I have enjoyed meeting you."

.   .   .   .

8

As the fly, containing the Lady of the Manor, trundled through the village, the Fallen Idol loomed in sight, a dark figure among the clustering cottage roses, depressed and depressing. He walked heavily, meditatively; not at his usual rapid pace, with coat-tails flying.

When the Lady of the Manor perceived him, she told the driver to stop. Then she waved the Fallen Idol to the window.

At sight of the face of his patron looking forth from the village fly, the Rector brightened, visibly. He hurried into the road, lifting his hat.

"How come you here, dear lady?" he inquired, in the manner which he considered at once courtly and deferential.

The Large Lady told him. "And I took luncheon at the Manor," she added. "Mrs. Herriot was unable to appear. But young Mr. Herriot entertained me quite charmingly. An exceedingly agreeable young man." She sat back, complacently, as if challenging the Rector to contradict her.

The Fallen Idol shot his face forward into the fly, rapidly opening and shutting his mouth, in a vain endeavour to speak. He looked at that moment exceedingly like a chameleon.

The Lady of the Manor observed him with distaste.

"What is the matter, man?" she inquired, crossly. Then the Fallen Idol found his voice.

"There *is* no Mr. Herriot," he trumpeted,

solemnly. "Your tenant has neither husband nor
son."

He made an impressive pause. It always annoyed him when the Lady of the Manor addressed
him as "man."

"Then who—what—?" Dismay was in her eye.

"Young Dick Cameron," said the Fallen Idol,
thickly. "The little scamp who pelted me with
cake in your dining-room, broke your china, and
insulted you in his boyish passion. He has gone
from bad to worse, as the years went by. He is
now living at the Manor. When I called unexpectedly, yesterday, Mrs. Herriot made an attempt,
which I soon exposed, to conceal him behind her
couch. Finding himself discovered, he took refuge
in abuse, and ordered me off the premises."

At the opening words of this astonishing statement, the Large Lady of the Manor rose to her
feet in the fly, as if in one vast, horrified protest;
then sat down heavily, in an attitude of absolute
dismay. But, as the Rector proceeded, a malicious
gleam showed in her eye. She signed to him to
open the door.

"Get in, man," she said. "I must hear more of
this. You can drive with me to the station."

The Fallen Idol wrenched open the door, and
stepped in. The Lady of the Manor made no
attempt to find room for him beside her. So he
seated himself, uncomfortably, upon the narrow
seat opposite, pulled the door to, and the fly
rumbled on, down the village street.

.   .   .   .

Dr. Dick rapped lightly on the door of the Little White Lady's room.

"Come in !" called her gentle voice, and he entered, gaily.

"Well!" he said, and, crossing the room, sat down in a chair beside her couch.

"Well?" questioned Mrs. Herriot; and her eyes were anxious.

"Oh, I behaved quite nicely. I kept her amused during the whole of luncheon, and I squeezed her hand at parting. We are now on terms of intimacy, not to say affection."

Merriment danced in his eyes.

Mrs. Herriot still searched his face, anxiously.

"I am afraid—" she began.

"You needn't be afraid," said Dr. Dick. "Nemesis stalked round the luncheon table, I admit; but in truly jocund mood. If you would like to be entertained for half-an-hour, I will recount the most amusing comedy you ever heard; namely, how 'the greedy little boy,' while still keeping his promise, and behaving quite properly, made the Large Lady of the Manor admit that she was a regular old tartar, unfit to give a children's party."

Then, with much delighted laughter, Dr. Dick told the story.

"So now," he concluded, "I have paid off the old scores. I always swore I would do it. I've had to wait twenty years, but I've done it at last, and done it thoroughly. I am even with them both. I can start with a clean slate. Little seven-year-old Dicky is avenged—and there's an end of it!"

But Mrs. Herriot looked grave. The recital of the scene in the dining-room, had failed to amuse her.

"My dear young doctor," she said, "I doubt if it will prove to be the end. No good ever comes of paying off old scores. A generous forgiveness is the only possible end to an old wrong. It appals me to think of the desire for revenge, harboured, during all these years, in so young a heart. You may have hurt them; but you have hurt yourself, even more. And you have certainly made two bitter enemies. I greatly fear this is far from being the end."

But Dr. Dick laughed, lightly. "The Fallen Idol can't hurt me," he said. "And I shall hear no more from the Large Lady of the Manor until leap year, which is so long ahead that she may, by then, be safely deposited side by side with her mother-in-law in Ireland!" Then, seeing the look of distress deepen on the Little White Lady's face: "Don't be sad," he said, "or you will spoil my pleasure. And, anyhow, one very nice thing has happened to me to-day. I have been taken for your son!" He leaned forward, with a softening of his whole mood. "I wish it were true," he said. "I should like to have been your son."

At last he had won a smile from her. She laid her hand gently on his.

"I should have liked to have been your mother, dear boy," she said, "but I fear you would have given me many an anxious moment. But now, will my doctor kindly consider whether I may be allowed to go down to the garden for tea?"

CHAPTER X

NEMESIS ARRIVES

MRS. HERRIOT was enjoying an afternoon drive. Her barouche, so well known in the park, drawn by a high-stepping pair of perfectly matched dapple-greys, bowled in stately fashion through the Surrey lanes, and along the wide roads on the common above Dinglevale.

At the sound of the measured klop-klop of the four pairs of hoofs, chance pedestrians turned, then stood still to watch the stately equipage go by.

The Little White Lady's turn-out was of a kind rapidly becoming obsolete; her dapple-grays seemed to come stepping out of a past century. Here was no trotting dog-cart, or rushing motor. No startling hoot preceded her; she left no bewildering cloud of dust behind. The old village women dropped long-forgotten curtseys, and went smiling on their way; the labourers touched their caps, as the carriage swept by; then wondered, in surly fashion, why they had done so.

With the passing of a great Queen, and of a great century, there seems also to have passed the spirit of courtesy and of gracious manners; the consideration of the rich for the poor; the respectful deference of the poor toward the rich. In this age of push and hurry, of attempts to level all class distinctions by those to whom the levelling means a step up, at the expense of others who stand higher, England is invaded by the spirit of Liberty, Equality, Fraternity—which practically means: I am at liberty to grab the things which belong to my brother—and the term "early Victorian" carries with it somewhat of a sneer. But a reaction must come before long, for Englishmen are stanchly conservative at heart, faithful to traditions of Church and State, loyal to the great names, which in the past have made Britain great. And supreme among these, standing for all which is purest, noblest, and most truly British, will ever be the name, Victoria.

Mrs. Herriot was enjoying her drive. Since recovering from her last attack, she had been so much better, that she was now able to go out driving, unaccompanied by her maid.

Ellen Ransom's presence in the carriage was apt to be oppressive, and did not by any means conduce to restful enjoyment. Her apology for being there at all, consisted in sitting bolt upright opposite her mistress, as far forward on the seat as possible, looking neither to right nor left, but fixedly on a spot a few inches above the white plume in Mrs. Herriot's bonnet.

"Do you think you could lean back, Ellen?" Mrs. Herriot would sometimes venture to ask.

But the gentle suggestion had no permanent effect upon her maid's respectful rigidity; and Mrs. Herriot would reach home, tired out by the contemplation of Ellen's stiff back, and wearied over fruitless attempts to induce Ellen to share with her the beauties of the scenery.

"I've no patience with distant views!" Ellen had once remarked to the housekeeper, on her return from a drive, in an unusually communicative mood. "What's the good of 'purple hills on the horizon' to me? What do *I* want with 'a wood of bluebells, and young bracken,' or 'golden gorse bestrewing this wide common, Ellen'? Give me a chair to sit on, a good cup of tea, and a plate of bread-and-butter within easy reach of m'own hand. I've no use for things I can't take a hold of. And when all's said an' done, distant views, purple hills, bluebells an' all, is in yer own eye."

"How do you make *that* out, Mrs. Ransom?" inquired the housekeeper, mildly, stirring her tea, but gazing out of the window, across the wide expanse of park, to the fir-crowned hills, dark against the pearly pink of the evening sky. The housekeeper was stout, comely, long a widow; and inclined to romantic ideas of life, when the *menu* was off her mind.

"Well—put out yer eyes," snapped Ellen, "and where's the distant view?"

"Where's your cup of tea, for the matter of that?" suggested the housekeeper, with what she hoped was a brilliant flash of repartee.

"Why, within reach of m'hand, where it's been all along!" replied Ellen, crushingly; and proceeded to drink it.

This was unanswerable and conclusive. The housekeeper's enjoyment of the sunset, was impaired by the uncomfortable suggestion that it was all in her own eye. Ellen Ransom plumed herself on her opinion. She ventured to repeat it, in more respectful terms, to Mrs. Herriot herself, during the next drive.

The Little White Lady smiled. "Ah, Ellen," she said, "how exactly you express the mental outlook of so many people. Their own inner vision is the measure of their distant view. My good Ellen, you are becoming a philosopher."

"Not if I know it, ma'am," retorted Ellen, who had a deeply-rooted prejudice against long names of which she did not understand the meaning. Yet she plumed herself still more on her opinion. But the Little White Lady smiled again, as she looked away to the golden battlements of the distant sunset.

Nevertheless, it was a decided relief to be able to leave Ellen at home, and to go out alone with Giles, her coachman, whose broad and comfortable back, seated high and immovable in front of her, inspired a sense of stability and confidence. Giles had been in the Herriot family for over forty years. From a slim stable lad, he had advanced to be a stalwart groom, and had finally become the portly personage who drove the pair, and made so fine a figure-head to Mrs. Herriot's stately outings. His weight and size appeared to have increased in exact ratio to his wages and standing. His general impression was not so much pompous, as full of benign dignity. Had he appeared in gaiters and a silk apron, instead of in the mulberry and silver of the Herriot livery, he would have looked as typical a bishop as any prelate in the House of Lords. He had a firm belief in the immortality of every horse he drove, and always spoke of them after their decease in the reverent tone in which we mention the dear Departed.

On this particular afternoon, Giles had chosen a drive which brought them home over the wide common above Dinglevale; and as Mrs. Herriot leaned back, enjoying the cool breeze, the scent of the golden gorse, the songs of the gaily soaring larks, a bicycle bell tingled sharply, and Dick Cameron, with a wave of his cap, shot past her.

This chance meeting gave the finishing touch to her pleasure, and as she bowled slowly homeward, she mused upon how much the bright companionship of her young doctor had come to mean to her.

On her return she rested in the drawing-room, deferring her move to the garden until the teatable should be laid beneath the shady trees, and Dick's gay whistle should be answered by the thrush.

He, meanwhile, after passing Mrs. Herriot's carriage, had ridden on to that distant Rectory, over the common where lived the patient who was slowly taking up life again, at the bidding of his strong will and of his absolute determination to win even the most losing game. Dr. Norton's verdict, "practically no hope," had sent Dick speeding there in double quick time on that Sunday morning, early in June. Now his actual medical visits were no longer needed, and his frequent friendly calls were made simply for his own pleasure, and to make sure that his patient was not shirking the difficult task of taking up a life which held but few of those things which make life worth the living.

It was during Mrs. Herriot's interval of quiet rest that the two-wheeled scarlet cart, pretentiously lettered "Royal Mail," trundled up the avenue. The ancient village postman, shouting "Woa, will yer!" to his old pony—which had already stopped and was standing stock still, its patient eyes turned wistfully towards the grass border—climbed stiffly down, rang the bell, and handed in a letter.

With this letter Ellen Ransom presently marched gravely into the drawing-room, and laid it on the little table at her mistress's elbow.

Mrs. Herriot, taking it up, glanced at the handwriting and postmark. A sense of pleasurable anticipation awoke within her. The letter came to her from a moor away in the Highlands. She genuinely liked the woman whose handwriting she recognised on the envelope. She expected to be amused by a chatty account of the doings of a

Scotch house-party, most of the members of which would be intimately known to herself.

She opened the envelope and drew out the closely written sheets, with a little smile of anticipatory enjoyment.

This letter seemed at once to bring her again into touch with the life which she had temporarily laid aside.

Dick Cameron was a dear boy, and amusing. But he was not in her set, never had been, and—it seemed to her, then—never could be. The delicate inflexions of Shibboleth, the tacitly understood pass-words into the inner circle, would always be beyond him.

In the generous friendliness of her warm heart, she had valued his skill, admired the undoubted power of his strong character, loved the frank gaiety of his nature, and enjoyed his society. But, as the quiet summer weeks, spent in the seclusion of this little Surrey village, slowly passed, a sense of loneliness and isolation of spirit had crept over her; a loneliness of which she had hardly been conscious, until this letter from one of her most intimate friends suddenly put her again into touch with the society she loved, the little world of people worth knowing, who came to her quiet house in Park Lane, counting it a privilege to drop in to tea, bringing her news of the doings of a wider circle in which she was held in high esteem, and where she would have been always welcome, had not her frail health prevented her from bearing the fatigue of a constant round of visits and functions.

So a slight flush of excitement and pleasure tinted the soft cheeks of the Little White Lady, as she unfolded the letter.

"Myra is sure to be amusing," she said to herself. "She will know all 'the latest,' and will give me an epitome, in her gay, kindly fashion, of what everybody is doing and saying."

She settled her cushions, drew her white shawl about her shoulders, and began to read.

There are people who invariably read their letters with an expression of countenance which betokens horror and amazement. Watching them, you feel sure the very worst must have happened, and you wait in suspense, words of anxious sympathy ready, until the letter is laid down, the tense frown relaxes, and you hear that somebody has decided to make the raspberries into jam; or that somebody else recommends a new kind of soap for the washing of pet dogs, excellent for the coat, and effective in—er—every way! Your suspended sympathy falls limp, and you reflect upon the uncertainty of the science of facial expression.

But Mrs. Herriot was not one of these stern and fearsome readers. She even read telegrams with unruffled brow, until their contents actually proved to be of an alarming nature.

Her gentle smile of pleasure held, through the first two pages of the letter. Then it faded, suddenly; and with it went every vestige of colour

from her face, leaving it very white and frail.
Yet, before she reached the final words, a hot flush
mounted from her chin to her brow, and an
indignant light shone in her eyes, causing her for
the moment to appear singularly young and alert.

"Oh, shame!" she whispered. "Shame!" and
made a movement as if to crumple up the letter
with both hands; then checked the impulse,
smoothed out the sheets, and laid them on the
table beside her.

There was a long silence in the room.

The Little White Lady lay very still, with
folded hands and stricken face.

The gay piping of the thrush in his bush, came
through the open windows unheeded.

Mrs. Herriot had passed through many hard
moments in the course of her life. This seemed
to her almost the hardest. It was characteristic
that she bore it silently, with folded hands. The
more her spirit writhed at the injustice, the malign-
ity, the shame, the calmer she outwardly grew.
In her bewildered pain she was trying to cling
firmly to a thing not always reckoned of supreme
importance by a woman—her sense of justice.

At last she said, with conviction: "It is entirely
his own fault; and mine, for not realising to what
his foolish behaviour might lead. But now the
question is, how best to put the matter right."

Then she listened anxiously for Dr. Dick's step
in the hall.

CHAPTER XI

"WHATSOEVER A MAN SOWETH"

"THERE is nothing whatever to be gained by being angry," said Mrs. Herriot, gently. "It is a waste of mental force and of physical energy. The only thing now to be done is calmly to face the situation in order to find out, if possible, what steps to take in an endeavour to retrieve the intolerably false position in which I find myself placed."

She leaned back in her chair, smoothing with her frail hands the open letter which lay upon her lap, as if the action might in some way help toward the unravelling of the tangle of circumstances brought to her knowledge by those closely written sheets. Then she glanced at Dr. Dick's broad and angry back, and awaited a reply.

Dr. Dick stood looking out of the window, his hand gripping the sash. He was so angry, that the words which crowded into his mind were all adjectives, not one of them, alas, fit for the Little White Lady's gentle presence.

Dick felt like a stalwart policeman, intent upon keeping back a crowd of roughs, all surging forward in a mad attempt to push into the presence of the Queen. Strings of violent epithets concerning the Large Lady of the Manor, the Fallen Idol, and the scented and coroneted missive of the Intimate Friend, rioted through his brain, forcing their way to his lips, and only held in check by his determination not to add to the pain and perplexity already lining the delicate face of the Little White Lady. One or two all-embracing and consoling verbs, dealing in a final and comprehensive way with the future condition and circumstances of the Lady of the Manor, almost fought their way at least into muttered expression; but Ellen Ransom's remark, made when she first introduced him into her mistress's presence: "You will please to remember, sir, that my lady is *not* deaf!" marched up as a stern reinforcement to the aid of his own strong endeavour. So Dick Cameron, of the ready tongue, stood silent, fighting down his fury, while Mrs. Herriot again smoothed out her letter, and waited patiently.

The sunny drawing-room of the old Manor House, usually so calm and quiet in its flower-embowered atmosphere, was charged with tense emotion.

How complete a change may be wrought in a peaceful home, by the advent of a letter. It accomplishes its rapid journey for the modest sum of one penny. It arrives at its final destination by means of the impersonal agency of the old village postman, who hands out the letters, and

9

trundles away down the drive in his smart Royal
Mail, jogging the mouth of his ancient pony.
But the letter he has left behind is opened and
read—and lo, the huddled figure in the livery of
the Crown, is transformed into a Nemesis of fate-
ful retribution.   Much of the mischief arises from
the fact of the crude intrusion of ideas, launched
forth on paper, by a mind wholly unacquainted
with the conditions and surroundings into which
its point of view is to be ruthlessly propelled.
How often a letter would be modified in tone, or
even posted in the waste-paper basket, if its writer
could but spend half an hour in the house where,
on the following day, that letter will burst as a
devastating bomb, reducing to shattered fragments
the peace and happiness of those who receive it.

There was a good deal of the bomb-like nature
about the letter, now lying open beneath the
fluttering fingers of the Little White Lady.   Its
scented fragrance and its embossed coronet supplied no balm for the cruel wounds it had inflicted;
in fact, they rather added to Dick's vexation, he
having a socialistic scorn of coronets, and a doctor's
wholesome abhorrence of all smells which were
not either antiseptic or disinfectant.

At last he spoke.

"I am awfully sorry that you should have the
bother of it, Mrs. Herriot.   But it is just like a
pack of gossipping women to make a scandal out
of nothing."

"It is hardly 'nothing,' " said Mrs. Herriot,

gently. "Nor does it mend matters to say hard things of my friends. Lady Airth's letter is written in a most loyal and generous spirit. She simply feels it right to acquaint me with this story, which undoubtedly originated with the owner of this house, but which is being circulated far and wide among my friends: that I have a young man staying here, whom I pass off as my son, and whom I attempted to conceal beneath my couch when the Rector of the parish paid me an unexpected visit. Naturally, my friends do not believe such a story, but everybody is talking of it, and they wish to be able to give it an authentic denial. It places me in a most awkward position, because, though it is most maliciously false in the spirit, it is practically true in the letter. You *have* been staying in this house for many weeks; you *did* conceal yourself behind my couch when the Rector called; and when that woman mistook you for my son, you did not set her right. On each occasion, my dear young doctor, you were playing your own game, regardless of consequences; on each occasion I feared you had made an enemy who would contrive that the consequences should be both painful and far-reaching."

"But why should the old beast have dragged *you* in?" demanded Dick, angrily.

"Because, unfortunately, I was 'in,' already. No scandal could be made of your presence here, excepting in connection with me."

Dick turned from the window, and looked at

Mrs. Herriot. He had never seen her appear so old and frail.

"It is absurd," he said. "All your friends must know that it is absurd! At your age—I mean—if my own mother had lived she would not have been fifty."

Mrs. Herriot smiled. "I know what you mean, dear boy. I might almost be your grandmother. But shall I tell you what a very wise woman, when she was even older than I am now, once said to me? We were discussing the question—which had arisen owing to the death of a sister who had resided with her—of the necessity of various changes being made in her establishment, so that she should not live alone with a young man who acted as her secretary, and who was to her as a very dear, adopted son. I remember saying: 'Why make any change? At your age, you can do as you please. Nobody would talk.' Her quiet smile was a mingling of proud dignity and wistful humour—she was a very great lady, in her day and generation. 'My dear,' she replied, 'no woman is ever old enough to be beyond the reach of scandal.' I was young myself then; it was in the first year of my widowhood. I have often thought of it since."

Dick left the window and took a low seat near the couch. The tension of the atmosphere seemed to have somewhat relaxed.

"What did she arrange about the secretary?" he asked. "Did she send him packing?"

Mrs. Herriot hesitated. "No; she—she kept him with her."

"She should have married him," said Dick, "and given the idiots something to talk about."

"She did," said Mrs. Herriot, softly, "and the whole world talked. But she lived to keep her silver wedding-day."

Dick threw back his head. His gay laugh rang out. "Bravo!" he exclaimed. "What a sporting effort! It reminds one of——"

"Hush," said Mrs. Herriot, quickly. "No names, please."

His keen eyes held hers.

"Was I going to name the 'very great lady' herself?"

"Possibly."

Dick whistled, then looked grave. "If so," he said, "she was, indeed, beyond scandal, and above reproach."

"Nevertheless, many people presumed to reproach her."

"There *are* tadpoles," remarked Dick, "whose sole conception of a star, is a reflection in their own muddy pool."

Mrs. Herriot laughed; folded the sheets she held, and slipped them back into the envelope.

Dick took heart. He had come through a bad half hour, during which he had feared he would never again be able to make her laugh; that their gay intimacy of friendship was over forever. He moved his seat nearer the couch, and sat twisting his strong brown fingers in and out of the fringe of her rug.

"Fancy you having had *her* as a friend," he said. His tone expressed some surprise, coupled with deference to the memory of a great personality.

Mrs. Herriot looked at him, gently amused.

"My dear boy," she said, "you would be considerably more surprised, if you could glance through an approximate list of the friends I possess to-day. Do you know that, if this story, to which your foolish escapades have given rise, is as widely circulated as I fear, I shall be required to make an explanation to several Royal Ladies—that is, if they graciously grant me the opportunity so to do."

But Dick had by then a firm hold on the fringe of the cashmere rug, and his strong young face looked unabashed, even by the mention of Royal Ladies—spelt with capitals—displaying the possible condescension of gracious curiosity. Also he came of a long line of Camerons, whose only method of explanation had been a swift drawing of the sword.

"Why should we bother to explain?" he said. "We know we were all right. If people choose to believe a pack of lies—let them!"

But that confident "we" was a mistake on Dick's part.

At that moment Mrs. Herriot was back—in thought—in her charming drawing-room in Park Lane. The door was being held open with extreme

deference by her old butler, and she was hearing
a kind voice say: "Pray do not rise, my dear Mrs.
Herriot. Allow me the privilege of taking this
chair beside your couch. Now, dear friend, if
you can listen without fatigue, I have much to
say to you."

Into this gracious mental atmosphere the uncompromising "we" of Dick the democrat, hurled
itself, with much the same disastrous effect as
when the stone, flung by his boyish arm so long
ago, went crashing through St. Peter's halo.

The Little White Lady bridled. With a quick,
apparently unconscious, movement, she drew
away her rug, and sat very erect against her
cushions.

"Indeed, I must explain," she said, "and you
hardly seem to realise in how painfully false a
position your folly has placed me. I shall of
course make it clear that you stayed here as my
medical attendant; but I must also be able to say
that you are here no longer. Will it suit your
plans to return to town to-morrow morning?"

Dick looked searchingly at Mrs. Herriot. He
had never before seen her vexed out of serenity.
He suddenly realised how cruelly she had been
hurt by the Lady of the Manor's spiteful travesty
of facts; and the painful position in which it.
might place her, unless she were able to give a
satisfactory explanation without delay.

"I am so sorry for the bother," he said gently,
"and for my share in it. Neither of these

unpleasant people could have worried you, but for
me.   Of course I will leave here at once; to-night,
if you like."

"No, not to-night," she said.   "But to-morrow
morning, early.   I shall reply to this letter by the
mid-day post.   Where do you stay in town?"

"I have rooms in Chelsea," replied Dick, in
which I store my few belongings.   I and a chum
of mine put up in them together.   He is away just
now.   I can turn up at a moment's notice.   It is
rather a rough-and-tumble arrangement, but I
shall hope to improve upon it when I get a practice.
I have never had a real home.   This jolly old
house——" he looked regretfully round the room,
then out of the window and across the lawn to
where the rustic table stood beneath the shady
trees, "this jolly old house, and these very delightful weeks with you, seem to me more my ideal of
home life than anything I have ever known."

This was a good deal for Dr. Dick to say.   A
few hours before, it would have met with a very
warm response from Mrs. Herriot.   But now
there rankled too freshly in her mind this
amazing sentence from the letter she had just
received:

"Needless to say, we none of us believe it, but
the story goes that a young man has been staying
with you at Dinglevale Manor, whom you pass
off to visitors as your son, home from diplomatic
service abroad.   That, far from being either your
son, or a diplomatist, he is known to various old

inhabitants as a ne'er-do-well, who left the village in disgrace, some years ago Also—I hate to write this, but you must know what is being said, in order to refute it—that on one occasion, when the Rector of the parish called unexpectedly and entered unannounced—this in itself stamps the story as untrue to those who are acquainted with your punctilious household: Jarvis, bland but adamant, and that good old dragon, Ellen Ransom —you concealed the said young man under your couch!"

Indignant, apologetic, and affectionate sentences followed; but through them all ran the earnest insistence of many friends for a detailed analysis of the "little fire," tiny spark though it might be, which had kindled these wild flames and columns of blackening smoke, belched forth by the lurid imagination of the Large Lady of the Manor.

Here sat the undoubted spark in the person of Dr. Dick—and not a very penitent or easily extinguished spark, either. Also Mrs. Herriot had temporarily lost her well-balanced sense of proportion. She forgot her exceeding need of him, which had been the primary cause of his sojourn at the Manor House. She forgot the purely professional aspect of much of their inter-course at the outset. It seemed to her that it had all originated in a bunch of golden roses and a pair of bright brown eyes—daring in their steadfast regard, solicitous, penetrating, tender? Yes; sometimes they had even ventured to soften into tenderness; and her mother-heart, lonely in its childlessness, had responded with an answering affection.

"I have been a foolish old woman!" exclaimed the dismayed mind of the Little White Lady. "And my folly deserves this outrageous chastisement. What did I know of this young man, excepting that he was a remarkably clever doctor, with an excellent gift of diagnosis, and knowledge of remedies?" Aloud she added: "Of course I can make it quite clear to my friends that you stayed here professionally—really, in the first instance, at Ellen's suggestion, owing to her anxiety about the nights. And, by the way, my dear young doctor, that reminds me—I have often wanted to ask you—how about your fee? Or perhaps I should rather say, your account? It has been such a long course of careful attention and treatment. I must be very largely in your debt. You will let me have your account before you go?"

A dull red crept into Dr. Dick's tanned cheeks. This mention of his fee followed so closely upon his unwonted lapse into sentiment concerning the sense of home his stay at the Manor had given him. It partook of the nature of the snub direct, though he instantly knew that it was not meant as such.

Yet his eyes hardened, and his tone was perfunctory as he replied: "You owe me nothing. I merely acted as Dr. Thompson's *locum tenens*. In due course you will receive an account from him."

"Ah, yes, for the first visits," said Mrs. Herriot. "But since his return—since you took the case over entirely, staying on here as my physician-in-residence! For that time, a long account is owing to you, and you must let me have it."

"Your kind hospitality, the honour of your friendship, and the pleasure of your society, have more than repaid any medical service I was able to render you," said Dr. Dick, with exceeding stiffness. In fact the formality of his tone was so much overdone, that Mrs. Herriot glanced at him quickly, to catch the twinkle in his eyes which should belie the gravity of his voice. But no gay twinkle was there.

"Very well," she responded, gently. "It puts our friendship in the primary place, which is kind in you, and pleasant for me. And may I remind you that you promised to show me the letter you received this morning, from your friend the Kensington doctor, giving full particulars concerning that practice, and his final terms for a purchase of the partnership?"

Dick drew out his pocket-book, in silence, selected a folded letter from among many papers, and gravely handed it to Mrs. Herriot. He was too deeply hurt to be mollified by this sudden display of interest in his affairs.

Mrs. Herriot slipped the letter into her reticule, without looking at it; then, rising, held out her hand to Dr. Dick.

"Come," she said. "A last little turn together

in the old garden, and then I must send for Ellen, and retire to my room. I am weary, and shall dine upstairs to-night, and take a quiet morning to-morrow. So we will say farewell, my dear young doctor, and close this pleasant episode in your young life and my old one, beside the golden rose-tree, which has yielded you so many buttonholes, and provided me with so many lovely bouquets. When we are back in town, when summer has merged into autumn, and autumn has given place to the stern gloom of winter; when roses bloom no longer in these Surrey gardens, but only behind plate-glass windows at the florists', I shall give a standing order for Rayon d'Or roses, and we will keep them in a silver vase on a table in my drawing-room, to remind us of the old Manor House, and these happy summer days." She looked up at him, with an anxious little smile.

The "we" was very neatly done. It counteracted the snub direct, of a few minutes before. It not only forgave Dick's use of the plural personal pronoun, but it also included him in a possible Park Lane programme.

Yet Dick was not by any means elated. He had deeply resented the sudden mention of his fee in that particular conversation. It would take more than a mere sentimental allusion to yellow roses to restore his mental equilibrium.

He drew Mrs. Herriot's hand within his arm, and stalked silently round the garden.

The Little White Lady looked like a fragile lily, promenading with a tall young fir-tree.

Presently Ellen Ransom appeared, and carried off the drooping Lily.

Then the Fir-tree sat violently down in a rustic garden chair, took out a pipe, and said: "Damn!"

CHAPTER XII

DICK lingered over dessert. It was his last dinner in the Manor House dining-room. He realised regretfully how different would be his surroundings on the following evening, and for many evenings to come.

He had dined alone; but all had been served with the same punctilious care as if Mrs. Herriot herself had been downstairs.

When Jarvis, placing the fruit and decanters within easy reach, noiselessly left the room, Dick peeled a peach, flinging angry thoughts at the Large Lady of the Manor; then pushed an easy chair into position between the table and the open French window, and lay back smoking, and looking gloomily out into the soft summer darkness.

No message had been brought down asking him to go up and say good-night to his patient. Mrs. Herriot had practically bidden him good-bye in the garden that afternoon, implying that he would not see her in the morning.

He somehow felt shunted and in disgrace; and the injustice of this annoyed him.

"Women have no sense of proportion," thought Dr. Dick to himself, "or if they have, they lose it the very moment the need for its proper exercise arises. Here we are, under exactly the same conditions as we were yesterday, as we have been during many weeks past. She has done nothing of which to be ashamed. I have done nothing but what was perfectly legitimate and right. Yet, just because a spiteful old woman makes up a story, and some of her friends exaggerate and repeat it, she herself looks upon our connection from their warped point of view, holds me at arm's length, with horrified eyes, while we discuss the letter; then, as a first step toward righting a wrong which never existed, gives me my dismissal; and, in order to put our friendship on a purely professional footing, asks for my bill! I suppose she does not see that all this is practically putting herself and me in the wrong, and that horrid old scandalmonger in the right."

Dick smoked on, crossly, reviewing in his mind all that had happened since he came in, unusually late, and found Mrs. Herriot, white and worried, with this meddlesome letter on her lap.

He wished he had not stayed to tea at the Rectory over the common.

He wished he had lightly laughed at the whole thing, from the first, instead of being silent and angry. She might have taken the cue from him, if he had only had the presence of mind to laugh.

Out in the soft darkness, a grasshopper suddenly began to chirp in the grass.

Dick leaned forward and hurled his peach-stone in the direction of the cheerful, worrying sound.

The astonished silence which resulted, won from him a grim smile. He wished he could throw peach-stones at all the Little White Lady's friends, and stop their silly talk.

Then he began to think rather darkly and heavily of the future. Unconsciously the house in Park Lane had lately been figuring largely in all his forthcoming plans. Mrs. Herriot had made him feel so much at home with her, that wherever she was, or would be, had seemed to be home; and a home in Park Lane was a very desirable home, and one from which great things might be accomplished and attained.

Now, he must go back to his Chelsea diggings; to his vague and uncertain prospects.

And this was all owing to that odious woman, with her cold voice and her hard eyes. It really dated from the day, so long ago, when out on that smooth lawn, and in this very room, she was unjust to the small boy whom she had asked to her party.

He did not regret, even now, that he had taken his revenge. He had a right to that. The injustice was, that it should be costing him so dear.

But he would be even with her yet. From the rock of apparent disaster, he would mount to the top of the tree.

The dining-room door opened, slowly.

Ellen Ransom, gaunt as ever, in unrelieved black merino, advanced into the room.

Dick looked up, expectant. A silent compact of trust and understanding existed between him and Mrs. Herriot's faithful attendant.

Somehow, to-night, Ellen seemed the one strand which, firm and unswerving, held him safely bound to her mistress, both now, and for the future.

She looked at him, with a slow crooked smile, and laid a note upon the table beside him.

"From my lady, sir," she said. "And I am to bid you good-night, and to say she is feeling more rested, and expects soon to sleep."

She turned and walked to the door.

"Ellen," said Dr. Dick.

"Sir?" said Ellen Ransom.

"I'm off in the morning early, Ellen. I'm going back to town. There is no more need of me here, apparently."

Ellen Ransom's solemn eyes met his, in the soft light of the shaded wax candles.

"That may be as it may," she remarked ambiguously. "The wisest folk at times cut off their own noses to spite their face. But you'll please to leave an address, sir, where I can telegraph."

Dick laughed. "All right," he said. "Good-night, Ellen."

"Good-night, sir," said Ellen Ransom.

10

As the door closed behind her, Dick turned and took up Mrs. Herriot's note.

All things seemed brighter. Ellen's stolid old face had done him good; her calm assurance was consoling, amid so many shifting sands of uncertainty. Somehow he felt he already had one foot planted firmly, with surmounting tread, upon the rock of would-be disaster.

He opened the envelope. Within was enclosed the communication from his friend, concerning the Kensington practice. Also a smaller envelope, endorsed: "Read letter first."

He unfolded the sheet and read:

"MY DEAR YOUNG DOCTOR:

"I find it difficult adequately to express my thanks for all you have done for me and been to me, during these past weeks. But I am perfectly conscious that your skill has given me that inestimable benefit: a new lease of life.

"This is a gift which can hardly be repaid. There can be no question, between us, of anything adequate in the shape of a fee, for such devoted thought and care as you have bestowed upon me. Yet I want to do something for you in return.

"Also, I want to make quite sure of having you always at hand, in the future, as my medical adviser.

"Therefore I wish you to allow me the great pleasure of supplying you with the sum required for the purchase of this partnership in the Kensington practice.

"I am perfectly aware that to accept this from me demands from you that form of generosity which is more rare and great than any generosity which gives—that higher generosity, which knows how to receive.

"Do not look upon it as a gift, or pain me by refusing it. It is not a gift; it is simply that which you have absolutely and honestly earned, by your clever care and kindness. It is also an investment on my part, by which I ensure my future comfort and safety.

"I have never written a cheque with greater pleasure or with a more grateful heart. My one prayer is, that the receiving of it may give you one half as much joy as the bestowing of it gives to me.

"I part with you to-morrow the more easily, owing to the happy expectation that I shall find you established in town on my return there.

"May the Divine blessing, my dear boy, rest upon your future life and work. Such will be the constant prayer of your old friend, and grateful patient,

"HELEN RAEBURN HERRIOT."

Tearing open the smaller envelope, Dick unfolded Mrs. Herriot's cheque, carefully made out, in her delicate handwriting, for the exact sum required for the purchase of the Kensington partnership.

During some minutes he sat quite still, mechanically folding the cheque and letter, and putting them back into the envelopes.

Then he suddenly sprang up, dashed out of the room, across the hall, and up the staircase, three steps at a time.

"Ellen! Ellen!" he called softly, as he ran.

Ellen Ransom was just leaving Mrs Herriot's room. She carried a tray in her right hand, and had closed the door with her left, as Dick reached her.

"I must see her!" he said.

Ellen Ransom kept her hand upon the handle behind her, and confronted him across the tray.

"She hasn't sent for you, sir."

"I can't help that! I must see her. Is she in bed?"

"Not yet, sir. She is lying on the couch, where she has just been taking dinner. The orders are, that she is to be left quiet to have her reading, and I am to return in half an hour."

"Well go along, Ellen," said Dr. Dick. "I'm going in on my own responsibility. I shall only stay a minute. Trot along with the tray. You can't come the mighty dragon over me, you know! I'm still the doctor in charge of the case."

Ellen smiled, grimly. But she withdrew her hand from the door-handle, and stalked off down the passage, without further protest.

Then, unannounced, Dick Cameron softly opened the door, and went in.

The large room was mostly in shadow, lighted

only by the shaded reading-lamp, close to the head of the couch.

The Little White Lady lay very still, in a soft dressing-gown of grey cashmere, her Bible, open, before her.

She looked up, as Dick entered, and her hands dropped upon the open page.

"I had to come," said Dick; then words suddenly failed him.

He knelt down beside the couch, and took her right hand in both his—the frail little hand which had just given him his great start in life, the chance he needed.

He held it, and tried to speak, but, for the second time that day, Dick Cameron found speech impossible. In the afternoon he had been dumb with anger, now he was dumb with gratitude.

He looked helplessly at the kind hand he held, twisting the ring she wore, as if the gleam of the emeralds might inspire him to adequate expression.

At last, lifting his eyes, he looked into her face.

Tears ran silently down the Little White Lady's cheeks, but her eyes were full of a tender happiness.

"You are too good to me," said Dick, brokenly. Then, suddenly, he laid his forehead upon the hand he held.

She lifted her left hand from her Bible, and placed it gently on his bowed head.

"God bless you, my dear boy," she said.

Dick knelt on for a few moments, conscious only of that touch of blessing.

Then he felt her remove her hand; and, rising silently, he turned to leave the room.

Pausing at the door, he looked back at her.

She lay with closed eyes, her folded hands resting upon her Bible. The lamp shed a halo of golden light around the sweet, calm face and silvery hair.

Dr. Dick softly closed the door and went downstairs.

The sense of her benediction went with him.

CHAPTER XIII

BY THE LIGHT OF THE MOON

IN the hall Dick found his bicycle, where it always stood, ready for sudden need. He wheeled it out, mounted, and rode off rapidly across the park and down into the village.

The post office was closed, but Dick made his way round to the back, up the little path among the cabbages, and found the old postmaster in his shirt-sleeves, having an evening pipe at his kitchen door.

"Simmons," he said, "it is a shame to trouble you after hours, but I want a wire to get through at the first possible moment in the morning. May I come in and write it, and leave it with you to-night?"

"Come in and welcome, Master Dick," said the old man, who remembered Dick in sailor suits. "Your message shall go through on the tick of eight to-morrow morning—sooner, if it can be managed."

He went into the dark little office, fumbled about for a few moments, and returned with a telegraph form.

Standing at the kitchen table, Dick wrote the words which definitely closed with the offer of the partnership in the Kensington practice.

Mrs. Simmons, wiping her hands on her apron, came in from the scullery, where she had been washing up the supper things.

She took up her position on one side of Dick; old Simmons, pipe in hand, on the other.

They watched him, with an air of fond possession, as he leaned over the table and wrote by the light of their kitchen lamp.

He belonged to the good old days gone by. He had been "little Master Dick" at the Rectory, in the time of the old Rector and his lady—*their* Rector, who had married them, and had christened their children.

Being past and over, the old days were remembered as having been altogether good. Being also gone, Uncle Andrew was canonized in their faithful hearts; in other words, his many failings were forgotten, his few virtues remembered and magnified.

Dick, though very much alive, shared in this glorification, by reason of his youthful connection with the good old days. So they suspended pipe and dishcloth to watch him, with kindly looks of admiration, as he wrote the firm clear words, each in its small appointed space, which marked so important an epoch in his career.

As he signed "Cameron" at the bottom of the form, he straightened himself, and saw the two pairs of kind old eyes fixed upon him.

"Hullo, Mrs. Simmons!" he said. "See how I break in by the back way when office hours are over. Too bad, isn't it?"

"La, Master Dick! You were never one to be stopped by bolts and bars. If there *was* a hole, you crawled through it; or if there happened to be a locked gate, you climbed over it. As I used to say to Simmons: 'The spirit of the boy, Simmons!' I used to say. And now, to be sure, sir, you *do* grow like your uncle!"

Dick rumpled up his thick crop of hair, with a vivid remembrance of Uncle Andrew's shiny baldness.

"My uncle would not be flattered, Mrs. Simmons. He considered his nephew a hopeless young scamp, to whom you were always far too kind. How well I recall your sweet-shop, with its rows of tempting bottles. Do you remember the *extra* bull's-eye in the ounce? That is a form of generosity which impresses the youthful mind and memory, stirring a deeper fount of gratitude than the gift of a thousand pounds could awaken in us, later. Why are the joys of childhood so much more vivid, and the sorrows of childhood so far more overwhelming than are the emotions of our older years, Mrs. Simmons? Somebody has given me a wonderful thing in the way of gifts, to-day. I am grateful, of course—immensely grateful. But why cannot I feel the enraptured admiration with which I used to regard you, when you would say, in a confidential whisper: 'There, Master Dick!'

and drop yet one more bull's-eye into the already over-weighted scale? Mrs. Harris, up the hill, would have taken one out. *You* dropped another in. You stood, to me, for Generosity incarnate! And I suppose my eyes were just on a level with the edge of your counter! Why cannot we recapture the fine emotions of our youth?"

"And beautiful bright eyes they were, too, Master Dick! I can see 'em now, a-looking up at me so searching, as you laid down your penny, though I don't remember the *extry* bull's-eye. But, bless your heart, you should have a whole ounce for nothing if I kept the old sweet-shop now! We handed that over to Charlotte, when we had to enlarge for the telegraph. She got married just then, and twins within the year. You remember Charlotte, who pulled you out of the duck-pond and carried you up to the Rectory, dripping? And I'm thinking young hearts are softer than old ones and more easily impressed, like a peach with the bloom on it. You soon rub off the bloom; then the fruit shrivels and dries up, till by-and-by you have nought left but the stone — like the old heart — a hard thing."

Mrs. Simmons' kind old face belied her words; but she was sometimes inclined to affect a pessimistic philosophy, chiefly in order to hear it authoritatively contradicted by Mr. Simmons.

He now rose at once to the bait, though he would not have presumed to answer Dick's question.

.' He laid down his pipe on the table, and held up a horny hand, in arresting protest.

"No, no, wife," he said, his fine old face illumined by the light of an inner certainty. "You're wrong there, my dear. We start with the stony heart, I grant you. But, by-and-by, we come to know the truth of the promise: 'A new heart will I give you; and a new spirit will I put within you. I will take away the stony heart out of your flesh; and I will give you an heart of flesh.' In the power of this truth, the old heart should be softer than the young one. Nor do you need to lose the bloom, for another promise says: 'Present you faultless before the Presence of His glory, with exceeding joy.' "

The rugged face of the old postmaster was illumined by the reflection of that "exceeding joy," even as the rocky peaks of the snow mountains gleam rosy and golden as they stand and face the glory of the sunset. When the Fallen Idol had stepped into Uncle Andrew's shoes, and made many changes in the church, old Simmons had responded to the insistent "Come! Come! Come!" of the chapel bell, and had there "sat under" simple Bible teaching, which had changed and softened his whole nature, and brought to him this radiant glory of eternal certainties.

Dick saw no sun, but he saw the brightness of the reflection. He did not, himself, believe in any of these facts; but he believed in the reality of the old man's faith, and would say nothing to dim or cloud it.

He took a handful of small change from his pocket, and laid the cost of his telegram on the table.

"I like your ideas, Simmons," he said, "and your way of putting them. Any theory which tends to keep humanity young and kind, is a thing to be cultivated. Now I must be off. I shall remember with satisfaction, when I wake up in the morning, that my message is speeding to town at the earliest possible moment. I shall be following it up, myself, without much delay. Good-night, Mrs. Simmons. I wish I still adored bull's-eyes, and I wish you still sold them. Good-night, Simmons. Finish the pipe I interrupted, and don't let your wife upset your simple faith with her philosophy. Yours are the views which make for health and happiness. Good-night, old friends."

Dick walked down the little narrow path between the cabbages.

He rode on through the village and turned in at the Rectory gate, where—years before—he had run into Grandaunt Louisa, trimming her roses.

He left his bicycle behind the laurels, making his way through the dark wood where the nut trees grew, and where you had to push aside the boughs to find the path. Then he slipped through the hedge, into the quiet churchyard.

He stood there, in the moonlight, beside his young mother's grave. The marble cross gleamed white against the purple shadows beyond. He could clearly read:

"Aged 26."

So he was older now than she had been when they laid her here. Poor young mother, who failed, and faded, and pined away, leaving her little son alone with Granduncle Andrew and Aunt Louisa!

The tall young man, on the threshold of life, stood looking down upon the quiet grave, a sense of pitying tenderness stirring at his heart.

And, as he stood there, he seemed to see a little lonely huddled figure, in a flannel shirt, sobbing out all the shame, and pain, and misery of that tragic day. He remembered how the little boy of seven had said: "I am never going to pray again in my whole life! But I'll come out on top of everything—always. And I'll do it by myself."

He had certainly kept to the first of these resolves. When his baby faiths slipped from him, he had quickly lost the habit of prayer. On the afternoon of this very day, an earnest heart, desiring his eternal welfare, had given him a beautifully bound little book entitled: *Great Souls at Prayer*, with the request that he would promise to use it every day. But he had answered: "Great souls don't pray! They shoot straight, and 'keep their powder dry.'"

Also, he had kept his word as to coming out on top. Not once had he failed in an examination. He had made the most of every chance—and his chances had been many. And to-night—at a bound—he was within definite sight of the tree-top. Once established in town, nothing would be able to check his steady advance. It might be uphill work; it might take years of strenuous endeavour —but he would get there.

He walked round to the porch, where he had first seen Mrs. Herriot.

Somehow he had felt, all along, that the Little White Lady was his mascot. To be quite honest, it had flashed into his mind, on that first Sunday afternoon, that she might think it worth her while to secure his constant attendance, by making it possible for him to obtain this practice within easy reach of her town house. He had been immensely grateful at first—not so much for the gift itself, as for the delicate wording of the letter, which had made it possible for him to accept the gift. He was grateful still. Yet, undoubtedly, Mrs. Herriot was correct when she impressed upon him that he had earned it. He had saved her life—or rather prolonged it; and the cheque he had just received was not a high price to pay for a new lease of life; especially as there was no doubt his patient could quite easily afford it.

Dick made the mistake, very commonly made by people with small banking accounts, of supposing that somebody with a much larger balance than his own could pay down a sum which would have been impossibly large to himself, without missing it. This expression, "without missing it," as applied to anybody, however wealthy, who possesses a rightly proportioned idea of the responsibility of money and its expenditure, is an ignorant, not to say an ungrateful, fallacy.

As a matter of fact, Mrs. Herriot had had carefully to consider which of her private investments she could most easily sell out, in order to meet this unexpectedly large call upon her bank account.

Dick left the porch and strolled round to the east window. As on that evening so long ago, Saint Peter loomed large and dim, the "plate" once more fixed firmly at the back of his apostolic head. Dick glanced at it, and smiled; then suddenly recalled the Little White Lady's tender words: "I fear the broken halo stands for an outward and visible sign of an inward and spiritual loss. Think of all you lost on that one day, poor little boy!"

He turned to the quiet grave, and stood again, one foot on the marble curb, looking down at the white cross.

"Poor pretty little Mummie," he said. "Your hair was so soft, your hands were so tender. You were made for laughter, and love, and life. Yet, in your Book of Life, Finis was written sternly on the twenty-sixth page, just when the interest was beginning, and all should have promised well. I wonder whether you would have lived, if you had gone with him. You stayed behind, so as not to leave your little boy. Yet, all the same, you left him. Never mind! He has always taken the will for the deed. But your life went with the soldier lover, for want of whom you died. And now, you lie here, with calmly folded hands, and he lies under the veldt, with a bullet through his heart. Yet old Simmons would say it is not the end, either for you or for him; old Simmons might even hold that somewhere in Elysian fields, you and your soldier lover are together now. I wish I could think it also, little Mummie of mine; but I know you to be here."

Dick turned, sadly, from the unresponsive grave.

Then, seized by the sudden need of living, understanding, human sympathy, he dashed through the dark hazelwood, found his bicycle where he had left it, rode up the hill, and sped swiftly over the wide common, until he turned in at the gate of that other Rectory, which he had left only that afternoon.

He rode up the drive, but not to the front door. Passing down a little side path, between laurel hedges, he came to a small garden-gate.

Leaving his bicycle here, he passed through, and walked across a moonlit lawn to a rustic verandah wreathed in clustering rambler roses, where a woman in a white gown lay back in a low garden chair. A crimson cloak was wrapped about her shoulders. She sat very still, her head reclining against the cushions. She appeared to be a tall, long-limbed girl. Her face showed white in the moonlight, her folded hands lay listless in her lap.

She saw Dick coming across the lawn, but she did not move, or even hold out a hand. Only as he came quite near, she gave him a smile of welcome.

"Well?" she said—and her voice was very low and sweet. "A late visit. Is it with intent to catch me disobeying orders?"

"No," he said. "I knew I should find you here. 'On such a night!' Could anybody be indoors? Also, all orders are superseded by the one paramount command to forget that you have ever been an invalid."

"Then why this late visit, doctor?"

Dick drew up a second chair, sat down, leaned forward, elbows on knees, and looked eagerly at the white shadowy figure so near him.

"Margaret," he said, "I have my chance all right. I told you I should. I have earned enough to buy that partnership in town. I telegraphed to-night closing with Graham's offer. I am off early to-morrow, and expect to start work at once. I am come to tell you, and to say good-bye. You, perhaps, better than anybody else, will realise how much it means to me. I am sorry I said that about your little book this afternoon. *You* are a 'Great Soul,' Margaret, and I dare say your prayers carry weight with the Powers that be. So I have come to you. In a moment of weakness, I felt I wanted somebody to be pleased, and to say so."

He paused, abruptly.

At once, from out the shadows, came a woman's hand, white and slim, but strong in its clasp of friendship.

"Dick, old boy," said the deep, quiet voice; "I am more than glad. I think I am thankful. Of course I had prayed. I know how much this means to you—and will mean. I believe I feel almost as much excited as I did on that memorable day when you threw the piece of cake, and sent the curate's tea streaming down his silk waistcoat. I can see you now, flinging defiance at them from the doorway. I don't know why that moment should so vividly come back to me. I suppose it has some sub-conscious connection with this present triumph. Anyway, I congratulate you, Dicky. I laughed then, in childish glee, thinking you such a hero! I laugh now, but almost with tears, because it means that I shall lose you. But I must not be selfish. It would be a poor return for all you have done for me. And I can desire nothing better for your future success, than that all your London patients, when you pay your farewell visit, should say, as my sinking heart is saying now: 'What on earth am I going to do without him?' "

CHAPTER XIV

AFTER THE MISCHIEF WAS DONE

DURING the days which followed Dick Cameron's departure, Mrs. Herriot found it difficult to explain or to understand her own feelings.

At first relief was undoubtedly paramount—immense relief in the fact that if any of her friends paid her a surprise visit, they would not find her having a tête-à-tête tea, in the garden, with the young man whom she had "passed off as her son," and "concealed beneath her couch."

But presently the reply to her letter of explanation arrived, and two or three other letters from friends in the same house-party, all making light of the whole thing and saying how preposterously absurd it was; nobody in their senses would have believed it; how stupid of the old cat who circulated it, to suppose for a moment that such a story could obtain any credence with those who knew Mrs. Herriot.

All this—after the hurt had been inflicted; after the delicate spirit of the Little White Lady had been put through the furnace; after Dick had been dismissed; after the mischief was done. How many of our "afters," mere valueless things, would have been priceless could they but have been "befores."

Then the Ronald Wests wrote from Gleneesh, where they were spending August with the Dalmains, claiming Dick as a great friend, whose skill and devotion had been worth everyth'ng to them during Ronnie's breakdown the year before; and Jane herself added a postscript: "Dick is a splendid fellow ! You could not be in better hands. We all rejoice."

With the sense of relief at his departure thus diminished in its value, the miss of his presence began to make itself felt. Mrs. Herriot gradually realised how her day had centred round his coming and going. At every turn she missed him. His was one of those vivid natures, taking so keen an interest in the small happenings of every day, as to magnify them into delightful importance.

Therefore—Dick gone—the Little White Lady's exciting, eventful days, suddenly became unspeakably flat; her drives, monotonous; her little walks round the garden, devoid of interest and adventure.

It was no good telling Ellen Ransom that by walking very softly over the noiseless turf, she had stood quite close to the thrush while he piped in his bush. Or that, by lying perfectly motionless for half an hour, she had coaxed the robin on to her couch, where he had roguishly pecked at her emeralds, and helped himself to little pieces of cheese out of her hand.

Ellen did not know the joke about the piping of the thrush; and the tone in which she would have said: "Indeed, ma'am," to the second little story, would have implied that, to her thinking, cheese was intended by Providence for respectable people, and not for robins.

Ellen was showing her disapproval of Dr. Dick's sudden departure, by being more stern and taciturn than usual, and by doing everything in jerks, as if each brush she took up, or each tray she removed, awoke in her a fresh impulse of resentment.

It was long since Mrs. Herriot had had strong young life about her—that abounding life which is so vitalizing to those whose pulses beat feebly, whose vigour is almost spent.

So she missed Dick physically as well as mentally, and it is quite possible she might have called him back, had not a very gay and very grateful letter arrived from him, full of all he was doing and arranging in town, and obviously rejoiced to be busy again, after his long holiday.

She could not call him back, yet she suffered in her solitude, the more because she felt she had acted upon an exaggerated impulse, and sent him from her sooner than she need have done.

Into this atmosphere, so sorely requiring fresh interest of some kind, there arrived yet another letter from the Countess of Airth.

"Are you able for calling?" the letter ran. "If so, you would be doing a real kindness by paying an informal, friendly visit to a very dear girl in your neighbourhood, who has been seriously ill, and is now passing through the weariness of convalescence at home, a process which is dragging on into weeks, when change of air and scene, and, above all, change of company, might have reduced it to days. I must tell you a little about her.

"Her name is Margaret Royston. It used to be Cray—she is a cousin of mine; but five years ago, just after her twenty-first birthday, she married Eustace Royston, to whom her father had lately given the living of Hazelmoor. He is owner of the Hall, and squire of the place. The daughters had always taken a great interest in the parish, so it seemed a most natural and suitable arrangement that Margaret, the eldest, should leave the home of her childhood to become mistress of the charming old Rectory, not five minutes' walk from her father's park gates, and only a stone's-throw from the church in which she played the organ, trained the choir, arranged the flowers, in short did everything which a musical, artistic, earnest-minded girl would delight to do. It *seemed* most suitable; but, alas, the most suitable marriages are not always the most successful. If she could have married the Rectory, the church, and the parish, omitting the Rector, all would have been well! It was the Rector item of the programme, which spoilt the perfectly suitable wedding plans, arranged by Margaret's parents. And yet I can hardly tell you in what way the excellent Eustace comes short. Perhaps it is negative rather than positive, but I should be inclined to describe him as a life-slayer. It seems to me that he crushes everything which is living and vital, clips the wings of all things which would mount and soar, dissects ideals, chills enthusiasms, blows out every torch which is not a little glim of his own lighting. He is the sort of person who openly and patently looks at the clock when you begin to tell an enthralling story. His sole form of sport and exercise is clock-golf, played on his own lawn. Margaret looks on, and admires, and keeps the score.

"Of course they have no children. It is impossible to imagine the excellent Eustace as the parent of anything more youthful or alive than sixteenth century prie-dieux, of which he has a fine, worm-eaten collection. They once stayed with us—the couple, not the prie-dieux!—and he looked with extreme disfavour on our romping infants. He always gives you the feeling that he himself stepped out of the Ark in a ready-made cassock, and therefore considers any other method of arriving upon this earth both improper and unsuitable.

"The effect upon Margaret of a course of five years of the excellent Eustace is, that she has been quietly and persistently nipped in the bud. At twenty-one she was a bright, expansive girl, abounding in enthusiasms, full of incipient possibilities.   She is now a silent self-contained woman; strong with the strength which is born of constant self-repression; beautiful, but no longer brilliant. Her music used to pour forth like the song of a soaring lark.   Now, she plays chants with precision; hymn tunes with accuracy; and very rarely sings.

"This summer she has been very ill. I hear Eustace was deeply concerned over the fear of losing her; and her mother, dismayed at the little inclination she showed to hold on to life.   Like Mrs. Dombey, she needed to make an effort, and she would not make it.   When all hope seemed over, they had a very clever new man down from town.   I did not hear his name, nor how they got him, but he pulled her through.   She is now convalescing at home, which accounts for this long letter.   I feel sure a visit from you would greatly cheer her.   I am writing by this post to tell her I have written to you.

"This is quite an epistle; but it was necessary, in order that you should understand Margaret. From herself you would never hear one word of this inner history.   She is absolutely loyal to Eustace. She never lets drop a hint that he is not all her heart and mind require.   For what I have told you, I draw on my own observation, supplemented by that of others.   Remember, the key to the whole situation is the terrible negative quality of Eustace Royston's mentality.

"I sometimes wonder what would happen, if

Margaret came unexpectedly into intimate contact with a real virile, vital *man*. Her starved nature would awaken, and leap up responsive. It would be like the first days of real sunshine at the beginning of Spring. All nature bursts forth at the call of the sun. Nothing can keep the golden crocus buried beneath the mould, when sunbeam heralds sound the *réveillé*. I remember being swept completely off my feet when I first met Jim; but, thank heaven, I was free, and he also! There are all kinds of crocus possibilities in Margaret's nature, should the sun appear. At present she dwells alone—with the Garden Roller! . . . "

Mrs. Herriot smiled, as she folded the letter.

"Myra's imagination is apt to be picturesque," she said; "and she is a strong partisan, where her friends are concerned."

However, she went to the writing-table and wrote a note; then sent it by hand, "*Bearer waits*" being written across a corner of the envelope.

When the answer came back, written in a clear characteristic handwriting, Mrs. Herriot ordered the carriage for three o'clock, and sat down to her solitary luncheon, cheered by the pleasant anticipation of an interest for the afternoon.

Soon after three o'clock, Ellen having jerked her into visiting array, the Little White Lady found herself driving over the common to that distant Rectory to which, all unknown to her, Dick had so often sped on his bicycle.

CHAPTER XV

"WE, WHO LOVE HIM"

"YES, it was Dick," said Margaret, "oh, of course it was Dick ! It could have been no one else. Yet the extraordinary part of it was that we thought him a stranger—some stray young man who happened to be acting '*locum*' to Dr. Thompson. My husband was much vexed at his being sent here, when I was too ill for a fresh mind or a strange face to be considered advisable. But Dr. Norton sent for him, and he came—oh, he came in an old college blazer, the most ancient white flannels, and tennis shoes! I had these particulars from my mother afterwards. I was too ill at the time to notice anything. And Eustace wanted to stop him from going up to my room. But stopping Dick is more easily said than done. The whole house was obeying him, without question, when he had been here three minutes. Eustace had gone to his study, and mamma was offering up raptures of silent thanksgiving. Mamma said she never saw anything like the way he quietly took control, changed everything in the treatment which he considered required changing, and did

170

things himself, instead of merely telling other people to do them."

Mrs. Herriot smiled. "He certainly has a commanding way, in an emergency," she said. "I remember how soon my maid, Ellen Ransom, a most difficult person to manage, humbly did his bidding."

"My first recollection," said Margaret, "is of a sense of coming back to earth quite unexpectedly. I suddenly felt able to open my eyes. Dick was kneeling beside me, holding something under my nose on cotton-wool. As I inhaled it I breathed more easily, voices sounded distinct again, and I could see clearly. The first thing I saw, was Dick's intent face bending over me. As I looked up into his eyes, he smiled and said very low, as if it were a secret between himself and me: 'You are going to live.' I waited a little while; there seemed no hurry about answering. I lay looking up into his brown eyes—Do you remember how brown they are?"

"Yes," said the Little White Lady, "they are very brown."

"As I looked they seemed to shine with assurance, growing brighter and brighter. Don't you think they are very bright eyes?"

"Yes," said the Little White Lady, gently. "I have always thought them quite the brightest eyes I had ever seen."

"Well, even then, as I looked up into them, they struck me as being curiously familiar. At last I said: 'Am I—am I—going—to live?' And Dick said: 'Yes, you are going to be quite well.' I said: 'Why?' Such a silly thing to say, wasn't it? But Dick smiled his triumphant smile and bending a little lower said: 'Because I intend to pull you through.' From that moment I never doubted that I should get well. I used to lie and whisper to myself: 'He intends to pull me through.'"

Margaret leaned back, looking past her visitor, with dreamy, unseeing eyes. She was trying to recapture the sensations of renewed hope and possibility, which those words used to awaken within her.

Mrs. Herriot used these moments of detachment, to study more closely the beautiful oval face, the broad low forehead, from which the soft hair grew in abundant waves, with gleams of gold in its rich darkness; the sensitive mouth, showing in repose lines of proud self-repression, coupled with a little droop of wistful sadness. Dark shadows beneath the eyes, blue veins on the thin temples, and the extreme whiteness and transparency of the hands, betrayed the fact of a long and severe illness; yet there was about Margaret Royston a look of returning health and beauty, which gave promise of complete recovery—if life did but hold something for which it was worth while to regain the full radiance of perfect health.

Mrs. Herriot's loving heart went out to this girl before her, with a fulness of perfect understanding. She knew she had to do just then with a mind which was opening and expanding at her touch, owing to the loss of self-control brought about by long weakness, and by the unexpected luxury of a sympathetic listener. The barriers of self-repression were down. The Little White Lady intended to walk in, but she did not wish to intrude. Exceeding delicacy and tact were required on her part, in order to allow Margaret to say all she wished, and yet not more than she would afterwards remember with comfort. A confidence which is regretted, is fatal to all further friendship. This silence gave to both a breathing space.

Mrs. Herriot looked round the pretty drawing-room. For a Rectory, it was unusually complete in its scheme of colour, its simplicity, and the excellent taste of its furniture. The style and atmosphere of the old English country-house had accompanied the eldest daughter from the Hall, to her new home. The mental influence of "the excellent Eustace" evidently did not waste itself upon inanimate objects. Margaret paid the bills, so Margaret had been left free to furnish as she pleased. But, in the very centre of the well-kept lawn, viewed through the open window, was a crude white-washed circle, marked round with Roman figures, a flower-pot sunk in the centre—the clock-golf which provided the Rector with sport and exercise. Myra's picturesque imagination had not here been at fault.

The silence was lasting a shade too long. Margaret would begin to realise that she had been expansive. So Mrs. Herriot thought well to break it, carefully.

"Those words of Dick's must have given you a mental suggestion of hopefulness and health," she said. "It is a pity doctors do not more often realise the extraordinary effect upon a patient's mind, of a mental suggestion."

Margaret smiled, and her grey eyes grew less dreamy.

"Well, certainly nobody had given me a mental suggestion of recovery until Dick walked in. Mamma, with streaming eyes, had entrusted me with a tender message to a little sister of mine who died twenty years ago; and Eustace, kneeling beside my bed, had repeated: 'Yea, though I walk through the valley of the shadow of death.' I seemed sinking away, without a hand held out to which I could cling, until Dick crossed the floor in his old tennis shoes! You know, he was sent for quite unexpectedly, in the middle of breakfast on Sunday morning. He had meant to take a day off, and had come down in his oldest flannels in order to start his holiday by mowing and rolling his landlady's lawn. When Dr. Norton's note reached him, he did not wait to change, but stuffed the pockets of his old blazer full of the things he was likely to need, and bicycled off, without losing a moment."

"Sunday morning?" said Mrs. Herriot, on her brow a slight wrinkle of perplexity, of doubt, of searching of memory. "Why, it was on a Sunday morning in June——"

"Yes," said Margaret, "it was on that very Sunday morning, as he was on his way back from here, that he attended you in the church porch. He told me afterwards how fortunate it was, that coming straight from my case, he had with him all the remedies needed for heart-failure."

"I see," said the Little White Lady, gently; and if there was pain in her eyes, the brave smile on her lips concealed it. "Dear old blue flannel coat! I remember comparing it to Nazareth, because it seemed at first so unexpected that everything we needed could come out of it. But, of course it is quite explained by the fact of his being then on his way back from you. It was fortunate for me that this happened to be the case. I do not think he would have had time to fetch what was required."

"No," said Margaret, gently. "Dick told me there was not a moment to lose."

"Then he has talked to you of me?"

"Oh, yes, often; not as a patient—I don't think he ever talks of one patient to another—but as a kind and wonderful friend. I am sure you can't know how much living at the Manor with you has meant to Dick. All his life he has been so homeless and alone. One does not say it in the least pathetically. He would not have had it otherwise. It has made him what he is. But he has been so independent—yes, that is a better word; he has never had anybody to consider, from the social or

family point of view. He told me once that it
seemed so new and curious to him to have to time
his work so as to be home punctually for his meals
with you. I well remember the pleasure in his
face, and the sudden softening of his voice, as he
spoke of it. Do you know, Mrs. Herriot, I think
the thing which has been worst of all for Dick is
that he grew up believing in nothing and nobody.
But now he believes in *you*. And this belief in
your goodness, and kindness, and sweetness, has
done more for him in a few weeks than any number
of creeds or sermons."

For a moment Mrs. Herriot made no reply.
Personalities were always difficult to her. Then
she said: "How soon did you find out that he was
an old friend?"

"Oh, quite soon; directly I was able to talk.
We had been playmates when I was six and he
was seven. I perfectly well remember the children's party at Dinglevale Manor, when he threw
the piece of cake at the curate. I was a shy, round-
eyed little girl, on that great occasion; and I
thought him so splendid, standing in the doorway,
hurling defiance at the grown-ups. He became
my hero from that hour. We often met and played
together. I lavished admiration and devotion
upon him, which he, in a lordly little way, accepted
and enjoyed. He used to show me the things
in his pockets, and occasionally present me with
a very sticky bull's-eye. I, alone, knew that it
was Dick who had broken the church window. I

remember well the proud burden the responsibility of this terrifying confidence laid upon me. Dick insisted upon our climbing a very high tree before he told me. He said we must be 'safely out of earshot.' I was doubtful as to the exact meaning of 'earshot,' but it sounded a warlike and a dangerous thing. Perched up together in the fork of a large bough, Dick told me that it was he who had put a stone through 'old Peter's plate.' He also informed me, in a very calm little voice, that he was consequently going to hell. I nearly fell off the bough! He caught and steadied me, just in time. I remember weeping copiously, from the double fright. I sometimes wondered he was not more annoyed by my tears. I understand now that they were a tribute enjoyed by his masculine vanity. He put his small arm round me, and said: 'Don't be a silly little girl, Magsy. You can't help being a *girl*, but you *can* help being silly.' Ah, how often, long years later, I used to feel that sturdy little arm round me, and hear Dick's clear, childish treble saying: 'You can't help being a *girl*, but you *can* help being silly.'"

Margaret paused. Her eyes were dreamy again.

Mrs. Herriot felt herself on the threshold of an inner sanctuary. She leaned forward and laid her hand gently on Margaret's knee. By virtue of that touch, she passed in.

"What happened next, dear?"

Margaret laughed. "Oh, my womanly devotion responded to the supreme test. I dried my tears, and said that if he was really going to hell, I would go too. But Dick said I must not do that, it was not a place for girls, and I should be very much in the way. I felt useless and inadequate, and wept again. Whereupon Dick searched his pockets and found a bull's-eye. It had lost its little paper bag, and had become mixed up with a good deal of string. Dick sucked it first, because it was dusty, and then gave it to me." Margaret smiled again. "You see I was right in telling you our original friendship had been a very intimate one! Then we both climbed down, and ran home. Not long after this, his father returned from India, and sent for him. I never saw him or heard of him again, until I looked up into his eyes, eight weeks ago, and heard him say: 'You are going to live. I intend to pull you through.' "

Mrs. Herriot leaned back, looking—not at Margaret—but out of the window, past the lawn with its white-washed clock, to the distant trees beyond.

"The very earliest friendships of our childhood," she said, with a certain detachment of manner, "always maintain a tenacious hold upon the heart and memory. I can look back, nearly sixty years, and remember, with a thrill of admiration, a charming little boy with clustering curls and a velvet hat, who rode a donkey with me on the sands at Broadstairs, during a happy summer holiday. I was strapped into one pannier, and he

into the other.   The donkey's name was Rosebud!
Next time I met him, he was a Cabinet Minister,
bald and portly, much weighted with the cares of
the state.   He took me in to dinner, and we bored
one another with social and political topics, until
we chanced to discover each other, and the mutual
link of Rosebud the donkey!   After which we
talked airballs, and sand-castles, shrimps and sea-
anemones, with so much vivacity and animation
that his wife raised her lorgnon several times, to
gaze at us.   Nevertheless, we each drove home
disillusioned.   Yet I always read his speeches now,
however dull and ponderous; and did I happen
to require a favour of the government, I should
know to whom to apply, endorsing my petition:
'For Rosebud's sake!' "

"*I* was not disillusioned," said Margaret, softly.
"Only—" she hesitated, then continued, in sudden
agitation: "Oh, Mrs. Herriot, I had prayed for
him for years!   I began doing so the very day
he told me he had broken the church window;
and it was such a shock, when we met again, to
find him an agnostic!"

"My dear!" said the Little White Lady, almost
sternly, "do not say 'agnostic' in the same horrified tone of voice as you would say 'thief' or
'murderer'!   Do you know the meaning of the
term 'agnostic'?   It was invented by Professor
Huxley in 1885, to indicate the mental attitude of
those who withhold their assent to whatever is
incapable of proof.   In regard to miracles and

revelation, agnostics neither dogmatically accept nor reject such matters; but simply say '*Agnosco*— I do not know.' The term is modern; but the attitude of mind is as old as human thought. It was an honest agnostic who raised at Athens the altar to the Unknown God, of which Saint Paul made his text on Mars' Hill, in preaching before the court of the Areopagus. We, to whom has been granted the inestimable privilege of a certainty of knowledge, should respect the doubts of the honest doubter, proving to him the reality of our faith, by the sincerity of our love."

Margaret's luminous grey eyes searched the quiet face of her visitor.

"I wish you could talk to Eustace," she said. "He declares Dick should never have entered this house had he known him to be an agnostic."

"I do not suppose my opinion would carry any weight with your husband, dear child," said Mrs. Herriot, gently. "But his Master's way of dealing with those who could not profess faith for lack of personal knowledge, might be illuminating and instructive. 'Who is He, Lord, that I might believe on Him?' questioned the man who did not know. And the answer was so convincing and so complete in its understanding tenderness, that it instantly called forth the worshipping response: 'Lord, I believe!' "

"Eustace has had several arguments with Dick," said Margaret. "But Dick invariably got the best of it. He kept perfectly cool, whereas

Eustace, who naturally feels strongly on religious matters, lost his—I mean, grew rather heated. It only made bad worse."

"Naturally," said Mrs. Herriot. "I never argue with Dick. I try, in my humble way, to live the things I believe, hoping thus to arouse in him a realisation of their reality. That broken halo stood for more than the mere shattering of stained glass. It was the wrecking of childhood's faiths and ideals. Poor little boy! We, who love him, must strive to restore to him, by faith and patience, his broken halo."

Suddenly—without any warning—Margaret burst into tears. She buried her face in her hands and sobbed, with no attempt at control.

Mrs. Herriot said nothing. She rose, moved over to the window, and stood looking out on to the rustic verandah, with its clustering rambler roses. She was wondering how often Dick's gay, cheery presence had made it a place of more than sunshine.

Presently the sobs grew few and far between, and finally ceased altogether. Then inarticulate words came from the depths of Margaret's chair.

Mrs. Herriot turned back into the room. She laid her hand gently on the bowed head.

"Tell me about it, dear child," she said.

"It is all very well to say 'we, who love him'—" began Margaret, in a choking voice; then broke off abruptly.

Mrs. Herriot let that pass.

"Tell me all about it," she repeated, gently, as though Margaret had not spoken. She stroked the coils of beautiful, bright hair.

Then Margaret lifted her head, caught the kind hand in both her own, and laid her cheek against it.

"Yes," she said, "I will—I will! Oh, you must think me so foolish, so distraught! But I hope you do not really think so badly of me as to suppose that I love Dick!"

Mrs. Herriot's gaze was an astonished question.

"My dear? I should think very badly of you if, after all he has done for you, and the sweet link with the long-ago past, you did *not* love Dick."

"But you forget that I am a married woman," said Eustace's wife, almost after the manner of the excellent Eustace himself.

The indignant blood mounted into the delicate cheeks of the Little White Lady.

"Oh, my dear," she said, "I cannot believe you to have that kind of mind! Are you one of those who think that there is only one sort of love possible, between men and women? Do you not know that a sweet pure-minded woman can give a man a strong and helpful love, which shall make him hold all women the higher for her sake; which shall move unseen to his side in the hour of temptation, coming as a bright silver shield between him and enticement; which shall remind him of a dead mother's prayers, of a little sister's kiss? Surely the Margaret who was prepared to follow little eight-year-old Dicky to hell, if need be, is able now to give a calm helpful love to the full-grown Dick, if he needs her sympathy and friendship."

The Little White Lady paused. Her breath came quickly. Her hand stole to the place where emotion was apt to cause a sudden stab.

While she spoke, Margaret's eyes had not left Mrs. Herriot's face. Now a sudden light illumined her own. It was as if a heavy cloud had lifted. Her eyes shone, her mouth was sweet and noble in its smile of unhesitating tenderness. For the first time, Mrs. Herriot saw Margaret Royston as she really was—as she always might have been.

"Oh, you are right!" she said. "Of course, when I think of Dick, and not of my own stupid self, I could do that—or anything else—for him. But may I tell you why I have been feeling troubled and uneasy, almost—yes—almost self-condemned, since Dick suddenly went away? I have missed him so much, so unaccountably more than I should have expected to miss him. Not only mentally, but physically. I feel so limp and listless, and as if life is an impossible effort, because there is not the hope of looking up to see him walking across the lawn. Oh, Mrs. Herriot—I don't want to make another trite or unworthy remark—but I *do* feel that it is wrong that any man who is not—well, who is not Eustace—should have so great a hold upon me, as to make that kind of difference to my life, by his presence or absence."

"My dear," said Mrs. Herriot, with gentle earnestness, "I quite understand your meaning, but I do not think you need feel condemned. Will it help you if I confess to you that I—an old woman of over sixty—miss Dick in precisely the same way? There is nothing foolish or sentimental, or wrong, in what we feel. It does not depend upon ourselves, but upon the vivid, vital quality of his own personality. He has, in a marked degree, that power which all doctors should possess —which every born doctor does possess—of imparting life and vigour. He acts upon a fading, worn-out physique, as sunshine upon a drooping plant. Just as nature responds to the call of the sun, and bursts into leaf and blossom, so we respond to his vigorous vitality. Also, we who have been his patients, have experienced the force of his strong will coming up under ours with the concentrated determination that we shall get well. It has drawn us into the intimacy of oneness of purpose with him. To ordinary patients it would begin and end at that; merely the satisfaction of success and augmented reputation, for him; undying gratitude, and a cheque, for them. But for you and me, my dear, it means more than this. For me—because he has become to me as a very dear son and companion, in my loneliness; for you—because there is the tender link of a childish friendship; for us both, because we earnestly desire his spiritual welfare. We must not allow any morbid selfishness on our part to creep in, spoiling

two friendships which are a divine gift to him, if
purely and faithfully kept in hand by us. By
means of his skill and devotion he has saved your
life and prolonged mine. Surely, that we should
give him, in return, a prayerful earnest affection
is not much to ask?"

There was complete silence in the Rectory
drawing-room. A noble mind, long forced into
a narrow groove, was fighting its way out into
light, liberty, and breathing space. An honest
conscience was facing a difficult problem, and
striving to decide aright. A woman's heart, deep
beyond all human sounding-lines, was trying to
find bottom with a two-foot rule.

Suddenly Margaret rose, came and knelt down
beside Mrs. Herriot, and took her right hand in
both hers, laying her cheek against it, with a confiding gesture, just as Dick had done on his last
evening at the Manor; only, in Dick's impulse
there had been gratitude; in Margaret's, there
was surrender.

"You are right," she said. "You have helped
me so much, and I will not fail. But he needs
you more than he needs me. He loves nobody,
and believes that nobody loves him; and he regards
this condition of things with entire complacency.
He remarked to me, the other day, that love and
ambition could never go hand in hand, citing
Napoleon as an instance. Dick often reminds me
of Napoleon. Look at that Capo di Monte
statuette of Napoleon on the top of the china

cabinet over there. See him bestriding a chair as if it were a charger, his arms folded on the back; a face of iron, beneath the cocked hat; a look of indomitable will, in every line of the calm figure. I bought him in Italy the year before my marriage, when papa and I went abroad together. I couldn't understand why he so fascinated me. He was terribly expensive, and most difficult to pack. I brought him home in my hat-box, to the ruin of my hats! I realise now, that, even then, he reminded me of Dick—little Dick who broke the halo, defied the world, and swore to come out on top, no matter who or what might stand in his way! Mrs. Herriot, Napoleon set his heel on a woman's heart, as he stepped up to the summit of his ambition. Dick, under similar circumstances, would do the same."

Mrs. Herriot smiled, her eyes upon the stern little figure of Europe's conqueror.

"Yet Napoleon adored Josephine," she said, softly. "He hurt himself, more than he hurt her. Yes, I saw it was Dick, as soon as I came in; but not Dick at his best. It is Dick fighting seven devils, and failing to cast them out."

"He puts success in his profession—getting to the top of the tree, as he calls it—before all else," said Margaret. "He congratulates himself on having nobody to consider, no home ties to hamper or hinder him. Yet, I believe, all unconsciously to himself, he really loves you. Who could help it, dear Mrs. Herriot! You are so kind, and sweet, and understanding. I have seen him pull out his watch, find tea-time nearer than he thought, and dash off instantly, saying: 'I must not keep my Little White Lady, waiting!'"

"Is that what he calls me?"

"Yes, always; and always with a softening of his voice, and of his whole manner. Oh, I wish he had not had to go from your influence."

"He has gone to town," said Mrs. Herriot. "I return home early next month. He will attend me there. I shall see him constantly."

"It was curious," remarked Margaret, "that he suddenly became possessed of the sum he wanted for that partnership, in the very nick of time. He had told me he should do so. I feared he might borrow it. But it appears he earned it. It was a large sum to earn."

The Little White Lady's eyes turned to the top of the china cabinet.

"Napoleons usually get what they want," she observed, softly; "and get it just when they had determined to have it."

"Well, Dick says it has given him his chance, and he means to take it. But it has taken him away from us."

"It has left me very lonely," said Mrs. Herriot. "Could I persuade you to spend a few days with me at Dinglevale? I would fetch you myself, take every care of you, and drive you home at a moment's notice, if necessary. It would be an immense pleasure to me, and would give you complete change of surroundings, without the fatigue of a long journey.

Margaret's delight was unmistakable. "Oh, I should love it," she said, "if Eustace will consent."

And then, though unwarned by rustling wings of his approach, they both looked up, and saw the black figure of the Rector, advancing over the lawn.

Margaret had ample time to fly back to her seat and smooth her tumbled hair, for he carried a spud in his hand, and rooted up the smiling little daisy faces as he walked. Even upon that well-kept lawn, starry white petals, centred with gold, had responded to the call of the summer sun. The Rector dealt a well-directed prod at each, and left them lying prone.

He reached the window.

"Margaret," he began, looming large between the lace curtains, "it is disgraceful that, do what I will, these objectionable weeds—" Then he saw Mrs. Herriot.

Margaret rose, hurriedly.

"Mrs. Herriot, will you allow me to introduce my husband? Eustace, Mrs. Herriot has kindly driven over from Dinglevale Manor. She heard of my illness from Myra."

The Rector leaned his spud against the window frame, removed his soft felt hat, then came in through the window, extending a cordial hand to Mrs. Herriot.

"Most kind," he said.   "*Most* kind."

Then he sat down, looking intently at Mrs. Herriot.

"A very fine day," he remarked with emphasis, and the decision of incontrovertible certainty.

"Very fine," agreed Mrs. Herriot, her mind paralyzed, by the gaze of the excellent Eustace, into the ineptitude of mere assent.

The Rector looked round the room, conscious of something missing.

"My dear Margaret," he said, his tone one of mild reproof, "have you omitted to ring for tea?"

Margaret flew to the bell.

"How careless of me!   Eustace, Mrs. Herriot knows Jim and Myra well."

The Rector rose, took up his position on the hearth-rug, parting his coat-tails for the benefit of the ferns and fuchsias with which Margaret adorned her empty fireplace.

He turned his gaze once more upon Mrs. Herriot.

"In fact," he said, "we are really having a continuous spell of summer weather.   Most unusual in this variable climate."

"We are," assented the Little White Lady. "Most."

Then she glanced at the firmly seated figure of Napoleon, in long grey overcoat, white breeches, top-boots, and cocked hat.   "He certainly *is* extraordinarily like Dick," she thought.   "I wish he would leap down from his exalted position on the cabinet, and help forward this conversation."

She looked back toward the mantelpiece. The Rector had had a fresh inspiration. He was gazing at her with renewed interest.

"Do you play clock-golf?" he inquired.

CHAPTER XVI

"SO THEY KNOW EACH OTHER!"

WHEN Dick came down to breakfast on the morning following Mrs. Herriot's visit to Margaret, he found among his letters an envelope addressed in the delicate pointed handwriting he knew so well.

He poured out some rather unsatisfactory coffee, helped himself to sausages and cinders, buttered a thick piece of sodden toast, and opened Mrs. Herriot's envelope.

After glancing at the first few lines, he pushed back his chair, walked over to the window, and stood in the morning breeze and sunshine to read the rest of the letter. Somehow it seemed so foreign to the stuffy atmosphere of London lodgings.

> "THE MANOR HOUSE,
> "DINGLEVALE.

"MY DEAR YOUNG DOCTOR,

"I have something to say to you which partakes of the nature of a confession, I had almost said of an apology!

"It has been borne in upon me, with a certainty of conviction, that I was unduly concerned over that false and scandalous report circulated among my friends and acquaintances by a person who shall be nameless—or rather whom we will continue to call 'The Large Lady of the Manor.' I was so greatly horrified that my name should be connected with such tales, and that any foundation of fact should lend them a semblance of truth, that I lost my sense of proportion, and sent you from me, in unnecessary haste, without just cause or due consideration.

"I feel I owe you the expression of my sincere regrets, and the affectionate assurance of how greatly I have missed you.

"All has worked together for good, so far as you are concerned, as I gather, from your letter, that your presence in town just now would have been imperative.

"But I earnestly hope we shall, at no distant date, resume in other surroundings our pleasant home-life together. I do not think it would be wise or well that I should ask you to live entirely with me. We do not wish to provoke question or comment, however absurd or unreasonable; besides, your work will make it needful that you should have independent rooms. But Ellen and I will take delight in arranging for you a study in my house in Park Lane, where you may always count upon undisturbed quiet. Also, at any meals which you can share with me, you will be most welcome; and any evenings you can spare me will be indeed a gift to my solitude.

"If you will look upon my house as home, my dear boy, and allow me to share in your work and interests, you will prove that you have generously forgiven an unreasonable regard for false conventions, and an undue concern for the mistaken opinions of others, which I fear must have disappointed and pained you.

"What gay little dinners we will have, and luncheons also! And why not even breakfasts sometimes, if my hours work in with your engagements?

"Let me hear how you progress. Run down and see me, if you feel inclined.

"I am keeping very well. I go out driving daily.

　　　　"Believe me,
　　　　　　"Affectionately your friend,
　　　　　　　　"H. R. H."

Dick folded the letter; then went back to his tepid sausages, with a very gay smile.

"No more fried cinders!" he remarked, as he crunched the first mouthful. "No more grey coffee; no more beastly greasiness. Buck up, Dick, my boy! There's no manner of doubt about hours working in!"

Another letter lay on the table, also in a woman's hand-writing—a large, clear writing this; full of unmistakable character.

13

Dick opened it and glanced at the signature. But he did not leave the table to read this letter. He propped it up against the coffee-pot, and helped himself to another sausage.

" HAZELMOOR RECTORY, SURREY.

" MY DEAR DICK,

"Your perfectly angelic Little White Lady has paid me a visit!

"She had not heard of me from you; but my cousin, Myra Airth, wrote asking her to call, and this afternoon she came.

"Dick, she is far more lovely than you ever told me. It almost took my breath away, when she came in! She might have stepped straight out of a sweet old picture. And it is not only the general effect, at a distance. The closer you look, the more lovely she is. I never saw such a skin! Her face is like an exquisitely cut cameo; and her little delicate hands so pretty in their movements, with the flash of the fine emeralds and brilliants on the third finger. Myra tells me that, owing to the coincidence of her initials her friends speak of her as 'Her Royal Highness,' and sometimes call her 'dear Princess.' I don't wonder! She is a most regal person; yet so gentle and gracious, and easy to talk to.

"But, indeed, you are wrong, Dick, when you sum her up as 'easily taken in.' On the contrary, I assure you, she is most extraordinarily intuitive and far-seeing. She reads character, and weighs circumstances, with swift and unerring judgment.

If you are making any calculations based on lack of perspicacity in your Little White Lady, unmake them, Dicky, or you will find yourself caught on your own hook!

"Needless to say, I am only chaffing, old boy. I know how high you hold her. But I assure you, she is more clever than you think. You should have heard her talk round Eustace, and get her own way, and on an important point for me, too.

"What do you think? To-morrow she comes in her carriage to fetch me, and I am to spend a week with her—perhaps longer—in your beautiful old Manor House. So I shall see Mrs. Maher-shalal-hash-baz, and the birds, and the garden, and have tea under the trees. And I shall get to know your Little White Lady really well. And I shall be back in the old dining-room, where we sat on high chairs when you petrified us all, by flinging the cake at the curate.

"I am so much excited at the prospect, I can hardly behave with proper decorum.

"Do you approve, doctor? You know, you advised change. Can't you run down one day, and see how the cure is working, and whether your two patients are good for one another?

"How go the London plans? Write and report progress, to Dinglevale Manor. A letter from you will be of thrilling interest both to your Little White Lady, and to

"Your little chum of old days,
"MARGARET."

Dick folded the three sheets—Margaret's rather bold hand-writing had run the letter into three—put them back into the envelope; tore it across, and then across again, and threw the fragments into the waste-paper basket.

Then he pushed back his chair, walked over to the mantelpiece, and filled his pipe.

This time he was not smiling. He looked remarkably like the Capo di Monte statuette of Napoleon. His brows were bent, as he lighted a match.

"So they know each other," he said, his pipe between his teeth, "the Little White Lady and Margaret. Now, how is that going to work out, I wonder?"

He lay back in the lumpy leather chair, with a broken spring in the seat.

As he smoked his brow cleared. The furrow of annoyance lifted; the bent look of concentration smoothed away.

He took Mrs. Herriot's letter from his breast-pocket and read it through once more.

He smiled again, as he folded it and stowed it safely away.

"All's well," he said. "No harm's done. But the Intimate Friend, who sports a coronet, seems for ever putting a finger in my pie! However, Park Lane is the next move. No going back to Dinglevale for me!"

He whistled gaily, as he pulled on his boots. It reminded him of the thrush piping in the bush;

also of breaking stupid rules in the hydropathic establishment at Leipzig.

Then he went out into the busy rush of a London morning.

. . . .

And in the peace and calm of the old Manor House, the two women who loved Dick waited expectant, hoping for the surprise visit, which never came off.

But by-and-by, Margaret's time was up, and she returned home to take up the daily routine of life with a fresh store of "courage and gaiety."

And Mrs. Herriot bade her household pack and make ready to return, with as little delay as possible, to her house in Park Lane.

CHAPTER XVII

AUTUMN IN PARK LANE

"CHECK!" said the Little White Lady, softly.

Dr. Dick hooked his feet round the legs of his chair, placed his elbows on the table, and gazed long and meditatively at the chess-board.

At last he lifted his right hand, let it hover for a moment over the battle, like a great brown hawk over a moor; then pounced suddenly down upon a piece, made a decisive move and leaned back in his chair, as if to say: "How's that?"

A fragile hand came forward without a moment's hesitation, guiding a bishop swiftly down his slanting course.

"Check!" said the Little White Lady.

Dr. Dick wound his feet round one another in a grotesque attitude beneath his chair, pondered long over the situation; then—in a slow, deliberate, masterly manner, he moved his king to the only possible square.

A quick flash of emeralds and diamonds, a sweep of lace across the board, and a knight, leaping over several crowned heads, planted himself belligerently upon the one square of the board on which his presence was least desired.

"Check!" murmured the Little White Lady.

"Oh, I say!" exclaimed Dr. Dick, breaking for once the rule of silence. "Now I must sacrifice my queen; and, adding insult to injury, she will be captured, poor lady, by that little brute of a pawn ! Wait a bit! Let's see. Can I save her?"

Mrs. Herriot smiled into his eager eyes, but offered no opinion.

After much contorting of his long legs and rumpling of his hair, Dr. Dick reluctantly captured the aggressive knight, placing his queen at the mercy of the humble foot-soldier.

But nothing happened to the queen. The knight's bold leap had left a vacant square in front of a hitherto unnoticed little pawn, whose own proud queen stood one square to the left exactly behind him. This little soldier now took an unostentatious step forward, leaving an uninterrupted vista of empty squares, down which her victorious White Majesty gazed in brazen triumph at the stricken Red King.

"Mate!" said the Little White Lady, softly.

Dr. Dick looked in bewildered astonishment at the chess-board, made one or two hopeless endeavours to find a man who could be brought forward to stand between his king, and the steady stare of the White Queen. But every line of route was blocked, every move had been forestalled.

"Mate it is!" said Dr. Dick. "And a jolly good one, too!" Then he threw back his head and laughed. "Shall I never beat you at chess,

Mrs. Herriot? Here we are at our tenth game, and not even a stale-mate to my credit! But you must admit I made a better fight over this one. And I am certain you did not see my masterly schemes over in that corner. All I wanted was a chance. If you had ceased checking for just one move, I could have got my chance, and turned the tables."

"The Emperor of Germany might reign at Buckingham Palace if we gave him a chance," mused the Little White Lady. "The secret of power lies in never giving a chance."

"Well, but," argued Dr. Dick, "you might just have chanced to start in with your checking fusillade one move later——"

"There is no chance in chess," interposed Mrs. Herriot. "It has all the certainty of a mathematical calculation. I could have begun checking exactly four moves earlier; but it made a better game of it to let you develop your plan to within three moves of a possible mate."

"Oh, ho!" said Dr. Dick. "Then you realised my invincible plan?"

Mrs. Herriot rearranged the pieces as they were before her first check move, then rapidly mated her own king.

"Was that it?" she asked.

"Yes," admitted Dick, ruefully, "but one move better. You are a masterly chess-player, Mrs. Herriot, and somehow I can't make it fit in with the rest of you! They say a really great chess-player must also be a great strategist, and a great politician."

"And does my young doctor deny me all potential possibilities of success in strategy or politics?"

"Well, I can't quite see *you*, Mrs. Herriot, marching to Westminster, and knocking off policemen's helmets, with a silk umbrella."

A delicate flush mantled the cheek of the Little White Lady.

"Are strategic politics and vulgar rowdyism synonymous in this country," she inquired; "or only in your own mind?"

"No, no, Mrs. Herriot!" said Dick, quickly. "I humbly beg your pardon. I forgot to whom I was speaking. The mention of politics set me off, because this afternoon I have been dressing the face of a young constable who will probably lose the sight of his right eye, injured by an umbrella thrust. It has put my blood up, where female politicians are concerned."

"I think we are discussing the ancient and noble game of chess," suggested Mrs. Herriot, with gentle dignity.

Dr. Dick pulled himself together. "So we are," he said. "And I am wondering whether I shall ever beat you. How long have you played?"

"For over fifty years," she said. "My father taught me the game when I was nine years old. He and I used to play together nearly every evening. Often my bedtime arrived before the

game was ended. We then stood the board on the
top of the piano or on a bookcase in my father's
study, and held ourselves bound in honour not to
look at it, until we sat down on either side of the
board next evening. I remember a game begun
on my twelfth birthday, which lasted three days."

"Who won it?" asked Dick.

The Little White Lady blushed and smiled.
The victory might have been yesterday. "I did,"
she said. "And I think my father was as much
pleased as I was; but he gave me no quarter. It
was a fair win. Certainly, we had a few peculiar
little ways of our own. One was an intense respect for the balance of power, and a nicety of
calculation in the matter, based upon our knowledge
of each other's game, which always enabled us to
gauge whether or not we were running a risk in
exposing a piece. Then, we never took advantage of an obvious slip. I can hear his quiet
voice now, saying: 'But—my child?' While I,
under similar circumstances would say under my
breath: 'Oh, *dear* Papa!' I have never yet found
anybody who could fully understand how enor-
mously this added to the grandeur and greatness
of the game, and to the glory and delight of ultimate victory. Then we extremely disliked what
my father called 'a slaughtering game.' We
never took a prisoner, unless the exigency of war
demanded it. In many of our best games every
man was on the board at the conclusion, saving
perhaps a knight on one side, a bishop on the other,

and a few pawns.   The fewer the prisoners we had taken, the greater the satisfaction of our win. Some years ago I played with a young American. He dashed about the board massacring my men, right and left.   His sole idea of plot appeared to be a succession of rapid little schemes for capturing my pieces.   And he succeeded.   My king was left standing alone and disconsolate.   Whereupon my opponent marched up, surrounded him, and brought about an extraordinarily clumsy finish, I being too bewildered even to make it stalemate.   In fact my chess mind was unhinged for months!"

Dick's delighted laughter filled the quiet room.

"Oh, well done, Stars and Stripes!" he said. "Hail, Columbia!   Now *I* shall know how to dash in and win."

"You dare!" laughed Mrs. Herriot.   "Who then would have to be called by the many syllabled name which signifies 'to rush upon the prey'?   No, no!   '*C'est magnifique, mais ce n'est pas la guerre!*'   And the quixotic method, so dear to my father and myself is perhaps hardly chess, either.   You and I will play according to the very best rules; then, whether we win or lose, we shall at least have the satisfaction of knowing we have played an excellent game."

"Whether we win or lose!" repeated Dick, in mock despair.   "My chances of winning being about on a par with the infallible method of tossing a coin: 'Heads I win; tails you lose!' "

"As I never toss coins," remarked Mrs. Herriot, "I am unacquainted with these infallible methods."

Dick looked at the clock, pushed back his chair, and rose.

"I suppose I ought to be off," he said. "I hate saying good-night, and turning out; but I often blame myself afterwards for having kept you up too late."

He walked over to the hearth-rug, and stood with his back to the fire. The autumn days were still warm and lovely; but in the evening Mrs. Herriot was apt to feel chilly, and enjoyed a cheerful blaze.

"What happens after I am gone?" inquired Dick.

"A great calm," said Mrs. Herriot, smiling up at him. "A stillness which can be felt; a brooding silence——"

"Oh, draw it mild!" laughed Dick. "I am not an earthquake, nor a whirlwind! Seriously—I want to know in my professional capacity—how soon do you go off to bed?"

"I do not 'go off to bed,' my dear doctor. I do nothing so rapid or so explosive as that. I enjoy the peaceful atmosphere of the great calm, for a little while; and then I retire to rest."

"How soon do you retire to rest?"

"I will tell you exactly what happens. First of all, I listen for the bang of the front door behind you. It reverberates up from below. It is your final good-night, e'er the silence falls. Then I ring for Ellen to tidy the room, and to bring me a glass of hot milk."

Dick looked round the charming drawing-room, so perfect in the taste shown in every detail of its arrangement.

"Does the room ever need tidying?" he asked.

"It does, my dear whirlwind, after your departure.   Look at that cushion on the floor, the rumpled chair-cover, and the screwed up ball of paper which represents a missed shot at the waste-paper basket; all, quite the right thing with a man about; but when the silence falls, at once they seem to require tidying."

"Sorry!" said Dick, picking up the cushion, and smoothing the seat of the easy chair.   "Well? When the havoc wrought by the earthquake has been set right, what happens next?"

"Ellen leaves me to have my quiet time for reading, the most precious half-hour of my day."

"What do you read?"

"I read a psalm," said Mrs. Herriot, simply, laying her hand upon the Bible at her elbow. "During the last forty years I have read a psalm every night before retiring to rest.   Then I ring again for Ellen; she carries the chessmen and the board, I carry my Bible, and we slowly mount the stairs, if the lift is not working."

Dick shook his head.   "We must absolutely put a stop to that walking upstairs," he said. "If you insist upon having your drawing-room on the first floor and your bedroom above it, you must really make arrangements for somebody to be always on duty to work the lift."

Mrs. Herriot smiled at his anxious face.

"I could not consent to change my rooms," she said. "This balcony, with the view across the park, is a constant delight; and the view from my bedroom window is even more beautiful and far-reaching. We use the lift, unless I am very late. Jarvis and Albert have orders not to wait up later than eleven——"

"When they go off to bed, leaving you to walk upstairs! They must not be so 'explosive'! Well, we shall hear what Sir James Montford says, to-morrow. You must promise to abide by his decision in these matters."

"My dear young doctor, I would far rather be guided by you. I think as highly of your opinion as of that of any specialist. This proposed consultation seems to me altogether unnecessary. I merely yield to your urgent insistence."

"I continue to urgently insist," said Dick, gravely. "Sole charge is too great a responsibility for me. I must have a specialist to hold over you."

He had thought she would smile at this; but a fresh train of thought held her grave.

"Dick," she said.

He started, and stood at attention. It was the first time she had called him by his name.

"I want you to ask your specialist to state quite clearly how long he gives me."

"No, no!" said Dr. Dick. "That would be a useless question. We never fix dates for our patients. The duration of life depends upon so many things, not under our own control. In your case it depends largely upon the care we are able to take in order to ward off these attacks. How far less frequent and less severe they have been lately. I wish I could be always at hand in case of need. It bothers me that you are not on the telephone. How would Ellen get at me if I was wanted at two o'clock in the morning? If I may not sleep in the house, will you authorize me to order the immediate installation of the telephone?"

"No," said Mrs. Herriot, firmly. "These modern innovations destroy all privacy. I should dislike the feeling that anybody's mind could intrude upon me, at all hours of the day or night. When my house door is closed, I prefer to be alone. A telephone would be to me like the peep-hole in the door of a prisoner's cell, through which any passing warder can look at will, thus giving the poor soul within no sense of privacy, either by day or by night."

"You need not let your number appear in the book," said Dick. "Ellen could have mine. That would suffice."

"Ellen dislikes telephones. She would rather 'walk on her two feet' to fetch you, than take down the receiver."

"Ellen is a silly old thing!" commented Dr. Dick. "She always talks of walking on her *two*

feet in moments of great stress and strain, as if
her usual mode of progression was to walk on *one!*
She has only once attempted to use a telephone,
and her chief grievance against it appeared to be
that she did not like to have people 'a-whispering
into her mouth.' Obviously, she had listened at
the mouth-piece, and talked into the receiver!
Ellen is a tiresome old stupid—when she chooses."

Mrs. Herriot was feeling too tired to defend
Ellen, or to argue further.

"Sir James shall decide," she said. "If he
orders a telephone, Ellen must learn to use it.
Now, before you go, let us talk of something more
interesting. Tell me what progress you are
making with the poor lady who thinks something
jumps out, every time she opens a cupboard; and
with the girl who fancies she cannot swallow, and
insists upon being a helpless invalid, when she
might be perfectly well."

Dick sat down again, and launched into an
eager account of his ideas concerning mental
cases, and his methods of dealing with nervous
patients, and sufferers from hysteria. This was
the particular line of medical work in which he
was most interested, and of which he was rapidly
making a speciality, owing to several cases over
which he had been signally successful. His somewhat original treatment, aided by the force of his
indomitable will and magnetic mental influence,
had resulted in complete cures, where almost all
hope of improvement had been abandoned.

Grateful patients, and still more grateful friends of those patients, had sung his praises. He was beginning to be summoned further afield than his own actual practice. He had always inclined toward the l'ne of study required by a mind and nerve specialist. Each case in which he was successful brought him two or three fresh patients, and an ever increasing reputation. The consulting-room in Harley Street began to seem not so very far off. Yet the necessary routine of a general practice, held him back. He could not afford to relinquish the partnership for which he had paid so high a price.

Mrs. Herriot was the enthusiastic sharer of all his hopes and plans, his interests and ambitions. He gave her no clue to names or whereabouts, but he told her details of his most difficult cases, discussing with her the line of treatment he proposed to pursue. Sometimes a shrewd remark of hers would set him thinking out fresh methods; always her sympathy was an encouragement, and her belief in him, an incentive.

On this particular evening, he sat opposite her couch, looking very much like the Capo di Monte Napoleon, his brows bent in a line of keen determination.

"Many of these cases," he said, "are too difficult to treat in their own homes. I'll tell you what I ought to have—what I *shall* have, some day—a house of my own, run entirely on my own lines, where I shall be able to manage them properly,

and send them out, cured. No; it would not be
in the least like a nursing home, nor a rest-cure
place. It would either be a large house, in which
each patient would have a complete private suite,
or a village of little bungalow cottages, each in its
own garden. I should choose some healthy place
—say the common above Dinglevale—within an
hour's motor run of my consulting-rooms. I
should have a staff of excellent nurses, all keen on
my methods, all well educated, and gentlewomen.
The patients would not be allowed to associate
with one another. Each would have her own nurse,
as her friend and companion. They would see no
one while under treatment, excepting myself, their
nurses, and the matron. I should have to have a
wonderful matron. So much would depend upon
her. She must be perfect, and a permanency.
In order to ensure the latter, and to hold her
completely loyal to the scheme, if she proved capable in every respect, I should probably marry her.

"My dear young doctor!" ejaculated Mrs.
Herriot, shocked into an exclamation. "You do
not marry merely to secure a capable assistant
in your profession!"

"*I* should!" laughed Dr. Dick. "What better
reason could there be?"

"Where would love come in?" inquired Mrs.
Herriot, gently.

"Love would not enter into my calculations,"
said Dick. "Love is a drag on the wheel. When
I drive the coach, I hold reins and whip, I drive

a fiery team, and I like all my wheels to run free and unhampered."

"There are steep hills on life's highway, dear boy, down which a headlong driver may come to grief."

"I am not afraid," said Dick.

A silence fell between them.

She was wondering whether a knowledge of her own life-story would teach him some of the lessons he needed to learn.

He was picturing the little group of bungalows, where his will would reign supreme, where all his theories could work out in practice; where he would build up for himself a world-wide reputation.

"How much capital would you need to start your plan?" inquired Mrs. Herriot.

"Ten thousand pounds would do it," replied Dick, promptly. "And we should soon be able to pay a high rate of interest on our original outlay. We should charge big fees."

"Margaret would have made a good matron," said Mrs. Herriot, "had she not been otherwise engaged. Margaret is a woman of remarkable ability, and great personal charm."

"Margaret is over-Eustaced," said Dick. "In other words she drives a fine coach uphill, with a drag on every wheel! Now I must be off, or you will sit here until past the bedtime of Jarvis and Albert, and insist upon walking upstairs. Goodnight, Mrs. Herriot. You will expect us at half-past two o'clock to-morrow afternoon?"

"And I am to remain in bed until then?"

"Please. You can come down for tea. I am dining at my club to-morrow night with two or three friends, but I can get off immediately after dinner, and will look in at about nine o'clock, if I may."

"Am I to wait in suspense until then, for Sir James Montford's verdict?"

"Certainly not. He will give it you himself, before leaving the house."

"Will it be his real opinion?"

"Undoubtedly," said Dick. "We are having him here in order to secure his real opinion. He will answer any question you like to put to him."

The Little White Lady looked very frail just then, seated upon her velvet sofa, a folding table in front of her, on which were placed her shaded reading-lamp, her Bible, and the chessmen. There was an appeal in her eyes, as she looked up at him, which suddenly went to Dick's heart.

"Oh, I do hate leaving you!" he said. "Shall I fetch my things and come back?"

"No," she said. "No, no, dear boy! Ellen is most capable. I am troubled for you to-night, not for myself. Now good-night, and God bless you."

She blessed him always, when he left her. She hoped her blessings might hover over him, like a flock of white doves, and come home some day.

He left her, and ran downstairs.

He remembered to close the front door quietly.

He did not know that really she loved hearing the bang.

Ellen brought the glass of hot milk, picked up the crumpled envelope and dropped it into the waste-paper basket; then retired as usual, leaving Mrs. Herriot to read her psalm.

The brooding silence fell; the great calm; the stillness which might be felt.

But it was some time before Mrs. Herriot opened her Bible. She sat toying with Dick's Red King, so easily mated by her White Queen.

She looked into the leaping flames of the fire.

She seemed to see the cosy little bungalows on Dinglevale common, each with its pretty garden, lawn, and rustic verandah—havens of hope for distraught minds, for weakened wills, for morbid bodies. Moving amongst them, Dick the Conqueror; Dick, doing noble work, along his own fine, vital lines; Dick, in his element, curing both body and mind.

She placed the Red King in the centre of the board, sweeping all the other pieces into the box. She was quite unconscious of doing this; yet she gazed long at it, while still thinking of Dick's scheme.

At last she said: "It is a fine thing to have before him as an aim and object, even if he cannot carry it out for many years to come. He is young yet; all the best of life lies before him. But the needed capital. How is he to earn so large a sum? Ten thousand pounds!"

She took up the Red King and laid it in the box.

"If only it were not tied up," she said. "If only it were not so cruelly tied up!"

Then she slipped the lid over the ivory chessmen, and opened her Bible.

The room was still, with a holy stillness. The Little White Lady was reading the 127th Psalm.

"Except the LORD build the house, they labour in vain that build it: except the LORD keep the city, the watchman waketh but in vain."

CHAPTER XVIII

"HOW LONG DO YOU GIVE ME?"

MRS. HERRIOT lay back upon her pillows, waiting until the consultation in the room below should be over.

A careful examination had been made by the great heart-specialist, whom she had consented to see, in response to Dick's earnest request. This over, the two doctors had gone downstairs together to the drawing-room.

She could just distinguish the low hum of their voices beneath her.

Ellen Ransom came in from the dressing-room, and fidgeted about at the washhand-stand and toilet-table.

Mrs. Herriot sent her away. She felt better able to await alone the return of the doctors.

The consultation was, in reality, a short one; but it seemed very long to the patient awaiting its conclusion in her room.

At last the hum of voices ceased below. She heard their footsteps on the stairs.

Her door opened, and they came in.

Sir James Montford looked cheerful. He was smiling pleasantly, and rubbing his chin.

Dick looked grave; very professional and quiet. He placed a chair, on the right side of the bed, for the specialist; then walked over to the window, and stood looking out across the park to the spire of Christ Church in the distance.

Sir James took the chair beside the bed, sat down well in view of the patient; very deliberately crossed his knees, placing his right hand between them. With his left, he alternately stroked his chin, or twisted a little charm on his watch-chain.

He began to speak in a carefully modulated voice, and talked for nearly ten minutes without telling Mrs. Herriot anything she did not know already, and without allowing her a chance to ask a single question. He praised Dick's care, method, and treatment, all of which were correct, and left nothing to be desired. He said the attacks were undoubtedly most trying, and likely to be injurious to the general health, as well as to the heart itself. They must be avoided—in fact, warded off, so far as possible. To this end, great care and constant attention would be needed. Over-exertion, either mental or physical, worry, anxiety, excitement of any kind, must be avoided. In case of an attack coming on, not a moment should be lost; there must be no delay, in summoning Mrs. Herriot's medical adviser.

"You cannot be in better hands," said Sir James with an inclination of his head toward the window, "than in those of my friend, Cameron. I fully endorse his prescriptions, his treatment, and the general rules he has laid down for the case. He will no doubt carry out one or two further suggestions which I have thought it well to make. Now, I hope we have not tired you out, Mrs. Herriot."

The specialist rose, with hand extended, his smile more pleasant and genial than ever.

At last the patient, waiting so patiently, had her chance.

"How long do you give me, Sir James?" she asked, in a very quiet voice.

Sir James Montford's face expressed extreme mystification.

"How long do I—? I don't quite grasp your meaning, my dear lady."

Dick, at the window, turned with a quick gesture of impatience.

"How long am I likely to live?"

Sir James beamed again.

"Ah, there you ask a question so often put to doctors, and one which it is so impossible for them to answer. The duration of life depends upon so many side issues, which they are powerless to determine. For instance, if you went out, and greatly overtaxed yourself—ran to catch a train, let us say, or hurried up a long flight of stairs at a concert hall, it is quite possible that fatal results might follow such imprudence. If, on the other hand, you take reasonable care, confine your exercise to short walks on the level, or to pleasant drives, behind horses you have tested and a coachman you can trust, there is no reason you should not live for years—and not merely live, but live a very agreeable life, seeing your friends, and able to enjoy the good things with which you are surrounded."

The Little White Lady turned her head and looked at Dr. Dick, but he had resumed his steady survey of the park.

Sir James no longer appeared to be in a hurry. He stood beside the bed, waiting with the utmost geniality and patience.

"Is there anything else you would like to ask me, Mrs. Herriot?"

"What did you say to Dr. Cameron, when he asked you how long I was likely to live?"

"Precisely what I have said to you, my dear madam: that the duration of your life entirely depends upon the care he is able to take of you, and upon your careful carrying out of his instructions. Now, Cameron, I think we must leave our patient to rest quietly."

Dick turned from the window, and opened the door. Then he looked at Mrs. Herriot. He read a silent appeal in her eyes.

"I will come back," he said, "in a few minutes." His smile was reassuring.

"Do," she whispered, and he followed Sir James down the stairs.

CHAPTER XIX

THE HERRIOT WILL

THE two doctors entered the drawing-room. Dick closed the door. Sir James walked over to the window.

"She has a charming outlook," he said. "I always envy people these delightful old houses, with their great balconies and pillars, and quaint variety of architecture. And what an expanse of park."

Dick glanced at Mrs. Herriot's empty sofa. He had not, until that day, been in her drawing-room without her. It gave him a depressing sense of unreality. He felt much as the guests feel who gather before a funeral, in an empty drawing-room, from which the presence which made its genial charm has gone forever; striving to talk to one another in hushed voices, while all the time they listen to those shuffling feet, carrying a heavy burden down the stairs.

"Poor little lady," said Sir James, turning from the window. "She certainly lives in a charming house. Well, I give her two years more, in which to enjoy it—possibly three, if you do not relax your care and attention."

Dick made no answer. His brows were bent, his face was rather set and white.

"You do not agree with me?"

"No, Sir James," he said. "I don't."

"You still adhere to your own opinion?"

"If you will excuse me for saying so, I do."

"Ah, well," said the great man, graciously, "time will show. Has she any near relations?"

"I think not; but she has many friends."

"She must be a wealthy woman. Who comes in for it all?"

"I have not the slightest idea," said Dr. Dick.

"Stay," said the specialist. "Let me see! Herriot? Herriot? An uncommon name. How long has she been a widow?"

"Over thirty years, I believe."

"Ah, yes, just so. Well, if I remember rightly, there was a very queer will case, after her husband's death, followed a year later, by some complication about a second marriage, involving a suicide, or a murder, or something equally unpleasant. The whole thing was hushed up at the time—private influence brought to bear; the family was influential. I know there was an erratic will, disputed by the relatives; but the will held good. If I remember rightly, the money was tied up under some odd condition which, failing to fulfil, she retained a life-interest only. Herriot was a crank. Yes, I remember him perfectly;

clever, quite a good fellow, in many ways, but a decided crank. He died thirty-five years ago. I can place the exact date, because I sailed for India just after. That is why I have only a hazy idea of the tragedy. But I remember the fact of the will case perfectly; given in favour of the will, which left her a life-interest and nothing more, failing the fulfilment of certain conditions, which I have forgotten. But if you are interested in the matter, Cameron, all you have to do is to go to Somerset House, pay your shilling, and look up Alexander Herriot's will. I have no doubt as to the year."

"I wouldn't be such a cad!" said Dick, hotly.

Sir James bridled, astonished and offended.

"Well, really! There is no need to stigma-tize——"

"I beg your pardon, sir. I spoke hastily, because I felt strongly. Mrs. Herriot is more to me than an ordinary patient. I am—I am much attached to her. She has been good enough to treat me in some ways as if I were her son. I feel for her the same respect as I should feel for my own mother. I could not pry into her private affairs."

"Pooh!" said Sir James, still inclined to be annoyed. "If she regards you as her son, my boy, all the more reason for you to know how the land lies. There is no secret about a will. It is public property. However—please yourself in the matter. Take care of the little lady, and she may enjoy her life-interest for several years to come, whatever eventually happens to the capital."

With which reiteration of his opinion, Sir James marched downstairs, entered his electric landaulette, and, with a rather casual adieu to Dick, was whirled swiftly off to his next appointment.

Dick turned, and dashed upstairs.

His relief was great at having got rid of the specialist. He had, of deliberate purpose, chosen a man whose opinion was of the best, yet whose personality would not appeal to Mrs. Herriot. Yet he had not realized how keenly he would dislike seeing her brought into contact with a coarse, unsympathetic mind, with a manner which could not fail to jar upon her sensitive susceptibilities. There were men he could have chosen, whose calm dignity, whose kindly choice of words, whose refined tact would have been infinitely comforting to the patient. Yet he had chosen Sir James Montford as best serving his own purpose, without realizing that the personality of the man would be almost as trying to himself as it undoubtedly had been to her.

It was an infinite relief to be alone with her once more.

He re-entered her room on the crest of this sensation, and coupled therewith was a sense of compunction over his own selfish disregard of her feelings in the matter.

A rush of tenderness filled his heart, as he saw the troubled, weary face of his Little White Lady on the pillows.

He went straight to her, knelt down beside the bed, and took her hand in both his own.

"I am so sorry," he said. "It has been a horrid tiring time for you. I hated to see him touch you! But he is really clever, you know; and his opinion is worth having."

She managed to smile into his anxious eyes.

"Then I hope, if it is worth having, he has confided it to you. He told me absolutely nothing more than I already knew. And do I look like a person who runs to catch trains, or scampers up long flights of stone stairs in a rush for the un-reserved seats at concerts? I know that the man has only seen me in bed; but is that the impression I produce, as I calmly recline on my pillows?"

"The man is a fool," said Dick, angrily. "He has the sort of mind which states a case in an exaggerated, preposterous way, in order to obviate any possible discussion or contradiction. It is a cheap attempt at a pose of masterly cleverness, which goes down with some people. I have heard that kind of man say to an anxious mother, earnestly asking instructions as to the diet of her sick baby: 'Don't give it beef-steak!' To some pawky minds that sort of remark passes for humour."

"Why did you bring a 'pawky' mind to bear upon my case? Did you think it would amuse me to be told not to run after omnibuses?"

Dick's face was full of trouble.

"I *am* so sorry," he said. "He is admitted to

be the best opinion going, on your particular form of heart trouble. I ought to have realized that you would not like his way of expressing things."

"Never mind," she said, gently. "It has at all events done one good thing. It has made me appreciate my own doctor more, if possible."

She looked up at him, her eyes full of affectionate trust and dependence.

Dick was deeply moved. For once he realized that he was receiving more than he deserved. He bent over her, very tenderly.

"You shan't be bothered again," he said, "if I can prevent it. But some of his suggestions are quite worth trying. We will talk them over this evening. What a blessing to be alone again! I could have kicked him downstairs, when he pretended not to understand your first question."

"He was fencing, to gain time," said Mrs. Herriot. "How long does he really give me, Dick?"

"Shall I tell you exactly what he said?"

She looked into his eyes. "Yes, I greatly wish to know."

Dick bent his head and, for a moment, leaned his forehead against the frail hand he held. When he raised it again, his eyes were steadier than his voice.

"My Little White Lady," he said, very gently, "if you *must* know, he gives you anyway two years, probably three, possibly more."

"And does my own doctor agree?"

"Oh, you know my opinion! No man living can fix a date for the duration of a life, when that duration depends upon the care taken. But, if we may measure the duration of your precious life by the care I intend to take of it, we may as well put it at once at twenty years."

"Twenty years?"

"Yes; twenty years."

"Did you say this to Sir James?"

Dick hesitated, but only for a fraction of a second.

"I said I did not agree with him."

"What did he say?"

"He said: 'Ah, well, time will show.'"

"That was clever," said Mrs. Herriot, with a gentle smile. "It put the responsibility of proof upon Time—where, after all, that responsibility already rests, for all future happenings. But now we are wasting your time; and we must call Ellen, if I am to be downstairs for tea. I shall expect you this evening."

He did not rise at once. He still knelt beside her. There seemed to be something more he wanted to say; yet he did not speak. His eyes were bright, with an intensity of feeling. Something in the atmosphere perplexed Mrs. Herriot, sounding an indefinite note of warning. The sense of his being there as her doctor, seemed obscured by the vivid realization of him as the handsome youth who had sent her the golden roses in a silver vase, telling Ellen Ransom they were a "fit emblem of her own golden heart."

15

She gently withdrew her hand.

"Go now, dear boy," she said. "I am tired, and wish to be alone."

She closed her eyes, in a finality of dismissal.

He did not rise at once; but she felt his lips very gently touch her hand.

Then the door closed behind him.

. . . .

On the pavement Dr. Dick stood hesitating.

His absolutely firm foundations seemed unaccountably shaken.

It had filled him with an altogether unreasonable annoyance to see another man listening to the heart of his Little White Lady. It had caused her suddenly to become dearer to him than she had ever been before.

She was too good—too lovely—for this noisy, vulgar world! Yet—she should not leave it, if his care and skill could hold her there.

He hesitated on the hard, solid pavement.

He was experiencing emotion—very slight emotion; but emotion of any kind had, so far, played no part in Dr. Dick's direct onward march.

This awakening of emotion had originated with his indignant reply to Sir James Montford's suggestion. The conversation flashed back into his mind, as he hesitated on the pavement. He heard himself say again: "Mrs. Herriot is more to me than an ordinary patient. I am—I am much attached to her. She has been good enough to treat me, in some ways, as if I were her son."

And the older man had replied: "If she regards you as her son, my boy, all the more reason for you to know how the land lies." He had thereupon, for the second time that afternoon, felt a desire to kick Sir James downstairs, a proceeding which might have resulted in disappointment for Sir James's many waiting patients.

This recalled to Dick's mind his own waiting patients.

He hailed a passing taxi.

It drew up.

He opened the door, stood with one foot on the step, and again hesitated.

All the crisp certainties of his life, seemed blurred and shaken.

The driver clicked down the red metal flag on his indicator. The bell tinged, sharply.

Dick Cameron regained, at sound of that smart ting, his hold upon the immediate happenings of the moment.

"Where to, sir?" jerked out the driver.

Dick gave the address of a patient in the furthest part of Kensington, stepped in, banged the door; and, as the taxi glided into the flowing stream of Piccadilly traffic, remembered with satisfaction the whole of his conversation with the specialist.

"I am glad I said 'cad,'" reflected Dr. Dick, with a grim smile. "It made the old bounder sit up!"

Suddenly he felt unable to give his mind to patients just then.

He leaned out of the window and ordered the man to turn back and drive to his club.

Arrived there he went up to the smoking-room, threw himself into a deep armchair, lighted his pipe and, taking out his pocket-book, looked through various prescriptions and notes upon the treatment of his patient, left with him by the specialist.

It did not take Dick long to master these.

This done, he smoked on, with knitted brows, absorbed in silent meditation.

Could Margaret have seen him just then, she would have thought him more than ever like her Capo di Monte Napoleon. She might also have remembered Mrs. Herriot's remark: "Yes, it is Dick, but not Dick at his best. It is Dick fighting seven devils, and failing to cast them out."

Presently he rose, squaring his shoulders; knocked the ashes from his pipe, and went out into the street.

He walked with his usual rapid stride; his look of decision and certainty.

Dick's temporary lapse into emotion was over, and with it had passed the hesitancy so foreign to his nature, so unhinging to his habit of mastering at once each event, however unforeseen, as it arose.

There was no drag on his wheel, as he steered a straight course along the Mall, and crossed Trafalgar Square.

CHAPTER XX

MRS. HERRIOT had never known Dick so restless, so preoccupied, so unable to give his mind to the simple pleasures with which they usually passed the time when he spent an evening with her.

He seemed harassed, and anxious, and so unlike himself that, every now and then, her quiet eyes searched his face with a look of real concern.

He appeared completely unable to put away the subject of the afternoon's consultation. They had fully talked it out, during the first half-hour of his visit, yet again and again he recurred to it, as if he had something further to say in the matter; yet broke off abruptly when that further point was reached.

Mrs. Herriot was gently patient with her young doctor's mood; in fact, she was infinitely touched to think that his solicitude for her should have taken so unnerving a hold upon him. When strong natures, not easily moved, betray emotion, that emotion carries with it an infinitely greater

229

significance than the easily ruffled surface of the more susceptible.

She, herself, had quickly recovered from the strain of the afternoon; in fact, the actual physical rest of the long day in bed gave her in the evening an unusual sensation of freshness and of vigour.

She would have enjoyed a keen game of chess; but Dick began by placing his king on the queen's square, and played so badly that she did not think it worth mating him, but quietly put all the chessmen back into the box, packing them in with her usual loving care. Dick hardly noticed that she did so. He was again talking of Sir James Montford's instructions.

She asked to see these, and the prescriptions. Dick at once produced his pocket-book. From amongst a good many letters and folded papers, he selected three. He placed his open pocket-book on the arm of his chair; then, leaning forward, handed her the papers one at a time, carefully reading through each one himself, before passing it to her.

"I doubt whether you will be able to make head or tail of them," he said. "He writes an abominable hand."

Mrs. Herriot put on her glasses, drew the reading lamp closer, and proceeded to try. She was not particularly interested in Sir James Montford's suggestions, but Dick had something on his mind, which he was either striving to keep from her, or endeavouring to tell her, she was not sure which. In either case, the sooner she found out what it was the better, both for him and for herself; and it seemed to her probable that it was connected with these papers.'

She tried to decipher the crabbed writing, the queer hieroglyphics.

As she did so, she knew Dick's eyes were on her face. She felt his look seize, and search, and sear her. It held a strange, eager, burning question. It set her heart beating with an indefinable fear, a dread of something in Dick which was to her an unknown quantity; which accounted for the atmosphere of restless strain with which she felt herself to be surrounded. She kept her eyes upon each paper in turn, purposely avoiding the searching question of Dick's.

As he passed her the third paper she noticed that his hand shook. Was this the paper of importance? She held it close to the lamp.

It was a prescription. She could make nothing of the hieroglyphics. But at the bottom ran three lines of ordinary script.

As she reached these, Dick leaned back suddenly; his elbow knocked the pocket-book off the arm of his chair. Its contents were strewn upon the floor.

With a muttered exclamation of annoyance, Dick leaned over the arm, picked up the pocket-book, passing it into his left hand, then dived again and with a long right arm proceeded to collect the scattered papers from the floor.

This little diversion removed his gaze from Mrs. Herriot's face, and somehow relaxed the tension between them.

She quickly made out the purport of the instructions which followed the prescription. As Dick sat up, restored his sheaf of papers to his pocketbook and held out his hand for the third paper, his face, flushed from bending over the arm of the chair, had lost the anxious pallor which had seemed so unfamiliar.

"I certainly cannot make head or tail of the prescription," she said, returning it to him, and settling the cushions more comfortably at her back. "So far as I am concerned, it partakes of the nature of your infallible method of tossing coin. But I conclude it to be important, for I see it is to be given without loss of time, immediately certain symptoms, presaging an attack, make their appearance. Is it a remedy you can leave with Ellen?"

"I could leave it with Ellen," said Dick slowly, "but it will be essential, in order to gauge its effects, that I should see you myself as quickly as possible after its administration. Somehow we must contrive to manage this."

"I wish the attacks did not so often begin at night," remarked Mrs. Herriot. Then she paused, astonished, for Dick had risen, lifted the table at which she was sitting, removed it bodily from between them, and was down on one knee before her, his strong hands gripping both hers,

his dark eyes—on a level with her own—holding
hers with masterful intensity.

"Now, look here," he said, and his voice was
firm and decided; all signs of restless uncertainty
had gone from him completely. "The time has
now come for taking this thing seriously. I am
tired of playing at being non-residing 'physician-
in-residence.' I have had enough of being a sort
of filial medical man—a little dearer than a doctor,
somewhat less useful than a son. Neither of
these parts will answer the purpose. We know
now the incessant watchful care you need, in order
to ensure even the added years of life of which
Sir James Montford holds out promise."

He paused. The world seemed to stand still
for one breathless moment, arrested by the sudden
break in the torrent of his words.

"Well?" said the Little White Lady; and all
the calm dignity of her gentleness made itself
felt in the unfaltering question of that single word.

Dick bent his head and answered, his eyes upon
the hands he held: "I want you to marry me,
Mrs. Herriot, so as to give me the right, and
the position, to take of you the full measure of
care which we know to be necessary."

A long silence in the room, broken only by the
clock which seemed suddenly to begin to tick
very loudly. Dick could hear his own pulses throb-
bing in unison with the insistent ticking of the
clock.

The hands he held were not withdrawn. For a

moment they gripped his; then, relaxing their hold, lay in his clasp, still and motionless.

Had he raised his eyes to the Little White Lady's face, he would have seen many and varied expressions flit across its frail loveliness. At first, speechless astonishment; then fear and almost horror; then indignation, flushing the pallor of fear. Then an unexpected gleam of humour, followed by a light of understanding tenderness, which chased away the more violent emotions, calming the countenance into its usual quiet look of peace.

But Dick did not lift his eyes. He kept them bent upon those passive little hands.

The silence lasted so long that the mind began to break away from the great issue at stake, and to fix itself on trivialities. The clock persistently reiterated *Which we! Which we! Which we!* varying it, every now and then, with *Know to! Know to! Know to!*

At last Mrs. Herriot spoke. The perfect self-possession of her quiet voice, breaking in upon the turbulence of his own emotion, fell upon the flame of his excitement, as a most amazing douche of cold water.

"I think, my dear boy, I must ask you to return to your chair. I shall be able to answer your last remark more comfortably if you are seated in your usual place. But first of all, kindly put back my table where it usually stands."

To his own immense astonishment, Dick instantly obeyed. He loosed her hands, rose to his feet, and carefully lifted back the table. Then he took his own seat, without protest; merely marking the fact that the situation was distinctly unusual, by lying back in his chair, his hands clasped behind his head, smouldering defiance in his eyes, awaiting a reply from Mrs. Herriot.

She was conscious of that sombre gaze. She did not look at him, but gave careful attention to her reading lamp, which showed signs of flaring up in natural resentment at the double move to which it had unexpectedly been subjected.

As she bent forward, carefully lowering the wick, a little smile of gentle amusement, played about her lips. Dick saw it, and it suddenly angered him.

"If there *is* a joke," he said, "don't you think we might share it?"

The Little White Lady turned her kind eyes upon him, crinkles of fun at their corners.

"Oh, you dear boy!" she said. "I was thinking of the matron who, if perfect, was to be made a permanency. Your reasons for entering upon the holy estate of matrimony, my dear young doctor, are as original as they are varied. You will require a revised version of the Prayer-book, setting forth a completely new list of the causes for which matrimony was ordained. You would also, I fear, require a Prayer-book which omitted to state that a man may not marry his grandmother!"

"If you laugh at me, Mrs. Herriot," said Dick, between his teeth, "I shall leave the ·house."

The sparkle of the Little White Lady's humour was instantly veiled by her tenderness.

"Dick," she said, and her voice was gravely gentle, "unless I were able to laugh at you, I should be obliged to ask you to leave the house. My dear young doctor, have I given you time to return to your senses?"

But now Dick's strength and tenacity of purpose began to reassert themselves.

"You sent me back to my seat, Mrs. Herriot, which perhaps I had no business to leave. But you can't order me back to my senses, because I never quitted them."

He leaned forward, elbows on knees, both hands outstretched, and spoke with quiet insistence.

"I offer you, for just so long as you need it, all the best of my time and skill. For just so long as it can reach and surround you, I offer you my life's loyal devotion. When I beg of you to marry me, I only mean by this: give me the right to dwell—no matter how restricted—under the same roof with yourself. Give me the right to be within instant call, if you should chance to need me. Give me the right to go in and out, before the world, avowedly holding as my most precious possession, the life which I am striving to prolong. I offer you all this, after hours of intent thought, during which I have reached the conclusion that this, which I offer you, is a thing you require, and a thing you will be justified in accepting."

"And—*why* do you offer me—all this?" The Little White Lady's quiet voice trembled.

"Because I love you," said Dick Cameron, simply.

Once more complete silence fell.

Again the ticking of the clock grew insistent, and carried on the theme. *All this! All this! All this!* it reiterated in the stillness.

"My dear boy, you amaze me!" said Mrs. Herriot, at last. "Now that I really grasp your meaning, I am touched beyond words at this expression of your devotion to me. You must forgive me if I say at once that of course I could not think of consenting to your proposal; I could not dream of taking advantage of the very generous impulse which your affectionate regard for me has prompted. But I am infinitely touched; I am sincerely grateful. In my long life—more than twice the span of yours, dear boy—I have been many times courted, and twice won; but I will tell you, frankly, that nothing so beautiful as this has ever before come my way. After to-night, we will never speak of it again. But you may always know that you have to-night given me a gift which I shall tenderly cherish in the storehouse of memory, as a lover of gems might lay away in a rosewood casket a diamond star, or a necklace of pearls. Your gift is not mine to wear or to use; but it is mine to possess, to keep, and to remember. Now let us close the lid, and turn the key. I hold it as my treasure—but locked away. So that at last, when Time has ceased to be, when Past and Future are merged into the great Present of Eternity, your mother and your wife shall greet me with smiling faces, glad—without regret—that their Dick's generous heart once did this for his Little White Lady."

She ceased speaking. She was weeping softly.

Dick's throat was dry.

The clock repeated *Did this! Did this! Did this!* but not in the tender tones of the Little White Lady. It seemed to tick out a threat, a menace, a reproach.

Dick leaned forward.

"I have no mother," he said, hoarsely, "and I want no wife. I want only you. Don't refuse me for an idea. Don't let conventionalities count. It will be so simple to do as I ask. You have no one to consult, nor have I. I was alone in the world, my Little White Lady, until I found you. Is it likely that I can risk losing you a day sooner than I need? I did not know how much I cared, until this afternoon, when I saw another man touch you, and trouble you, and presume to call you 'our patient,' as if he and I shared you alike. Don't refuse me, offhand, Mrs. Herriot, as if I had made a preposterous suggestion. Do let it remain in abeyance for 'a week at least, while you think it over quietly. I admit that it only to-day came into my mind, as a way out of the difficulty. But ever since your return, as you know, I have chafed at being forced to leave the house at night—the very time when you might need me most. I hardly need say that, if you thus trusted yourself to me, I should treat you always with exactly the same respect and reverence, as I should have owed to my own mother. I should be at hand, if you sent for me; and out of the way, if my presence was not required. I should merely wish to have the right to tend and serve you. Will you take time, and think the matter over?"

"My dear young doctor," said Mrs. Herriot, "I cannot imagine the possibility of feeling able to give you any answer other than a very tender, very grateful, No. However, if you prefer to receive that decisive refusal a week hence, rather than to-night, surely I owe it to the marvellous generosity of your devotion, to humour you in this. Now, bid your old friend good-night, dear boy, and go."

Dick stood up at once; threw back his head with his old determined smile, and stood for a moment looking down upon her.

He had won his last point. This had restored his confidence in his own powers. He was himself again—confident, assured.

She dismissed him, with a little wave of her hand, and he went at once.

He knew he was leaving behind him the full force of all he had wished to say.

Just for one moment he turned, at the door, and waited.

She wondered—then remembered.

"God's blessing go with you, dear boy," she said; and he went out, smiling; leaving his Little White Lady alone to meditate.

She sat very still in the silence, as one who dreamed—a strange and lovely dream.

It was so wonderful to be cared for thus for herself alone.

Not for one moment did she contemplate the possibility of accepting his offer; but whether she accepted it or not, his brave young love had been poured out at her feet. And it was such a beautiful love—undisturbed by passion, unmarred by any thought of self-seeking; a strong, simple, honest love, such as in her long, sad life—first tragic, then empty—she had never known.

She had been dismayed, startled, almost angered by his offer, until she had understood. When she understood, she was touched, uplifted, made rich indeed. The fact that she was frail, and worn, and old, only made it the more wonderful that she should be cared for, considered, wanted— thus.

She sat on, in the great calm, the brooding silence, the stillness which might be felt.

Truly her whirlwind had whirled her well-nigh off her feet; her earthquake had wrought an upheaval which stirred her to the depths.

She drew the lamp nearer, opened her Bible, and was turning to the Psalms, when another passage catching her eye in passing, arrested her attention.

"And after the wind, an earthquake . . . and after the earthquake, a fire . . . and after the fire, a still small voice."

The Little White Lady's hand still trembled from the surprise of her great happiness. She laid it on the open Bible.

"'And after the fire, a still small voice.' Speak, Lord," she said, "for Thy servant heareth."

Then she looked up, and saw, beneath the chair in which Dick had been sitting, a folded sheet of white paper, lying on the floor.

16

CHAPTER XXI

THE FOLDED PAPER

MRS. HERRIOT, from her seat upon the sofa, considered that half-sheet of folded paper, lying under Dick's chair. It had evidently fluttered there, when he knocked over his pocket-book, and, as he had merely leaned over the arm of the chair to gather up the scattered contents, it had remained beneath unnoticed.

It looked very much like one of the prescriptions Dick had shown her that evening. Possibly it was a prescription of his own, or medical notes of some important case. Anyway, having fallen from his pocket-book it was likely to be important, and must be safely kept for him.

Mrs. Herriot rose, pushed the chair slightly to one side, slowly stooped, and picked up the folded paper.

At first she thought it was just a blank half-sheet. Then she saw that the inner side was covered with words and figures, hastily scribbled in pencil.

Merely to determine the question of its importance or non-importance, she took it back with her to the sofa, and, seating herself, held it within the halo of golden light beneath her shaded lamp.

It seemed to her rather sweet to hold in her hand a paper of Dick's. Even in pencil, and obviously scribbled hastily, his small, perfectly clear, handwriting was so forcible and characteristic.

Mrs. Herriot bent over the paper. One glance would indicate the nature of its contents.

Yes——

One line did that.

Dick had written at the top:

Notes of the Herriot Will.

Clause V. Concerning conditions of re-marriage.

This half-sheet of note-paper represented a very business-like and accurate examination of the will of Alexander Herriot. Its entire gist, in greatly condensed form, appeared upon that folded sheet. Also, in one corner a sum of many figures, which was obviously a calculation of the approximate annual income brought in by Mrs. Herriot's life-interest in the capital.

It did not take her long to master the contents of the half-sheet. The facts were very clearly stated; besides, she already knew them well.

Laying down the paper, she folded her hands upon it. She usually folded her hands when she wished to think calmly and deeply. Anxious thought, with her, so often merged almost unconsciously into prayer, and then the folded hands were ready.

Dick's paper of notes, beneath the folded hands of his Little White Lady, lay within the halo of light shed upon the table by her reading-lamp. Those frail hands trembled no longer. They were clasped in absolute stillness.

"Oh, poor boy!" she whispered; "*poor* boy! How best can I help him? How can this be made to work together for his eternal good? Any mistake on my part might make of it an irrevocable loss."

She pondered silently. She had no time to think of her own pain. Besides, hers was pain, only—just a thing to be borne. Dick's was pain and wrong—and needed setting right.

She had no time for long consideration. At any moment Dick might return to retrieve the paper. The first essential was that he should not know she had seen it. If he found it on the floor, he would be doubtful. He would not dare ask her, and he would always be doubtful. If she destroyed it, he would be even more doubtful; besides, she had no intention of destroying it. It was far too important a factor in her future, and Dick's.

She rose, moved to her writing-table, tore a sheet of note-paper in half, took it to the lamp-light, wrote a few lines upon it in pencil, folded it, and dropped it upon the floor, beside the chair; returned to the writing-table, and concealed the waste-paper basket behind the window curtains.

Then she rang the bell for Ellen Ransom, took her seat upon the sofa, drew her Bible into the circle of light, and found her psalm. Dick's memoranda of the terms of the Herriot will, she slipped into her Bible at the 139th Psalm.

Ellen Ransom came in, carrying the glass of hot milk. She found Mrs. Herriot reading her psalm.

"Tidy the room, Ellen," said Mrs. Herriot, without looking up.

Ellen smoothed the seat of Dick's easy chair, straightened the corner of a rug, rucked up by one of its castors, and caught sight of the piece of white paper lying upon the floor. She picked it up, glanced at it, and turned mechanically toward the waste-paper basket.

It was not in its usual place beside the writing-table.

Ellen hesitated.

Mrs. Herriot did not lift her eyes; she certainly did not speak; yet it seemed to Ellen that her mistress said: "Put it in the fire, Ellen."

In thinking it over afterwards Ellen knew that Mrs. Herriot had not spoken, had not even looked up, while she stood hesitating with the scrap of paper in her hand; yet, at the time, it seemed to her that some one said: "Put it in the fire, Ellen."

She walked across the room, and dropped the half-sheet of note-paper into the bright heart of a burning coal. As it stiffened and turned over, it slowly opened, and, just before flames darted up reducing it to shrivelled blackness, she saw pencil writing upon it.

It did not occur to Ellen that she could have made any mistake in putting it into the fire. The accepted way of dealing with all papers thrown upon the floor, was to hurry them into the waste-paper basket, or, failing that, into the fire.

The Little White Lady went on reading her psalm.

Ellen walked in silence to the door. Just as she reached it, Mrs. Herriot spoke.

"Ellen?"

"Ma'am?"

"I may be rather late to-night, Ellen. Do not return until I ring, whatever the hour. I rose so late, that I am not fatigued. But turn on the lights, in my bedroom now. The doctor grows anxious, if he thinks I sit up late. He may pass the house again, before long. If he does so, he will look up, hoping to see lights in my chamber overhead. So turn them on, Ellen. Then wait in the work-room until I ring."

Ellen went out, closing the door.

Mrs. Herriot moved to the electric switches, and turned off all the lights, leaving the room in darkness save for the leaping firelight and her own shaded lamp.

Once more she returned to her seat upon the sofa, rested her left elbow on the table, shaded her eyes with her hand, and went on reading her psalm. It chanced to be the fifty-fifth.

She paused at the twelfth verse, reading it and the two following verses, very slowly.

Then she turned to the Prayer-book version of the same psalm, and read that rendering of

David's pathetic reproach—the heart's sad indictment of a trusted traitor, whose kiss turns a mere chance of war, into a veritable Gethsemane of suffering.

"For," read the Little White Lady, "it is not an open enemy that hath done me this dishonour; for then I could have borne it.

"Neither was it mine adversary, that did magnify himself against me; for then, peradventure, I would have hid myself from him.

"But it was even thou, my companion, my guide, and mine own familiar friend."

The room was very still. The chastened look of suffering on the Little White Lady's face was sad to see.

"But it was *even thou*——"

The door opened, noiselessly, and Dick came in.

He stopped short, in blank astonishment, as he saw her sitting there in the lamplight.

She looked up, met his startled eyes, and gave him a gentle smile. Perhaps that smile cost the Little White Lady more than all else she was to do and suffer.

Dick came forward. He was bareheaded, but he wore his overcoat. His appearance gave the impression of breathless haste, suddenly checked into silent stealth.

"I beg your pardon, Mrs. Herriot," he said. "I had no idea you were still here. I thought you would have gone up some time ago. I hope I did not startle you. I feel like a burglar! Did you

take me for a burglar, just for a moment? The
fact is, I came back to look for—my pocket-book.
Did I leave it in my chair?"

"You had better look and see," said Mrs.
Herriot. "I have not noticed your pocket-book.
Ellen has tidied the room, but I do not think she
found any pocket-book."

"May I have a look?"

He searched, feverishly, in the chair in which he
had sat. He plunged his hand down into its
depths, into the cracks and crevices around and
behind the cushioned seat. He looked beneath it,
under the rug; everywhere.

Then he stood erect, anxious, dishevelled, his
dark eyes sombre in the unusual pallor of his face.

"It is not here," he said. "Obviously it is not
here. I must have dropped it elsewhere. I am so
sorry to have disturbed you."

He turned toward the door and was leaving the
room, when again he met her eyes in the lamplight. Something in the quality of her look made
him pause and come back. He suddenly remembered the thing that was now between them.

He came and stood beside her table, resting his
hands upon it, and looking down upon her.

"Why are you so late to-night?" he asked, in a
tone of affectionate authority. "You ought to be
in bed."

"I spent the whole day in bed, my dear doctor.
Besides, I had had considerable food for thought
this evening. Now, I am reading my psalm."

"Which is it to-night?" asked Dick.

"The fifty-fifth."

"Tell me something you have found in it," said Dick.

Mrs. Herriot drew the Bible toward her and, bending over it, read: "And I said, 'Oh that I had wings like a dove: for then would I fly away, and be at rest.'"

Dick laid his big hand on hers, covering it suddenly, as if he were capturing a little bird.

"Don't spread your silver wings and fly away, just yet, my Little White Lady," he said, tenderly. "I want you so!"

She looked up at him; a depth of great tenderness was in her tired eyes.

"I know you do, my dear, dear boy," she said. "I know you do."

Her heart was filled with the spirit of the faithful Shepherd, who leaves the ninety and nine righteous sheep penned into their fold of safety, and yearns after the reckless wanderer, now a prey to the wolves of the wilderness.

During some moments, Dick stood in silence beside her.

Then he said: "Are you thinking over my request?"

"I am," she said. "And since you left me, I have realised it in a fresh aspect—not merely as it affects myself, but as it might possibly affect your future. In order to explain this to you, I shall have to tell you my life's story. Do not come to me to-morrow, nor the next day; but three days hence, dine with me early—I think we might say seven o'clock. This will give us a long evening afterwards."

"Thank you," said Dick, "I will."

He knew himself dismissed, yet he lingered.

"Mrs. Herriot, do you forgive me for springing upon you a proposal which was, I know, startling, perplexing, and—perhaps—distasteful to you?"

She looked, not at him, but straight before her, into the shadows.

"My dear boy," she said, "if there is anything in that which you have done to-day, which seems to you to require my forgiveness, it is yours, freely and fully. But all you said—and said so finely—however unexpected it may have been, calls for my gratitude rather than for my pardon."

"Yet I have your pardon?" insisted Dick.

"You have," said the Little White Lady, very low.

He lifted her hand to his lips, then left her.

She sat listening.

Dick's movements were · unusually quiet to-night. After he had closed the drawing-room door, she did not hear him go downstairs.

Nearly ten minutes elapsed before the hall door closed, also quietly, and she heard his quick step on the pavement below.

Then she rang the bell.

Ellen arrived.

Ellen's face wore the grimly satisfied expression,

which always meant a recent conversation with Dr. Dick.

"What did the doctor want, Ellen?" inquired Mrs. Herriot.

"Asked if I had found his pocket-book when I tidied the room."

"Had you found his pocket-book, Ellen?"

"I had not, ma'am."

"What else did the doctor ask, Ellen?"

"Whether I had noticed a folded bit of paper on the floor."

"Had you noticed a folded bit of paper on the floor?"

"I had, ma'am; and I picked it up and put it on the fire. As I told the doctor, I 'm sorry if I did wrong; but scraps of paper rubbishing up the floor, I always pops into the basket or the fire."

"What did the doctor say to that, Ellen?"

"Oh, he laughed!" Ellen's grim face momentarily showed a fleeting reflection of Dick's gay smile. Mrs. Herriot could picture exactly how he had laughed in the immensity of his relief. "He laughed, ma'am, and said his rooms would be the better for my tidyings, and a few good bonfires! Which I 'ave no doubt they would," added Ellen, with conviction.

"What else did he say, Ellen?"

"He asked if I had read what was on the paper. I said no, I don't tidy the room in m' glasses; and I had thought the paper was blank until it opened as it scorched, and I saw pencil writing inside. But it was too late then to pick it out."

"Did the doctor seem to mind its loss?"

"No," said Ellen, "thanks be! He said it was notes about a patient of his, and he had done with them. He only came back about it, because it was a nasty sort of thing to leave lying about, and he thought if you got hold of it, ma'am, it might worry you."

"Worry me?"

"Well, you see, ma'am," volunteered Ellen, with unusual loquacity and illumination, "doctors 'ave to know things about our insides, which would send us plump into our graves if we knew them ourselves. Only God Almighty, as made us, knows how we ever keep going at all. Mrs. Jarvis went to hear a lecture on Insides, with a magic lantern. When she come home, she told me one or two things, but I would hear no more. 'Mrs. Jarvis,' I said, 'they showed their good sense in 'aving a lantern. But you and me sit here in the light, and I tell you plainly, I'll hear no more. We can't help *having* insides, but we *can* help talking about 'em; or, for that matter, knowing about 'em. The *outside* of the cup and platter for me, Mrs. Jarvis,' I said, 'which is scriptural and therefore conclusive.' We then gave our minds to our supper, which when lost sight of, is best forgotten, and left to Providence."

Ellen closed her mouth, with a snap. The stimulating effect of Dick's conversation and

Dick's praise, had trapped her into unwonted eloquence.

She took up the chessmen and board, and stood waiting her mistress's pleasure.

"Did the doctor ask you whether I was likely to have noticed the paper, Ellen?"

"He asked if it was lying where you might have chanced to see it."

"What did you say?"

"I said no, it was lying under the chair. I shouldn't have seen it m'self if I hadn't bin straightening the rug. Then he said, did I think you saw me pick it up? I said: 'No, sir. My lady was intent upon the Scriptures, and that being so, I could 'ave picked up a barrowful of rubbish and wheeled it away, without her noticing!' That seemed to satisfy him. He told me to be sure and not to mention his having asked about it; and to try and get you to bed quickly, ma'am. Then he ran downstairs."

Mrs. Herriot smiled. "I see, Ellen. Well, as you always obey the doctor's orders implicitly, you may ring for the lift and we will go up without delay."

She raised her Bible, made sure that the half-sheet of folded note-paper was tucked in safely at the 139th Psalm; then followed Ellen across the shadowy room, into the waiting lift.

"A barrowful of rubbish," she said to herself, "and Ellen wheeling it out! One could hardly be credited with a more complete and comprehensive lack of observation."

The irony of it appealed to her; little crinkles of amusement appeared once more at the corners of her eyes. Ellen and her barrow were so deliciously out of place in her dainty drawing-room; the suggestion of a rubbish heap on her velvet-pile carpet was so delightfully incongruous. Only—it was such a pity that the rest of the conversation would preclude her from saying to Dick, next time he flung a crumpled envelope at the waste-paper basket and missed it: "Ring for Ellen and her barrow!"

Thus, as so often happens after a time of deepest tragedy, the Little White Lady's hours of pain closed in a gleam of humour.

CHAPTER XXII

TO BE BURNT—UNOPENED

MRS. HERRIOT had told Dick not to come to her until three days had passed. But at one o'clock the next morning, within three hours of their final parting, his night-bell rang. Jarvis was at the door, with a taxi.

During the long hours which followed, Dick many times feared that his Little White Lady was about to spread her silver wings and fly away.

He bitterly reproached himself with being the cause of the over-excitement which had brought on the attack. Had he been less impetuous, had he worked up more carefully and gently to that which he had to say, it would not have reacted with so much severity upon her nervous system; she might have been spared this agony of suffering.

Dick cursed himself for a fool, and watched beside her with a remorseful tenderness, which seemed to increase his power to hold her in life, leaving nothing untried which might relieve her distress.

During the long hours of the night, he was perplexed by the look of agonized anxiety which she constantly turned upon the little table at her bedside.

Her Bible lay upon it, and it seemed to Dick that her distress of mind was somehow connected with the Book.

He was sitting beside her bed at four o'clock in the morning, when he surprised one of these looks of anguish. He had thought she slept; and, taking his eyes from her face, had laid his fingers on her wrist, and looked down at his watch. When he looked up, her eyes were open and fixed again upon the table.

He put away his watch, leaned forward, and carefully took up the treasured Bible, holding it in both hands.

It was years since he had held a Bible between his hands. It brought back strange and undesirable memories of Grandaunt Louisa.

"Would you like me to read you a psalm?" he asked. And he opened at the 139th, where there happened to be a marker.

He could not quite hear himself reading a psalm aloud; but he would do that, or anything, to remove from her face this look of distress.

However, he was obviously making things worse instead of better. In obedience to an imploring wave of her hand, he closed the book. Then he bent over her.

"What is it you want? Don't attempt a sentence. Say it in single words. I shall understand."

"Book—lock—key," whispered the blue lips of his Little White Lady.

Dick got up, walked to a mahogany chest of drawers, well in view of the bed, pulled open the right-hand top drawer, and looked in. It seemed full of lace and ribbons—little billowy heaps of lace, with strings and bows of pale lavender-coloured ribbon.

Dick shut the drawer in a hurry. He did not know much about lace, and he knew still less about the gauzy things, with ribbon threaded through them. But he knew enough to realize that a heavy book must not—even in a moment of the greatest stress—be laid upon the top of them.

He tried the left-hand drawer. Here he found himself on less mysterious ground. Rows upon rows of silk stockings lay neatly in this drawer. There was plenty of room. He left it open, came back to the bed, took up the Bible and carried it over to the chest of drawers in full view of those watching eyes. Then he deposited the Little White Lady's cherished Bible, safely on the top of the silk stockings, took the key from the right-hand drawer of mystery, locked the drawer which now contained the Bible, and brought the key over to the bed.

"You saw me lock it up," he said. "Here is the key."

He slipped it under her pillow.

She looked relieved, but was whispering again. He bent over her.

17

"If—I—die——"

For some time she could get no further.

Then she began again.

"If——"

"Yes, I know," said Dick. "Don't try that again. I quite understand. If you die—which I am not going to let you do—I am to do something. Now tell me, in one word, what."

"Burn," whispered Mrs. Herriot.

"Burn?" thought Dick. "Burn! Now, in the name of all the martyrs, when and where, and what am I to burn?"

Suddenly it dawned on him.

"Yes," he said. "If you die, I am to burn your Bible?"

"Unopened," whispered the Little White Lady.

"Yes, of course," said Dick. "I quite understand. I am to burn your Bible, unopened. Well, you may trust me, most faithfully to do it, Mrs. Herriot."

She closed her eyes quite restfully; and before long, to his immense relief, she slept.

Dick had ample time for meditation.

"Now why on earth," he thought to himself, "am I to burn my Little White Lady's Bible, unopened? It is the most original Bible story I know. Anybody would have expected her to leave it to me, after binding me by a sacred and tiresome promise to read a chapter every day. Instead of which, I am to burn it, unopened."

By-and-by, when she was better, when she was

able to be downstairs again, and he had the triumphant pleasure of seeing her sitting on the sofa, behind the low table, with her Bible close at hand, laid in the halo of golden light cast by the shaded lamp—his sweet Little White Lady, just her own self again, only a little older, a little frailer, a little more ethereal—he wondered once more: "Why did I have to promise to burn that treasured Bible, unopened?"

But he never spoke of it to her. He would as soon have thought of mentioning the mysterious drawer, full of gauzy things and lavender ribbon. Both these mysteries had come beneath his ken, merely because he had been alone with his Little White Lady when she so nearly unfolded her wings and left him.

"It is no business of mine to question why," thought Dick. "And I should most certainly have burnt the Bible. But Ellen would have had to undertake the other drawer."

So Mrs. Herriot lived to read her psalm again each evening; and presently she felt well enough to have Dick to dinner, and to tell him her life story. It was exactly three weeks after the day of the consultation.

CHAPTER XXIII

ROSEMARY, FOR REMEMBRANCE

"SIT there," said Mrs. Herriot, "in your usual chair. Make yourself very comfortable, Dick, because we are going to have a long quiet talk. I want to tell you my story from the beginning, and I do not want to feel hurried."

"Why should you feel hurried?" said Dr. Dick, looking at the clock. "We have dined early, and quickly—for us. The whole delightful evening lies before us. But, if you grow tired, or the story proves too long, we can say: 'To be continued in our next, and I can come back to-morrow.'"

He dropped the cushion over on to the floor, lay back in the large chair, crossed his knees, and fixed eyes, earnest with attention and bright with expectation, on Mrs. Herriot.

She looked very calm and sweet, seated in the lamplight, her table in front of her; her Bible and chessmen close at hand. She wore a soft Chudda shawl of purest white over her evening gown; and, as she talked, she every now and then drew it more closely round her shoulders with a graceful movement which reminded Dick of a dove spreading, and then folding, its white wings.

The art of gracefully wearing a shawl is rapidly becoming a thing of the past. It calls for the drooping shoulders and the delicately poised head and neck, which do not belong to this generation. The grandmothers of the future—the hockey-girls of to-day—will be a fine, stalwart race of old ladies, but their sons and grandsons will never see them —as Dick now saw his Little White Lady—folding soft cashmere shawls around them. The swing of the tennis racket, the throw of the cricket ball, the free wielding of golf clubs undoubtedly make for fine development of figure, for square shoulders and athletic limbs, but not for the eventual wearing of shawls.

In her young days Mrs. Herriot had been a charming croquet player; but the most violent exercise in which she had ever indulged, had been an occasional game of battledore and shuttlecock. Even this she had left behind with her teens, but always retained a vivid recollection of the glow and excitement of the sharp "tang! tang!" on the parchment, and the swift flight of the feathers in their velvet-covered cork crowns.

Quite recently, at a crowded reception, Mrs. Herriot had found herself seated near a group of young men who were discussing an absent friend.

"Battledore and Shuttlecock did for him," said a tall, sunburnt young fellow, just home from a winter holiday at St. Moritz. "He took Battledore too high; went over Shuttlecock, and broke his jaw and three ribs."

Mrs. Herriot was amazed. She beckoned the brown youth, whom she happened to know, and as he bent over her, she looked up at him and said gently: "Your story is most astonishing. *I* never considered battledore and shuttlecock dangerous."

"No more they are," agreed the sunburnt young man, heartily, "if you are reasonably careful. You see Jack was trying to drop a second from the top, and like a silly ass, he did n't break enough; took the Rise too high, Battledore, higher still; and shot clean over Shuttlecock. He broke his jaw on his skeleton, and his ribs as he rolled over, but he 'll be home again next week, none the worse."

Mrs. Herriot was more amazed than ever. Her congratulatory smile carried with it no attempt at comment. The conversation of the youthful generation was so apt to be beyond her. But how—oh, how!—could even the youthful generation break its jaw on its own skeleton? She had never heard of a skeleton toboggan, and had not the least idea that the remarks to which she had listened, referred to a reckless rider on the famous Cresta Run.

So the Little White Lady and her soft Chudda shawl were distinctly "early Victorian"; yet to Dick's watchful eyes they made a sweet restful picture, as he lay back awaiting the unfolding of her life story.

Calm and uneventful it would probably be,

yet relieved from monotony by gleams of gentle humour and little sparkles of gay wit; while, through it all, undoubtedly would flow the loving, lovely spirit of his Little White Lady, leaving in her wake a blessing upon all she touched in passing, just as the speeding vessel leaves behind it a path of gleaming white to mark its passage over the trackless sea. Life's ocean might sometimes have proved rough to her, and sometimes dark and stormy—she had implied as much; yet Dick felt certain she had always had her path of light ahead, and always left her track of blessing behind.

These thoughts passed lightly through his mind, as he watched her settle her cushions, adjust the wick of her reading lamp, and draw her shawl more closely around her shoulders.

Then she met his eyes with her own clear penetrating look, and they both smiled. It was one of the long, silent smiles which had so early become a habit of their friendship. They never spoilt its sense of comprehension by hurrying it away in speech.

Dick was thinking: "However mild it is, I shan't be bored, because I enjoy watching her pretty hands in the soft light, and I like the sort of up-and-down music of her voice."

And Mrs. Herriot was thinking: "Can I tell him all, without startling him too much? Or will the heavy shadow of those dark happenings in the past, for ever after, cloud the bright sunshine of his thoughts of me?"

"Anyway, I shan't be bored," thought Dick, still smiling.

"Anyway, I must tell him all," thought Mrs. Herriot, and her smile faded.

Then she began to speak, slowly and carefully, as if drawing up facts from a deep well of experience and memory.

"The tragedy of life, my dear young doctor, for me, personally, arose from the fact that I always so greatly longed to be loved for myself alone."

She paused, as if to let that thought sink in.

Dick suddenly stirred in his chair.

"Well, I should think you always had your wish," he said. "Everybody who knew you must have loved you; and anybody who loved you would love you for yourself alone."

Her quiet eyes searched his face. Dick's fell before them.

"I have never been loved for myself alone," said the Little White Lady. "Now listen. And when I pause, considering how to proceed, do not feel obliged to speak. Silent pauses are so helpful to the mind.

"My girlhood, spent alone with my dear father, was very simple and happy. Our little cottage in Devonshire placed us in a setting which, as I look back upon it, seems to be banked with primroses, and over-arched with apple-blossom; fragrant without, peaceful within. His had been a life devoted to scientific investigation. Even when his active researches were over, and he was no longer able to write and to lecture, we lived in an atmosphere of ever fresh mental discovery. He had a valuable library. The great minds of all the centuries dwelt with us in our little home. We desired no other guests. The ever varying charms of spring, summer, and autumn in Devon, were our constant delight; and, during the long winter evenings, chess was our recreation.

"We paid occasional visits to London, staying with my father's first cousin, Constantia Herriot, in her great gloomy town-house in Portman Square; a place always connected in my mind with rep curtains, toast-and-water, and a queer assortment of deep-voiced, oddly-dressed women, all more or less cut after the pattern of Cousin Constantia, who gathered in her ugly drawing-room to discuss—no, it would be more correct to say, to lay down the law concerning all social and political problems which chanced to come within their massive ken. Few of them were married, and of those the majority had had no children of their own, yet with the inflexible sternness of total inexperience, they decided all the most delicate questions relating to marriage, and to the upbringing of children. They ground the iron heel of their systemized charity, into the despairing hearts of the suffering poor. They made the lives of officials and dependants a burden to them. They worried busy statesmen on to the very borderland where courteous attention merges into bored irritation. They wrote social and political novels, in which well-known people figured in the most transparent of disguises, doing and saying utterly impossible things; and they appeared at Cousin Constantia's receptions dressed in such a queer diversity of extraordinary clothes, that I used to imagine them as having one large wardrobe, filled with a heterogeneous collection of garments, to which each went in turn, pulled out the first thing which came handy, and put it on!"

Dick laughed. "I know the kind of woman," he said. " I've seen them, and heard them talk."

"I think not, my dear boy," said Mrs. Herriot. "They were before your time. Like the Great Auk, they are extinct and, mercifully, have left no eggs behind them! The present race of advanced and advancing women, may be mistaken in many ways, and trying in others, but at least they have hearts, and they have enthusiasms. Cousin Constantia's heavy brigade had neither. They lumbered along to the tune of 'All the world is wrong, and here we come to tell it so.' The modern progressive woman, with all her faults and mistakes, is keenly ready to put her shoulder to the wheel in helpfulness. She says: 'All the world is wrong, and here I come to put it right.' The women of Constantia's following, contented themselves with sitting in judgment, and pouring forth illogical suggestion, and ill-considered denunciation.

"Constantia was their high-priestess; her house

was their rendezvous; her hard, cold mind, their refrigerator.

"My father used to laugh at them. His gentle sense of humour was tickled. He loved to quote concerning them, King Solomon, wise old Marcus Aurelius, and his constant and intimate companion, William Shakespeare! All these had much to say, which came most aptly to hand, regarding Cousin Constantia's advanced women and their views.

"But her brother, Alexander Herriot, considerably younger than herself, who had equal rights in the Portman Square house, and usually lived there, quarrelled bitterly with his sister, thwarted and crossed her at every possible opportunity, never losing a chance of advancing views and rules of life which differed from her own. Yet, by natural disposition, he was kindly and pleasant, much attached to my father, for whom he had a genuine admiration, and mildly tolerant of me, as a harmless nonentity who, being a young woman, did not count amongst the things of importance; yet, not being one of his sister's set, need not be regarded as a positive nuisance, but might even, under some circumstances, prove to be a negative blessing. I always felt, during those visits, that Cousin Alexander, tolerated me for what I was not, rather than liked me for what I was.

"My father was the only person toward whom Cousin Constantia showed the less brusqueness of manner which passed with her for tenderness.

During his closing days when, though attacked
by no fatal malady, the bolts and bars of all the
doors and windows of his physical being seemed
gently to fall away, allowing the captive spirit
liberty to respond to the call of the Unseen, he
confessed to me that, as a very young man, before
he met my mother, he had fancied himself in love
with the stateliness of Cousin Constantia, and
had proposed marriage to her.   She had refused
him, without hesitation, and with considerable
asperity.   Yet, as the years went by, the remembrance of this feat of temerity on the part of her
scholarly cousin, apparently invested him, in her
hard mind, with a certain halo of romance, which
resulted in invariable rudeness to my unoffending
mother, and in consistent kindness to himself.
My father failed to notice the rudeness—an in-
nately courteous person is always slow to perceive
or to comprehend rudeness in others—but appre-
ciated the kindness, as a phenomenon which could
not be scientifically explained, but which held
advantages to be accepted with gratitude.   Hence
our half yearly visits to town, occasional cheques
from Cousin Constantia, which added substan-
tially to our well-being and comfort; hence also
the alarming fact that, when my dear father's
will was read, he had left me to the care of Cousin
Constantia, as my sole guardian.

"I was then nineteen, very shy, very simple;
deeply versed in prophets, poets, and philosophers,
but wholly ignorant of modern life, and of the ways

of the world in which I was now left practically alone.

"Our principal means of support, my father s pension, ceased with his life. In order to have more to leave to me, he had lately tried to increase his slender capital by speculative investment, with the result that he had lost it nearly all. There were, after his death, a certain number of liabilities to be met. The little home in Devonshire, with all the cherished treasures it contained, had to be sold. With my own pocket-money I bought in these chessmen,"—Mrs. Herriot laid her hand upon the cedar-wood box beside her,—"my father's Bible, his favourite edition of Shakespeare, and as many as I could afford of the other books, which had been to us a constant source of interest and delight. You can see them all, in the little mahogany bookcase over in that corner."

Dick got up, walked across to the old-fashioned bookcase, took out the volumes, one by one, looked at them, and replaced them with reverent care.

They were none of them books which held any appeal for him; but he wanted to give Mrs. Herriot a few moments' pause. Also, for himself, he wanted to escape from the spell of the "up-and-down music" of her voice, and the unaccountable fascination he was experiencing, as he listened to this quiet unfolding of her story. It was not so much that which she had already told him, as a sense behind it of greater things to come. The atmosphere seemed charged with dramatic presage of future tragedy.   Its very calm awakened a sort of nervous apprehension, as does the heavy stillness on a summer's day, when each fluttering leaf hangs without motion, each twittering bird sits silent; all nature holds its breath and listens, to catch the first low rumble of the coming storm.

Dick was thrilled with interest, yet scarcely knew why; he was apprehensive, yet did not know of what.   He wanted to escape, yet could not go; and would not have gone, if he could.

He turned the pages of a rare edition of Æsop s Fables in the original Greek.   His eye was caught by the "*Ho muthos deloi*" which marked the close of each fable and introduced the moral it was intended to teach.   It reminded him of construing in his schoolboy days, and of how infinitely easier to translate was the Greek in which the Fox flattered the Crow, than that in which the tiresome old moralist pointed his moral.   Dick could recall going triumphantly to the top of the class on the Fox's remarks, but finding himself at the bottom when the moral chanced to come to his turn.

As he closed the valuable old book and replaced it in the shelf, he found himself wondering what the "*Ho muthos deloi*" of Mrs. Herriot's story was likely to be.   That it held a moral, he had no doubt.   Would it be easy of translation, or would it send him to the bottom of the class?

Dick could not see himself at the bottom of

anywhere now. He was stepping up rapidly,
gaining ground every day. The tree-top of his
ambition, though lofty, was well in sight.

"*Ho muthos deloi*" held for him no terrors. The
very fact of the "*muthos*" did away with the importance of the "*deloi.*" The great truths which
might have cried "Halt!" to the forward march of
his ambition were to him but fables; no more
alive than the grotesque figure in a stained-glass
window; of less value than fragments of broken
glass upon a tesselated floor.

Yet there had been a time when that broken
glass had been a halo; and also a time when he had
prayed each morning, encircled by his mother's
tender arms:

> "Take me by the hand and lead me,
>   In the way I ought to go;
>   Thou canst make me good and happy,
>   Only Thou canst make me so."

"*Ho muthos deloi!*"

"Bother the moral!" thought Dr. Dick. "I am
unnerved by my Little White Lady's sentimental
setting of clustering apple-blossom and banks of
primroses. Let us get on to Act II., Scene I.
Background: Constantia's stuffy rep curtains.
Only bird allowed: Constantia's swearing parrot,
shrieking the nineteenth-century equivalent of
'Votes for Women!' I am sure she had a parrot,
and I am certain it swore. The little 'cottage in
the country' was too idyllic for this wicked world.
So R.I.P. to the old Professor, who must—I admit—

have been worth knowing, and ring up the curtain on Cousin Constantia's ugly drawing-room in Portman Square. Cousin Alexander at present requires kicking; but I suppose he must be allowed to figure largely in the next act."

Thus Dick tried to lash himself into levity; then turned from the bookcase and came back into the soft circle of light cast by the Little White Lady's reading lamp.

He had meant to make several remarks and comments.

He made none.

He took his seat in silence. Mrs. Herriot slipped a folded paper, at which she had been looking, back into her Bible; adjusted her lamp, drew her shawl more closely around her, smiled at Dick, and went on with her story.

CHAPTER XXIV

THE DEAD HAND

"COUSIN CONSTANTIA came to the funeral. She wore the most extraordinary higgledy-piggledy of mourning array. Even in the utter bereftness of my sorrow, it occurred to me as we went, in the only fly the village could produce, at a foot's pace, to the churchyard, that she must have fished it at random from out the Universal Wardrobe of the Heavy Brigade. It was a warm day in July. I remember she had on a very ample trailing skirt of black grenadine, flounces all up the front, and a polonaise gathered up, very bunchy, at the back. Over this, a tight-fitting coat of black astrachan, very thick and woolly. On her head, a high felt hat, not unlike a Prussian Chasseur's, with a plume of black cock's feathers. I call them 'black,' because I know Cousin Constantia intended them to pass as such; but, as they jauntily waved in the breeze and sunshine, they stood revealed an unmistakable, glowing green!

"Though I had not much to expend upon it, I had taken great pains over my simple mourning, because my father had always liked my dress to be neat and dainty. For his sake, I had tried to look cool and fresh, though my dress had to be sombre. He always liked white; so I wore a white silk kerchief folded at the neck, and I remember fastening in a sprig from his rosemary bush, with a little pearl brooch which had been my mother's. It was on a Sunday morning that her earthly life had ended; and each Sunday, when I came down ready for church, and found him waiting in the garden, he used to give me a sprig from that bush, and put another in his own buttonhole, saying softly: 'Rosemary for remembrance.' I gathered the sprig for myself on that day; and thought of them both, as I whispered: 'Rosemary for remembrance.'

"I only tell you this to explain that, though in black attire, I was trying to feel fresh and dainty, in the dark recesses of the village fly.

"But Cousin Constantia had travelled third class—a thing she and her following always did; not of necessity, but on principle—and had had a long and dusty journey. Half way to the church, she noticed that her astrachan coat was full of dust. Whereupon she proceeded to beat herself all over with her large black-gloved hands, and we emerged from the fly, into the radiant sunshine and flowery green around us, completely smothered in railway dust.

"I tell you this absurd little detail—trivial it now seems, though it reduced me to tears at the time—because of the light which it throws upon Cousin Constantia's character. She always beat her dust over other people. If she wanted to launch a cruel criticism, or to make a censorious remark, she did so, absolutely unconscious of the hurt feelings or the wounded susceptibilities around her. Many a time, later on, when I writhed under her apparent unkindness, or saw others do so, I had a vision of her beating the dust out of her own impossible fur coat, completely unaware of the fact that she was smothering me in the very thing of which she herself wished to be rid. I did her the justice to believe that her mental and moral dustings often gave pain which, owing to her selfish lack of imagination, she was totally incapable of realising.

"When the funeral was over, Cousin Constantia returned to spend the night at the cottage. Then the will was read. All that evening Cousin Constantia merely snorted. But the next morning she informed me with decision, and a certain amount of abrupt kindness, that I was to live in future at the house in Portman Square, as her secretary and companion."

"Surrounded by the magenta rep curtains?" remarked Dick. "What a contrast to the apple-blossom and Devonshire primroses!"

"It was," said Mrs. Herriot. "A terrifying contrast. But now I must advance more speedily with my story. I feel I have been taking up our time over trivialities; yet a certain amount of detail was needed in order to give you a clear idea of the combination of circumstances and of characters which led to the developments which followed.

"I spent a year in the gloomy house in Portman Square, acting as unpaid secretary and companion to my Cousin Constantia. I need not weary you with a recital of the trials and humiliations of that sad time.

"It was chiefly enlivened by the fact that I became the unwilling and often unconscious cause of contention between Constantia and her brother, Alexander Herriot. They had long wrangled vaguely over social problems, and political matters. I now became an ever-present pivot upon which their quarrels turned. Constantia was bent upon training me along the narrow groove of her advanced ideas. Alexander wished me to remain an ornamental little nonentity. In their kinder moments they both treated me as if I were a caged wild bird, which they each wished to tame and teach. Alexander's method was to pay me continual gratifying little attentions, and to laugh perpetually at his sister, behind her back. Constantia took me with her to all her lectures and debates, and taught me the war-cries and catchwords of the Heavy Brigade, in much the same way as she taught them to her parrot."

"Then she *had* a parrot?" exclaimed Dick.

"Indeed she had! A most unpleasant bird. One of my duties was to feed him, and to superintend the cleaning of his cage. He used to shriek with laughter when Cousin Constantia found fault with me; and if I attempted to make an original remark, he either said: 'Silly little fool!' as a derisive ejaculation, or 'Hark at her!' in a weary, conclusive tone of voice. Either of these comments had an equally silencing effect upon my very shy attempts at conversation; but they delighted Constantia, who was never tired of saying how absolutely to the point were all the remarks of her parrot. His name was 'Tobias.' Constantia called him 'Toby,' but allowed nobody else to use the endearing diminutive. When Alexander and his sister were quarrelling, I have seen Tobias almost fall from his perch, convulsed by a perfect ecstasy of demoniacal laughter. He was the only person to whom Cousin Constantia ever said 'Darling!'"

"What an odious bird!" said Dick, laughing; immensely pleased at having divined the parrot, before he was mentioned by Mrs. Herriot. "I hope he met with an untimely end."

"Tobias is still alive and well," said Mrs. Herriot, "and likely to survive us all. He lives alone with Constantia's maid. She left the poor woman a pension to be paid during the lifetime of the parrot. Consequently Tobias is much pampered and cherished. He is rather bald and infirm, very old, and cross, but he still remarks: 'Silly little fool! Hark at her!' when I visit the maid. It recalls my young days!

"But here I am again, dwelling on unimportant details, instead of advancing toward the main

issues. Dick, I fear I am somewhat of a coward.
I dread telling you of the events which followed. .
I am postponing, with paltry comedy, the moment
when grim tragedy must stalk in."

Dick leaned forward. He was at his best
just then. He put her comfort before his own
curiosity.

"Don't tell me anything which it pains you to
remember," he said, and his voice was very gentle,
and full of understanding sympathy. "Why
should you?"

"Hush!" she said. "I must. Listen! When
I had lived a year with my Cousin Constantia,
Alexander Herriot asked me to marry him. He
was actuated, I believe, by two motives: genuine
pity for me, and a desire to annoy his sister. Her
lack of kindness toward me had increased. Everything I did, or attempted to do, met with her
contemptuous disapproval. My life was hopelessly sad and disappointing.

"Alexander, who never forgot his warm regard
for my father, took my part, and really behaved to
me with consistent and charming courtesy and
kindness.

"Old Mr. Herriot had divided his money
equally between his son and daughter; but it was
expressly stated in his will, that if Alexander died
unmarried, his share of the capital and of the house
and furniture, should pass to Constantia. If he
married, it became absolutely his, to do with as he
pleased. I think this put the idea of marriage into

Alexander's mind, as a more or less trying necessity.
Since his college days he had always been looked
upon as a confirmed bachelor, and I suppose his
father wished him to marry, in order to carry on
the family name. I was less likely to prove
troublesome as a wife, than any other young
woman of his acquaintance; yet I represented the
fascinating fact that his marriage to me would be
more profoundly distasteful to his sister than any
other union he could compass.

"So one evening, when Constantia's temper had
been more imperious and trying than usual, when
she had departed, leaving me in tears, to a select
gathering, in the drawing-room of one of her
followers, where the housing of the poor and the
feeding of the improvident were the problems to
be discussed and considered—Alexander sought
me out and said, very kindly and affectionately:
'Look here, you poor little white bird! We have
had enough of this! You come of age in a few
weeks. Say nothing to Constantia, but immediately after your birthday, I will marry you;
we will go off to Devonshire together, and explore
the lanes and woods you love so well; and we will
find out what has become of the little cottage
where you lived so happily with your father. I
am sure he would have been willing to trust you to
me.'

"I dried my eyes and looked gratefully at
Alexander Herriot. It did not for a moment occur to me to refuse this unexpected loophole of

escape. I knew nothing of love or marriage. I thought him very kind; and the prospect of seeing my little home again, seemed a joy beyond all earthly expectation. He was twenty years older than I, so I concluded he knew what was right.

"So we ran away from Constantia, and from Tobias, and from the terrible tramp of the Heavy Brigade in Portman Square; and the week after my twenty-first birthday I married my cousin, Alexander Herriot.

"Of the time which followed, I prefer not to speak in detail. My husband soon wearied of the Devonshire lanes. Life was monotonous without daily contentions with Constantia. Letters of fury arrived from her. He answered them on paper, but looked forward with keen enjoyment to answering them in person. Then I discovered, to my dismay, a thing which had not dawned on me before: that he had no intention whatever of making a new home for himself and for me. He retained his rights in the house and furniture in Portman Square. Our brief holiday over, he and I were to return and to take up our abode with Constantia.

"My married life with Alexander Herriot, in his sister's house, lasted seven years. They were not happy years, Dick. Up to a certain point he was loyal to me; he protected and defended me. He insisted upon my rightful position in the house being accorded me. But he had never really loved me; and he was the kind of man whose affection is turned to contempt and irritation by the very fact of marriage.

"My little son—the much desired heir to the Herriot name and fortune—born a frightened, trembling baby, died in my arms, when only a few days old. I was never given another.

"My heart was numb; my arms were empty; my youth was slain.

"At the end of six years, my husband developed symptoms of that most terrible of all maladies, to alleviate which so little can be done, even now; against which, in those days, practically nothing was attempted. From the first there was no hope. He lingered through many weary months of ever-increasing suffering. It tried him beyond bearing.

"Having to witness this real tragedy of pain and despair, brought out all the best in poor Constantia. She became really kind and considerate to me, and, as a rule, extraordinarily patient with him. After all, when parents are gone, there is no closer tie than that between brother and sister. The daily life does not reveal it; but let either be in an extremity of any kind, and at once the call of the blood responds, where all other calls might fail. Even a wife must stand aside, as the sister steps in to the brother; or the brother holds out a strong right hand to the sister, in response to the cry which has reached him, of her overwhelming need.

"I found myself more and more left on one side, and ignored, as the tie between brother and sister grew into a closer intimacy of dependence.   Yet I was still the object of their occasional arguments and discussions.

"A favourite subject with Alexander was the probability of my re-marriage.   He spoke of it as calmly as he might have mentioned the likelihood of Constantia thinking it advisable to engage a new maid.

"Constantia, who had so greatly resented my first marriage, was filled with angry irritation at the idea of my venturing to transgress in the same way a second time.   If she could have lighted a funeral pyre and condemned me to be Suttee, she would have done so, without mercy and without compunction.   But the more she scouted the idea of a future second marriage for me, the more set upon it Alexander grew.   It became with him almost an obsession.   He used to recur to it again and again, talking of it to his sister, in my presence, until I fairly wept with pain and humiliation.

"On one of these occasions she remarked: 'My dear Alexander, you forget that the greatest compliment a woman can pay to the memory of her first husband is to take a second.   I very much doubt whether the experience of married life which Helen has enjoyed with you will be likely to encourage her to embark a second time upon the treacherous waters of the uncertain ocean of matrimony.'

"'Don't quote your sour-grape speeches to me,' said Alexander, irritably.   'Keep them for the

ranting ranks of the great Unwanted and Unwed.
Helen has been a good little wife to me. I have no
cause for complaint, nor have I given her any.
But she need not therefore pose, either as the
strong-minded female who can stand alone without the support of a husband, or as the disconsolate widow whose heart lies buried in her first
husband's grave. After my death, she will behave
as a rational nice-minded woman should behave;
wear widow's weeds for a year, with due decorum;
then gracefully discard them, and marry the first
decent fellow who wants her. *I* shall see to that.'

"'I have no desire ever—*ever*—to marry again!'
I exclaimed, goaded at last into speech.

"'Hark at her!' chuckled Tobias.

"The brother and sister took not the slightest
notice either of my interruption or of the parrot's
remark.

"'Your authority will be over by then, my poor
Alexander,' sneered Constantia. 'You will no
longer have any say in the matter.'

"'Shan't I?' said Alexander Herriot. 'You
wait and see! A Dead Hand may still hold the
reins. In fact, the Dead have sometimes a more
conclusive "say" than the Living. They are beyond the reach either of argument or of entreaty.'

"Constantia laughed.

"'*My* authority will still remain,' she said, 'and
her own inclinations. It is not at all likely that
our gentle Helen will do violence to either.'

"'Silly little fool!' said Tobias.

"'Wait and see,' said Alexander Herriot.

"Perhaps this conversation should have prepared us for what followed.

"When my husband's will was read it appeared that he had left his whole fortune to me on the understanding that I had a life interest only, if I died a widow, but if I married again, the entire capital became mine to dispose of as I pleased; with the proviso, that if the man who married me was willing to take the name of Herriot, a sum of ten thousand pounds became his on the wedding-day. If I remained a widow, the entire income from the capital was to be mine for life, without restrictions; but on my death the capital— over which as a widow I was to have no control —was to go to the male Herriot nearest of kin, then living. Failing any such, to the funds of a city corporation of which Alexander Herriot had long been a member. My power to exercise any control whatever over the capital depended entirely upon whether or not I married again."

Mrs. Herriot paused, and looked at Dick.

"Am I making it clear, my young doctor? I want you to understand the exact terms of the will, because of their important bearing upon that which follows."

"I quite understand," said Dick. "You make it perfectly clear. It was an unusual will, but evidently made to ensure the fulfilment of a definite purpose. It does not seem so erratic, when one is in full possession of the facts."

"That is why I gave you the facts in somewhat amplified detail, before telling you the terms of the will. Undoubtedly my husband's mind was largely influenced by his own father's will, which left him the capital if he fulfilled a condition which might reasonably have been expected to ensure an heir, and the carrying on of the Herriot name in conjunction with the Herriot wealth. As a matter of fact the family has now completely died out; and the capital, at my death, will go to swell the funds of an already over-wealthy society. But that which surprised me most about Alexander's will was that he left the entire income of his money to me. During his life-time I had had a small allowance which barely sufficed for my dress, and which—when in generous mood— was occasionally supplemented by Constantia. She had fully expected the money to be left to her, subject to a small annuity to me; an arrangement which would have made me once more dependent upon her. I am afraid the leaving to me of the entire fortune was a parting shot at his sister, and a vindication of the stand he had always taken with regard to my position; yet I like to hope that it was also a permanent continuance of his kindly feelings toward me, and of his abiding affection for my father.

"Constantia was furious, and insisted upon disputing the will, on the ground that her brother's mind had been affected by his illness, when he made it. She took the case into court, but the will was upheld, and I found myself in undisputed possession of seven thousand a year, and the half share in all properties and furniture.

"Constantia's eccentric action in the matter had, however, disastrous results where my comfort and peace of mind were concerned, in that it gave most unfortunate publicity to the fact that Alexander Herriot's widow would be a desirable wife for the impecunious. Before my year of mourning was over, all sorts and conditions of men had discovered that they were not only willing, but anxious to take the name of Herriot, and to console me in my loneliness. I grew to have an almost morbid dread of the appearance of a fresh suitor, eager to qualify for the privilege of carrying on the Herriot succession, with the honorarium it entailed of a settlement upon him of the useful sum of ten thousand pounds on his wedding-day.

"Poor Alexander had undoubtedly been extraordinarily clever in the drawing up of the conditions of his will. They worked precisely as he had foreseen; only, he had failed to recognise in me a strength of character which suffering had developed, or to comprehend that my wedded life with him had generated in me a passionate desire to be loved, some day, for myself alone.

"His was indeed the kind of will in which the Dead Hand strives still to hold the reins and to keep control over the Living. I saw just such a document described the other day, in the review of a book, as 'a will beloved by novelists.' I can only say, it is well that such wills should be beloved by somebody! They are certainly not beloved by those who have to suffer the consequences they entail, and the unnatural developments for which they are responsible.

"Probably some of the men who sought my hand in marriage, were fully worthy of a woman's trust and regard. Possibly some of them may have genuinely loved me, and might have won my love in return. But the shadow of that Dead Mind hung black over the dawning of a possible love-match, obscuring its radiance, turning the gold of a genuine devotion, into the dross of mere grasping after pecuniary gain. All men to me seemed fortune-hunters, all marked attentions, mercenary.

"In the second year of my widowhood, to avoid this persecution and to escape from Constantia's society, I bought the little cottage in Devonshire, where I had spent such happy years with my father, furnished it with great simplicity, persuaded a friend to accompany me, and quietly disappearing from London society, went down to spend the summer in the restful privacy and the complete seclusion of that old-world village."

CHAPTER XXV

THE STALWART STRANGER ,

" AND now," said Mrs. Herriot, "let me stead- fastly withhold myself from all unnecessary details, and go straight to the main issues."

"I like the details," objected Dick. "I could come back to-morrow evening, and during as many more evenings as necessary."

But Mrs. Herriot waved him into silence.

"No, dear boy, no! By-and-by we will return and gather up any details you may care to hear. My story in its main facts must be completed to-night. I could not sleep on the consciousness that you know a part but not the whole. So hush, while I take you to an early summer's evening, when I walked alone along a Devonshire lane. I constantly went out by myself. Complete solitude refreshed my' weary spirit; my father's old companions were mine once more; great minds of the past walked with me. I was no longer lonely or alone.

"Yet that lane was far away from my little cottage; and the nearest farmhouse was fully a mile off.

"Presently I heard the sound of a horse's hoofs behind me. They approached at a rapid trot; but the rider drew rein just before he reached me, and walked his horse slowly past. He did not look at me, but his face was turned my way, as he looked over the hedge of clustering wild roses, straight into the golden glory of the sunset.

"He was the most strikingly handsome man I had ever seen. Dark, ruddy, stalwart, and strong, he rode his horse with that easy air of command, which gives to the onlooker the impression that the animal moves obedient to the dominant will of the rider, rather than to the touch of his hand on the reins.

"He seemed unconscious of the fact that he was in the saddle, or of anything around him, save the glory of the distant sunset behind the purple hills.

"His fine profile was illumined by the glow, but his dark eyes seemed quite undazzled. Looking straight and full at the sun, they shone golden and tawny, in the reflected light.

"He walked his horse until almost at a turn of the road; then, breaking again into a quick trot, disappeared from view. It seemed to me evident that he had reined up just behind me in order not to trot, in rapid startling fashion, past a woman walking alone in a narrow lane; and the unobtrusive courtesy pleased me. I liked the fact of this impersonal attention from the Stalwart Stranger. His horse's hoofs died away in the distance. He was quite out of sight when I reached the corner.

"On the right of the lane ran a high stone wall, soft with velvety moss, and green with ferns—their graceful frondes hanging from every crack and cranny in the wall. Above this wall, a bank sloped steeply into a dark wood, already full of shadows. On the left of the lane was a deep ditch, behind which rose a hedge, one mass of eglantine, and of a climbing, flowering creeper, we used to call 'Traveller's-Joy.' On the other side of this hedge, considerably higher than the level of the lane, a wide field sloped gently down into the valley. Beyond, on the further side of a rushing burn, rose steeply the purple hills. Beyond them the sunset.

"A thrush sang out clear and sweet, in a hawthorn bush close beside me; then fell silent, as I passed.

"An intense sense of solitude came over me; and yet an indefinable feeling of being watched—and by other eyes than the bright, anxious eyes of the thrush guarding his nest in the hawthorn.

"I quickened my pace, in another moment I should have been running, but two men leapt suddenly from the ditch, the one before and the other behind me. They did not speak or make a sound, but the man behind pinioned my arms, while his comrade snatched a locket and chain from my neck, forced off my rings, and then began tearing at my pocket, with his huge dirty hands.

They were powerful men of the tramp type. I was helpless in their grip.

"I shrieked for help, though I knew no help was near, yet I shrieked again and again, and it did not seem to occur to them to stop my cries.

"Suddenly I heard the soft thud of a horse's hoofs on turf, galloping up on the other side of the hedge; the brown face of a horse with wide-spread nostrils and starting eyes appeared over the wild roses; above it the splendid head of the Stalwart Stranger against the crimson sky.

"I shrieked again: 'Help! oh, help!'

"In another moment he had flung himself straight from the saddle over the hedge, dropped into the ditch, and leapt up into the lane.

"The ruffians loosed me, and turned upon him, two to one. He came at them as if they were mere ragged urchins, playing a rough game. With one blow of his right fist, he knocked the man who had robbed me backwards into the ditch, where he rolled over and lay motionless, almost hidden by foxgloves and bracken. With his left he caught the other fellow by the throat. There was a short scuffle, then the man wrenched himself loose, and fled down the lane.

"The Stalwart Stranger seemed about to make off in pursuit, but I clasped both hands around his arm.

"'Oh, don't leave me!' I cried. 'Let him go! Let him go!'

"He turned and looked at me. He smiled, as

if to reassure me; but his nostrils dilated like those of his horse, and his eyes flashed quickly to right and left. If tramps had come down from the wood, and up from the ditch, and over the wall, while I clung to his arm, I should not have been afraid!

"'You poor little lady!' he said. 'What a fright the ruffians have given you!' Then he laid his left hand over both mine, still clasped round his sleeve. 'You should not walk alone in these out-of-the-way places. What are your people thinking about?'

"'I have no people,' I said, meekly. I could not resent the masterful manner of his reproof and question. He had earned the right to be masterful. His virile strength thrilled me. The touch of his hand laid over both mine gave me a sense of unutterable peace and safety. 'I am living with a friend in a little cottage,' I added. 'It is two miles from here. It has been my home for years, and I never heard of there being any danger in these lanes.'

"He laughed. 'We are not far from the Doone country,' he said. 'I was thinking of the wild Doones, as I rode along. I believe I passed you about ten minutes ago, did n't I? . . . Ah, I thought so. I should have been five miles from here by now; but just round the next bend I passed a gate, and the meadows looked tempting for a gallop. So I put my horse over, and chanced to double back along the way I had come. We were at the bottom of the meadow just below, when I heard your first cry for help. It did not take us many moments to reach the hedge, and then it was quick work and soon over. Had they time to rob you?'

"'Yes,' I said. 'The man in the ditch has my locket, my rings, and I think the contents of my pocket. But do leave them with him, and let us come away.'

"The Stalwart Stranger laughed. 'No, no,' he said. 'The man is my prisoner. I must pick him out of the ditch and march him off to jail.'

"'Oh, pray do not do that!' I exclaimed. 'I cannot bear the idea of people being in jail, and especially for attacking me. And I should so hate to have to appear against him.'

"My rescuer considered this. 'True,' he said. 'You are right there. A police court is no place for a lady. I must manage otherwise. But, first, I will find your trinkets.'

"He stooped above the ditch, and turned the man over.

"'Is he dead?' I asked. 'Have you killed him?'

"'Not a bit! I only did what we call knocked him silly. In fact, I believe he is shamming insensible now; which is, perhaps, on the whole, a sensible thing to do.'

"He took a piece of whipcord from his pocket, pulled the man's arms behind his back, and tied them firmly together. Then he hauled him bodily out of the ditch and deposited him in the lane.

"'Stop shamming,' he said, 'and sit up.'

"The man sat up. He looked dazed and sheepish.

"The Stalwart Stranger searched his pockets, and produced my rings and locket. From an inner breast-pocket in the tramp's ragged coat, he drew a small revolver. 'Hullo!' he said. 'Loaded! You're a nice customer!' Then he searched the ditch, and found my purse and handkerchief.

"'Is that all you have lost?' he inquired.

"'All,' I said. 'Oh, do take me away!'

"He put his hand upon the knotted cord at the man's elbows.

"'Stand up,' he said; and jerked him on to his feet. 'Now look here, my man! I ought to march you to the lock-up, but—as you heard while you lay low in the ditch—this lady has begged you off. However, you must earn your liberty. Right about face, and walk on ahead of us until you come to a gate into the field, then stop. If you attempt to bolt, I shoot.'

"The man walked on. The Stalwart Stranger and I followed. He drew my hand within his arm. I was thankful to lean on him.

"Arrived at the gate, we looked over, and saw his horse quietly grazing in the middle of the field.

"'Now,' said the Stalwart Stranger, 'I want my

horse, but I do not choose to leave this lady's side.
I am going to untie your arms.   If you catch the
horse and lead him here within five minutes, you
may go.   If you attempt to mount him, or if you
bolt, I shall shoot instantly; and I may as well tell
you, I am a crack shot, my man.'

"He opened the gate, untied the cord, and put
the man through into the field.   Then, still keeping me close beside him, he swung the gate to,
and leaned over the topmost bar, steadily covering
the tramp with his own revolver.

"There was a splendid look of power about the
Stalwart Stranger as he stood thus.   My nervous
tremors left me completely.   We laughed as we
watched the shambling, anxious gait of the tramp,
as he crept up behind the horse.

"In five minutes, or less, the horse was standing
beside us in the lane, the ruffian had been dismissed
with a few curt words of warning, and my rescuer
turned to me

"'May I see you safely home?' he asked.

"So he slipped the reins over his arm, and we
walked home together in the sunset.

"At my little garden gate we parted.   'I am
staying at the inn,' he said.   'May I call in the
morning to make sure that you are feeling no ill
effects from this shock and fright?'

"I gave him leave to call.

"He drew out a pocket-book, and handed me
his card.

"'Just to prove that I am not a wild Doone,'

he said, with his delightful smile, 'but a quite respectable person, with a town address.'

"Then he mounted his horse, lifted his hat, and rode off toward the village.

"I went slowly up my little garden path, past the rosemary bush. 'Rosemary, for remembrance!'

"The happenings of the past hour seemed a strange, startling, impossible dream. But all through that evening the thing which held first place in my mind, which gave me a wakeful night, which was still vividly with me when I arose in the morning, was the curious thrill of joy and peace, stirring, yet calming, which had passed through me, when my Stalwart Stranger of the Sunset laid his left hand over both mine, as they clung round his right arm. It had stirred in me a sensation hitherto unknown. It seemed to belong to another world—a world of which I had never trod even the borderland. Or was it that it made all this world seem different? Anyway, as I looked from my window in the early dawn and saw the pearly mist melting away before the upward march of the rising sun, it seemed to me that I beheld a new heaven and a new earth wherein dwelt—romance. I looked toward the Doone country and wished my Stalwart Stranger were indeed one of the wild Doones. But his card, lying upon my dressing-table, told me that his club was in St. James's Street, and that his name was 'Alexander Ross.'

"He called on the following morning to inquire; he came to tea in the afternoon. He took us a wonderful excursion the next day, up the lovely Doone Valley to see the ruins of the old stronghold of the Doones, the stream up which John Ridd climbed to find his Lorna, and the little church of Oare, through the window of which Carver Doone fired the shot at the wedding.

"Alexander Ross stayed on at the village inn, and made no secret of the fact that he stayed to be near us; and every time his eyes met mine, every time his hand touched mine, I experienced the strange thrill which had given me a new heaven and a new earth.

"Nor did I fear to let the rapture grow, because here was a man who knew nothing of the Herriot will, who had not even known my name until he heard it from my own lips. I always remember my pleasure in the fact that the first time he wrote to me he spelt the name wrongly.

"To cut a very long story short, Dick, love—deep, passionate love—had come my way at last; and, at the end of ten days, I was engaged to be married to Alexander Ross.

"Before I consented to be his wife, we had a long talk, and I told him the whole story of my first marriage and of my husband's will. He took it very simply.

"'I have no objection to taking the name,' he said. 'It is a good old name, and even if it were not, so long as I get you, I shall not complain at getting a new name with you.   I am "Alexander" already; but you must never call me so.   To you I must always be "Alec," with no memories of any one else to spoil it.   And if, having gathered my little wild rose in the Devonshire lane, she proves to be a grand "Reine d'Or," that fact does not lessen her sweetness, or make her less dear to her lover.'

"So at last I was loved for myself alone.   I had my wish, and my happiness seemed complete.

"Before pledging myself finally, I asked Alec whether we should be of one mind concerning those Divine things which meant most in life to me.   I told him frankly of my love for my Bible— my father's Bible; of how I never went to rest without reading my psalm for the day; of how crushed and lonely I had felt in soul, during all the years of my first marriage, because the things most precious to me had meant nothing to Alexander Herriot.

"Alec looked at me with honest eyes.

" 'Dear,' he said, 'I am something of a black sheep, I am afraid.   But I had a pious old mother. Her prayers have followed me through all my wanderings; and, at last, they have guided me to you.   You will win me back into the old paths. Never fear!'

"So I rested content.   When Alec said 'Never fear!' a woman's fears all spread their fluttering wings and flew away.

"We returned to town, saw my lawyers, settled all business matters, and fixed our wedding-day."

CHAPTER XXVI

THE GLORY FADES

"CONSTANTIA was abroad. It saved much harassment that she was not at home to be consulted; that the vials of her wrath would be poured out in letters, which, after all, could be burnt when read. So all went forward easily.

"But suddenly Alec insisted upon our marriage taking place a week earlier than the date originally fixed. He gave me no definite reason, excepting that he could not wait; but to a woman who loved Alec that was reason enough.

"He had planned that we should go abroad, and travel during several months. There was no need to have a settled home until we pleased. He wished to show me Switzerland and Norway during the summer; Italy and the Riviera later on. I had never really travelled, and it seemed an entrancing dream to be taken to all these places by Alec—places I had visited in books, dwelt in with my father as we sat together in our cosy cottage home; but never really seen.

"On our wedding-day we were to go to a charming riverside hotel on the Thames, not very far from town. Alec said he had engaged a suite of rooms on the ground floor. The sitting-room opened on to a lawn, which sloped gently down to the water. We should sit under big trees in the moonlight and watch the silver river flowing by. He would not tell me where it was. He said it was so perfect that no one on earth should know where we were spending the first ideal days. I should have liked to have left an address behind with a few friends; but nothing seemed really to matter as I should be with him; also I knew I could write, as soon as I wished to be in touch with the outer world once more. Meanwhile I was living in a dream-world of my own, alone with my Stalwart Stranger of the Sunset. And I longed to be away in the quiet country again. Alec in town clothes, was not quite the same as Alec on horseback, in rough tweeds and gaiters.

"I had an indefinable sense that he was not altogether at ease in my set and amongst my particular friends. He captivated most of the women, but he avoided the men; and, as the days went by, began to make various excuses for coming to see me only when he would be likely to find me alone.

"The evening before my wedding-day I had a somewhat unpleasant shock. A friend of mine, a charming and delightful woman, whose gladness in my joy had been very warm and genuine, wrote to tell me that her husband had just ascertained that Alec was not known at the club, the address

of which was printed on the card he had given me.
It was an old and very exclusive club, and I had
mentioned to her, the day before, the fact of his
being a member, when she had very tactfully
tried to find out how much I knew of his antece-
dents. Her letter begged me to postpone my
marriage until I had made a few inquiries concerning my lover's family and previous history.
'An old Scotch family, of which most of the members appear to be dead, is so very vague,' she
wrote; 'and the one fact which could be investi-
gated turns out to be inaccurate. Dear Helen,
let an old friend implore you not to make the fatal
mistake of trusting yourself, for life, to a possible
adventurer.'

"I burnt the letter with indignation. Nothing
would have induced me to inquire privately into
any statement of Alec's, nor would I have author-
ized anybody else to do so. But, even though
promptly destroyed, and loyally dismissed from
my mind, the letter cast a slight shadow over the
radiance of my joyful anticipation of the morrow.

"I could not speak of it to Alec. It had arrived
after we had parted for the last time. I should
not see him again until we met at the church on
the following morning.

"Could I have shown him the letter, and have
heard him laugh it away with some joke about
being a wild Doone, and carrying me off to an
unknown happy valley, I should have gone to my
wedding with a more restful heart. As it was,

I seemed to have lost the magic of some sweet spell which had been cast over me since he had laid his hand upon mine, when calming my fears in the Devonshire lane.

"As I walked up the church, and took my place at his side, I seemed to see him, for the first time, as not being quite one of us; as having about him a certain restlessness and recklessness, which laughed instead of explaining; which put a woman off with a kiss, when she had requested a statement.

"It was too late to go back; nor would I have gone back if I could. I loved him. Yet I know there was an anxious doubt in my eyes as they met his on our wedding morning, instead of the clear shining of perfect love and trust, which he had always before seen in them.

"This may have accounted for the change in his manner as we drove away together from the church.

"The glow and the glory of the charm he had held for me had faded, suddenly.

"I knew he was conscious that it had faded; yet he did not seem inclined to take the trouble to bring it back. He could have brought it back, with a word or with a touch: I loved him so!

"He was very gay and charming at the breakfast. My own pride in him revived, as I saw the admiration and interest with which other women regarded him. I felt sure all would be well when we found ourselves, at last, alone, under the shady trees, beside the silver river. After all, what man ever showed to advantage on his wedding morning?

"When the carriage was at the door to take us to the station, just as I was bidding my friends good-bye in the hall, a telegraph messenger ran up the steps.

"Alec, waiting at the hall door, took the telegram from the butler, glanced at it, tore open the envelope, read the message, then slipped it into his pocket, merely saying: 'No answer.'

"The butler hesitated, then dismissed the boy. As he tucked the rug around me, in the carriage, a moment later, he said in his usual low respectful tones: 'The telegram, ma'am, was for you.'

"As we drove off I turned to Alec. 'Was that telegram for me?' I asked.

" 'Certainly not,' said Alec, 'or it would not be in my pocket. It was from a friend of mine in Scotland, who was rushing down by the night mail in order to be present at our wedding, but who has been delayed by an accident on the line. Half-a-dozen carriages derailed. Nobody badly injured, but the line blocked. I had heard already of the accident, but did not know, until this moment, that my friend was in it.'

"There seemed no more to say; there was no more to say. Yet why, oh, why, did the glow and the glory of the sweet spell vanish again? Why did he know it was vanishing, yet make no attempt to bring it back?

"At the station he put me into the compartment

reserved for us in the train, and went off to the cloak-room, to which he had already sent his own luggage.

"The long platform was somewhat crowded. I stood at the window watching for Alec's return. Suddenly I noticed two men walking up and down together, evidently keeping an eye upon our carriage. Their faces seemed strangely familiar, yet I could not recall under what circumstances I had met them. They wore rather shabby black clothes, and gave one the impression of having belonged to the men-servant class, but of being out of employment and down in the world.

"The train was due to leave in three minutes, yet Alec had not returned. I leaned from the window in some anxiety.

"The two men stationed themselves close to the door of our compartment. I heard one say to the other: 'He has seen us, Bill, and will get in lower down. We shall have to travel with the lady, and tell our little tale on the journey.'

" 'No, no!' said the other. 'Here he comes.'

"Then I saw Alec striding down the platform. The men went to meet him, and, in that moment, seeing him—handsome and fearless—come toward them, two to one, I remembered where I had seen those heavy, evil faces before.

"They were the tramps of the Devonshire lane!

"They came toward my compartment, one on either side of Alec, talking low and insistently, their looks threatening and sinister.

"He walked between them, erect and fearless. He laughed as he walked.

" 'What a pair of blackguards!' His gay voice reached me at the window. 'But you 've come to the wrong shop for blackmail, my friends. I paid you what I promised. I admit you earned it well; but it was ample payment. Not another stiver do you get out of me! Besides, you arrive a day too late.'

"He opened the door of the railway carriage and stood beside it, debonair and defiant.

" 'This lady is my wife,' he said. 'A man should have no secrets from his wife. You are welcome to tell her anything you like.'

"The men scowled and pushed forward. Their faces were almost in the railway carriage. In their eagerness to make me hear, they both spoke at once.

" 'It was all a put-up job.'

" 'He hired us to do it.'

" 'We was no more tramps, than you are!'

" 'We had watched you for days, to pick the best place.'

" 'He was after your money. He paid us well; but considering how much he got himself, we thought he might just as well pay us a little better.'

"They stopped for want of breath.

"The guard came by, whistle in hand, trying to close the carriage.

" 'Come,' said Alec, gaily. 'You have said quite

20

enough. I can tell my wife the rest. I have allowed you full value. Now you will know, you pair of silly fools, that I am not the kind of man you can blackmail. Be off! If it were n't my wedding-day, I would chuck you both under the train.'

"He pushed them on one side, sprang into the carriage, and pulled the door to. The guard whistled and waved his flag. The train started.

"At that moment there was a sudden commotion on the platform. Apparently a woman was running along beside the train. One voice shouted: 'Jump in here, ma'am!' Another: 'Hold her back!' Somebody else said vaguely: 'Why don't they stop the train?'

"It all happened in a moment, as we began to glide out of the station.

"Alec leaned out of the window to look. Then he drew back, pulled up the glass, drew down all the blinds with three rapid movements of his arm, and swung round upon me.

" 'I 've had enough of this,' he said, 'and I 've had enough of waiting. Come to me, Helen.'

"But I shrank into the furthest corner.

" 'Explain about the tramps,' I said.

" 'My dear girl,' he answered, 'there is nothing to explain. The scamps told you themselves. They were not tramps at all. They were two chaps I got hold of in town, who wanted to earn an honest penny. They faked themselves rather well on the whole. The entire scene was got up simply to provide me with a good introduction

to you. You should feel flattered that I took so
much trouble to obtain it. Most men would have
waited until you returned to town, and then would
have asked to be introduced to you at an evening
party. I, being by nature somewhat akin to the
wild Doones, preferred a rescue in a Devonshire
lane.'

" 'Why did you desire an introduction to me?'
I asked, with trembling lips.

" 'Because I wished to marry you,' he replied,
with absolute *sang froid*.

" 'You wished to marry me, before you had
even seen me!' I cried. 'Why! Oh, Alec! Why?'

"But I knew the answer before I put the
question.

"I, who had thought that at last I was loved
for myself alone, had been married by the man
who had won my whole love, simply and solely
for my money.

"It suddenly struck me that Tobias ought to
have been there, to shriek at me, with shouts of
derisive laughter: 'Silly little fool!'

"I need not record the whole of that sad conversation. He answered all my questions quite
freely, seeming, if anything, amused that I should
know of his cleverness. He had not seen the
Herriot will case in the papers himself, being
abroad at the time, but had been told the whole
story by a friend on his return. He came to town
in order to see me, and to find out particulars.
He was not sure of the exact terms of the will, so

he went to Somerset House, paid a shilling, and
read it through."

"Cad!" exclaimed Dick, suddenly.

He had not uttered a syllable for so long that
the sudden vehement ejaculation startled the
Little White Lady.

He had been sitting very still, shading his face
with his hand, as he listened.

She paused and looked at him. A sombre fire
of indignation was in his eyes.

"Cad!" he said again below his breath.

Mrs. Herriot smiled, rather wistfully.

"It is not a pretty word, dear boy," she said;
"yet I must admit I am glad to hear you use it.
The calculating coolness of this action on the part
of the man who wooed and won me, hurt me almost
more than anything else he did. Well—he verified
the will. Then he traced me down to Devonshire
and laid his plans. You know the rest.

"With extraordinary coolness and bravado,
he admitted all this. His fine eyes did not cease
to sparkle with amusement, though he must have
seen the anguish of my pain.

"At last I cried: 'And, I so trusted you, so
wholly loved you, that yesterday I made my will,
leaving you my entire fortune, and to-day, after
the wedding, I signed it.'

"'Very good of you, dear,' he said. 'But it
was rather due to me, wasn't it? If I had not
married you, you would not have had it to leave.'

"'I shall change it,' I cried. 'I shall leave

my money to Constantia, to any one—but not to
the man who has so deceived and wronged me!'

" 'I doubt whether you can, legally, will your
money away from your husband,' he said,
'but we can see about that, when we return
from abroad.'

" 'I shall not go with you!' I exclaimed.

" 'Oh yes, you will!' said Alexander Ross.
'Whatever motives may have actuated the winning,
nothing alters the fact that I have won you; and
I mean to keep you. You love me, my little
gentle lady. I am your husband, and more than
that—I am what every woman likes that her husband should be—I am your master. You can't
leave me, and you will have to forgive me. I told
you I was a black sheep, but that you could redeem
me. Well, you must redeem me now! You had
to marry some one; and, owing to that cursed will,
you were bound to be married for your money.
It might have chanced to be an ass, or a prig, or
a hypocrite; instead of which, it is a *man*—and a
man who has told you the honest truth. Come!
Make the best of it. Surrender, and forgive him!'

"He caught me in his arms, standing up in the
railway carriage, and held me close to him. His
spell was over me once more.

" 'Oh, Alec, I love you!' I said.

"He laid his lips fiercely on mine. I almost
swooned beneath their touch.

"He had made an effort to win me back. He
had thought it worth the trouble. It had cost

him only a few minutes' eloquence, and one embrace.

"And I had surrendered. If he wanted my money, he should have it. So long as I was with him, and he loved me, nothing mattered.

"I was still in this frame of mind, when we reached the beautiful riverside hotel, where he had engaged a suite of rooms. I remember unpacking in my bedroom, which communicated with the sitting-room, while he had a pipe in the garden.

"It was the first time I had been alone since I knew the truth concerning his shameless courting of me; yet I would not allow myself pause to think.

"'He loves me! He loves me, and he wants me!' I kept on repeating, feverishly. 'It might have been an ass, or a prig, or a hypocrite; but it is a *man*—a strong, masterful, splendid *man*—and I love him; and I don't care *what* he has done! All love worth anything has to stand a test. This is my test. I will not fail. I will reclaim him, by showing him a perfect love, and a complete forgiveness.'

"I knelt beside the bed; and, flinging my arms across it, tried to pray. But I could only repeat, unceasingly: 'O God, I love him! I love him! I love him!'

"At last I whispered: 'O God, answer his dead mother's prayers.' This calmed me; and, rising, I changed into a white evening gown; then went out to join him in the garden.

"The smooth lawn was there, the shady trees,

the swiftly flowing silver river. But where was
the trustful bride, radiant in her pure happiness?
Where was my Stalwart Stranger of the Sunset?
The man I loved, the unscrupulous adventurer who
had trapped me into marriage, sat on a rustic seat
beneath the trees.

"I moved across the lawn, and sat beside him.
He put one arm around me, but did not remove his
pipe from between his teeth. With the ceasing of
the necessity for pose or pretence between us, he
unconsciously dropped his good manners. It was
a little thing, but to me it seemed significant. My
heart sank within me. The glow and the glamour
once more slowly faded.

"At dinner all need for firm restraint being
over, he let himself go still further, and took too
much wine. Then a coarseness of mind showed
itself, which wounded and terrified me. Half-way
through the meal, he called for champagne. The
waiter handed him a wine list.

"'Now then,' he said to me, laughing loudly;
'I have a threefold choice. Of course there is
but one champagne worth drinking—the Widow!
But my choice is threefold, because we can either
have *rich* widow, *sweet* widow, or *dry* widow. Well,
I have married the *rich* widow; and I have proved
her to be a *sweet* widow! I think I had better order
the *dry* widow, because, Lord knows, I don't want
any tears, and just now a deluge seemed threatening. I'll drink to the sweet, rich widow in
Veuve Clicquot, dry, extra quality. Here, waiter!

Number 43, in ice.' Then, leaning across the table toward me, he explained, thickly: 'Only the *dry* widow, in ice; not the sweet and rich!'

"I declined to touch it when it came; so he finished the bottle of 'dry widow,' while the poor little, rich widow sat trembling, and every hope of sweetness vanished from her wedding-day.

"Dinner over, he took my arm and lurched me along the passage to our private sitting-room.

"The mental agony for me of the hour which followed, I cannot describe in detail. I had never before been in intimate contact with a mind from which alcohol had taken every kind of restraint.

"He lounged in an easy chair facing the French window, but some distance from it, at the further end of the room. A table was on his left, upon which stood a large brass lamp, burning brightly. Wax candles were alight on the mantelpiece behind him.

"I remember I sat between him and the window, with my back to it. He had bidden me close it, because the night air from the river blew in, damp and chilly.

"He lay back in his chair, smoking, and noted my nervous terror with an expression of heavy amusement.

"A veil had been ruthlessly torn from my eyes. The face which had seemed to me so strong and splendid in its manly beauty, now showed coarse, cruel, and ruthless. I loved it still; but I loved it with a horror, which caught me by the throat in a suffocating grip.

"He flung remarks at me, which seared my mind, as hot iron sears soft, shrinking flesh.

"I felt as a terrified rabbit must feel, in the firm and pitiless hands of the vivisector. There seemed no hope, no way of escape; none to take pity, or to come to my aid.

"Suddenly I remembered that he had faithfully promised to read my psalm with me on our wedding evening. I knew a promise sometimes keeps its hold over the man who has made it, even when his brain is beyond all other control. It was a forlorn hope; but, with the remembrance of my Bible, Omnipotence seemed to come to my aid.

"I rose, fetched it from my bed-chamber, leaving the door of communication ajar; drew my chair to the table, and, with trembling fingers, found my evening psalm.

"I began to read aloud. He listened in amazed silence to the first few verses. Then, bursting into a wild peal of laughter, he poured out such a torrent of obscene blasphemy that, to my terrified spirit, it seemed as if hell itself had opened before me, and let loose a legion of reckless, mocking demons. The remembrance of those moments has sometimes given me hope that Alexander Ross himself, having long yielded to the power of evil temptations, was then no more responsible for that which he did and said, than was the poor demoniac of Gadara for his reviling of the Christ, at Whose

blessed feet his own great need had laid him
prostrate.

"It seemed to me in those terrible moments,
that indeed I heard demons speaking through the
lips of the man whom, in my unguarded folly, I
had trusted, loved, and wed.

"Closing my Bible, and clasping it in my hands
I rose, left the table, and moved to the French
window. I stood on the left side, leaning against
the window frame.

"Then, for the first time since we had returned
from the dining-room, nothing intervened between
Alec and the window.

"In despairing silence my whole soul cried out:
'O God, make me a way of escape! O God, deliver
me from the terrors of this night!' Then falling
back, instinctively, upon the old Church collect
I knew so well, I found myself repeating wildly,
clasping my father's Bible to my breast, and looking with hopeless eyes out into the purple shadows
of the soft summer night: 'Lighten my darkness,
I beseech Thee, O Lord; and by Thy great mercy
defend me from all perils and dangers of this night;
for the love of Thy only Son, our Saviour, Jesus
Christ. *Amen.*'

"Gazing out through the long window, at first I
could see only myself reflected, a slight girlish
figure in white, leaning helplessly against the
window frame; behind me, the brightly-lighted
room, the lamp on the table, the large heavy
figure in the chair, lying back in evening dress,

awaiting, in amused tolerance, my next move. I could see the expanse of his white shirt-front, the flushed, handsome face above it; the crisp thickness of his hair.

"I peered into the plate glass, trying to see the lawn, the seat beneath the shady tree, the river beyond.

"I wondered whether, if I suddenly wrenched open the window and fled to the river, I should find any place wherein I could hide from him; and, creeping away under cover of darkness, find my way to the station; and so to the safe shelter of my own home in Portman Square. Yet fleeing thus, in a thin evening gown, with no money, and without hat or cloak, I knew I should at once be taken for a poor demented creature and detained until the man from whom I fled arrived to claim me. To escape by the door and make a scene in the hotel would be equally hopeless. I had arrived there as his wife; the church had bound me to him; the law would hold me to him. 'Till death us do part' must stand. I was in his power. No human hand could release me.

"Yet an unfaltering human hand was at that moment nearer than I knew."

CHAPTER XXVII

THE UNFALTERING HAND

"AN unfaltering human hand, Dick, was, at that moment, nearer than I knew.

"Gazing through the plate glass window, I suddenly saw something which was not a part of the reflection.

"My eye was caught by a little shining ring quite near the glass of the further pane. I focussed my eyes upon it, as it gleamed in the lamplight, and tried to see what it was.

"At first I saw only that little shining ring, gleaming bright out of the darkness.

"Then slowly—as the focus of my sight grew accustomed to looking beyond the reflection, I saw, behind the shining ring, the white, set face of a woman. Her dark eyes stared into the room, without flinching or blinking.

"Then I saw that the bright ring was the rim of a revolver barrel. The woman held it in her hand, and was looking steadily along it. It pointed past me, straight at Alec.

"I shrank back, clutching the window frame for support.

"I tried to cry out, but my throat contracted, and no sound would come.

"Before I could speak or move, there was a loud crash, and a splintering of broken glass.

"I felt myself spinning round with closed eyes, and with a smell of powder in my face.

"When I opened my eyes, my back was to the window; I was looking up the room.

"I saw Alec still seated in the chair, but a small dark hole showed in the centre of the left side of his stiff shirt-front.

"As I gazed, petrified with terror, a bright red stain like the vivid leaf of a Virginia creeper in autumn, appeared on the white expanse, around the small dark hole. It quickly spread and grew, like a large angry hand, with fingers pointing downwards.

"Then his head dropped forward on his breast; his massive figure shrank together, and seemed to crumple up in the chair.

"The window beside me opened quietly. A tall woman stepped in, leaving it open behind her.

"I felt the damp breath of the chill river air blow upon my face.

"The tall woman held the revolver in her right hand.

"'I must make quite sure,' I heard her say, as if to herself, as she walked across the room.

"I saw her place the barrel of the revolver against the temple of the crumpled figure in the chair.

"Then I screamed loudly, one piercing scream of horror.

"There was the deafening crash of a second explosion. All became black around me, and I felt myself swaying and sinking slowly—slowly; catching at the curtains as I fell, while palpitating waves of darkness overwhelmed me.

"But at that moment, strong arms closed around me; a deep tender voice, reaching me in the depths through which I was falling, said, close to my ear: 'Ah, poor child, poor child!'

"My last conscious sensation was of being gathered up and lifted, my head resting against softness, instead of striking the hard floor.

.　　.　　.　　.　　.　　.　　.

"My moments of complete oblivion—Nature's merciful provision when the mind can bear no more—must have been very few.

"When I returned to consciousness and opened my eyes, I was lying upon a couch. A woman knelt beside me, her arms wrapped round me, as I lay, my head pillowed against her breast.

"My first conscious realization was of the gentle strength of those arms; the wonderful tenderness of that bosom. I pressed my face closer to it, and closed my eyes. Never before had I experienced a woman's tenderness. I did not yet remember why I needed help and comfort; but I knew that whatever help or comfort I needed, those arms could give; that tender bosom could supply.

"I opened my eyes again, and looked up into her face.

"She was bending over me, a look of infinite compassion in her deep-set, steadfast eyes. I have seen that look since then, in the eyes of the Madonna, as painted by the most inspired of the old Italian masters.

"'You poor child!' she said; and her voice was very soft and low. 'You poor little white dove! Lie still a few moments longer, and do not try to think. You are quite safe. No harm can come to you now.'

"I heard a sound of running footsteps, and the approach of many voices.

"'Don't leave me!' I whispered. 'I can't remember why; but I know I am afraid.'

"The strong arms tightened. 'I will not leave you, child,' she said.

"The door of the room burst open.

"The room seemed suddenly filled with cries and exclamations.

"Somebody said 'Suicide!' Another voice replied, 'No, murder!'

"Two or three women screamed.

"The woman kneeling beside me did not stir.

"'Don't stand gaping there!' said a man's voice, angrily. 'Fetch the proprietor of the hotel, and a doctor, and the police. Who are these women?'

"Nobody answered; but yet other hurrying feet

arrived. They seemed all to pause at a certain spot, and there stand transfixed.

"'What are they looking at?' I whispered; and tried to lift my head.

"She pressed it down against her. 'Don't look,' she said. 'You poor wee bairn, don't look!'

"I thought how pretty was the soft burr of her Scotch accent.

"A fresh tramp of feet. Then a voice of authority in the room.

"'Who did it? Who are these women?'

"'The young lady on the sofa is his wife, sir,' somebody replied.

"'No,' said a firm voice, just above my head. '*I* am his wife. This young lady is a girl he has deceived, and with whom he went through the ceremony of marriage to-day. I am his wife. My name is Janet Ross.'

"'Have you any idea, madam, who shot him?'

"'*I* did,' said the firm voice, clearly.

"Dead silence in the room.

"'You had better send for the police and for a doctor,' continued the firm voice. 'The doctor is not needed over there, but will be sorely needed by this poor young lady. You need not lay hands on me, my man. I shall not stir from here until the doctor comes.'

"The hubbub in the room seemed hushed into awed silence.

"Suddenly I remembered seeing Alec crumple

up in the chair, with a red stain spreading over his shirt-front.

"I srceamed again. I could not help it. The strong arms tightened, rocking me gently.

"'Hush, poor bairn!' murmured the tender voice. 'Try not to think, and do not listen.'

"My head was pressed yet more closely to that tender bosom, and a hand was laid gently over my ear.

"After that I heard only a hum of voices, until somebody touched my wrist, and the hand covering my ear was suddenly removed.

"—— 'a great shock,' the firm voice was saying. 'But she will be safe in your hands. I can furnish you with her address in town. Yes, she believes herself to be his wife. But it is not so. I am his wife. I travelled from Scotland by the night mail; but, owing to an accident, was too late to stop the marriage. I followed them here. . . . Yes, that is mine. Be careful! Four chambers are still loaded.'

"Again a silence in the room; a sense of many minds nonplussed.

"Then a gruff voice, speaking for the first time, said: 'I arrest you, Mrs. Ross, on your own confession, on the charge of murdering your husband. I must trouble you to stand up.'

"I heard the clink of metal. The arms tightened round me.

"'Quite right, constable,' said the firm voice, without a tremor. 'I shall not make any attempt

to escape you, or to evade the law. Had I wished
to escape, I should have had ample time to have
done so, by that window. There is a boat moored
at the landing stage. I pull a steady stroke. I
could have been a mile down the river by now,
leaving no trace behind. I could have taken the
train at the next town, and the death of Alexander Ross would have added yet another to the
number of unsolved mysteries. As I remained
patiently here, awaiting you, you need hardly
suppose I shall now attempt to escape. I will
accompany you wherever you wish, and give you
any information in my power, but not until I have
carried this young lady out of this room, placed her
on a bed, and left her with the doctor and a maid.
Arrange for me to do this, doctor——' the firm
voice softened into pleading. 'You will know
why the poor little lady must not change hands
in this room.'

"The doctor turned and spoke to the constable.
I heard him say 'shock,' and 'any further scene
avoided.' 'You can come too,' he added.

"Then, without loosing me, the woman, in
whose arms I lay, rose to her feet, lifting me as
easily as if I had been a little child.

"'No, not in there,' she said. 'A fresh room—
a room she has not seen. Away from here, down
the passage—anywhere!'

"'Follow me,' said a man, whom I afterwards
knew to be the proprietor.

"I felt myself borne from the room, carried

along a corridor, and up a staircase. The firm step never faltered. I put up my arms, and clung round her neck. I heard the doctor following; behind him, a heavy tread.

"'Oh, don't leave me!' I said.

"As we mounted the stairs, there came a breathless whisper in my ear: 'Quick, child! Slip your hand into the bosom of my gown. Yes: there under your cheek. You will find a letter. Draw it out. Oh, hasten, hasten! Now hide it—anywhere, anywhere! Show it to nobody. They will conclude it was your own, if they find it upon you presently. Read it when alone, so soon as you are able. Then burn it. But tell nobody; show it to nobody. I only want that *you* should understand.'

"Still shielded by her arms, I crushed the letter into the front of my gown.

"We entered a quiet room. A maid was lighting two candles on the dressing-table. A bed stood against the wall.

"Gently she laid me down. Just for a moment her cheek rested against mine.

"'Try to sleep, poor bairn,' she said. 'And remember all the time that you are safe—quite safe. Nobody can harm you, now.'

"She loosed her arms from around me. I felt them going. I flung mine about her neck.

"'Oh, don't leave me! Don't leave me!' I cried.

"The doctor's hands took mine, and drew them down.

" 'Be gentle with her,' said the tender voice. Then the firm voice—and now I knew them to be one and the same—rang out: 'Now, constable! I am ready.'

"I heard two rapid clicks and the chinking of a steel chain.

"I sat up quickly. Instantly the tall figure turned and walked toward the door. But in that one glance I had seen that the hands, which had ministered to me so tenderly, were locked together in steel handcuffs.

"Oh, they might have spared her that! They might have spared her that!

"At the door the policeman took her by the arm. They passed out quickly. She was gone!

"Then I screamed again.

"The doctor hastened across to shut the door.

"I sprang from the bed.

"No strong, prompt arms were there to save my fall.

"I stood for a moment with hands outstretched.

"Then the floor seemed to come up suddenly and strike me. I sank into depths of impenetrable silence and blackness; and I knew no more."

CHAPTER XXVIII

A MIND DISTRAUGHT

DICK got up, walked over to the window, moved aside the curtain, and stood looking out on to the park.

The whirl of the London evening traffic was passing by beneath him. Swiftly moving cars glided to and fro; taxi-cabs dashed past with a hoot and a flash; an occasional brougham went by more slowly, to the accompaniment of the steady klip-klop of horses' hoofs.

The twentieth century was there all right. It was a relief to verify it.

Thirty-five years had elapsed since the broken-hearted, desolate little bride swooned, and struck the floor.

The man who crumpled up in the chair, with the red stain, like the fingers of an angry hand, spreading over his breast, had lain thirty-five years in his grave.

The woman who sent him to that grave? What of her? She still seemed to walk, locked in steel handcuffs, the relentless grasp of the Law upon her shoulder.

Dick pressed his forehead against the cool window-pane. He felt thankful his Little White Lady could not know through what a purgatory her story had put him.

He came back to her; he sat down beside her on the foot of her sofa.

"I cannot let you tell me any more to-night," he said.

She turned to him, smiling gently. Her face was very white and tired, but filled with a quiet peace. In view of his own agitation, her calmness surprised him.

"I would rather finish my story this evening," she said. "Look! It is not really late. I will tell you the remainder in more condensed form. I could not sleep to-night, feeling you did not know all which had led to the terrible step taken on that evening by Janet Ross—a woman whose chief characteristics had always been devoted love, and self-forgetting tenderness."

Dick laid his fingers on Mrs. Herriot's wrist.

"Of course I want to hear the rest," he said; "and I can well understand your wish to finish it. An unfinished story, especially such a story as this, tries the teller of the tale, even more than the listener. Yet the strain upon you of such a recital must be immense. I cannot sanction an effort which might mean an attack to-night."

"My dear young doctor," she said, "I think the relief is greater than the strain. Also, I have an object in telling you my story; and an object

accomplished always means peace of mind.   It
is a human repetition of the Divine 'I have
finished the work which Thou gavest me to do.'
In the strength of that assurance, the soul passes
peacefully from the upper chamber of communion,
to the shades of Gethsemane, or even to the hill
of Calvary."

"*Ho muthos deloi*," mused Dick to himself.   "I
thought so!"   Aloud, he said: "Very well; only
do not tax yourself too heavily."

He returned to his chair, without further protest.

"I will briefly give you Janet's history," resumed Mrs. Herriot, "without details as to how it
came fully into my possession.

"She was one of the many instances in which a
truly noble woman succumbs to the fascination of
an utterly bad, unscrupulous man.   She was a
fully trained hospital nurse when she met Alec
Ross.   By the way, I ought to mention that all
through the story I have called him by his real
name 'Alec Ross,' and not by the name which
he assumed when he laid his plans for entrapping
me.   To my own mind this keeps the story clearer,
and saves confusion in that portion of it, subse-
quent to the appearance of Janet.   After all it
matters but little what we call him; he had passed
under many names, and had dishonoured them
all.   But Janet will always be Janet Ross—she
could be nothing else!   She stepped in as Janet
Ross; as Janet Ross she lives to me for ever."

The Little White Lady's cheeks were flushed;

her eyes shone. Dick marvelled, but made no comment.

"He was five years her junior," continued Mrs. Herriot, more calmly, "a handsome, adventurous boy. She came beneath the spell of his extraordinary fascination; yielded, married him, and thenceforth poured out upon him the whole wealth of a woman's great love and matchless devotion. Undoubtedly he loved her; first with passion, then returning always—as to a haven of sure refuge— to the tenderness of her arms, the comfort of her love, the unfailing certainty of her patience and forgiveness.

"During the early years of their married life they lived together in California, a wild life of liberty and adventure. She learned to shoot and ride, sharing with him, as mate and comrade, all his interests and pursuits; yet all the while holding him to her, by the unfailing sweetness of her womanly nature. .

"Gambling was his besetting sin. In a gaming saloon out West, with a swift shot, forestalling another man's fire, he took a life. He was acquitted in that land of lax laws, and got off scot-free; but the incident brought about a steady deterioration in his own character. The mark of Cain upon him appeared to be a cheapened idea of all human values—life, faith, honour—all these lost their worth in his estimation. In killing another man, and not suffering for the action, he had slain all the best in his own inner life.

"Not long after, he speculated to great advantage in some mining enterprise, made a fairly large fortune, and returned with her to live in Scotland, their native land, dear to them both.

"They bought a fine old place, with plenty of shooting and fishing, and all might have been well; but his insatiable passion for gambling took a fresh hold upon him. It was first revived by card-playing after dinner at the houses of friends; then by flying visits to Monte Carlo, and other continental gaming resorts. To these he never took Janet. She awaited his return, in an anguish of suspense, amid the purple heather, stately firs, calm beauty of moor and hill, in their lovely Highland home.

"One day he came back to her ruined; announced that the place must be sold, and that they must start out again on a life of uncertainty and adventure.

"She was heartbroken, yet her tenderness never failed. During three days and nights he rested in the comfort of her love; remorseful, crushed, full of regrets and good intentions.

"But, on the fourth morning, he flung down a newspaper he had been reading, sprang up, full of fire and vitality, and told her he had thought of a plan which would retrieve their fallen fortunes. He borrowed money for current expenses, bade her a wild, passionate farewell, and disappeared completely for five months.

"At the end of that time he returned, handsome and debonair as ever, possessed of the sum of thirty thousand pounds.

"He completely refused at first to tell her how he came by it; implying it was a huge stroke of luck at Monte Carlo. But her suspicions were aroused, she remembered certain things she had seen in the newspapers; put two and two together, and finally drew from him a by no means reluctant confession of what he had done.

"Passing under an assumed name, he had gone through the ceremony of marriage with a comparatively friendless young heiress, secured the reversion of her capital, and taken her to Switzerland for the honeymoon. There had been a glacier accident; the bride had vanished down a crevasse; the bridegroom had returned to England alone, secured her fortune, and booked his passage, with much publicity, to America. The day after 'Eric Macleod' reached New York, Alec Ross boarded a liner sailing for Queenstown, and within ten days turned up, successful and unsuspected, to find his anxious wife awaiting him in the Highland home.

"She forgave him the bigamy, and tried, beneath the spell of his influence, to believe in the accident; but her soul was tormented by the horror of the almost certainty that the unfortunate bride's fatal slip on the glacier had not been caused by her own foolhardiness.

"A year or two elapsed, and then the same

thing happened again; and again, though he would not admit it, the unhappy wife felt practically certain that the money had not been won at the gaming tables, but that he had come back to her once more a murderer.

"That her devotion to him still held, can only be explained by the fact, well known to all students of criminal psychology, of the extraordinary hold sometimes retained by an utterly bad man upon the life and affections of a truly good and noble woman. How far, in these cases, magnetism merges into mesmerism, it is difficult to determine.

"He was soon off again on various adventurous journeys, apparently of a less sinister nature. Then came a reckless fling at Monte Carlo, and once again ruin stared them in the face.

"He disappeared, and she heard nothing of him for six weeks. Then a friend, who had recognized him in London, wrote and told her of his impending marriage with me. It was the first time she had become aware, beforehand, of his dastardly plans. All the woman in her awoke in a frantic desire to hold him back from doing this thing, and to save me—his hapless victim.

"Knowing the irresistible influence he had over her when with her, she did not at first venture to follow him, but having ascertained his address, the name under which he was passing, and the date fixed for the wedding, she wrote to him urging him to give it up and return at once to her. She taxed him, directly, with the murder of the poor girl who had perished in Switzerland, and declared that her silence should no longer make of her an accomplice in his career of heartless crime. Finally, she warned him that if he did not return within a week, she should come South, and acquaint me with the truth.

"He replied, telling her that expostulations were useless. He must have my money, and could only obtain it by marrying me. She need not be jealous, as I was a silly little fool for whom he felt no particle of affection; all his love was hers, and as soon as he was 'through' with me, he would come back to her, give up gambling, and never leave her again. But, should she attempt to thwart him, he would instantly shoot me, and himself, leaving her desolate, with both deaths at her door. If she would be wise and faithful, make no foolish move, and ask no questions, he would probably be at home again with her in a couple of months. He was taking me to Norway and Switzerland, and should leave the rest to Providence. 'It is not *my* fault if glaciers are slippery, and women lose their heads in awkward places,' he concluded, with horrible levity.

"This was the letter Janet left with me, just before her arrest; believing that to have my eyes fully opened to the character and designs of the man, would best help me to recover from the shock of his death.

"Shortly after receiving Alec's letter, she heard from the friend who still watched his movements in London, that the date of the marriage had been put forward a week; the wedding was to take place on the following morning.

"Meanwhile, her own conscience and power of independent action, once awakened, refused to be silenced.

"She caught the night mail, and would have reached London several hours before the time fixed for my marriage, had it not been for the unfortunate accident at Crewe.

"From there she telegraphed, urging me not to marry Alec, or at all events to wait until I had seen her, and heard what she had to tell me. This message had been delayed several hours in transmission, yet it arrived in time to have stopped me from going away with him, had not Alec himself intercepted it.

"She reached London too late to go to the church, so came straight to the house, only to learn that we had left for the station, ten minutes before; and that her telegram to me was in Alec's pocket.

"Frantic with anxiety, she followed us, but in those days of old four-wheelers, progress was slow, and we had trotted rapidly to the station in my own carriage and pair.

"She reached the platform after the train had actually begun to move; but recognized Alec at the window of our compartment, and saw his instant recognition of her.

"With the departure of the train she felt helpless, not knowing our destination; but there, by a strange irony of fate, the 'tramps' came to the rescue. They had marked Alec's unmistakable look of dismay at sight of her, and the lowering of the blinds. Eager to spite the man who had scorned and flouted them, they told her the name of the station for which we were bound. They had seen it on the paper, in the window of our reserved compartment.

"'I must follow my husband there,' she said, hardly knowing that she said it; and at once the 'tramps' had the key to the situation.

"They made the most of it. Perhaps, in common with most scoundrels, they had a streak of human kindness and sympathy in their warped natures, and felt genuinely sorry for the white-faced despairing woman, who stood rooted to the platform as if at the end of all possible endeavour. Perhaps their rough sense of justice led them to wish to undo the wrong they had helped to do to me. Undoubtedly their anger against Alec sought some means of revenge.

"They ascertained that the next train to Riverslea left in two hours; found a quiet table in a corner of the station restaurant, and suggested that the worn-out traveller should have some refreshment; offered to procure her ticket for her; and, in their rough way, showed her all possible kindness.

"Too dazed and stunned to realize into what queer companionship she had fallen, she accepted their help gratefully; struggled to swallow the food they set before her, felt refreshed by a cup of tea, and then listened, in grief and dismay, to the story of the mock attack in the Devonshire lane. Perhaps the heartless, fiendish cleverness of this scheme, revealed to the mind of Alec's wife, better than anything else could have done, how utterly hopeless it was to attempt to redeem Alec; how impossible to rescue, by any appeal to his sense of right, the poor little friendless widow, whose person and whose fortune had fallen into his hands. The 'tramps' ' story of his picturesque treachery, revealed to her a side of his nature she had not before realized in actual detail. It was the last straw upon the heavy burden of her despair.

"After they had found her an empty compartment in the slow train for Riverslea, one of them stepped into the carriage, while his comrade kept guard outside.

"'Look here, lady,' he said. 'He's a dangerous customer to deal with, if you get him at bay. Here's a thing might come in handy, just by way of a threat in case of need. You can have it for a sovereign, and welcome.'

"He took a small revolver from his pocket, and, with a quick shuffling air of secrecy, pressed it into the hands of Alec's wife.

"It was the weapon Alec had supplied for use in the mock attack on me, in the lane, and which he had afterwards laughingly presented to the man, as compensation for a black eye, which had not been a part of the bargain.

"The 'tramp' told Janet this; but she had already recognized in it an old revolver of Alec's, in fact the very 'gun' with which he had shot the man in the Californian gambling saloon. She had often implored him to throw it away, or at any rate to sell it. It had seemed to her the original cause of the fatal deterioration in her husband's character.

"She now took it mechanically, gave the tramp a sovereign, and slipped the weapon into her bag.

"'Mind how you hold it, ma'am,' he turned back to say. 'It is loaded in every chamber.'

"Janet gave a wan smile, more pathetic than tears.

"'I have loaded and fired it many times, my friend,' she said. 'My husband used to call me the finest woman shot in California.'

"As the train moved on and she found herself alone, she tried to face the situation and to realize exactly what she meant to do. The story told her by the men whom Alec had hired in order to compass his infamy, had aroused in her a passionate desire to come to my help and to rescue me from his hands. To such a nature as hers, the wronged and the weak always held a special appeal.

"Alec's need of her was that which had all along called forth her deepest tenderness. My dire need now turned a large portion of that tenderness upon me. She resolved to save me that very evening, not only from the probable death which threatened me, but from immediate dishonour.

"Yet her stunned brain showed her no possible way of doing so.

"She drew out Alec's letter, and read it again. Then there dawned upon her all the horror of his threat to shoot himself and me, if she appeared, leaving both deaths to lie at her door.

"This definite threat of Alec's, completed the full measure of her despair. Whether she arrived to save me, or left me to my fate, my death seemed assured. Yet, if she appeared, and he fulfilled his threat, Alec would pass into eternity not alone a murderer, but also a suicide.

"Suddenly, in her distraught mind, a startling thought took shape. Supposing she—she who loved him so—shot Alec—shot him with her own strong, tender hands? This would put a stop, once and for ever, to his career of crime. She would save me, and—her own life being forfeited—she would soon be sent, by the legitimate way of the law's death penalty, to rejoin Alec in the great Unknown; for, wherever that might be, her love would find him out, and she felt sure he would still have need of her.

"At once this idea took possession of her mind, to the complete exclusion of all else. It seemed the *only* way.

"As twilight fell, and the train glided on into

22

the shadows of meadow, wood, and river, it grew to seem the *right* way.

"How came the revolver in her possession, if not placed there, by Divine interposition, for this very purpose? No thought of herself entered her mind. Unhinged though it undoubtedly was, it instinctively held its natural noble balance in regard to proportions. Her wounded, bleeding, yet enduring love for Alec, came first. Then her yearning pity for me. Lastly, her firm belief in the unfaltering finger of that Hand which points out by signs and tokens the things which are to be—the relentless law of just and inevitable retribution.

"Alec's life had been forfeit by Divine laws when he took another man's, with that very weapon, twelve years before.

"Because men, through laxity of justice, had spared him, another life had followed the first; another death lay at Alec's door.

"Now—just as he planned to compass a third— the weapon with which he took the first was placed in the hand which loved him best, in order that the long-delayed penalty might be exacted and his soul saved from contracting further stain of sin.

"Of course the ethics of this were all wrong; but we must remember they were evolved by a mind undoubtedly distraught. Starting from a false premise, dream-like they developed along a line of reasoning which seemed to prove wrong to be right.

"So, at Riverslea, a calm, white-faced woman left the train, passed unnoticed out of the station; and, finding her way along the river path, soon discovered the sloping lawn and brightly-lighted windows of the Royal Hotel."

CHAPTER XXIX

WITHOUT EXTENUATING CIRCUMSTANCES

MRS. HERRIOT shivered and folded her shawl more closely around her.

Dick got up, put coal on the fire, stirred it into a bright flame, then returned to his seat in silence.

"I must take you back now," said Mrs. Herriot, "to the poor desolate little bride, who found herself no wife, but still a widow; and, overwhelmed with trembling thankfulness at her deliverance, hardly realized the horror of the deed which had set her free, nor the dread consequences thereby involved.

"Days passed before I could be moved, the severe strain and shock having produced complete nervous prostration.

"Kind friends arrived, and surrounded me with loving care; foremost and kindest of all, the woman whose warning I had resented and ignored.

"But as life, consciousness, and realization returned, my one vivid sensation was the remembrance of those strong shielding arms around me, of resting my head against that tender woman's breast. I only rested when, in fancy,

I felt them round me again; I only slept when, under the influence of narcotics, the pillow beneath my cheek became again the motherly bosom of Janet Ross.

"I longed for news of her, with a longing which consumed me; but the doctor—it is a tiresome way doctors have, Dick!—absolutely forbade all mention of her name or of the tragedy.

"At last I remembered the letter with which she had trusted me. I feared it must have fallen into other hands. I dared not ask; but as soon as I found myself alone, I rose, crept to the dressing-table and made a search. There, in a small drawer, unnoticed and forgotten, I found a handkerchief, a chain and locket, my rings, and the letter, evidently placed there by the maid who had undressed me, and who was not allowed in the room after the arrival of the trained nurse. So the letter, which could have revealed so much, had kept its secret.

"As soon as I could safely do so, I read it; and then, indeed, I realized from what I had been saved by Janet Ross. In the first horror of the discovery, in the first rush of my gratitude, wishing to do her bidding, and to keep my unspoken promise—alas, I burnt that letter! Later on, I would have given all I possessed to recover it.

"I was eager now to be at home, able to see my lawyer, and free to communicate with Janet. I proved, in actual fact, your favourite theory, my dear doctor, that nervous prostration

is soon overcome by an effort of will, energized
into action by the force of an absorbing new idea.

"Before long, I was out of the hands of the
doctor and nurse; and, accompanied by my kind
and trusted friend, returned to my home in Portman Square.

"I sent for my lawyer, told him everything,
and implored him to obtain for me immediate
access to Janet.

"Influential friends of Constantia's came to
our aid.   Dabbling in reforms at least brings you
into touch with people whom it is sometimes useful
to know.

"All difficulties were removed, and I was allowed
free and private access to Janet whenever I pleased,
during the weeks which elapsed, between her
committal and her trial.

"Oh, Dick! Never can I tell you what Alec's
noble wife became to me, during those weeks.
It was she who strengthened, cheered, and com-
forted me, rather than I, her.

"But, alas, no arguments, no prayers, no
entreaties, would move her! She absolutely refused to admit, or to put forward, any extenuating
circumstances.

"She wished to die—Alec's wife wished to die.
She used to say to me, her large hand gently strok-
ing mine into stillness—she was the tallest woman
I have ever seen—'He wants me, my bairn. My
poor boy wants me. There is no place either in
heaven, earth, or hell where a man can do without

his own woman's love. And there is no place, either in hell, earth, or heaven, where a woman's love will fail to follow and to find her man, when he needs her.'

"At the trial the crime appeared to be merely that of a jealous wife, who had followed and shot her husband in cold blood, because he had gone off with another woman. There was even an attempt to make out that the first shot had been aimed at me, and the second alone intended for him; the first, fortunately missing me, had chanced to strike him. At this suggestion on the part of counsel for the Crown, a slow smile passed over the face of 'the finest woman shot in California.' It was her only change of countenance, during the whole trial. It did not favourably impress either the judge or the jury.

"They found her guilty, of course, and with no recommendation to mercy.

"I had insisted, through my own lawyer, upon employing counsel to defend her, and to set up the plea of insanity. But it was not entertained for a moment. No doctor would certify that calm, strong woman insane. Yet I know her to have been insane upon that one point, because never, for a single instant, could she realize the shooting of Alec Ross to have been a crime.

"So they—so they—they condemned her to death."

"But they did n't hang her!" exclaimed Dick. "They could n't hang her! Why in America she would have been triumphantly acquitted, and cheered as she left the court. Of course a British jury has no more sentiment than a horsehair sofa! Besides, no doubt, by the judge's ruling, they were bound to convict. But an almost immediate reprieve must have followed."

Dick's impetuous young voice fell silent.

Tears were flowing down the Little White Lady's cheeks. For the first time her hand stole to her heart.

"They hanged her," she whispered.

Dick got up, and once again walked over to the window. He was ashamed of his own emotion.

The taxi-cabs still rushed by, with a hoot and a flash.

The street lamps still burned.

There was no rain or mist outside; yet, as Dick stood at the window, all the lights were blurred; the scene was dimmed.

He fought in silence with his emotion.

Within, the Little White Lady wept softly, and her weeping brought relief.

Presently Dick came back.

He knelt down beside her and took both her hands very gently in his.

"Truly, my Little White Lady," he said. "I can allow you to talk no longer. Let me stay quietly with you for a few minutes, and then ring for Ellen."

"I would rather finish now," she said. "It is so nearly done."

So he knelt on beside her, holding her hands while she finished.

"I suppose they would have reprieved her, had it happened now," she said. "But thirty-five years ago, it was less unusual to carry out the capital sentence on a woman. She did not desire a reprieve, and would allow no steps to be taken. Her quiet courage never failed.

"I saw her, the day before—to say good-bye.

"'May I tell Alec you forgive him?' she said.

"'I forgive him the wrong he did to me,' I answered. 'I cannot forgive him the wrong he did to you.'

"Her face was illumined by a radiant smile. 'There is no need you should,' she said. *'That* has been long forgiven.'

"I don't know how I left her. A young wardress carried me out. She seemed kind and capable, and to have some feeling.

"'Oh, will you be there to-morrow?' I said.

"'Yes, ma'am,' she answered. 'I shall be with her to the end.'

"'Oh, I do implore you,' I cried, catching hold of her hard hands—'I do implore you to make things as little difficult for her as possible. I understand no payment from friends is allowed; but, if you will promise me to be good to her, I will befriend you all your life. You can turn to me, if ever you are in need.'

"She looked surprised, but her stern face softened.

"'I will do what I can, ma'am, though I fear it won't be much. But indeed you take on about it far more than the poor thing herself. Can't you get comfort from the thought that this time to-morrow it will all be over?'

"But that gave me small comfort.

"'She is giving her life for mine!' I cried.

"The wardress evidently thought me demented. She hurried me along the stone passages to the room in which my faithful friend, and my old lawyer waited.

"At the door, I made her pause.

"'Will you promise to come and see me,' I said, 'as soon as possible afterwards, and to an-swer any questions I feel able to ask?'

"'I will come, ma'am,' she answered, 'on my first day out. We are n't allowed to say much; but I will tell you all I can.'

"I gave her my address. 'What is your name?' I asked. It was Ellen Ransom."

Dick started. "Ellen? Our old Ellen? Oh, I see! Of course. That completely explains Ellen."

"Yes, it explains Ellen. Dick, I don't know how I lived through the hours which followed. A strong sleeping draught was given me at five in the morning.

. . . .

" In the afternoon, Ellen arrived.

" She told me—all I asked.

" A year or two later, when she was tired of the

gruesome prison work, she came to me to know if I could find her some other employment.

"I had just taken this house, and was leaving Constantia's. She and Tobias had become more and more impossible. I at once engaged Ellen Ransom as my personal attendant. She has been with me ever since."

"Did you live here alone?" asked Dick.

"Yes, dear boy, alone. I made many friends, and some of these came to me on long visits. I spent many winters abroad at Cannes, Mentone, and elsewhere, but especially in lovely Florence. There, in the Villa Trollope, where George Eliot wrote *Romola*, where those ideal poet-lovers the Brownings used to visit, where everything breathes forth an atmosphere of literature, art, and priceless memories, I had a suite of rooms, and spent many happy weeks each year, usually accompanied by some bright young friend in full mental sympathy, who could not otherwise have afforded the change and pleasure. But, in my own home, I have always lived alone; and I suppose my heart never really recovered from the shock of the terrible happenings of which I have been telling you. I have never been really strong, or able for much strain or exertion, since that evening in the Riverslea hotel."

"My poor Little White Lady!" said Dick, tenderly. "To think that you—you, of all people —should have been the central figure of so ghastly a tragedy! Yet, notwithstanding it all, you have contrived to keep that exquisite air of aloofness from all which is sinful and sordid; an atmosphere which not only makes one feel 'here evil is not,' but 'here evil is unknown.' I am acquainted with some old ladies, whose personal lives have no doubt been most decorous and virtuous, yet, as you look into their clever wrinkled faces, the knowledge of sin seems to look out at you from their shrewd eyes. They are ready to talk quite lightly and glibly, perhaps even racily, of the vilest things, especially when they find themselves alone with younger members of their own sex. They may be impeccable, themselves, but their minds seem seared by an intimate knowledge and appreciation of the sins of others. I should have said—of you—that sin, in any gross form, had never come your way. Yet now I know that sin, of the vilest type, enveloped your sweet life in tragedy. Yet it has left you unsoiled, unseared, pure as the dove with silver wings. And more than that—your recital of these happenings, though mercilessly clear in its portrayal of the wrong, leaves one hating the sin, sorry for the sinner, and realizing that honour, faith, and self-abnegation may have their place, even on the darkest page of human tragedy. I am conscious that this tale of wrong, far from debasing me, has raised my ideals. I suppose the fact of the matter is this: if your own heart is true, your own mind pure, if your spirit walks radiant on the mountain-top, breathing an atmosphere exalted and refined, no circumstances can debase it, no outward things, however much they may surround, can soil or defile it. In fact your atmosphere is created, not by what has *happened* in your life, but by *what you are.*"

Dick paused. He was still kneeling beside her, holding both her hands. His eyes shone very brightly in the golden halo cast by her shaded lamp.

Mrs. Herriot, though deeply moved by her young doctor's words, was dumb. Praise or appreciation always had this effect upon her. Her lips could never make response, because her spirit instantly exclaimed: "What am I, that this should be thought and said of me!"

Suddenly Dick bent his head and kissed the hands he held, many times, reverently, tenderly.

"My Little White Lady," he said, "I am so glad that you are you! It has given me something to believe in, in this world."

He kissed the little hands again—so soft, so transparent, so frail. He liked the fact that they looked old, and yet were white and pretty. He hated to think that Alec Ross had ever held and kissed them. An immense pity for the little bride of thirty-five years ago was surging through Dick's manly heart. Her sorrows might have been yesterday.

He looked up into her gentle eyes, with fire in his own.

"Oh, I love you!" he said. "I love you for yourself alone, just because you are you!"

She drew her right hand from his grasp. She passed her fingers softly through his hair, searching his face with a long earnest gaze.

Dick's look did not falter before hers. Dick's impulse, at that moment, was absolutely honest and genuine.

The Little White Lady smiled—and it was a very tender smile.

"And I love your love, dear boy," she said. "It greatly comforts me to-night. It helps me to forget my sorrow at the loss of my own little son; though, had he lived, he would now have been several years older than you, Dick. But— my dear young doctor—look at the clock!"

Dick turned and looked. He was on his feet in a moment.

"What have I done!" he said. "To let you talk for so long, and then to start talking myself. You must be completely worn out. And now, am I to go? Am I to leave you here, not knowing whether you are able to sleep quietly, or whether the strain of this long talk is resulting in wakefulness and pain? I do beg of you, Mrs. Herriot, as it is now so late, to let me stay here to-night. I came straight up here from Hollymead—I spent last night with the Wests. I had not time to go to my rooms, so left my bag here before I went round to my patients, and Jarvis provided me with a dressing-room. Don't turn me out to-night.

Think of the comfort of knowing that Ellen could fetch me in two minutes, if you were not well!"

"Yes," she said, "it would undoubtedly be a comfort."

She hesitated, pondering. "Very well, dear boy. Just this once. Now ring for Ellen."

Ellen Ransom appeared. She showed no surprise either at the lateness of the hour or the presence of the doctor. She carried the usual glass of hot milk, but also, on a little tray, a large plate of sandwiches and a syphon of soda water.

Mrs. Herriot smiled at Ellen's forethought. Where the doctor was concerned, she had lately developed a way of taking the initiative.

"Quite right, Ellen," she said. "The doctor must be hungry; and as I have kept him so late to-night, he will sleep here. Will you see, presently, that a room is made ready? I will read upstairs, and you can take up my milk."

Ellen Ransom seized the chessmen and board, and the glass of hot milk. Triumph was in her eye. It had long been the wish of her heart that the doctor should sleep in the house.

Mrs. Herriot and Dick followed slowly, she carrying her Bible.

As they passed through the drawing-room door, they perceived Ellen at the foot of the flight of stairs leading to the floor above.

"Lift!" said Dick, in a peremptory monosyllable.
Ellen made an apologetic movement toward the brass gate of the lift.

"Mr. Jarvis and Albert did not wait," she said.

"I can work the thing," cried Dick. "Give me a moment in which to run down."

But Ellen shook her head. "I am sorry, sir. Mr. Jarvis said I was to say the lift is out of order, and is not working to-night."

"The lift *must* work—" began Dick. But Mrs. Herriot interposed.

"You go on before, Ellen. I will bid the doctor good-night, and follow slowly."

Dick frowned. "Is this the sort of thing which happens when I am not here?" he asked.

"Not often," she answered. "But, as you know, lifts are apt sometimes to get out of order. Stairs are always there."

She put her hand on the banisters.

"You shan't walk up!" said Dr. Dick.

"What alternative do you suggest?"

"Let me carry you," he said.

"Carry me?"

"Yes, my Little White Lady. Let me carry you upstairs, as I used to do at Dinglevale, and as —as *she* carried you. It would comfort me to-night to carry you—as she carried you."

Mrs. Herriot understood.

"Can you carry my Bible too?"

"You shall carry your Bible, and I will carry you."

"Very well, dear boy."

His arms were very strong and tender.

He mounted slowly.

He was carrying the bride of thirty-five years before.

"Are my arms strong, too?" he asked, his face very close to hers.

"Very strong."

"And tender?"

No answer.

"And tender, my Little White Lady?"

"Dear boy, I can't answer questions when I am being carried upstairs!"

"Will you answer one question when we reach the top?"

"Perhaps."

He set her down near the open door of her room. Ellen was striding about, tall and gaunt, within.

For an instant he kept his young arms about her, as he ventured his question.

"Are you going to give me the right to take care of you always?"

"To-morrow evening," she said, "I will finally answer that question. Now, good-night, Dick; and do not expect to be called. I feel particularly well, and not in the least over-tired. Ellen will come down and tell you when your room is ready."

She passed in, and closed the door.

Dick ran lightly down the stairs. He felt happy and hungry. The long strain was over. Carrying her upstairs had been a curious vent and

23

relief. The strain upon his muscles had eased the tension of his mind. He wished she had been heavier. He wished there had been three flights instead of one. He had wanted a real call upon his physical strength.

Well, anyway, he had swung upstairs with her, sparing her all exertion.

He hoped his arms would haunt her, with a sense of strength and tenderness, as the arms of Janet Ross had done.

Now he was jolly hungry, and ready for the sandwiches!

Was there ever such another blackguard as Alec Ross?

He ran lightly down the stairs.

And in the silent, dimly-lighted drawing-room, the Shade of the Prophet Nathan waited.

CHAPTER XXX

"THOU ART THE MAN!"

DICK sat down in his own chair, drew the plate of sandwiches toward him, and fell to, hungrily.

Mrs. Herriot's place was empty.

The table looked strangely empty also, without her Bible, her chessmen, and the board.

The shaded lamp alone stood upon it, casting its circle of golden light.

The soda water fizzed into the glass. The sandwiches were really appetizing. Ellen was a useful, thoughtful old soul.

A prison wardress! Fancy! Of course, that explained Ellen. How like Mrs. Herriot to make a maid of her; always considering the good of others before her own comfort; faithful during thirty-five years to a promise, and to a debt of gratitude.

Dick pushed away the syphon and the empty plate.

He lay back in his chair, looking at the sofa where the frail, dainty little figure had sat in the lamplight.

The room was very quiet. In the shut-in silence he seemed still to hear the up-and-down music of her voice.

He thought of her, preparing for rest, in the room overhead, attended by—the prison wardress.

Then he thought of that other woman, attended on her last short earthly walk, by Ellen Ransom; the walk which led to a felon's grave, within stern prison walls.

The tall figure of Janet Ross held his imagination. She seemed to him not unlike another grand woman he knew—strong, capable, tender. It struck him that Janet was Jane—gone wrong. Might not Janet have been just as fine, just as good, just as happy and helpful, had the circumstances been different? Love, which had made the one, had blighted the other. How far are we responsible for the havoc wrought in us by circumstance?

Dick pondered this.

Then he dwelt on the extraordinary contrast between the tall Scotch woman and the fragile Little White Lady. Yet both had loved, to the fullest measure of their capacity, the handsome scoundrel, who played with women's hearts as lightly as he flung the dice.

What a beast! Great Heavens, what a beast!

The Shade of the Prophet Nathan drew nearer.

If Alec Ross wanted money, being utterly

unscrupulous, he might have turned forger, or
sharper, or gentleman cracksman. There are all
sorts of villainous ways of making money, other
than trampling upon women's hearts!

Possessing such riches as the entire love of so
grand a woman as Janet, he might at least have
left the poor unawakened, trembling heart of the
Little White Lady a one; she, who asked only to
walk in solitude at sunset, where thrushes sang
in the hawthorn, lambs gambolled in the meadows,
wild roses clustered in the hedge.

Lambs? Yes, a poor little white lamb. No,
what was it? A little ewe lamb—ruthlessly
sacrificed in its innocence, by the man who already
had so much.

As in the case of King David of old, Dick's
anger was greatly kindled against the man.

"He deserved to die," thought Dick. "I am
glad she shot him. But shooting was too good
for such a scoundrel. The cold-blooded way he
plotted and planned to get hold of her money!
Going to Somerset House and reading her
husband's will——"

The Shade of the Prophet Nathan lifted an
accusing finger. The silent words came forth
at last, in the stillness of the empty room: "THOU
ART THE MAN!"

Dick Cameron dropped his head upon his hands.
"Cad!" said his accusing conscience. "Oh,
double cad! He was an adventurer. He did

not know her. She had done nothing for him. I knew her well; knew all her gentle sweetness; and—she had done so much for me already. She trusted me. I had won her trust."

Her trust! Her trust! Her trust! ticked the clock.

"She gave me her sweet friendship; she took me to her heart; she treated me as a son; she made me welcome to her home; and I—turned traitor!"

Traitor! Traitor! Traitor! ticked the clock, in merciless reiteration.

Dick lifted a haggard face.

"But she does not know," he said. "Thank heaven, she does not know! No actual harm is done. She will refuse me finally to-morrow. That will wipe out the wrong. Then I can start in, loving her for herself alone; and I shall keep her trust, right to the end."

The end! The end! The end! ticked out the pendulum.

"The end of all my hopes," thought Dick. "She will be gone. Nobody will know or care about my work and plans. I shall drudge on, for years, going the hateful round, at the beck and call of every fool who has ruined his digestion, of every kid that needs a pill, of every silly woman who wants somebody's attention fixed upon her morbid mind and body. I, who could be doing really great work, must trundle round as an ordinary practitioner, wasting my best years scraping together the capital needed to start my theories working."

He gazed before him, moodily.

"And such men as Alec Ross gamble away thousands for their own selfish pleasure. I want it, for the good of humanity."

His eye fell once more upon the empty sofa; the shaded lamp left solitary upon the table.

"Well, she does not know," he said, "so no harm's done."

Harm's done! Harm's done! Harm's done! ticked the clock, conclusively.

The door opened, and Ellen Ransom came in.

·Dick did not stir. Ellen Ransom gave him the creeps to-night.

"Your room is ready, sir," she said. "We have prepared the room in which you dressed."

"Thank you," said Dick.

He did not move, or look at Ellen.

She advanced to the table, took up the empty plate and the syphon of soda water, then put them down and waited.

Dick felt her green eyes upon him. He ignored this, until he could bear it no longer.

Then he turned abruptly.

"Well?" he said. "Do you contemplate putting me to bed, Ellen? I am quite used to going to bed by myself. Really I am!"

Ellen stood her ground.

"Sir," she said, "I want your advice."

"My advice? Oh, I see. What's the trouble, Ellen? Heart, liver, or stomach?"

"Sir," said Ellen, with dignity, "I am a respectable woman!"

"My good Ellen, quite respectable women occasionally have indigestion; and I have even known a lady of title, with a liver."

"Sir," said Ellen, "if I had such a thing, I should know better than to mention it."

"Then for what portion of your exceedingly well-ordered anatomy do you require my advice?"

"My conscience, sir."

Dick laughed, rather mirthlessly.

"Pluck it out, and cast it from you, Ellen."

"I cannot, sir. It is a matter which concerns my lady."

Dick sat up, instantly attentive.

"Ah! Your conscience at once becomes a thing of importance. Mention the symptoms."

"Many years ago, sir, I told my lady a lie."

"Why did you tell her a lie, Ellen?"

"To make her happy."

"An excellent reason. Stick to the lie, and keep her happy."

"Sir, I cannot. When she looks at me, so clear and believing, the lie comes back, and I know I shall have no rest until I tell her the truth."

"Would the truth pain her, Ellen?"

"It would, sir."

"Then bother your conscience!" cried Dick, irritably. "What on earth does your conscience matter, compared with her comfort? If I had told her fifty lies to make her happy, I should stick to them, every one."

"Fifty lies might not be so bad as *one*," said Ellen, shrewdly.

"Well, out with it," cried Dick. "When I know what it is, I shall be better able to advise you."

"A good many years ago," began Ellen, slowly, "a dear friend of my lady's died—a very sudden death."

Dick felt a cold shiver down his spine.

"Well?"

"I was with her at the time."

"Yes?"

"My lady was much distressed about it. She sent for me, and asked particulars of the—the accident. With the tears running down her pretty face she asked if her friend had left any last message for her. My lady was young then, and her poor eyes were fairly starting out of her head. She loved the friend who met with the sudden death."

"Well?" said Dick, impatiently.

Ellen as usual declined to be hurried.

"I said: 'Yes, she did. She told me to say she sent her love and died calm, and happy, and resigned, and may we meet in the sweet by-and-by.' My lady dried her eyes, gave a sad little smile, and said: 'Did she really say that, Mrs. Ransom?' 'Ma'am, she did,' said I."

"Well, that was all right," said Dick. "Wasn't it?"

"But, sir, *she didn't!*" moaned Ellen, lugubriously.

"Didn't *what?*" cried Dick. "Didn't dry her eyes?"

"Sir, it is of the other lady I am speaking. From the time we called her in the morning, she spoke no word but 'please' and 'thank you'; she was a very pleasant-spoken lady. But just before she died, she cried out one name—yet that name was not my lady's. And when I think, that just to please and comfort her, I made up a dying message, and so to speak took the lady's last words in vain, it haunts my conscience, and I feel I ought to go to my lady and say: 'The poor thing never so much as mentioned you, ma'am. The only word she said before she died was '*Alec!*'"

Dick leapt to his feet. His overwrought nerves could bear no more.

"Oh, confound your old conscience!" he cried. "If you told her a thing to lessen her grief and pain, don't regret it now. Don't be a selfish old fool, Ellen! What do our own qualms matter—yours or mine—compared with the causing her one moment of fresh sadness? We must bear our own burdens, but never lay them upon her."

"Then you don't think I ought to tell her, sir?"

"I forbid you to mention the subject. I'll strangle you first!"

Ellen Ransom's mournful face brightened. Nothing pleased her so much as when the doctor did what she called "let fly." Also, it gave her a sense of pleasurable importance that he should even contemplate strangling her as a possible necessity.

"Very well, sir," she said. "I will be guided by you. I only want to do what is right by my lady. As you say, m'own peace of mind don't matter."

"You are a good old soul, Ellen," said Dick, walking to the door. "But don't start sporting a morbid conscience. Good-night. Call me immediately if she seems unwell."

"I will, sir. But she settled off very peaceful and happy. I think she likes feeling you are in the house."

Dick shivered as he went to his room. He was thinking of "the accident." Then suddenly he laughed. Poor Ellen's idea of an appropriate last message was grotesquely quaint. He wondered how far Mrs. Herriot had been taken in by it. 'The sweet by-and-by' was so unmistakably Ellen!

"Oh, my poor Little White Lady!" he thought. "We deceive her right and left. But she has had enough to bear, without sharing the burden of our sins. Anyway she shall be safeguarded from further sorrow."

He paused outside the door of her room. All was quiet within. He felt certain she slept. Had she been lulled to rest by the remembrance that his arms had been strong and tender?

He felt completely reinstated in his own esteem.

A wrong which is unconfessed and undiscovered

is very quickly condoned and forgotten by the wrong-doer.

It was a great saving of anxiety to be sleeping in the house.

The bed Ellen had prepared for him was a luxury of comfort calculated to lull the most restless mind to slumber. Dick stretched his limbs upon its springy softness, comparing it with the lumpy discomfort of the bed in his rooms.

In two minutes he was dreaming of the little group of bungalows on Dinglevale Common. Mrs. Herriot, young and active, was installed as matron. He was not sure whether he had married her. He hoped he had done so, but had no means of finding out. Ellen, in trousers and a smock-frock, was head gardener, and marched about saying: "Sir, I am a respectable woman!" Margaret was one of the patients. Dick stood beside her bed, searching his pockets for a bull's-eye—the one essential thing her case appeared to require. He found one at last; but, just as he put it into her mouth, she turned out to be the Large Lady of the Manor.

The shock of this transformation woke him. He started up shouting: "Margaret!"—then remembered where he was; laughed at the thought of Ellen in trousers; turned over, and fell into a deep and dreamless slumber.

CHAPTER XXXI

FOOL'S MATE

BEFORE starting on his rounds the next morning, Dick paid Mrs. Herriot a professional visit.

She had remained in her room, resting; but her night had been good, her sleep peaceful, and he found her pulse stronger and more regular than usual.

Dr. Dick's manner was grave, and more distinctly professional than was his wont at the bedside of his Little White Lady. He made no allusion to the happenings of the previous night, nor to the conversation impending for that evening. He satisfied himself that she was none the worse for the long hours of harrowing retrospection. Then he rose to take his leave.

She detained him a moment, searching his face with eyes which questioned.

"My young doctor," she said, "will you tell me, once again, exactly what Sir James Montford said about the probable duration of my life?"

"He said another two years, Mrs. Herriot, or

even three; with great care, possibly more. He spoke quite hopefully."

"But—you did not agree with him?"

"No. I did not agree with him."

"How long do you give me, Dick?"

"I told you on the day of the consultation, Mrs. Herriot. As it entirely depends upon the care taken, I am going to take such care, that it ought to mean twenty years."

"Then you give me twenty years?"

"I am going to give you twenty years, if care can do it."

"In that case, I shall live to be a very old woman, Dick."

"You will never be old," he said. "You have a young soul. I never think of you as old. You are one of heaven's evergreens."

"You must think of me as old to-night, dear boy. I am going to talk to you in a very elderly way— very, *very* elderly, Dick!"

He coloured, painfully.

"Mrs. Herriot, wouldn't you rather drop that subject and not return to it again? I have realised my folly, and my extraordinary presumption. I am ashamed that you should even be troubled to say 'No' to my request."

"'Trouble' is scarcely the right word, Dick, to describe the anxious thought with which one considers a problem set before one, by the loving devotion of another heart; a problem rendered difficult by many complications; perhaps, most of

all, by the tender, grateful response of one's own
nature. No woman, however old, can receive a
proposal of marriage from any man, however
young, however impossible to consider as a pro-
spective husband, without experiencing a thrill of
humbling elation over the fact that she has been
chosen, sought, and wanted; that any man should
come to her, desiring to lay a life's devotion at her
feet. I do not yet know, dear boy, exactly what I
intend to say to you to-night. But whatever it
may be, it will certainly be softened by gratitude
and inspired by tenderness. Do not come to me
until nine o'clock this evening. Now, I must not
keep you. I shall think of you as giving your
while mind to the many patients who await
you."

When Dick had left the house, Mrs. Herriot
rang her bell.

"Ellen," she said, "the doctor gives me an
excellent report to-day. I wish to rise at once.
And will you be good enough to tell Giles to be at
the door with the carriage at twelve o'clock. I am
going to take a short drive before luncheon."

While Ellen Ransom went downstairs with the
order, Mrs. Herriot lay quite still, her mind
concentrated upon a step she contemplated—a
step requiring a good deal of tact, and a certain
amount of quick, outwitting diplomacy.

"It is essential I should know," she thought.
"I must find out, definitely. Without that certainty, I cannot come to a decision."

Soon after twelve o'clock she was handing her card to Sir James Montford's pompous butler, with the gentle, confiding smile which usually gained for her whatever she wanted.

"Kindly take this to Sir James," she said. "I want him to see me between appointments. He will understand that I am not able to wait long. I shall only require a few minutes of his valuable time." Two or three words were pencilled upon the card.

In the crowded waiting-room, Mrs. Herriot's mind followed her young doctor, going his rounds from house to house, wasting much precious time in the tedious transit from one place to another.

When would his position be such, that patients would flock to him, waiting anxiously the summons to step across his hall into the quiet room where they would find him seated at his table, ready to give them the full benefit of his instant keen attention? The tree-top stood clear in Mrs. Herriot's vision. She felt almost as anxious concerning its ultimate attainment, as did Dick Cameron himself.

The door opened.

"Step this way," said the butler.

Several people made tentative movements, and half rose. But his eye sought and summoned the delicate figure of the Little White Lady. She followed him across the hall, into the heavy silence of the consulting-room.

"How kind of you, Sir James," she said, "to

see me so promptly. I will only take up a few minutes of your most valuable time."

The great man released the hand which seemed lost in the large clasp of his own, waved her to a chair, and seated himself at his table, pushing aside the notes of his last case.

"Delighted, my dear Mrs. Herriot," he said, cordially, taking up her card and studying it with attention, as if it conveyed to his mind the entire reason of her visit. "I only trust your desire to see me, does not represent any serious return of distressing symptoms."

"Not at all, Sir James. I am feeling better than when you kindly saw me at my house, in consultation with Dr. Cameron. But I feel sure you will understand my wish to have a few words with you in private relating to the opinion you formed of my condition, on that occasion."

Sir James revolved in his chair, and glanced searchingly at the gentle face of his patient. Its frail delicacy was obvious, but its expression was calm and peaceful. His hand sought the gold charm on his watch-chain, with the somewhat restless movement she remembered.

"Certainly, Mrs. Herriot, certainly. So far as I remember, there remained nothing further to be said. But any question you may wish to ask——"

"Circumstances have since arisen, Sir James, which make it absolutely imperative that I should have a definite idea as to how long—humanly speaking—I am likely to live. I know you told

24

me there was no reason I should not, with care, live for years; but I am well aware that, at a consultation, it is not always considered wise to acquaint the patient with the exact conclusions at which her medical men arrive. May I now beg of you to tell me quite frankly your real opinion on the matter?"

Sir James spread out his hands, expanding into a smile of extreme sincerity and candour.

"My dear lady," he said, "I gave you at the time my honest judgment, so far as it was possible to form an opinion, as to the probable course of your malady and duration of your life. If you like, I will examine you again; but there is no probability of any further examination leading me to alter my verdict. I remember I said two years, possibly three; with great care, even more."

"Is that what you told my own doctor?"

"I said to Cameron exactly what I am now repeating to you."

"But—he did not agree with you?" suggested Mrs. Herriot, softly.

Sir James's hand again sought the charm upon his watch-chain.

"No," he said, rather testily. "Young men are apt to be tenacious of their own opinions and unwilling to defer to the more mature judgment of others. But it was unnecessary that he should have worried you with the mention of any difference of opinion between himself and me."

"Sir James"—Mrs. Herriot's voice was even

more quiet than before—"in response to a very earnest appeal on my part, Dr. Cameron told me this morning how long he gives me. It is because I could not quite believe him—and it is so essential I should make no mistake—that I have come, unknown to him, direct to you."

Sir James Montford bounded in his chair.

"Unwarrantable!" he exclaimed. "I can only say it was absolutely unwarrantable of Cameron to have done such a thing. Even had I confirmed his opinion, instead of distinctly differing from it, no man—unless the circumstances are most exceptional—has any right to tell a patient that she can only live six months. Such a death-warrant can but hasten the disaster, which it is a medical man's business to avert, or at all events to delay. You were quite right to come to me, my dear Mrs. Herriot. I do not wonder you felt disturbed. I beg of you, in justice to your own condition, to dismiss Cameron's most injudicious statement from your mind, and to take comfort from my renewed assurance of a distinctly more hopeful view."

The colour had faded from Mrs. Herriot's face, but a look of triumphant peace lent to it a radiance which illumined its extreme pallor.

"Did my young doctor tell you at the consultation, Sir James, that in his opinion, I could not live more than six months?"

"He did, my dear madam. But—although I admit he has had plenty of opportunity to acquaint himself very fully with your condition, under varying circumstances—I did not agree with him. That he should have given you the hopeless suggestion of his view, rather than the encouragement of mine, merely proves that he is not a fit man to have charge of so important a case. I shall take the first opportunity of telling him so. Meanwhile, my dear Mrs. Herriot——"

"Meanwhile, Sir James," said the Little White Lady, rising, and illuminating by the sweet radiance of her smile the gloom of the consulting-room,—"meanwhile, I must not take up your valuable time any further. I thank you for your consideration and kindness; and may I suggest that you do not mention this interview to Dr. Cameron? It would greatly disturb him. I am afraid I ought to have told you at the outset of our conversation that, confident in the care with which he surrounds me, he promised me this morning twenty years of further life. He mentioned no other period, and it would trouble him to think that I should accidentally have discovered his true opinion. I am sure you will pay kind regard to my wishes on this point."

Mrs. Herriot laid down her two guineas, and departed.

It had been a short game of chess, ending—as usual—in victory for the Little White Lady.

As Sir James sat heavily down at his table, and

laid a blank sheet of paper on the blotter, he
realized how short had been the game, how complete the victory.

It almost savoured of Fool's Mate!

CHAPTER XXXII

"I WILL NEVER FAIL YOUR TRUST"

DICK'S condition of mind as he entered the drawing-room and saw Mrs. Herriot awaiting him in her usual seat behind the little table, defied analysis.

He felt as a schoolboy feels when summoned into the presence of the Head Master, knowing that a wise reproof awaits him, yet thankful that his principal delinquency, which would have merited severe chastisement, and probably expulsion, is undiscovered.

The previous night, he had so lived in the happenings of thirty-five years before, that he had seemed to be carrying the shrinking, frightened little bride up the stairs in his strong young arms; and so eager had been his desire to protect and comfort her, to succeed where other men had shamefully failed—that it had seemed quite natural to stand with his arms still wrapped about her, and put his question once again.

But now, in her calm grace and dignity, she was very much Mrs. Herriot of Park Lane; her silvery hair mildly rebuked his youthful audacity; her

374

supposed need of him no longer seemed to justify the magnitude of that which he had asked of her.

She greeted him in silence, putting her hand into his with a smile which searched his soul; and, though silence was constantly her way of expressing much, it now added greatly to Dick's perturbation.

As he sat down, he hurried his confusion into speech.

"Shall it be chess?" he said. "I must not let you talk too much to-night. It is long since we had a game. Perhaps I should win! I always think perhaps I shall win, until you beat me again. And even then I say to myself: 'I believe I shall win next time!' I suppose the only way to attain to ultimate victory is never to admit that you are completely beaten. Even in Elba, Napoleon scanned the horizon, and I am not in Elba yet."

"No," she said. "Not chess to-night, Dick. An explanation and a decision lie before us. I have perforce kept you so long awaiting it, that I feel I owe you the decision at once; yet I must preface it with the explanation. Lean back in your chair, dear boy, and on no account interrupt me while I try to say, honestly and clearly, that which has to be said.

"Three weeks ago you took me completely by surprise by suddenly asking me to marry you. I suppose no woman was ever more amazed than I, at such a proposal, from a young man whom I had come to regard almost as a son. Yet the reasons you gave for making it, all did credit to your unselfish devotion; also, I must admit you pleaded your cause well, and almost justified an apparently impossible proposition."

Mrs. Herriot paused. A little thread of flame was darting fitfully up the chimney of the lamp. Bending forward she carefully adjusted the wick.

Dick kept his jaw firmly set in determined silence. The least he could do was to pay careful regard to her express request that he should not interrupt. It also delivered him from the difficulty of feeling it necessary to speak, without having the faintest idea what to say.

The lamp having been gently reminded to curb its darting impetuosity, and the soft wings of her shawl folded more closely around her, Mrs. Herriot resumed her explanation.

"When a woman receives an offer of marriage, her first instinctive thought is of herself. I challenge any woman to deny this. The fact of a man seeking her in marriage is so intimately personal a thing, that the first instinctive thought, even of the most unselfish, must be of self. 'Do I love him? Does he really love me?' Or if—as in our case—the actual romance of love does not come in: 'For what reason does he desire marriage with me? Will life with him mean happiness?' Then, 'What will my friends think of the match?' And, finally, the inevitable, 'What will people say?'

"On that evening, three weeks ago, when you

made your proposal, my young doctor, I admit my first thoughts were mainly of myself. Astonishment, alarm, and indignation swept over me in quickly succeeding gusts. But when I realized exactly what you intended to convey by your offer, and the chivalrous devotion it implied, I felt the injustice of my first emotions, and I trust I answered you with tenderness and with gratitude. Yet my thoughts were all of myself; of how unheard of, such a step would be for me; of what my friends would think if they knew such a thing had been even suggested; of the nine days' wonder to my little world if I, at my age, married again—and married so young a man. Looking back upon that evening, I realize that all my thoughts, while you were present, centred in myself.

"But—after your departure—when I was left alone—my whole point of view was suddenly readjusted. Self stepped into the background, as self should always do, when important matters are at stake. I suddenly realized what a marriage with me would mean to you—to your whole future career.

"I had not then told you of Alexander Herriot's will, but it had been often in my own mind, because I so greatly regretted that its terms absolutely prevented me from doing that which I already desired to do: namely, to adopt you as a son, and to leave you so well off that you would not only be set free from the drudgery entailed by the necessity of making a living, and have ample time to continue your studies with a view to specializing in one branch of your profession, but also have the capital with which to launch your schemes for the betterment of so many poor suffering people. This seemed to me a most noble use to which to put the Herriot money; yet, alas, I possessed no control over the capital, and, having during all these years had no one for whom to save, had always expended my full income, only putting by sufficient to leave Ellen an annuity, and substantial legacies to Giles and to the rest of my household.

"In thinking over your proposal, I saw at once, dear boy, that to go through the ceremony of marriage with you—for I, of course, understood that this was all your suggestion meant—would give me immediate right to bequeath the whole capital to whom I would. Instead of passing into the coffers of an already over-wealthy institution, the Herriot money could, without defrauding anybody, be used in the splendid way in which I know you would use it.

"The end appeared to justify the means. The enormous gain for you, seemed worth the misunderstanding, the criticism, the possible ridicule to which I should undoubtedly lay myself open."

Mrs. Herriot paused and, looking across at Dick, seemed to allow, even to invite, a comment.

Twice Dick essayed to speak. His throat contracted; his mouth was dry.

At length he said: "You—you put it all on the

question of money. You don't seem to take into consideration my—er—what I——"

He broke off. His eyes fell before the gentle inquiry of her look.

"My dear boy, I remember all you said, perfectly. Of course there was no suggestion of any idea of pecuniary benefit, in the beautiful tender things you said to me on that evening. But cannot you see that I could never have even considered the question, if my own comfort in having you near me, always at hand with the right to tend and care for me, had been the main issue involved? No woman of my age could feel herself justified in accepting such a sacrifice from a young man on the very threshold of life."

"It would not have been a sacrifice," said Dick, huskily—misery in his eyes. "It would have been a privilege."

Mrs. Herriot ignored the interruption. Her pause had not been intended to call it forth.

"But, day by day, during the past three weeks, I have been realizing more and more clearly the immense difference to your whole life—to your future career—which would result from the possession of a fixed income, and of a substantial capital. You have done so much for me, that I feel I could bring myself to do this—even this—for you, if I were sure that I am not likely to live many months longer. But if I am to live through another year; or, as Sir James Montford says, two years, possibly three, I cannot feel that it would be right,

for any consideration whatever, that I should
consent to lay upon your young manhood the intolerable bond and burden of a merely nominal
marriage. Do you think it possible, Dick, that
Sir James was wrong, and that I am not likely to
live through another whole year?"

She watched him anxiously, as she put the
question. In her mind was Sir James Montford's
statement, that any doctor would know that to
tell a patient she had only six months to live would
inevitably hasten the disaster which it should be
his business to avert. She was putting Dick's
devotion through a crucial test. Would it stand
the test, or no?

His head had dropped into his hands some time
before—just after she ignored his last comment.

At her question, he slowly lifted a haggard face
and looked into her eyes.

"Sir James Montford is known to be one of the
best authorities on the heart, in London," he said.
"His words to me—repeated several times—were
exactly what I told you. For my own part, as
I have said before, if care can do it, I shall keep
you here as long as Sir James said, and longer."

His head dropped into his hands once more.
He did not see the rush of thankful tears which
filled his Little White Lady's eyes to overflowing.

Dick, little dreaming he was being tested, had
stood the test. However much his ambition
had led him astray; although his passion for
self-advancement had caused him to do her one

grievous wrong; he would not now sacrifice her to gain his end; he would lose the advantage for which he had planned, sooner than win it at any risk of cost to herself. His plot had seemed heartless; his deception of her, unworthy; but his devotion was genuine; his tender care of her would not fail.

She longed to put her arms about him, draw that haggard, troubled face to rest upon her bosom, tell him she knew all, and had long ago forgiven; and then, enfolding his shame and contrition within the shelter of her understanding love, reinstate him on the path of rectitude and honour.

Had Dick raised his eyes to hers once more, this must have happened. She could not have borne to see again that haunted look, as of a soul in despair, in those bright brown eyes, usually so gay and fearless.

But he did not lift his head; and the irresistible impulse of her tenderness passed.

Much had yet to be done before Dick would be ready to understand, to the full, a love which, knowing all, yet gave all, and forgave all; causing even his wrong-doing to "work together" for his eventual good.

The Little White Lady was planning to be a Divine Parable to her young doctor, who would have pushed aside the inspired page of the fifteenth chapter of Saint Luke, with a smile and a jest. Religion must be *lived*, if the mind of the agnostic is to learn to know its vitalizing power, and accept its eternal truth.

And the Living Parable, however much she longed to spare the wanderer pain, must adhere to the Divine order. Although the Father's love yearned out to him, unutterably, the son had to reach the point of voluntary confession, before he could be reinstated to full privilege in the home he had forsaken.

Mrs. Herriot looked at the broad shoulders, and the bowed head. Was he, even then, making up his mind to confession?

She waited, giving him time—giving him full opportunity. But Dick did not stir.

Then she wiped away her tears as silently as they had fallen, and nerved herself for that which must next be done.

"Dick," she said, "this long preamble brings us at last to my decision. I ought to tell you that, before making it, I paid a private visit this morning to a heart specialist."

Dick, starting, sat up, instantly alert and anxious.

"Whom did' you go to?" he asked, quickly. "You should not have done so, without telling me." Then, covering his anxiety with an attempt at banter: "I am offended, Mrs. Herriot. It was not etiquette."

"Just now we are not standing upon etiquette, my young doctor; and I doubt whether the full measure of twenty long years, would ever find us offended with each other.   To my thinking, offence has no possible place in a genuine friendship. The one pained always forestalls offence by the realization of non-intention to wound, on the part of the other.   Well, I would rather not tell you to whom I went, but I returned armed with the opinion of a man whom I fully trust, and whose verdict carries more weight with me than that of Sir James Montford."

"And it was——?"

"That he does not think me likely to live longer than another six months."

"Then all I can say," cried Dick, hotly, "is that if he told you so, he is not a man whose verdict need carry any weight.   Dismiss it from your mind as the haphazard conclusion of a bungler!"

"I think not, Dick.   I am inclined to consider it more correct than Sir James Montford's.   This being so, it has helped me to arrive at last at my decision."

Mrs. Herriot drew her Bible toward her, folded her hands and rested them upon it, as if the sense that it lay, in its entirety, beneath them gave her the required fortitude for her next sentence.   The large emeralds she wore on the third finger of her left hand, gleaming like green ocean pools in the soft radiance of the lamplight, almost covered the thin wedding-ring, placed upon that finger by Alexander Herriot, more than forty years before.

Dick's heart stood still on the threshold of the wonder, the surprise, the supreme responsibility of that which he suddenly realized Mrs. Herriot to be going to say.

She spoke very slowly, very deliberately. There was about her an air of sublime detachment from this world of change and transition, of sordid judgments, and mixed motives.

The soul of his Little White Lady seemed already about to spread its silver wings and leave him.

He listened as she spoke, awe and reverence in his eyes.

"For the sake of your future, my dearest boy; for the sake of your great work; for the sake of all that which I firmly believe you will eventually be and do for the glory of God and the good of mankind—I am willing to marry you, as soon as the matter can conveniently be arranged. I love you as a mother might love a very dear son. I am trusting you as a very dear son should be trusted by his mother."

Dick stood up.

For a few moments he was quite speechless.

Then he knelt down beside her and placed his right hand over both hers as they lay folded upon her Bible, thus covering the gleam of the emeralds, and the uncontrollable trembling of those frail little hands.

"My Little White Lady," he said, "I will never fail your trust—so help me God."

CHAPTER XXXIII

DICK COMES HOME

THEY sat together, as they had so often sat before, in the quiet drawing-room of the house in Park Lane—Dick and his Little White Lady. They had just finished an absorbing game of chess, in which, as usual, she had beaten him.

Outwardly there appeared to be no change in their relations.

Yet, on that afternoon, they had stood together in Marylebone Parish Church, in the presence of a few trusted friends; she had put her hand into his, and had heard him promise, with a depth of fervent earnestness in his voice, to love and to cherish her, "till death us do part."

There was a pathos, on this occasion, about that solemn sentence, known only, in its full significance, to the two who, at the Church's bidding, uttered it. They knew that unless death were going to part them soon, they would not be standing there to be united.

All necessary preliminaries had been easily and quickly arranged. There was no need for Dick to fulfil the clause in the will, concerning the taking of the Herriot name. All would so soon be his, that the making over to him of ten thousand pounds on the wedding-day would have been a needless formality.

"Shall you mind," the Little White Lady had asked, rather wistfully, "if, during the short time remaining to me, my friends continue to call me 'Mrs. Herriot'? I should find it somewhat difficult to accustom myself to anything else."

"You will always be 'Mrs. Herriot' to me," Dick had answered, gently. "Excepting for legal purposes, I do not see why you should be troubled with any other name."

He was eagerly anxious to make all as easy as possible for her.

As soon as the quiet service was over, he had brought her back to her own home—now his also; and, leaving her to rest undisturbed, had gone off on his usual rounds.

Between tea and dinner, by Mrs. Herriot's special request, her lawyer had waited upon her. Thus the first time she signed her new name, was in bequeathing the whole of her fortune—with the exception of a few legacies to her household un- conditionally to Dick Cameron. When all for- malities were completed and the will duly signed and witnessed, her mind was at rest.

So the evening of their wedding-day found them quietly playing chess; and if Dick's game was a little wilder than usual, Mrs. Herriot made no comment thereupon. She quietly mated him, marshalled the pieces in unbroken ranks once more, and saying: "A fresh chance, my young doctor, with a new game. Bend your whole mind upon the board. You are not in Elba yet!" moved forward the White King's pawn two squares.

Dick smiled, and conscientiously did his best.

At ten o'clock they packed away the chessmen, closed the board and placed the cedar-wood box upon it. Then Dick pushed aside the higher chair upon which he had been seated, drew forward the easy-chair usually his, and lying back, his hands clasped behind his head, let his eyes dwell tenderly upon the restful picture of his Little White Lady turning the leaves of her Bible, in the golden halo of her shaded lamp.

Presently she looked up, met his eyes, and smiled.

Dick returned the look. One of those long understanding smiles, from the first a feature of their friendship, passed between them.

In his buttonhole was the opening bud of a Rayon d'Or rose. As she looked into its golden heart, and then back into her young doctor's eyes, it vividly recalled that first interview in the Manor House at Dinglevale, when he had given her leave to speak, if she had anything of real importance to say; and she had said: "What a perfectly lovely golden rose!"

"Are you happy, dear boy?" she asked. "Are you quite content?"

"Very happy," he answered, "and very grateful to be so wonderfully trusted. I should be happier still, if I did not feel unworthy. I suppose no man on earth ever feels fully worthy of a really good woman's supreme trust."

He fell silent, and she made no comment. She did not protest against his sense of unworthiness; she did not question it. When his mind turned along that line of thought her silence always gave him opportunity to follow it up further, if he so desired. But Dick went no further.

Presently he pulled himself together with an effort.

"It is so wonderful to me," he said, "to sit here, knowing I am at home. All my life long, I have not really had a home."

"And during all these long years," said the Little White Lady, "my home has not had a master."

Dick coloured. "I am not that," he said.

"Dear boy, it is my wish that you should take your rightful place in our home. Are you pleased with your rooms?"

"Indeed, I am!" said Dick, warmly. "The new study was a great surprise, arranged so perfectly, with everything a fellow could need. How did you know all a man wants and likes in his own particular den?"

She smiled. "A little imagination is a useful thing."

"Imagination?" questioned Dick. "Surely this required something more practical."

"Imagination, correctly defined, is essentially practical. People too often define imagination as a gift for inventing the wildly improbable. Imagination is really the faculty which enables you to put yourself into circumstances which do not happen to have been your own, and to realize exactly how people would feel and act in those circumstances. An imaginative writer is by no means a writer of the impossible, or even of the improbable. Wild tales result only when the gift of imagination runs riot."

"I see. Well, a very perfectly controlled imagination was brought to bear upon the arranging of my study. By-and-by, when Graham has secured a third partner, and I am able to drop all the drudgery, I shall work there a great deal. I must write some theses and articles, and do a lot of reading, to pave the way for future developments."

"There will be no hurry, my young doctor," she said, softly; adding rather wistfully: "All the best of life lies before you."

"I know," he said. "Yes, I know. Thanks to you, there is no need for hurry."

After that they sat long in silence.

There was no need for hurry.

Dick broke the silence once. "It is nice not to be turning out," he said.

She looked up and smiled. Her thoughts had reached the same point, just at that moment.

Presently she bent over her Bible, once more turning the pages.

"I am going to keep you to your promise, Dick," she said. "Let us now read our evening psalm."

Dick produced at once the beautifully bound pocket Bible she had that morning given him.

He had known all along that this was coming! It was almost the only thing she had asked of him —to share with her the reading of her psalm, every night.

It seemed such a little thing for her to ask— she, who was giving him all.

He would do it willingly. He would do it with apparent appreciation and pleasure.

He remembered Alexander Herriot, who had shown no sympathy with the things which meant most to her. He remembered Alexander Ross, who had poured forth mocking blasphemy when the terrified little bride, of thirty-five years before, called Omnipotence to her aid over the open pages of her Bible.

She should realize the contrast now.

He leant toward the lamp, and began a hasty search for the Psalms. At first his little Bible appeared to contain nothing but Job and Jeremiah, but at last he chanced upon Proverbs; then, working backwards, found himself safely in the Psalms.

He glanced furtively at the Little White Lady, hoping she had not noticed how he floundered. But she seemed intent on her own page. He quickly moved the purple ribbon which had led him to Jeremiah. It should henceforth remain in the Psalms. He would not be caught again.

Then the Little White Lady looked up.

"The Ninetieth Psalm," she said; "and you shall read it to me, Dick. We will not read alternate verses. A change of voice spoils any passage, especially the lovely poetry of the Psalms. We will take it in turns to have the privilege of reading, or the delight of listening. To-night, I will listen, and you shall read. To-morrow, I will read, and you shall listen." She bent over the page, shading her face with her hand.

Dick had not bargained for this, but he did not demur. She should realize the contrast between himself and those who had disappointed and failed her.

He began nervously and in a great hurry, and arrived at the end of the second verse completely out of breath.

The Little White Lady looked up, quickly.

"Oh, Dick!" she said. "Forgive the interruption, but I must tell you before we go further: this verse with which the psalm opens is my favourite verse in the whole Bible. 'LORD, Thou hast been our Dwelling-place, in all generations.' I should like it put upon my tombstone. It is so deeply restful. It explains the past, it embraces the present, it gives absolute confidence for the future. Its matchless dignity, stability, and assurance are unsurpassed. And do you notice that it was written by Moses, of all people! I suppose no Bible character changed his earthly dwelling-place more often, or with more startling variety of surroundings. Born into a humble Hebrew home, in the land of Goshen; when only three months old, he was floating homeless on the broad river Nile, in a little ark of bulrushes. Found and adopted by a princess, his next dwelling-place was the palace of the Pharaohs. Grown to manhood, he had to flee from Egypt to the land of Midian, where we find him dwelling as a shepherd in the house of Reuel, the priest. There he was 'content to dwell,' though feeling himself indeed 'a stranger in a strange land.' By and by he received his commission to lead out his own people from their captivity in Egypt, to freedom in the Land of Promise. Then began forty years of desert wanderings, homeless, uncertain, ever travelling to and fro. And at last, death—alone on a mountain-top, within sight of the earthly Canaan, yet unable to pass in. Did ever human heart experience such vicissitudes? Yet this is the man who sang with sublime assurance: 'LORD, Thou hast been our Dwelling-place, in all generations.' Dick, I love that we should enter upon our home-life together, in this earthly dwelling-place, by reading 'the prayer of Moses, the man of God.' Begin again, and read it slowly, dear boy, so that our hearts may have leisure to respond to its pathos and its melody."

Dick had had time to regain his breath, and to have his voice well under control.

With an interest which surprised himself he read, slowly and clearly, the grand old words of inspired trust and confidence; his own mind, as he read, passing beneath the spell of their power and of their beauty.

"LORD, Thou hast been our Dwelling-place, in all generations.

"Before the mountains were brought forth, or ever Thou hadst formed the earth and the world, even from everlasting to everlasting, Thou art God.

"Thou turnest man to destruction; and sayest, Return, ye children of men.

"For a thousand years in Thy sight are but as yesterday when it is past, and as a watch in the night.

"Thou carriest them away as with a flood; they are as a sleep: in the morning they are like grass which groweth up.

"In the morning it flourisheth, and groweth up; in the evening it is cut down, and withereth.

"For we are consumed by Thine anger, and by Thy wrath are we troubled.

"Thou hast set our iniquities before Thee, our secret sins in the light of Thy countenance.

"For all our days are passed away in Thy wrath: we spend our years as a tale that is told.

"The days of our years are threescore years and ten; and if by reason of strength they be fourscore years, yet is their strength labour and sorrow; for it is soon cut off, and we fly away."

Suddenly Dick realized, as he read those solemn words, that this was the burial psalm. To-day was their wedding-day—his and his Little White Lady's—yet he was reading one of the psalms appointed for the burial service. His voice faltered and shook. "Soon cut off, and we fly away." He always thought of her as spreading soft wings, white as the wings of a dove, and flying away. "Soon cut off—Soon cut off." The words sounded as a knell in the quiet room.

He hastened on, to the brighter promise of the final verses.

"So teach us to number our days, that we may apply our hearts unto wisdom.

"Return, O LORD, how long? and let it repent Thee concerning Thy servants!

"O satisfy us early with Thy mercy; that we may rejoice and be glad all our days.

"Make us glad according to the days wherein Thou hast afflicted us, and the years wherein we have seen evil.

"Let Thy work appear unto Thy servants, and Thy glory unto their children.

"And let the beauty of the LORD our God be upon us; and establish Thou the work of our hands upon us; yea, the work of our hands establish Thou it."

Dick reached the end almost unexpectedly. His voice suddenly ceased.

Then, in the silence, his Little White Lady lifted her face, and Dick was amazed at its extraordinary radiance. She seemed completely unconscious of herself and of him; transported from all earthly surroundings.

In time he was to grow accustomed to this radiant detachment, always produced in her by the reading of the Word. But, on this first night, it arrested him, and he looked at her in wonder. Her face was a vivid exposition of the closing verse of the Psalm. "Let the beauty of the LORD our God be upon us."

Presently she began to speak—very softly and tenderly—commenting upon each verse; dwelling on the whole with loving, lingering touch.

Dick listened, spell-bound; his attention riveted not so much by that which she said, as by her manner of saying it. The keen delight in every thought; the vital, vivid belief in every truth.

Dick would have expected to be hopelessly bored by the exposition of a psalm.

He was not bored at all.

When at last she said: "And now, shall we pray?" Dick quietly knelt down beside the table, folded his arms upon it, and bowed his head upon them. Unconsciously he thus came within the halo of golden light shed by the shaded lamp.

The quiet voice beside him spoke words of reverent trust, of confidence and love.

Then, as his Little White Lady concluded, voicing her request in the closing words of the Psalm he had just read, Dick felt her soft hand laid gently upon his head in blessing.

"Let Thy work appear unto Thy servant, O LORD; establish Thou the work of his hands; yea, the whole future work of his hands—establish Thou it. Thus shall we be satisfied and made glad, and we shall rejoice indeed, during all the days to come."

Dick's face was grave as he rose, and stood silently beside the table. He hesitated, then made an effort.

"I wish it all meant more to me," he said, slowly. "You know, I can't honestly say it means anything at all."

"Never mind that, dear boy," she said. "The great facts remain unchanged, whether you believe them or not. We will pray about your work every evening. And now—it has been a long day —I suppose we had better ring for Ellen."

Dick walked over to the bell; then hesitated.

His Little White Lady was so good to him; she had done so much for him—she was so dear. He felt suddenly reluctant that the day should be over; rebellious at the fact that he must let her go.

"Could n't I carry up the chessmen?" he asked. "Why, I could carry you, and the Bible, with the chessmen and board thrown in!"

She smiled. "No, thank you, my young doctor. The lift is working to-night. And I think we will have Ellen. I do not want her to feel superseded, or to imagine herself deprived of any of her duties. Besides, I would rather we should say good-night where we have always hitherto said it."

Dick's eyes were mutinous.

"I hate handing you over to a stiff old dragon like Ellen," he said, "who marches you off and puts you to bed, as if she were snuffing out a candle! It will snuff out my light when you are gone," added Dick, as a romantic after-thought. He liked the simile. It was expressive, and poetic —of a sort, if he could contrive to put it more grammatically. "It will snuff out my light that you should go," he repeated, gloomily.

The Little White Lady did not speak. She smiled into his eyes, and pointed to the bell.

"Why should Ellen sleep in the room adjoining yours?" continued Dick. "She snores like a grampus! I heard her—twenty to the minute, regular—when I was sitting up with you last time you were ill. I don't think much imagination was brought to bear upon the arrangement which put me at the very further end of the passage! If I had Ellen's room, you could call me if you felt ill in the night. *I* don't snore."

"Thank you," said the Little White Lady, gently. "I do not wish to make any change. I am used to having Ellen close at hand; and her snoring never disturbs me. If I am asleep, I do not hear it; and if I am awake, I am glad to be sure that some one else is sleeping peacefully. Ring the bell, Dick."

Still Dick hesitated.

"Please ring the bell, Dick."

Dick rang the bell.

The Little White Lady rose, took up her Bible, and moving over to the hearth-rug stood beside him.

"Dear boy, it means so much to me to know you are at home beneath my roof, and need not go out to lonely, perhaps comfortless, rooms."

Ellen came in, with the usual glass of hot milk, also a syphon and a plate of sandwiches. Ellen was extraordinarily disguised by the fact that she had fastened a large rosette of white satin ribbon beneath her chin, with a black safety pin. She was so intensely conscious of this, that, as she entered, a wedding-favour seemed to advance into the room, with Ellen attached.

"Take up the chessmen, Ellen," said Mrs. Herriot. "I will have my milk upstairs to-night. You can ring up the lift, at once."

The favour, and Ellen, went out.

They looked at each other and smiled. Ellen's white satin bow had helped them.

Mrs. Herriot moved toward the door. Dick walked beside her. She slipped her Bible beneath her arm.

At the door she turned, putting both hands into his.

Dick raised them, and bending his head, kissed them each in turn, with quiet reverence, very tenderly.

"Good-night, my own Little White Lady," he whispered.

"Good-night, dear boy," she said.

She passed out on to the landing.

Ellen waited, a grim sentinel, beside the lift.

Dick, with his hand on the drawing-room door, stood watching.

Mrs. Herriot entered the lift; the brass gate clanged. The lift slowly mounted. The last thing Dick saw was Ellen's white bow, ascending.

Then he closed the door, and walked up the empty drawing-room.

He sat down in his own chair, drew the lamp close to him, and taking out his pocket Bible, read again the one verse in the psalm which had been passed over by his Little White Lady without comment.

It was the eighth.

"Thou hast set our iniquities before Thee; our secret sins in the light of Thy countenance."

CHAPTER XXXIV

THE MASTER OF THE HOUSE

ON the days which followed the announcement of the wedding in the *Times*, a good many letters arrived for Mrs. Herriot. Very few of them were seen by Dick.

Friends made appointments by telegram, and called.

She usually arranged to receive them at an hour when Dick would be out.

Whatever explanations had to be made, she made them, unsupported. In the evening he found her calm and placid as usual; her mind absolutely free for his interests. In reply to Dick's rather anxious inquiries, she merely said that she had had a very pleasant afternoon.

One day she told him that a few of her particular friends were coming to tea. She would like him to be in, if possible.

Dick turned up at tea-time, and found the drawing-room full of people.

It was somewhat of an ordeal for the young doctor. Mrs. Herriot, fully realizing this, watched him anxiously. But he faced it with a straight-

forward directness of bearing which made him at
once master of the situation, completely disarmed
criticism, and surprised and delighted Mrs. Herriot
herself.

There was no trace of the rather boyish manner
to which, in the intimacy always existing between
them, she had grown accustomed. He appeared
amongst her guests as a man whose profession had
accustomed him to being the immediate centre of
attention, upon entering a room.

He very quietly and simply took his place as
master of the house, treated her guests with
charming courtesy and tact, and herself with a
deferential consideration and a watchful solicitude, which completely captivated those who had
been prepared seriously to question the wisdom
of the step she had so unexpectedly taken.

Lady Airth was present. She immediately
acclaimed Dick as the man who had saved the life
of her cousin, when everybody else had given her
up; said how charmed she was to meet him, and
promptly asked him to dinner.

This marked friendliness on the part of so
popular a person as the Countess of Airth and
Monteith, at once decided the few who still wav-
ered, as to their attitude toward Dick Cameron;
and the whole atmosphere expanded into un-
qualified cordiality.

Mrs. Herriot watched him with an added secret
anxiety. Would this evident appreciation on the
part of all her friends go to his head? Would he

26

be betrayed into any youthful gaucherie which would stamp him at once as not quite of her world.

But Dick did not lose his head. He received all flattering advances with the complete lack of self-consciousness, the quiet self-respect of a clever man of the world. He expanded somewhat to Lady Airth, simply because he genuinely liked her, and felt the magnetism of her charming personality. But to those who would have misconstrued response on his part to their effusions, he displayed a quiet reserve of manner which discouraged any attempt at patronage, while responding with perfect courtesy to their friendly advances.

To Mrs. Herriot, who knew her set well, and could gauge exactly what they would say afterwards, as distinct from what they were saying now —this afforded immense satisfaction and pleasure.

She had not before seen her young doctor in a social *entourage*, and his pranks at Dinglevale with the Fallen Idol and the Large Lady of the Manor had not given her cause to be very sanguine. Accordingly she was surprised and delighted.

When Lady Airth, as she took her leave, bent over her and whispered: "He is *quite* delightful! Had I a heart to lose, I should certainly leave it behind!" The Little White Lady blushed and smiled, and felt altogether proud and happy.

She had expected, personally, nothing but pain and annoyance from the step she had taken for Dick's sake. Yet here was unalloyed pleasure!

When Dick came up from speeding the last
parting guest—who chanced to be his particular
friend, Helen West—he found Mrs. Herriot standing at the window watching the sun as it set
behind the great trees in the park. He had been
showing Helen his study, and they had had a few
minutes of the bright *camaraderie*, which had
marked their friendship from the first. She had
said a few indefinite, but tactful and kindly things,
about his marriage; showing, if not comprehension,
at least a total absence of misunderstanding and
of any inclination to criticise or to condemn.

Feeling pleased with himself, and with Helen,
and gaily at peace with all the world, Dick ran
upstairs, entered the quiet drawing-room, so lately
filled with the babel of many voices, and saw his
Little White Lady, in the soft sunset glow, standing alone at the window.

Coming back and finding her thus, alone, having
the right to remain, when all the rest had gone;
realizing for the first time the position she had
given him in her house and toward her friends—
Dick was suddenly arrested by the fact of how
much she had done for him; the extraordinary
selflessness which had sacrificed everything for his
advancement and future benefit, the sweet mystery
of the tie between them.

His rapid step was checked. The gay remark
on his lips, remained unspoken. He advanced
slowly, in silence, and stood behind that little
fading figure, waiting in the sunset glow.

"Come here, Dick," she said, and held out her right hand without looking round. "I want you to enjoy with me a thing I have enjoyed for years. I never grow weary of viewing the sunset from this window."

Dick took the outstretched hand, held it closely in his own, and stood beside his Little White Lady.

"It varies according to the seasons," she said. "It almost seems to vary daily. But always there is glory—even glory in the stormy sky, when the sun says good-night through rifts in angry purple clouds. But the sunset I love best is at the close of a hot summer's day. For, as the sun sinks level with the distant spire of Christ Church, the whole park becomes wrapped in a mist of soft, shining gold. Golden clouds veil the foliage of the trees; clouds of gold hang over the parched grass; far and near is one bright shimmering, billowy sea of glory; from out of which rises the spire of Christ Church, a tall, graceful beacon, against the sunset sky. I used to watch it come and go—this misty sea of gold—wondering whence it came, and why it went. At length, one day, I understood. It was the dust of London—the hot, dry, weary dust of a hot, dry, weary day! But the sun, in stooping toward it, in shining through it, turned that parched dust to gold. Then I made it into a parable, and thus enjoyed it more."

"Tell me the parable," said Dick, and drew within his arm the hand he held.

Leaning on him, she answered: "There are in

life, so many sordid, common things, so much which falls below our vision of the beautiful, our ideal of the noble, our conception of the true. But love, in stooping to think kindly, to speak hopefully, even of these common, sordid things, changes them to pure gold."

She leaned her cheek against his coat sleeve. Her eyes still dwelt upon the sunset.

"Do you not think so, my young doctor?"

"I think *you* bring out the best in everybody," said Dick, rather huskily, "providing there is a 'best' to be brought out."

"There is always a 'best,'" said the Little White Lady. "But I was not thinking of myself."

CHAPTER XXXV

MARGARET INTERVENES

AT breakfast the next morning, Mrs. Herriot looked up from a letter she was reading.

"Margaret writes, asking whether I can see her at half-past four to-morrow. Business brings her to town, and she seems to wish to see me. I think I will say 'yes,' and give her tea."

Dick folded a letter he had just taken from its envelope. He was looking perplexed, and not altogether pleased.

"It will break into your rest, between your drive and tea," he said. "Why should not Margaret come at five?"

"No; she may be planning to catch an early train home. I can rest earlier, and be quite ready to receive her at half-past four. Dick, I have not seen Margaret since she lost her father last month. I think she may want to talk with me about her future plans. I hear the old home and the whole estate have been left to her, jointly with her mother, during the latter's lifetime; to Margaret, unconditionally, after her mother's death. This must somewhat complicate matters for her. I

406

doubt whether the excellent Eustace will wish to live at the Hall. He is the kind of man who prefers to dwell in a house of such a size as to enable him to make his voice heard all over it, if he so desires. He would feel somewhat lost at the Hall."

Dick laughed. "He is a domineering, sanctimonious beggar!" he said. "I can't imagine what Margaret was dreaming about, when she married him."

"Margaret *was* dreaming," said Mrs. Herriot. "That was the mischief. So many girls dream until after the wedding. Then comes the awakening. However, we must not allow ourselves too much latitude in criticism. Margaret is our friend, and absolutely loyal to her husband. In faithfulness to her, we must respect her loyalty. But I think, Dick, if you do not mind, I will see her alone. She may wish to talk things over privately with me."

For the moment Dick made no reply. He was thinking in perplexity, of the letter he had been reading when Mrs. Herriot looked up from her own and spoke.

Dick's was also from Margaret. It was very short, and curiously abrupt. It had neither beginning nor ending.

"I wish to see you alone," it ran, "before I see 'Mrs. Herriot.' I am asking her to receive me at half-past four. But I shall arrive soon after four o'clock. Please be in.

"MARGARET."

Dick was puzzled. He would have handed the note across to Mrs. Herriot, asking her opinion, but it occurred to him, as a possibility, that Margaret might have some news of importance to communicate and, fearing it might worry Mrs. Herriot, wished to ask his advice before seeing her. It was tiresome of Margaret, and seemed unnecessary. But he could not risk any possible shock or worry for his Little White Lady. A word with Margaret, beforehand, must be managed.

"I should like to come in to tea," he said, "Margaret is such an old friend of mine. Directly tea is over, I can go out, and leave you alone."

"Very well, dear boy," she said. "Of course, personally I prefer having you."

Dick chanced, the next day, to have a full afternoon. He tried to hasten his rounds, so as to be back in Park Lane at four o'clock. At the last he was unexpectedly delayed. As he came in sight of the house, Margaret's taxi was just moving off. Margaret herself was passing in at the open door. It closed behind her, before Dick could reach the steps.

He was vexed at this. He had intended meeting her in the hall and taking her straight to his study.

He let himself in with his latchkey, and ran quickly up the stairs.

He met Jarvis coming away from the drawing-room, having shown Margaret in.

"Mrs. Royston, sir," he said. "And she asked for you."

"All right," said Dick. "I was expecting her. She will stay to tea. But do not bring it until half-past four; and on no account let Mrs. Herriot be disturbed before that time. If she sends down to know whether Mrs. Royston has arrived, send up word that I am with her."

His heart was light. He felt unaccountably happy just then. He loved doing the honours in his Little White Lady's beautiful house. He rather enjoyed receiving Margaret there. And Margaret, of all people, would understand what wonderful possibilities the future now held for him.

He opened the door and went in.

Margaret Royston stood in the centre of the room. The simple mourning she wore, added to the extreme distinction of her appearance. Her face, always lovely, but inclined, as Dick had seen it hitherto, to be spoiled by a weary, listless expression, was now almost startling in its beauty, as she turned at his entrance and faced him.

There was nothing listless about Margaret now. Her face was pale certainly—pale as white marble; but it was marble on fire!

"Hullo!" said Dick. "This *is* jolly!'

He shut the door, came forward, and, with a smile of genuine pleasure, held out his hand to Margaret.

Margaret looked at him—looked at his outstretched hand; then deliberately put hers behind her.

"I shall never shake hands with you, again," she said.

Staring at Margaret in bewildered astonishment, Dick put his hands into his pockets.

There is no harder blow to pride than to have a proffered hand refused. There is no way of severing a friendship more trenchant and complete.

Dick walked over to the fireplace; then turned on the rug and faced the old friend who had dealt him this blow.

"Margaret," he said, "what's up?"

"Nothing's *up*," she said. "But you're *down* —down as low, in my estimation, as a man can fall. You have married Mrs. Herriot for her money. Oh, you needn't trouble to deny it! I know all about the Herriot will. Mother remembered the case, and the main details of the tragedy which followed. But to make sure— when news reached us of this amazing marriage— she looked it up in the old files of the *Times*. And there we found it all complete. There was no need for *us* to go to Somerset House and get the information for a shilling. Ah, you wonder how I know of that transaction! A cousin of Eustace's, who had seen you at Dinglevale, happened to be there, examining a document connected with a case he was defending. He heard you ask for

Alexander Herriot's will, and saw you taking surreptitious notes. He chanced to be staying with us when we saw the announcement of the marriage in the *Times*. This is how I know. I might very well have guessed your motive, remembering your scorn of love and your constant declaration that love and ambition could not go hand in hand. But there was no need to guess. I had proof positive. Oh, Dick! How could you do it? That saint! That perfect saint of sweetness, gentleness, and goodness! Had you no regard for her white hair? Had you no respect for her social position, for the large circle of friends who held her in highest esteem—that you must sacrifice her, of all people, on the altar of your ambition, making her a laughing-stock to the whole world?"

Margaret paused abruptly. Dick's face had become white and hard, at the opening words of her indictment. It had turned ashen when she mentioned Somerset House. But before the sudden fury in his eyes at her last words, even her brave and angry spirit momentarily quailed.

His jaw had been set in dogged determined silence, as he calmly faced her. It was as if the Capo di Monte Napoleon had at last risen from his chair and stood confronting her upon the hearth-rug.

But now he spoke—in a voice more terrible because its tones were low and intensely restrained.

"If you say one word of all this to *her*, or

mention her money or the will," he said, "I'll kill you!"

The threat revived Margaret's waning courage. She laughed.

"I dare say you will," she said. "But you're welcome to kill me, so long as you don't harm her. You are already a murderer of love, of loyalty, and of honour; of all tender respect; of all one's belief in disinterested devotion. To kill one's body would be the lesser crime. However, I have not come here to say a word which could add to *her* trouble, so you need not be afraid. I have come to tell you that I know you for what you are, and to let you know what I think of you, and what any honest man or woman, knowing the facts, would think of you. And I have come to satisfy myself, if possible, as to how you are treating her, and to find out what measures you took to coerce her into this marriage. I dare say you think it is no concern of mine. But I love her, Dick Cameron; and love—*true* love—gives rights, which self-seeking ambition dare not gainsay. I spent three happy weeks, at Dinglevale, with your Little White Lady. I learnt to know her, as *you* will never know her. I learnt to trust her and to believe in her with my whole soul. I learnt to love her, as I love no other woman upon the face of this earth. I should have been craven to have stayed away without moving hand or foot to help her if she needed help; without confronting the man who had sacrificed her upon the altar of his selfish, mercenary ambition, in order to tell him what I think of him!"

Margaret paused, not for want of words, but for lack of breath.

A little gleam of angry amusement passed into Dick's hard eyes.

"I don't care one single, solitary damn what you think of me," he said.

The scornful smile on his white face maddened Margaret.

"I don't suppose you do!" she cried. "I dare say you are proud of your visit to Somerset House——"

The door opened quietly, and the Little White Lady came in.

She realized at once the tense atmosphere of conflict in the room. She glanced at the two angry young faces, at the two tall figures confronting one another in a fury of mental strife.

She turned and slowly closed the door, giving them time to loose their eyes from one another, and fully to realize her presence. Then she came forward, smiling.

"Dear Margaret," she said, "am I late, or are you early? I was timing myself to be down well before the half hour. However, Dick was here; so you have not been alone. Ring for the tea, Dick. If Margaret has had an afternoon of shopping, she will be in need of a cup of tea. Now come and sit beside me, Margaret. Dear child, in spite of the strain and sorrow through which you have passed, you are looking far stronger than when I saw you last."

At the first sound of her voice, Dick had regained immediate control of himself. He rang the bell; then came forward, moved her table up to the sofa, and arranged the cushions behind her.

As he did so she leaned back, looking up into his face, and there was in her eyes such a tenderness of deep affection, that Dick's sore heart bounded, with a sudden rush of relief and gratitude.

"Has it been a good afternoon, dear?" she asked, speaking in low tones, yet distinctly audible to Margaret.

"Full up," he said, "and quick work to get through, because I wanted to be home early."

"Then you also will be glad of tea. And I have been resting; and no amount of work makes one long for a reviving cup of tea so much as does an afternoon siesta. So we are all three glad that here comes the tea! Draw up your chair to the table, Dick. We are such a cosy little party, that everything is within reach."

It took all Mrs. Herriot's tact, and an inexhaustible flow of charming conversation, to justify "cosy" as in any sense an adjective descriptive of that little party.

Margaret and Dick both addressed remarks to her, but neither spoke a word to the other. Dick did not once look in Margaret's direction. Margaret scarcely took her eyes off Dick, and a growing look of amazement and dismay was in them, as she noted the perfect understanding evidently existing between him and his Little White Lady; his tender deference to her; her affectionate pride in him.

In this calm atmosphere of refined domesticity, her own tempestuous outburst now seemed an absurd nightmare, the causeless ravings of a deranged mentality. Yet the facts—the facts which had goaded her to this visit—still remained. No explanation exonerating Dick, could possibly be forthcoming.

Presently, in obedience to a look from Mrs. Herriot, Dick rose.

"I am afraid I must be off," he said. "I have heaps of writing to get through before dinner." He bent over the head of the sofa. "You will send for me if you want me?" I shall be down-stairs in the study."

Then he bowed, gravely, to a tall vase of flowers just beyond Margaret's troubled face, and went quickly out.

The Little White Lady sent a smile after him, a smile which lingered on her lips after the quick closing of the door.

Then she folded her white shawl about her, settled herself into the cushions, and turned to Margaret.

"Now—we can talk," she said.

CHAPTER XXXVI

"I TRUST YOU"

"NOW we can talk," said Mrs. Herriot, as the door closed behind Dick. "And how much we have to say. It made us all rather shy at tea. I half wanted Dick to keep away this afternoon, letting me have you alone. But he was anxious to be back for tea. He is very faithful to the old friendship, Margaret. It has that tenacious hold upon his mind and heart which the close companionships of our extreme youth always retain. I trust you will let it permanently abide as an influence for good over our dear Dick. But now you have much to tell me. How is your mother? What are the home plans? Ah, how deeply I have felt for you during these sad weeks. I know the blank, when a dear father is taken. Tell me all you can."

Margaret did so, and began to think that her visit—excepting for her outburst to Dick—was going to result in nothing save a talk about her own affairs.

Then suddenly, when she least expected it, Mrs. Herriot said: "Was it a great surprise to you, Margaret?"

Margaret did not pretend to misunderstand.

"A tremendous surprise," she said.

"I do not wonder at that," remarked Mrs. Herriot, gently. "And I feel I owe you more of an explanation than I should accord to anybody else, because I know your very true love for Dick, dating back to so dear a childish friendship, and subsequently based upon a real interest in his spiritual development. Will you listen, dear Margaret, and try to understand, while I explain to you the situation, and my reason for taking the important step, which has no doubt occasioned considerable comment and criticism amongst my friends?

"Dick stands to me in the position of a very dear and most completely trusted son. He treats me with the tender respect and reverence with which a young man of his age, and fine, manly character, would treat his mother. There is nothing more than that in the tie between us. Yet, after much careful and prayerful consideration, I went through the ceremony of marriage with him, in order to be able, legally, to fulfil that which had long been my earnest wish and desire—to leave him my whole fortune; thus enabling him, unhampered by the necessity of earning his own living, to be free to devote himself to his profession along the highest lines, and eventually to develop plans and schemes which will, I believe, place him in the very front rank of mental specialists, and result in much

27

benefit to sufferers from nervous and mental disorders.

"Owing to the peculiar terms of my late husband's will—intended to affect me in my younger days, but having equal force now—I could only do this by contracting a second marriage. If I died a widow, I had absolutely no control over my capital!

"Such a way out of the difficulty, as a marriage with Dick, would, I admit, never have occurred to me, but our dear boy amazed me one day by earnestly asking me to marry him, in order that he might be constantly near me during the short time which is likely to remain to me of earthly life; prolonging it, if possible, by his skill and devoted care.

"I need hardly tell you that I should not have accepted so great a sacrifice from him for such a reason. But his proposal made clear to me this other possibility —a matter of far greater importance than my own comfort and pleasure in his presence in my home. Thus, after much careful consideration, I felt justified in taking the step. Before doing so, however, I ascertained that, in the opinion of a medical man in whose judgment I place implicit reliance, I am not likely to live many months longer. So this nominal marriage with me will not stand in the way of Dick's future happiness, or have time to grow into a burden. Meanwhile, I think it is a real joy to him to have a home of his own; and no words can express what he is to me, in his perfect care and thoughtful solicitude."

Margaret's lips were trembling. "But Dick knew——" she said, and stopped.

"About my husband's will? Oh yes, of course Dick knew! I told him myself, in fullest detail, not only about the will, but the complete history of the tragedy it brought into my life. He was deeply moved, and, though it increased his desire to shelter, with a real manly tenderness, the life which had been so sorely tried and disillusioned, he practically withdrew his proposal, asking me not to refer to it again. But by that time my mind was so fully set upon securing for him the reversion of my capital, that I could not bring myself to give it up. By the way, Margaret, what did I hear you saying to Dick, as I entered the room just now, about a visit to Somerset House?"

Margaret was too much taken aback by the suddenness of the question, to make any attempt at parrying it.

"I told Dick that he had been seen at Somerset House examining Mr. Herriot's will, and making notes of its contents."

"Of course. He went there in order to make sure of its exact terms. In fact his little paper of notes is here. I happen to have put it, for safety, into my Bible."

With unruffled serenity of manner, Mrs. Herriot drew her Bible toward her, opened it, found the folded sheet of note-paper—that sheet which had torn her own heart so cruelly; unfolded it, with a gentle smile of affectionate complacency, and held it so that Margaret could see, in Dick's neat hand-writing: *"Notes of the Herriot Will."* Then she replaced it, and closed the book.

Margaret sat speechless.

The Little White Lady folded the soft wings of her shawl about her, and leaned back amongst her cushions.

"One thing I must beg of you, dear Margaret," she said. "Do not mention to Dick that I have shown you this paper; in fact, do not allude at all to the will, or to the pecuniary benefits which will accrue to him from his marriage with me. It is a subject upon which he is, as you may suppose, very sensitive. When I gave him my decision, I was explaining very fully my feeling with regard to what it would mean to his future, and I shall never forget the despairing tones in which he said: 'You put it all on the question of money!' So can I rely upon you to avoid the subject with him; and not to allow this story of his visit to Somerset House to go any further?"

"I promise," said Margaret.

Mrs. Herriot leaned still further back, against the cushions. Her hand stole to the place where the warning stab was apt to make itself felt.

"You are tired," said Margaret. "I have tired you! I must go." The grey shadow on the delicate face, alarmed her. "Shall I call Ellen, or send for Dick?"

"No, no!" whispered Mrs. Herriot. "Dick must not suspect any possible cause of fatigue in our conversation. He so quickly grows anxious over me, and never allows a thing which has tired me, to happen again. Oh, Margaret, no words can say how perfect our dear boy is to me! Will you always remember that I told you this? If, when I am gone, he ever comes to you in distress of mind, will you tell him I told you that his perfect care of me and goodness to me, since the hour when he promised to love and to cherish, have been beyond all words? Will you tell him this, Margaret?"

"I will," said Margaret, "if—if he ever turns to me."

She could not keep back her tears, as she knelt beside the sofa. She took the frail hands in hers, and laid her cheek against them.

"Mrs. Cameron," she said— "I must call you so, just once, because in my wicked heart I swore I never would—I want to confess before I go. My life with Eustace has made me so narrow and hard. I love you, and I love Dick—more than all else in this world; yet, when I heard the news, I wronged Dick in my heart. Can you forgive me?"

"My child," said the Little White Lady, "love can forgive all wrongs, intentional or unintended. The only unforgivable thing is a love which calls itself love, yet fails to forgive. Now we will both forget what you have just said. The one thing in which we must never fail is in our absolute loyalty to our—to our husbands. Good-bye, Margaret. God's blessing go with you; and remember—I trust you." .

"I will remember," whispered Margaret, her lips against the shining golden circle, guarded by the three emeralds—the wedding-ring which bound Dick to his Little White Lady. "I will remember, and I will not fail."

"I trust you to be good to him always," said the voice she loved, again; and with those words for ever in her heart, Margaret went out.

CHAPTER XXXVII

DICK WIELDS THE LASH

MEANWHILE Dick walked restlessly to and fro in his study.

He lighted a new meerschaum he was colouring, then discarded it for his old briar, and bit hard into the stem.

He sat down at his table, trying to correct the proof of an article on which a good deal depended. Printers awaited it. It must catch that evening's post. Yet, after a few minutes of attempted concentration, he pushed it away, leapt up, and resumed his restless pacing to and fro.

What was going on in the drawing-room upstairs?

A weaker nature would have remained there, ignoring Mrs. Herriot's signal to depart; afterwards pleading obtuseness, or the interest of Margaret's presence. But Dick had the courage of genuine strength. Yet, once below, intolerable suspense seized upon him.

He trusted both the women who were now, no doubt, discussing the situation.

Margaret, worse luck, was in possession of his

shameful secret. But she would not wilfully betray him to Mrs. Herriot.

Margaret evidently had a fierce temper when thoroughly aroused. No wish to spare *him* would enter into her calculations. But Margaret had said: "I have not come here to say a word which could add to *her* trouble." So consideration for Mrs. Herriot would keep her silent. But—supposing an allusion to the scene at Somerset House slipped out, accidentally?

Dick now knew—he had been told in unmistakable language—what a woman such as Margaret thought—what any outsider would think—of his conduct. Somewhere at the back of his mind he was aware that a horror of shame awaited him, when he should have leisure to think over that conversation.

But just now he could think of nothing save the dread of disillusion and pain for his Little White Lady; the wrecking of her content with him; the spoiling of the happiness of their peaceful home-life. So few months remained in which his careful devotion could in some measure repay all she had done for him. And now a chance word might spoil it all.

He wished he had throttled Margaret, before Mrs. Herriot came in.

No, that would not have mended matters.

He wished he had taken her forcibly downstairs, shoved her into a taxi, given the man a couple of sovereigns, and told him to drive to

Hazelmoor, never stopping until he got there. Would two sovereigns have been enough?

Dick began calculating the mileage, in order to decide the point; then laid down his pipe on the mantelpiece, and laughed bitterly at his own mental perturbation.

Yet—so much was at stake! So much was at stake!

What would she say, if she knew of that visit to Somerset House before his proposal—before his protestations of devotion, which she had described as "chivalrous"? He knew what Margaret, a mere outsider, had said. He had had a sample of the merciless judgment which had given him no quarter, made no allowance for mixed motives, or for possible regrets.

If this was the world's judgment, the world's sweeping condemnation, what might not the woman he had thus wronged, say? What would not that gentle, trusting heart suffer? He did not mind so much what she would *say*. It broke him to think what she would *suffer*.

He thrust his hands deep into his pockets, and walked up and down the room, his chin sunk upon his breast, his brows bent, his jaw set. It was as if the Capo di Monte Napoleon had not only arisen from his chair, but now paced the floor in helpless captive strength.

Sombre fury against Margaret arose in his breast.

He remembered catching her, years ago, just

in time to save her from falling off the high bough
of a tree they had climbed together.

He wished he had let her fall!

She might have broken her neck!

Then she could not have come travelling up to
town, bent on wrecking the happiness of himself
and his Little White Lady.

A gentle knock at the door.

"Come in!" he called; and his own voice sounded
hard and tragic, beyond recognition.

He turned to the mantelpiece and fumbled for
his pipe, his eyes upon the door.

He hardly knew what it was he dreaded.

Ellen's knock was not so gentle. It was curt
and knuckly, though respectful.

The door opened, and Margaret stepped in,
closing it behind her.

His anger against her flamed more fiercely.
The very revulsion of feeling caused by his relief,
accentuated the fact that she had contrived to
give him yet another fright.

Margaret came bravely up to him. Her sad
eyes were almost on a level with his own.

If looks could slay, Margaret would not have
left that room alive. But her consciousness of his
anger was drowned in the depths of her own
remorse.

"Dick," she said, "I have come to ask you to
forgive me. I know now that I wronged you
shamefully; I misjudged you cruelly. You are

perfect to her, and you have been true to yourself. It is I who imagined wrong, where no wrong was. Oh, Dick! Will you forgive me?"

Dick set his teeth.

"No," he said, "I will never forgive you."

He saw Margaret flinch and whiten, as if each word were the bite of a lash.

The sight relieved his strained nerves. Margaret should suffer as he had suffered, if that were possible.

"Oh, Dick," she pleaded, "can't you—can't you—" in her helplessness she fell back upon the trite old saying—"Can't you forgive and forget?"

The demon of rage in Dick grinned delightedly. Here was a fine opening for a fresh application of the lash. It was like a foolish move on the part of an opponent in a game of chess. He took instant advantage of it.

"Certainly I can forget," he said. "From this hour, I shall wipe you, and your words, and your suspicions, and your odious insinuations, clean out of my mind. But—if by any chance I ever *do* remember—I shall not forgive."

Margaret moved toward the door.

Half-way there she turned and came back.

"Dick, may I explain? It happened because I have cared so deeply, I have cared for so long, about—about your spiritual life. I have prayed so earnestly that you might be great, and good, and do right in all things. I have prayed that faith in the beliefs you have given up, might come

back. I think I was so angry when I thought—
what I did—because of all my prayers——"

Dick burst into harsh laughter.

"Then heaven defend me from your prayers!"
he said, "and from all the canting hypocrites who
say: 'Charity suffereth long and is kind; Charity
thinketh no evil,' and then take away a man's
character and ruin his life, without giving him a
chance to defend himself. If the God you believe
in, treated you as you treat others, you'd have
small chance of sitting on damp clouds, twanging
Jews' harps throughout eternity!"

He laughed again. In that moment his soul
felt at one with the blasphemous soul of Alec Ross.
Nothing seemed too bad to think or to say. He
turned to the mantelpiece, and took up his pipe.

Hell seemed to open at Margaret's feet. A great
gulf yawned between her and Dick; between Dick
and heaven; and the gulf was of her own making.

In her despair she made a desperate move.

"Oh, Dick," she said, "have pity upon me and
forgive me. I am so miserable and brokenhearted."

She came close to him, and laid her hand upon
his shoulder.

"Dick, it was because I love you, that I was so
angry. It was a case, all over again, of a broken
halo, and of a fallen idol. Ever since we were
boy and girl together, I had always thought there
was no one like you. I had shrined you in my
heart and kept you there. Oh, Dick, I am not
afraid to tell you, because I am absolutely loyal to

Eustace, and you are absolutely loyal to your—
to your—your Little White Lady. But my
blindness and misery and folly all came from the
fact that I love you—Dick, I love you."

Then indeed had poor Margaret put the lash
into the relentless hands of the Capo di Monte
Napoleon.

Dick took his pipe from between his teeth,
turned slowly and looked her up and down with
cold, scornful scrutiny; took in her sweet loveliness,
her noble stature, her womanly grace, her humble-
ness, her overwhelming remorse.

Then he walked to the door and opened it.

"Will you oblige me," he said, "by leaving my
wife's house?"

Margaret stood for one moment as if turned to
stone—petrified by horror and amazement.

Then the queenliness which bides its time somewhere in every true woman's nature, stepped
forward to the rescue.

"Oh, my dear Dick!" she said. "I have indeed
put it into your power to deal me a blow which has
taken the form of a quite insufferable insult. But
you must remember—if ever your power to forget
proves less adamant than your determination not
to forgive—that we are now quits, for you have
been even more cruelly unjust to me than I was
to you."

She paused and regarded him calmly, as he
stood holding the door open that she might pass
out.

She smiled, and that cold, proud smile won reluctant admiration from the man at whom it was directed.

"But now, considering the probable presence of Jarvis in the hall, I must ask you to escort me from Mrs. Cameron's house, with the same courtesy as you would show to any other woman whom she honours with her friendship."

Margaret swept from the room.

Dick walked beside her.

"A taxi for Mrs. Royston, Albert," he said to the man in the hall.

He stood with her on the step, while a taxi which had passed was making up its mind to turn and come back, in response to the shrill summons of Albert's whistle.

"Good-bye," said Dick, as the taxi drew up, and Albert opened the door. "I hope you will catch your train."

"Good-bye," she responded, bravely. "There are plenty of trains at this time of day."

She entered the taxi. "Tell him Charing Cross, please," she said to the footman; then, leaning forward, smiled a farewell to Dick Cameron.

The taxi-driver tinged down the indicator.

Suddenly Dick ran down the steps.

He put his head in at the window.

"Margaret," he said. "I beg your pardon. Now we are quits. We will both forget, even if we can neither of us forgive."

"We will, both, forget *and* forgive," said Margaret.

"All right!" said Dick. "Shake hands on it, Margaret."

He thrust his right arm in at the window.

Her hesitation only lasted long enough for her to hear a gentle voice whisper: "I trust you to be good to him always."

Then she put her hand into Dick's.

The taxi sped swiftly on its way.

Dick went back into the house, into his own room, and shut the door.

"Phew! What a scene!"

Yet only two words of it all stood out, in the background of his mental vision; and those two words had been uttered by himself: "*My wife.*"

He had ventured to call his Little White Lady that—yet the earth had not opened and swallowed him up!

A strange new sense stirred in his heart; a joy of manly pride in the fact that she was his to protect and guard, his to shield and defend. Moreover, he owed her fidelity of thought, of word, and of act. No younger woman's charms could make him swerve for one instant from that fidelity.

This new aspect in which he could be loyal to her was balm to the wound inflicted on his pride by the fact that another knew of his former disloyalty.

He put all unpleasant memories of the past into

the background; and dwelt deliberately on the beautiful present, which was still his.

Obviously Margaret had told her nothing.

Yet—had she?

He must make sure at once.

He ran upstairs, two steps at a time, and entered the drawing-room.

CHAPTER XXXVIII

THE APOTHEOSIS OF THE EXCELLENT EUSTACE

M RS. HERRIOT was seated on the sofa, an open telegram in her hand.

"Dick," she said, "I was on the point of sending for you. Look! This has just come for Margaret. She left half an hour ago. It is from her mother, and says: 'Come home immediately.' What can we do?"

"There is nothing to do," said Dick, lightly. "Margaret is 'coming home' as 'immediately' as train can take her. I saw her into a taxi. I should think the excellent Eustace has a toothache. Shall I go down by 'special'?"

"Don't joke, Dick. It may mean serious sorrow for Margaret. Let us hope not."

Dick crumpled up the telegram, and made a shot at the waste-paper basket.

He had not come up to talk of Margaret.

He dropped on one knee beside the table, and laid his hand over the hand which wore his wedding-ring. He did not know how recently Margaret's lips had rested against it; how lately Margaret's tears had fallen upon it.

"You look so tired," he said. "Did Margaret say anything which worried you?"

"No," she answered. "Nothing which need have worried me. Naturally I felt grieved over her anxieties and sorrows."

Dick felt himself pursued by Margaret's sorrows —past, present, and impending. But he restrained all signs of impatience.

"Did any comment she made about us—you and me—trouble you at all?"

"I think she was inclined to misunderstand, as I suppose we must expect some of our friends to do. I felt we owed Margaret more of an explanation than we should feel it necessary to make to most people. So I made it, and put everything right."

"Easily?"

She smiled. What did he call "easily"?

"Quite easily, Dick."

He could not hold back a sigh of relief. No harm had been done.

The sweet sense of possession again stirred in his heart.

She was his; nobody should take her from him. Nobody! Nothing! Death should not take her from him. He would fight Death, day by day, hour by hour. Who was the fool who had told her she could only live six months? He knew his business—worse luck; but how dared he tell her!

His clasp on her hand tightened.

"I ought to be reading proof," he said; "but I

am going to stay with you. It is so perfect to be left by ourselves, when tiresome people like Margaret take themselves off, at last."

But she drew away her hand, and gave him a playful pat.

"You are wrong there, dear boy. Margaret is not tiresome. Few people are dearer to me than that very noble girl. Also, if my doctor exercised his usual wisdom, he would see that my extreme fatigue really requires absolute rest, and he would order me to dine upstairs. Shall we summon Ellen?"

Ellen was summoned, and Dick's proof caught the post. But he felt he had really had a surfeit of Margaret when, on tearing open a little note, with which Ellen, after beating a loud tattoo on his door, marched into his study, he read:

"The thought of Margaret's telegram still gives me anxiety. Will you send a reply-paid, asking whether she has reached home safely, and found all well?

"H. R. H."

Dick smiled. He was glad she had kept to the old initials.

He glanced at the clock. There was just time to get a wire through, and to receive a reply.

He wrote it, and handed it to Ellen.

"I wish she wouldn't worry herself about other people's bothers," he said. "Tell her I will send up the answer directly it comes. I say, Ellen! Fetch me at once if she wants me."

"I will, sir," said Ellen, emphatically, as she went out.

The answer arrived, while Dick was finishing a solitary dinner.

But he did not send it up to Mrs. Herriot's room. He sat staring at it, blankly, for a few seconds.

Then he took a half sheet from his note-book and wrote:

"Reply just come. Margaret reached home safely and is all right. Send for me if you need me. Sleep well. Good-night.   DICK."

He finished the contents of his plate, mechanically; then, declining anything more, rose and went to his study.

He stood beside the mantelpiece, where he had had his final fierce duel with Margaret, so short a time before; where he had flung at her so cruel an insult, in response to her piteous appeal for pardon.

For once his natural selfishness stood at bay— dumb, dismayed, at the blow which had fallen upon the woman who had been his playmate and friend.

Taking the telegram from his pocket, he read it through again. It was signed by the doctor whose urgent call had first sent him to Margaret in her hour of need.

It was very clear and unmistakable.

"The Rev. Eustace Royston in attempting to save a child was knocked down by a motor-car this afternoon and killed instantly. Mrs. Royston has returned.

"NORTON."

So the life-slayer, as Lady Airth had dubbed him, the man who disliked all children, considering them unnecessary incumbrances, had lost his own life in an attempt to save that of a little child.

Truly a man's instinct is sometimes nobler than his reason.

How many times friends would quote beneath their breath, in speaking of the excellent Eustace, Malcolm's tribute to the Thane of Cawdor: "Nothing in his life became him like the leaving it."

These thoughts lay vaguely at the back of Dick's mind; but his more defined feelings were for Margaret. Yet when, at length, his foremost idea crystallised itself into words, neither Margaret nor Eustace had place in the sentence.

"She must not know until to-morrow morning," he said; and, putting away the telegram, was soon deep in the study of a work on the treatment of neurasthenia, by a great German specialist.

But, in her widowed home, Margaret Royston wept with a passion of self-reproach, which her mother could not fathom; because, on that very afternoon, in her talk with Mrs. Herriot, she had allowed herself to say the first disloyal word which had ever passed her lips during all the years of her married life with Eustace.

CHAPTER XXXIX

STILL WATERS

A S calm succeeds storm, in nature, so in life, a time of peaceful quiet often follows hours of mental stress and strain. The sunshine of unclouded happiness, illumines each opening day; birds of bright promise sing; the bloom and blossom of fulfilled hopes, make fair and fragrant life's highway.

The weeks succeeding Margaret's stormy visit were happy, though uneventful, to Dick and his Little White Lady; uneventful, except for the ever-increasing interest of his work, which daily became a more direct preparation for the greater things to be accomplished in the future.

The news of Margaret's tragic bereavement, though gently broken by Dick on the following morning, came as a great shock and grief to Mrs. Herriot, emphasized by the fact that Margaret had been with her at the very time of the fatal accident.

Her wish to go to Margaret in her trouble was firmly overruled by Dick, who well knew that the intense power of sympathy—sympathy in its true meaning, "a feeling-with"—which was so strongly hers, wore out that failing heart more quickly than aught else.

Constant letters passed between them, however; and, though they were not shown to Dick, he was often given information as to how matters went with Margaret.

"They will close the Hall and go abroad, probably to Italy, for the winter," said Mrs. Herriot one evening, looking up from a letter of many sheets which had arrived by the late post; "Margaret and her mother together. I think it is a good plan, though I wish poor Mrs. Cray were a more cheerful companion for Margaret. It is so sad—a mother and daughter both widowed within the year. In the spring they will return, and Margaret writes quite hopefully of taking up life again in the old home of her childhood. It will be lovely there in spring and early summer. Perhaps you will go and see her, Dick. You might run down on the anniversary of the day when you came to the rescue and saved that precious life."

"Certainly we will go, if you wish," replied Dick, quickly.

He could not bear the way in which she now left herself out of all plans, even in the immediate future. Each day he grew more eager not to lose her; and yet each day he saw her gently fading and failing.

Her eyes were now raised to his in question and

reminder; but hastily averting his own, he hurried into further speech.

"I am glad she feels able to 'take up life again.' As a matter of fact she now really has a chance to begin to live for the first time! She has been pretty well snubbed and squashed and jawed out of existence, all these years."

"Hush," said Mrs. Herriot. "We must not forget the noble rule: *'De mortuis nil nisi bonum!'* It often comes to me as a thought of exceeding peace and sweetness, that Death, in taking us away, covers us with a beautiful veil of protecting charity, through which our virtues—had we any—shine and are remembered, but our faults are hidden and forgotten. I like to think of how, when I am gone, those who might now speak of me unkindly, will remain silent; while those who speak, will only say kind things. If I then think of earth at all, I shall think of it as such a loving place."

She was lying on her couch. Dick got up, moved the little table, sat on the floor beside her, and leaned his head against the soft white rug which covered her.

"My own Little White Lady," he said, "nobody could ever speak unkindly of you! But do not talk of dying, as if death were near. Don't you remember? My constant care, is to mean twenty years! I cannot bear it, when you talk of going. Don't you know that I can't live without you?"

Her hand dropped to his head. She softly stroked his hair, looking into his earnest eyes.

"We have been very happy together, Dick. Has it been a real home to you?"

"It has been, and is, the only home I have ever known—the only home I shall ever know," said Dick. "It has made life altogether different to have you to care for, and you to care. If you leave me, I shall be utterly, altogether, completely alone."

She put her hand over his eyes. There was a quality in their brightness which she could not bear to see. That there should be unshed tears in those brave, brown eyes at the thought of losing her, made life so sweet to the Little White Lady, that it grew difficult to face, with resignation, the call which she knew drew daily nearer, and more insistent.

Yet her work for Dick was by no means finished. Much yet remained to be done.

He took her hand, slipped it under his cheek, and lay twisting their wedding-ring and the emeralds which guarded it.

Uninterrupted silences had always been a habit of theirs. They were apt to last longer now than they used to do.

She watched his face, noting its look of strength and gravity; realizing how much he had grown and matured since she had given him the position, the possibilities, and the responsibilities of wealth.

She realized, also, the gradual change which had

come over his mental point of view; the unconscious growth of reverence for the things she held
most sacred; the greater tolerance toward those
from whom he differed; the dawning belief in love,
sincerity, and goodness. Yet his attitude toward
the Unseen was still *agnosco*, "I know not," rather
than *credo*, "I believe." He seemed no nearer
any definite profession of faith. If she must
leave him, having given him wealth, position, belief
in earthly love, alone, her work would indeed be
unfinished; her aim, unaccomplished.

Yet to-night, though absolutely free from pain,
she felt that strange flagging of life at its very
centre, which seemed to her a warning that not
very long remained.

It was so marked on this particular evening,
that it gave her a sensation as of falling gently
through space, and yet remaining amid the
surroundings of her own drawing-room, held there
by the fact that her eyes were fixed on Dick,
and that she could still feel him twisting her
rings.

Suddenly she said—and it seemed to her that her
voice came from very far away: "Not alone, dear
boy.. I shall not, by going, leave you alone—
but free. Free to find the woman who can truly
be your mate and companion, the mother of your
children, your wife in every sense; a true help,
meet for you. She shall wear the emeralds, and
your wedding-ring."

"I don't want her!" said Dick, abruptly. "I

don't want to be free! I don't want anybody but you."

His voice brought her back with a jerk. She had hardly realized that she had spoken. She had said more than she had intended to say. Presently she seemed to be gently rising up—up, among the stars.

She smiled upon him from afar.

He threw his arm across her, and took her other hand firmly in his. She felt his fingers steal to her pulse. Then she fell suddenly asleep.

While she slept, a strong stream of life seemed pouring into her. She felt it first in her hands; then all over her, like warm wine in every vein.

After a few minutes she awoke.

Dick was still on the floor beside her, his eyes fixed on her face. Both her hands were clasped tightly in his.

She was safely back on her sofa.

She smiled at him.

"Better?" he asked.

"Much better," she said. "Quite rested. I have had what people used to call 'a little nap.' In my young days, people constantly took little naps. In this twentieth century, life moves too rapidly. Naps are almost obsolete. How long did mine last?"

"Barely five minutes," said Dick. "Yet it has worked wonders."

"It has," she said. "I feel strong and well again—almost young. I will sit up now. And

Dick? Have you time? Just one game! Then our reading. After which, I will retire early to rest, leaving the remainder of your evening free."

The game was brisk and gay; but Dick stood no chance. His Little White Lady had awakened from her nap, with her chess mind in great form.

He watched the swiftly moving hands, through which his strong vitality had poured.

If strength of will could hold her here, he would not let her go.

So the cosy days of winter passed; and Spring awoke, at the call of the thrush. And Mrs. Herriot saw, from her balcony, a thing she had hardly expected to see again: the exquisite budding green of the trees in the park; and the golden crocuses, uplifting joyous faces to the warmth of the March sunshine.

CHAPTER XL

"I WILL ARISE"

"TO-NIGHT we have the 139th Psalm," said Mrs. Herriot, "and it is my turn to read, I am glad; for of all the wonderful psalms in this wonderful Book, this, to my mind, goes deepest. It is the great Psalm of Life—the finite linked on to the Infinite, Omniscience taking cognizance of each one of us in perfect knowledge, complete understanding, yet fullest tenderness of forgiveness and enabling power. See how it opens, Dick. 'O LORD, Thou hast searched me and known!' Jehovah—me! Wide as the poles apart, yet linked by that searching knowledge."

A folded piece of paper marked the psalm, in Mrs. Herriot's Bible.

Before beginning to read, she took it from its place between the leaves and laid it on the table beside her, at her left hand, beyond where Dick was sitting.

Then she bowed her head.

"O, Spirit of God," she said, "Thou Who searchest and knowest every thought of our hearts

446

—even the most secret—be with us, in power, while we read Thy Word this night."

A sense of awe came over Dick. For the first time in his life, he was distinctly conscious of an unseen Presence, of a Power which shook his soul; of a Voice which spoke to him in the secret chambers of his own inner being, even while he sat listening to the quiet tones in which Mrs. Herriot read the mighty words.

"O LORD, Thou hast searched me, and known *me.*"

She paused, and looked up.

" '*Me*' is in italics, Dick. It is not in the original. Each soul for itself supplies the ellipsis."

She bent again over the page.

"Thou knowest my downsitting and mine uprising; Thou understandest my thought afar off.

"Thou compassest my path and my lying down, and art acquainted with all my ways.

"For there is not a word in my tongue, but, lo, O LORD, Thou knowest it altogether.

"Thou hast beset me behind and before, and laid Thine hand upon me.

"Such knowledge is too wonderful for me; it is high, I cannot attain unto it.

"Whither shall I go from Thy spirit? or whither shall I flee from Thy presence?

"If I ascend up into heaven, Thou art there: If I make my bed in Sheol, behold, Thou art there.

"If I take the wings of the morning, and dwell in the uttermost parts of the sea;

"Even there shall Thy hand lead me, and Thy right hand shall hold me."

Mrs. Herriot paused, and looked up.

"That always makes me think of Jonah," she said. "I feel sure the Prophet Jonah must often have recited this psalm. It so exactly describes his experience. Do you remember, when he made up his mind to disobey, when he fled from the presence of the LORD? He took passage in a vessel just putting out to sea. How perfectly, in poetic phrase, we have here the description of a sailing boat spreading its white sails at dawn: 'If I take the wings of the morning.' But even there, though it meant passing through shipwreck, disaster, the plunge into the deepest depths of the sea, even there darkness could not hide him, despair could not overwhelm him, Omniscience followed him, Omnipotence led him, the right hand of Divine Love kept hold of him; darkness became light; God brought him through!"

The radiance of delight in the Word, illumined the Little White Lady's face. She looked at Dick.

In his eyes she saw something which made her very heart stand still.

Instinctively her left hand stole to the folded paper beside her, and covered it.

She went on reading.

At the 17th verse she paused.

" 'How precious also are Thy thoughts unto

me, O God!' It is wonderful that knowing all about us, His thoughts of us should yet be precious thoughts, Dick. The thoughts of earthly friends, when they find out our wrong-doings, are scarcely precious thoughts. They are apt to be hard thoughts, possibly unjust. But God's thoughts are precious to us, because if our realization of His complete knowledge is followed by full confession and repentance, it means full forgiveness, the perfect atonement of the precious blood.

"Let us pass on to the last two verses, Dick. They form the most helpful prayer for every human soul. Along the lines of this prayer the heart which has wandered furthest away, can come home to the Father's House. It courts full knowledge; it asks to have all the worst, as well as all the best, known; so that Divine Omniscience and Omnipotence combined, may lead the wanderer home. I have prayed this prayer constantly, all my life long. Oh, Dick—my own dear boy— if I could know that you sometimes prayed it too!

"Search me, O God, and know my heart: try me, and know my thoughts: and see if there be any wicked way in me, and lead me in the way everlasting."

Mrs. Herriot was shielding her face with her hands. Her reading had merged into prayer.

Dick sat staring straight before him at the round glass lamp-shade. Where had he heard that prayer before? When had he last heard that prayer, in somewhat different form?

29

Suddenly he remembered. His mind went back twenty years. He saw himself in the church at Dinglevale, a small boy of seven, standing beside Grandaunt Louisa in the Rectory pew, gazing up at the hole in the stained-glass window. It was the Sunday after he had broken the halo. The Fallen Idol was declaiming the Prayer-book version of this very psalm. Dick could hear again his sonorous voice: "Try me, O God, and seek the ground of my heart: prove me, and examine my thoughts." Then Aunt Louisa's black kid finger had come down with an admonitory point upon his own book, and Dick could hear his childish voice uplifted: "Look well if there be any way of wickedness in me: and lead me in the way everlasting."

Twenty long years ago! And all that time he had gone his own way, believing in nothing, sticking at nothing, living for self-advancement. And yet—here he found himself, confronted with this very psalm, in the golden halo of light cast by the lamp of his Little White Lady, whose gentle voice and tender loving-kindness had brought him at least to wish he believed, to wish he could pray, to wish he could think her cherished Bible true.

Was it possible that, after all, a Higher Hand had been leading him all the while? Was it possible that an Almighty Power knew all; yet, knowing all, still wished him well; still held open for him the gate to a way everlasting?

·   ·   ·   ·   ·   ·   ·

Suddenly Dick pushed back his chair, and knelt down.

"I will pray it too," he said. "Perhaps as *you* are here, God will listen to me."

Mrs. Herriot took her hands from before her face, and folded them upon her open Bible. Then she sat very still, and waited.

"Search me, O God—" began Dick, and stopped.

The room was very quiet. No sound broke the stillness, save the solemn ticking of the clock, and the occasional low crackling of the fire.

With a sudden movement, Dick flung his arms across the table and dropped his head upon them.

"O God," he said, "forgive me! and help me to tell her the whole truth."

She turned and looked at him, and the yearning tenderness in her eyes spoke a love which was too great to spare him.

She did not speak. She saw the clenched hands and the heaving shoulders. She had to let him fight it out alone.

Presently Dick muttered: "I don't know if you will ever be able to forgive me. I shall never forgive myself. But to tell you the truth seems the only atonement I can make. Perhaps if God really knows all about it, He will help you to understand."

Long minutes passed before anything more happened.

Once she heard a hard, dry sob. She longed to

lay her hand upon his head. But she could only sit and wait; praying, as she waited, that the power which was working mightily, might win a complete victory.

At last Dick lifted a haggard face, and looked at her.

"Before I asked you to marry me," he said slowly, "before I ever even thought of it, I heard about the Herriot will. Sir James Montford told me. I went to Somerset House and looked it up. I found all the particulars about a second marriage giving you power to leave the capital. I knew, if I could persuade you to marry me, you would leave it to me. I wanted it, so as to get ahead in my profession. I asked you to marry me on that very evening. I had a paper of notes of the terms of the will, which I had scribbled down, in my pocket-book at the time. I dropped it here. That was what I came back for, when I told you I came to look for my pocket-book. Ellen had picked it up and burnt it.

"I can't expect you to believe it, but every word I said about wanting to take care of you and to be on the spot at night was true. Only I still put the other first; I still thought about the money.

"Then you told me the story of Alexander Ross, and all that you had suffered, and that night—" Dick's voice broke—"oh, my Little White Lady, I can't hope you will believe it—but that night I thought only of *you*. And when I went downstairs, after carrying you up, and realized that I was no better than Alexander Ross, in fact worse than he, because you had already been so good to me, I felt glad—honestly glad—that you were going to refuse me. I thought I could then begin over again, with the wrong I had done you wiped out, and feel I was doing all I could for you—as much as you would let me do, with no unworthy motive at the back of it. But then——" Dick's voice broke again—"then you, in your great and generous goodness, little dreaming what I had done, accepted me; and, for the very reason for which I—in the first place—had asked you. You accepted me, and I could not draw back, though I felt such a knave and a traitor; and somehow, I could not then tell you the truth. My one hope was that you would never know. Because—oh, my Little White Lady—I knew you thought well of me, and loved me a bit; and your love meant so much to me; I could not risk losing it. And I had grown to love you so awfully much—not for anything you could do for me—but just for yourself alone, just because you were you. And I couldn't bear the thought of making you suffer, as I am afraid I am doing now. But, to-night, I understood that—if there is an Eternity—I should make you suffer more by not telling you, while I have the chance, than by telling you. So I have told you the exact truth. And if, some day, you can feel able to forgive me, and to tell me so, it will help me to believe that there *is* a God, somewhere or other, Who follows a fellow down into the darkness, and gives him a hand up when he is in despair."

Dick's slow, difficult utterance had come to an end at last.   He lifted his eyes from Mrs. Herriot's folded hands, on which he had fixed them, and humbly, wistfully, looked into her face.

So great a glory of love and tenderness illumined it, that Dick gazed at her, bewildered.

"Oh, my darling," she said, "my own dear boy, I forgave you, long months ago!"

"How could you forgive," he stammered, "when you did not know?"

"But I did know.   I have known all along.'

"You—have—known?" he said.   "How?"

She took up the folded paper, opened it, and placed it in his hand.

"It was I who found it," she said, "not Ellen. I found it directly after you were gone.   I understood at once what had happened.   I kept the paper.   It has been in my Bible ever since.   I knew you would tell me all about it some day."

"But in that case," stammered Dick.   "Why did you——"

"Why did I marry you, Dick?   Because I completely forgave you.   Because, knowing you so well, I saw how the temptation had arisen, and I believed in the good, while realizing the wrong. Because I loved you so truly, that my one desire was to make things—even your great mistake— work together for your eventual good.   So I trusted you, and gave you all; and, oh, my darling, you have not failed my trust!"

Dick was holding the paper of notes, mechanically folding and unfolding it.

Suddenly it dropped from his fingers. He stood erect, his face livid, his hands clenched.

"Oh, my God," he said, "I'm broken!"

She pushed away the table from between them, and held out her arms.

"Dick," she said, "come to me."

And the next moment Dick's head was in her lap, his arms were flung up around her, and he was sobbing much as the little Dick of long ago had sobbed with his face hidden in the turf, beside his mother's grave. For the strongest man, when his deepest depths are reached, has the heart of a little child.

What his Little White Lady said, and how she soothed him, is known to Dick alone. He will hold it in his heart until he dies—and after.

Presently she drew his head from her lap, to rest against her bosom, wrapping her arms around him, as if to shield him from all further pain.

"Dick," she said, "you believe in my love, because, knowing all, I could do this for you. But my poor earthly love is but a pale reflection of the love of God. Cannot you believe that He has known all—far more than I have known, who only knew one thing—yet, knowing all, He has kept a hold on you, working all things together for your eternal good. So that now—now that you are brought to pray, 'Lead me in the way everlasting,' the everlasting way through Gethsemane to Calvary, then to newness of life by Union with the Risen Christ; uplifting of purpose through ascension of heart with Him, power to live out that purpose, through the Indwelling Spirit given at Pentecost—all this opens out before you, awaiting only the grasp of faith, the 'I believe' which transforms *promise* into *possession*. My own dear boy, does the light break in on the darkness? Do you begin to see and to understand?"

And Dick answered slowly, because he was so anxious to be perfectly honest.

"Helen," he said—for she had said that to him, which made any other name impossible—"your love and God's are so mixed up in my mind, that I think I shall have to get them sorted a bit, before I know exactly what I *do* believe. But I don't suppose He minds that, because, if He knows all, He knows that I *had* to see something really Divine, before I could believe. I should have gone on for ever like the man you were talking of the other day, who said: 'Who is He, Lord, that I might believe on Him?' unless I had had the actual experience of 'Thou hast both seen Him, and it is He that talketh with thee'; unless, right in my daily life, I had seen the Divine."

"But when did you see the Divine?" she asked. "When and where, Dick?"

And he answered, reverently: "I saw the Christ in you."

Was she rewarded then for all she had suffered, all she had done; the self-sacrifice, the patience, the forgiving love?

Anyway, her tears fell on his face; and in thinking of them, afterwards, he felt sure they were tears of joy.

Suddenly he held his breath to listen; for a moment she wondered to what. Then she knew, for he rested upon her heart.

He raised his head, still kneeling at her feet, and looked at her with anxious eyes.

"You are tired," he said. "My Little White Lady, you are tired. I have put you through so much. Have you any pain? Do you feel faint?"

She smiled into his eyes. "No, my young doctor. I feel quite well—quite strangely well; and happy beyond all earthly words to express. But I will leave you now, and go to rest. No, do not ring for Ellen. I can call from the foot of the stairs, or ring the lift-bell. I want you to stay here, just as I leave you, for a little while. I want you to kneel on, as you have been kneeling now. But the earthly messenger will have slipped away, and nothing will intervene betwixt you and the Lord. You will be able to say: 'O LORD, THOU hast searched me, and known——.' You now need no go-between. So I leave you, my own darling boy, to your Lord and mine."

She put her hands on either side of his face, and looked long into his eyes.

Then she bent forward, and laid her lips on his.

It was the first time his Little White Lady had ever kissed him.

It was the first time Dick had received a kiss of love from any woman's lips.

To him it seemed a strange, sweet benediction; a mystery he could not fathom, a wonder he could not explain. For one long moment, her gentle soul and his seemed one.

"Good-bye," she said, "my own dear boy, good-bye."

"Not 'good-bye,' " he whispered; "only 'good-night.' "

"Ah, yes, of course," she said; "only 'good-night.' "

Slipping from his detaining arms, she rose.

"Good-night, my Queen," he said.

She bent over him, smiling.

"No, my young doctor. I like the old name best."

"Good-night, my Little White Lady," said Dick; and felt her go.

As the door closed behind her, he did as she had asked. He knelt alone, where she had so lately sat, folded his arms upon the velvet couch, and leaned his head upon them.

The spirit of prayer awoke within him.

Divine love reached and found him.

Dick came home to the Father's House.

CHAPTER XLI

IN THE NIGHT-WATCHES

WHEN, at length, Dick rose and stood by the fire, the hands of the clock were nearing the hour of midnight.

He was surprised to find how long he had been kneeling; how far advanced was the night.

He took up the pocket-Bible; then looked for the folded paper, which had fallen from his fingers. Immediately it came back to him that he had seen the Little White Lady drop it into the fire, as she passed from the room. It was the very last thing he had seen her do.

Oh, the completeness of her forgiving love!

He now understood why he had once been made to promise, when illness seized her unexpectedly, that, if she died, he would burn that treasured Bible, unopened. Thank God, she had lived to receive his full confession, and to burn the paper, herself.

The chessmen and board lay forgotten on the table. It was the first time he had known her to go upstairs without them. He made sure that the box was safely closed, put it straight upon the

459

folded board, then turned out the lamp and crossed the room. At the door it struck him that he might as well carry up the chessmen himself, and keep them in his own room. He knew how precious they were to her. He thought it would please her that he should have remembered to carry them up. He went back and fetched them.

He switched off all the lights, and softly mounted the stairs.

Outside the Little White Lady's door, he paused to listen.

All was quiet within.

He was passing down the passage to his own room, when the door of the dressing-room opened, and Ellen appeared on the landing, a candlestick in her hand.

Ellen was a fearsome object at night. Her hair was all scraped back from her long face. She looked as a horse does, at the moment when the bridle is being pulled over its head; but, in Ellen, it was a permanent condition.

Once in the intimacy of a long night-watch, when they were both busily engaged in making coffee, Dick had asked Ellen why she did her hair that way, at night. With the nearest approach to a giggle ever arrived at by Ellen, she had told him she was "saving her parting." Dick was not much the wiser. He concluded that Ellen took off her parting at night, and put it in a drawer.

However, he was too well used to Ellen in night-array to be startled by her sudden appearance, though she wore the purple dressing-gown, covered with orange dragons and scriggly yellow snakes. She had bought it at a sale for sixteen and eleven pence ha'penny, and had been immensely pleased because the first time she had had occasion to call Dick in the night, while wearing it, he had found time to whisper: "By all that's gorgeous, Ellen, that dressing-gown must have belonged to the Empress of China!"

Dick little knew how his every word was remembered and treasured by the queer old mind of Ellen Ransom. In a drawer, with her black gloves and odds and ends of lace and ribbon, she kept a red penny account-book, gradually filling with stiff and laboured writing. The title-page held this inscription:

"Things sed by the Dokter to Ellen Ransom,
for my Eye only."

This limitation of readers for so unique a work was a pity. Mrs. Herriot's kind eye, and the merry eye of "the Dokter" himself, would have read it with many a twinkle of delighted amusement.

He now confronted this apparition of Ellen by candle-light on the silent landing, startled only by the sudden fear lest she had been sent to summon him.

"What's up, Ellen?" he said. "Is she ill?"

"She is not, sir," replied Ellen, in a sepulchral whisper. "I left my lady most comfortable and quiet, asking for a pencil, and almost asleep as I gave it her. She came up so cheerful and easy, and took the stairs without effort."

"Took the stairs!" exclaimed Dick.

"The lift, sir, was not working."

Dick groaned. "Why on earth didn't you call me?"

"She was half-way up, sir, before I had time to turn round. She hardly seemed to know she was walking upstairs. She took them as if she was treading on air. 'Let me call the doctor, ma'am,' I said. But 'I can't have him disturbed just now, Ellen,' said she."

"Well, another time, fetch me without asking. Good-night, Ellen. Why aren't you in bed?"

Ellen advanced as he retired. She looked like an anxious old horse leaning over a gate.

"I waited up to let you know, sir, that I took and told her, to-night."

"Told her what?"

"Told her the truth, sir. I couldn't keep that lie on m' conscience no longer. 'The doctor will be angry with me, ma'am,' I said, 'but speak I must!' 'The doctor won't be angry, Ellen,' she said, smiling. 'He will understand that I should wish you to have the comfort of speaking.' So I up and told her."

"Oh, Ellen, Ellen," said poor Dick, "I should dearly like to throw you over the banisters! But the pot must not call the kettle black. She had already had to-night more to bear than was good for her. What did she say?"

"She took it very quiet, sir. I think she had known all along."

"I dare say she had," said Dick. "There is not much she does not know. The moral of which is: never attempt to deceive her again. I suppose she forgave you?"

"She said, sir, that a kind intention, even if mistaken, did not call for forgiveness."

"That was like her," remarked Dick. "Always absolutely just. Well, go to bed, Ellen. If you hear a sound in her room, go in. And if there should be the slightest need, fetch me instantly."

Dick went to his room, closing the door without noise.

The house was quiet, with that intense sense of stillness which falls as the hour of one approaches.

Dick laid his watch on the table, emptied his pockets, and took off his coat.

Then he stood stock still beside the dressing-table, considering.

So she had walked upstairs! And, after the long strain of her talk with him, had had to meet Ellen's troubled conscience, and Ellen's confession; no shock in itself—for "the sweet by-and-by" had always been obviously Ellen!—but bringing back, most vividly, the tragic happenings of long ago.

"Oh, my poor Little White Lady," groaned

Dick, "we have given you an awful lot to bear!"

He kicked off his shoes, opened his door very quietly, and stood listening.

Then he walked down the passage and listened intently at the closed doors.

All was perfectly quiet, excepting that, while he still waited, Ellen started a low, contented snore. It was like the purring of a satisfied old cat.

Dick smiled as he walked noiselessly back to his room.

"Sleeping the sleep of the Just," he thought. "Poor old Ellen! I wonder how many worse busters she has told, and forgotten, in the thirty years during which she has worried over this one."

Back in his room again, he tried to undress, but was seized by a fit of intolerable anxiety.

Supposing the deathly faintness came on, and she could not even press the bell at her bedside, which rang in Ellen's room?

What if she called Ellen, but refused to have him fetched until too late for remedies to be of any use?

He walked up and down the room.

She had become so wonderful, so precious to him now. He could not face the possibility of losing her.

He had not yet allowed himself to realize all it meant—this strange sweet glow and glory in his heart. But he knew his Little White Lady loved him, with a love altogether above his comprehension, altogether beyond his experience. Yet the depths of his nature responded, just as, to-night, his soul had responded to spiritual truths which were as yet mysteries, but which he accepted in simple faith, and knew he would, day by day, go on to fully apprehend.

Earthly and heavenly love, in the fulness of their perfection, had been revealed to him together; and his heart stood still on the threshold of these holy sanctuaries; his wondering mind believed and accepted, but postponed full understanding, until the first bewilderment should be past. "Ye must be born again," sums up, in one significant sentence, the childlike attitude of mind which accepts, at first without question, that which is altogether beyond the grasp of unaided human intellect; then grows up, by slow degrees, to the perfect stature of full spiritual comprehension. "The natural man receiveth not the things of the Spirit of God, for they are foolishness unto him; neither can he know them, because they are spiritually discerned." "Whosoever shall not receive the Kingdom of God as a little child, shall in no wise enter therein."

Still in his shirtsleeves, Dick sat down and read through the story of the Prophet Jonah. His mind was gripped by its rugged dramatic power. Here was a man who deliberately turned from his God, who declined to obey the Divine command, yet—when humanly speaking, life was over—was brought up from despairing depths and given a second chance.

Then Dick, turning back to the 139th Psalm, read it through again, with the experience of Jonah fresh in his mind. He realized its striking application, and it brought him once more to the fourfold petition with which it closed: "Search me . . . try me . . . know me . . . lead me."

He knelt and tried to pray that he might be worthy of the great earthly love which had led him to realize the Divine, but, even as he prayed, a terrible sense of loneliness overwhelmed him.

He had nobody on earth save her, and she was so frail, her hold on life was so precarious.

If he could only see her, for one moment; hear her voice again, hold her hands in his, and know that she rested peacefully, he would be content.

He went to the dressing-table and looked at his watch. It was nearly two o'clock.

He had promised never to go to her room, unless she sent Ellen to fetch him.

His sense of loneliness and anxiety became almost unbearable, yet he could not break the promise, made at the time when she did so much for him.

Suddenly he picked up his coat, and put it on.

He knew he was released from that promise. He could not explain how; but he knew it.

He opened his door, and walked quickly down the passage.

The hall clock was striking two.

Outside her door he paused.

All was quiet within.

He would enter noiselessly. If she slept, he could slip out again. If she were awake—— If she were awake! Oh, blessed, tender Little White Lady of his own! If she were awake, he would explain; and surely he could trust her to understand.

Dick put his hand upon the door-handle, softly turned it, and stepped into the room.

CHAPTER XLII

THE WINGS OF THE MORNING

THE night-light burned beside the bed.

As he stood immovable, listening, Dick suddenly knew that he was alone in the room.

Yet the form of his Little White Lady lay upon the bed.

He closed the door, turned on the electric light, and walked forward to the bedside.

Did she sleep?

Yes—she slept.

As he looked down at that peaceful face, at those folded hands, he recalled the words she had read that very night in the room below: "When I awake, I am still with Thee."

His Little White Lady had wakened already, in the radiant glory of the Presence of her Lord.

Dick dropped on his knees beside the bed. He laid his fingers on the wrists, he listened to the silent heart—mechanically, hopelessly. He knew, already, that there was nothing to feel, nothing to hear, nothing to be done.

His Little White Lady had spread her soft, silvery wings, and flown away.

Dick could see just what had happened.   Prayer
had merged into sleep, and sleep—earthly sleep—
had gently changed into that other slumber, from
which his voice could never waken her.

"When I awake, I am still with Thee."

He looked around.

On the little table beside her bed lay her Bible,
open at the fly-leaf.   It bore her full name, in
·ink, in her own handwriting.   Beneath was
written in pencil:

"For Dick,
from his Little White Lady"

and the date of the evening before.

Between the Bible and the night-light, lay a
half sheet of white paper, and upon it gleamed
her emerald ring.   On the paper was traced in
pencilled letters, faint and scarcely legible: *"For*
Margaret."   But a line had been drawn through
those words, and below appeared, in firmer writing:
"For my Dick's wife—some day."

Dick folded the paper and slipped it, with the
ring, into his waistcoat pocket.   "I am glad she
did not leave it to Margaret," he thought, "because now it will always be mine.   I shall never
want another wife—Oh!" he cried, sharply; for
in that moment he first realized that she had gone
from him.

He covered those folded hands with his own,
and laid his forehead upon them.

At length he rose, and stood looking down upon the quiet face.

Already the Hand of Death, passing gently over it, had worked that strange miracle which foreshadows immortal youthfulness in the Life to come. All lines had been smoothed away. A look almost of youth was growing on the peaceful face.

Dick remembered how he had once said to her, standing just there, beside the bed: "You will never be old. You have a young soul. You are one of heaven's evergreens!"

How true it was! The worn-out body lay here, but the lovely soul had passed on into the immortal glory of a fuller life.

Then Dick remembered that for years he had scoffed at the idea of resurrection, and denied the future existence of the soul.

She had several times been distressed at chance remarks he had let fall, implying his disbelief in a future life.

He turned, and taking up her treasured Bible —her last gift to him—he closed it, and held it firmly between his hands.

The face of his Little White Lady seemed to smile in its long sleep. Did she know what her young doctor was going to do?

The softly shaded light, hanging above the bed, shed a halo of glory around the pillow, shining upon the silvery hair, illumining the gentle face.

And, in that sacred moment, Dick Cameron's broken halo was restored to him, complete.

He laid his left hand upon those folded hands; he raised her Bible in his right, and, with unfaltering voice, he said:

"I believe in the forgiveness of sins, the resurrection of the body, and the life everlasting."

Then he went to call Ellen Ransom.

THE END

The
Thunderhead Lady

By Anna Fuller and Brian Read

*With about 40 Line Drawings. $1.00 net.
By mail, $1.10*

"Wanted: By a Harvard Graduate, a permanent position as husband. Carefully trained by an anxious mother, and used to feminine domination."
So begins a clipping from the Boston *Herald*, written in jest, and printed from bravado, which elicits a reply from a chance reader and results in the correspondence that forms the substance of this little skit. From mock seriousness the writers drift off into more or less casual chat upon books and people, illumined from time to time with a touch of romance. The whole forms a bit of light reading which should appeal in equal measure to the thoughtful and the frivolous.

New York **G. P. Putnam's Sons** London

CPSIA information can be obtained
at www.ICGtesting.com
Printed in the USA
BVHW010438051221
623257BV00002B/136